Dancing with Demons

A Novel

Patricia Easteal

Publisher:
ASPG (Australian Self Publishing Group)
P.O. Box 159, Calwell, ACT 2905 Australia
Email: publishaspg@gmail.com
http://www.inspiringpublishers.com

National Library of Australia Cataloguing-in-Publication entry

Author: Patricia Easteal

Title: **Dancing with Demons/**_Patricia Easteal_

ISBN: 978-1-923087-90-3 (Print)

ISBN: 978-1-923087-89-7 (ePub2)

ISBN: 978-1-923087-88-0 (eBook)

CONTENTS

1. Introduction 1

2. The Toddler Princess: The Shrinks' View 14

3. The Princess Years: Unearthing with Dr Jaye 38

4. Puberty Deep Colour Blue:
    Intellectual Sub-Committee 60

5. Rebellion: Listening to Therapists
    and Drunkalogue 75

6. Teen Risk-Taking: PGA's Preliminary Hearing 91

7. Sharing Frankie's Diary with Dr Jaye 111

8. Summer of 17: An Open Meeting 124

9. Sharing Frankie's Uni Journal in Therapy 140

10. Rape: A Head Committee Meeting 149

11. Six-Week European Bender: An Open Meeting 161

12. Frankie's 18th Summer: Open Meeting, Part 2 174

13. Dissension in the Head: A Corner Turned 184

14. Michael (Tapes 1 and 2): Head Committee Meeting 190

15. Michael (Tapes 3 and 4): Head Committee Meeting 201

16. The Return of the Binge: Listening in on Therapy 210

17. Tom (Tapes 1 and 2): Head Committee Meeting 219

18. Tom (Tapes 3 and 4): Head Committee Meeting 229

19. Sharing the Tom Era Reflective Journal in Therapy 239

20. Frankie's Co-Alcoholism Bottom: Open Meeting 250

21. Sharing Frankie's Consciousness-
Raising Journal with Dr Jaye 260

22. In Between Rehabs: 12-Step Reps
Subcommittee Meeting 272

23. Getting Triple F Sober: PGA Award Ceremony 284

24. Epilogue (More About Francine):
Sharing with the Committee 297

1
INTRODUCTION

The ~~christening~~[1]

The central character is called Triple F, embodying the three first names she's known by throughout her life: Franny, Frankie, and finally, Francine.

Princess Franny

First comes Franny, the little girl whose mother, Miriam, castigates within her head, 'Franny, you really just are the most ungrateful child.'

At the age of seven, Franny watched the Oscars on TV, fantasizing about her future moment of glory when her name is announced as the Best Actress winner. Was this a flaw in her character, or do all little girls – or North American ones – harbour such dreams? Disconnected by the surround sound of abuse, Franny lives in her head – a relatively safe space. The downside to this sanctuary is that the fantasies inevitably translate into a deficit of surprise and a surfeit of disappointment; reality always falls short of the imagined utopia.

---

1   She can't be christened though as her grandparents who fled the pogroms in Eastern Europe would turn over in their graves. If her parents hadn't abandoned their religious practices, she might have had a *Brita* and been given a Hebrew name like Mazal, which means good luck.

Young Franny is a bundle of worries – from fears of being struck by lightning or an airplane crashing into her house, to developing cancer. Beneath these fears lies a reservoir of shame, hurt, and anger.

F***ed-up Frankie

Later in high school, when the teacher asks, 'Frankie, what's the problem? You're turning very pale,' Frankie passes out, a consequence of her harrowing episode the previous night with a razor blade. As Triple F matures into adolescence and young adulthood, Frankie struggles to live with her own traumatic experiences plus the emotions born from Franny's childhood trauma and sexual assault.

Frankie tries every means she can find to silence the relentless internal negativity: drinking, starving herself, using drugs, over-eating, vomiting, overworking, and any other activity she stumbles upon. Yet, none prove effective. Instead, these suppressed emotions manifest as obsessive-compulsive, depressive, and anxiety disorders, leading her to seek further self-medication.

Work in progress: Francine[2]

Upon relocating to Australia in her early-thirties, Frankie morphs into Francine. She discovers healthier coping mechanisms and adds Antipodean twelve-step members and mental health practitioners to the myriad voices already residing rent-free inside her head. Some aspects of her personhood remain unchanged. Like Frankie, Francine continues to be an outspoken advocate,

---

2 Although most of this story takes place during Franny and Frankie's time, Francine, the 'work in progress', is seen and heard as she looks at her past selves and through the reflections of those who witness the post-trauma awakening and recovering years in the southern hemisphere.

and, like both Franny and Frankie, she seeks approval.[3] This trait is evident when she encounters two female proselytizers at her Melbourne doorstep, offering religious tracts about the eve of a male God apocalypse.

'Sisters', she wants to yell righteously. 'The apocalypse is now. Just look around. There's patriarchal violence and cruelty everywhere. We're living lifetimes overshadowed by the disempowerment and subjugation from men! We neither want nor need another dominating male adding to the existing gender inequality and oppression!'

However, her desire to appease others curbs this outburst. Instead of embracing her feminist identity, Francine adopts another persona: the recovering alcoholic with pre-existing spirituality. She attempts to influence those who aim to convert her. Sermonising in the doorway about the gender-neutral force that 'saved' her from a life of addiction and pain, Francine articulates why many women, like herself, have moved away from a male Christian God. They aren't seeking further punishment but are turning towards a loving entity that transcends gender or anthropomorphic form.

Introducing Triple F's crowded head

There's no questioning the cacophony inside Triple F's mind, with the consistent chanting of the grey matter choir.[4] However,

---

3   Speaking out for marginalised women could be an odd career choice for someone craving universal acceptance as there are some who neither appreciate the message nor the messenger.

4   Not everyone in Triple F's life is heard – take Jake, for instance. Other than occasionally chanting blame for his victimisation, he rarely speaks. This may reflect his stammer-induced selective mutism during the ten years Franny and Jake were co-residents in Henry's kingdom. There were few words spoken by Jake to be replayed.

they merely provide backup for the **head**liners – those who have passed through Franny/Frankie/Francine's life and continue to remain within her, henceforth termed the 'head committee' (and its associated sub-committees).[5]

Some of the voices are permanent fixtures, while others come and go. Though earlier voices tended to be critical and demeaning, a couple of them were uplifting. There's the voice of older sister Sandy who, despite Franny's status as the family favourite, constantly assures her younger sibling of her worth. And there's another comforting presence, the embodiment of Triple F's spiritual core. Before embracing twelve-step programs, she referred to this essence as her Personal Guardian Angel (PGA) and later, after encountering Al-Anon in her mid-twenties, her higher power (HP).

Picture, as Triple F does, these voices congregating around a boardroom table (although PGA/HP might be conceptualised as hovering).[6] Sometimes, only a select few are present, like the 'Former and Current Triple F Shrinks'. All (sub) committees convene – especially during Franny and Frankie's time – to analyse and debate the worth of Triple F's emotions, thoughts, and actions.

Membership has expanded over time with affirmative Australian voices becoming more prevalent as Francine heals. While this shift doesn't completely silence the long-standing voices of shame and fear, Francine cultivates mindfulness. She learns to recognise and counteract the negative messages. She learns to dance with demons.

---

5   Having one's parents and significant others' opinions replayed within is likely not uncommon. Visualising them as head committee members might be less common.

6   Triple F has always heard words and ideas visually. This picture came to her after seeing a boardroom table on a TV program.

An ad hoc meeting

Sessions in the cerebrum may occur without notice. One example is the mental chatter that arises when Francine spends money on her children, regardless of their age.

For instance, her first full-time job in Australia required regular interstate travel. While her employer provided a per diem, she chose low-cost accommodation, using the extra money to purchase at least one special gift per child. Whilst browsing the toy department of Myer and overpriced sports clothing outlets, the chairperson would call the meeting to order:

'Really, Francine, you are a spendthrift. Didn't I raise you to save money? Haven't I shown you by my example? Where did I fail? What did I do wrong?'

Guess who? That would be the Jewish mother, Miriam, whose middle names might as well be Guilt and Shame.

'She just buys the children gifts to ensure they will love her. She's filled with a recognition of her inadequacies as a human being,' observes the rational and omniscient father, Henry.

'We entirely agree with the latter comment. However, we understand that these manifestations of low self-esteem are partly due to birth order and your narcissistic patriarch,' opine five of Triple F's therapists in unison.

Sister Sandy proposes: 'I used to create reward charts for Franny, like one for brushing her teeth. She'd earn a silver, gold, or red star each time she did the job and received a reward – a small gift I'd buy for her. Franny loved opening these surprise presents. These were rare light moments in her childhood. Makes total sense to me that Francine is replicating the practice with her kids.'

'Buying a child something, if you have the means, can be a healthy expression of your love,' say the newer age counsellors.

'Just do what you feel deep down is right. That is your higher power's voice,' declare the twelve-step program people, who are omnipresent since they have become long-term, permanent residents to ensure they never miss a meeting.

'Sure, we liked the presents, but we love our Mum cuz she's our Mum. We know that she constantly thinks about us and supports us,' concur the four adult children – Samuel, Daniella, Rosa, and Peter. Nonetheless, the youngest, spawn of Richard the third (husband), borrowing from his psychoanalyst's view, adds 'She has been overly involved in our lives – a "smother mother", if you will.'

Mental health subgroup: control

One cerebral working group, comprised of mental health professionals familiar with Triple F, convenes regularly.

Today's discussion centres around the 'big C'. There is consensus that *control* is a major issue for her, but differences arise concerning its origins and effects. For example, Gabe, the first counsellor Frankie saw, and a twelve-step program advocate, aligns with the neo-Freudian school of thought, emphasising parental influence.

'This kind of control is central to the conditioning *we* attribute to dysfunctional families and unhealthy societies. The child witnesses their father's aggression towards the mother or siblings, as in Franny's history. She can do nothing but survive. Survival is working out tactics to avoid becoming a direct target. The less internal control one has, the greater the external control one seeks – a classic paradox.'

He continues, 'Growing up amidst violence, the child feels helpless. Striving for control gives an illusion of power. Such individuals feel secure when in control. Conversely, relinquishing it is daunting. Unconsciously, we anticipate the terrible things that might transpire if we let go. No matter how dire the present is, we manage because we know the rules. We play the game and predict the next move. At times, adults like Francine and me, who grew up amidst violence, may still experience hyper-vigilance, even when in recovery. We are unconsciously in self-protection mode.'

'All an illusion, but that's OK. An illusion is as good as reality if you believe in it. Indeed, a peculiar aspect of control is its illusionary nature. Those caught in an unconscious quest for control grapple to maintain that feeling. A bulimic who sees a binge as three Tim Tams devoured and then expelled: a matryoshka doll of control within control. This is Franny, who navigated her early childhood by learning to master her emotions.'

Next to speak is Fred, the Australian Cancer Society support person. Without a university degree, he's initially reluctant to participate but believes that, given his successful work with Francine for months preparing for her quit smoking day, he's gained insights into how control manifested in her life.

'The reality, though, is that whatever she did – from throwing up biscuits to smoking two packs of cigarettes a day – Triple F seldom, if ever, truly felt in control. I can give you an example. During our time together, her fear of flying escalated to a phobia. With someone else at the "controls" at *10,600 metres*, the illusion Gabe mentioned disappears. Yet, the need for it, I believe, assisted Francine in quitting cigarettes. She thought about getting the other 'big C' and stopped smoking to lower the odds – essentially to exert control over the risk of cancer.'

Dr Jamyang, whose Tibetan name fittingly means 'gentle voice', (referred to as 'Dr Jaye'), the Asian-Australian psychiatrist with whom Francine has been in therapy the longest, clears her throat before responding to Fred's last comment.

'There are no coincidences. None. Henry was a war bomber pilot hero. His princess daughter develops a phobia concerning aircraft. She can't fly at night … intriguing, isn't it?'

Dr Jaye, not one of the more vocal or confrontational members of this sub-committee, but like PGA, she mirrors Francine's presence in a somewhat silent manner, offering validation. As today's keynote speaker, she proceeds to examine the connections between trauma, control, and major depressive episodes.

'Francine and I have acknowledged that change is a challenge for her.[7] As a survivor of complex trauma, she's familiar with the ominous feelings accompanying change. This sense of dread is alien to those who must be the captain of the ship, the leader of the troops, the general in the army. And yes, as Francine noted, these metaphors are inherently masculine. The significant shifts in her life, occurring in rapid succession, were, in my educated opinion, the trigger for her major depressive episode.

'In one consultation, Francine shared that just before her seven-month torturous period of undiagnosed depression began, she was pushing baby Peter in his pram to the neighbourhood shops and stopped mid-stride, saying to herself: "How did I get here? A short time ago, it was North America, Tom and academia. What the hell am I doing in Australia with another child and both a different partner and occupation?" She described to me how, over the three years leading to that moment of existential confusion, she had moved (both metaphorically and literally) to avoid a direct collision with a meteorite. The impact was inevitable, and she had no sway over its "life-changing *impact*." She is fond of wordplay, isn't she? Particularly accidental ones.

---

7   Covid restrictions' lifestyle changes have proven to be an exception. Being in 'lockdown' can be comfortable for someone with agoraphobic tendencies. Further, wearing a mask is quite comforting to those like Francine who have histories of serious upper respiratory illnesses.

'Francine went on to describe how these life changes took place, in her words, "like hurtling intergalactic debris," resulting in one catastrophic outcome – the script was obsolete. This was a new Australian-made production. Until around the eighth year of therapy with me and two decades attending Adult Children or ACA meetings, she believed that there were *correct* feelings and thoughts. However, she felt she could, at best, only guess what they might be. She observed those around her. Everyone appeared as though they did not have to guess but simply knew. The "haves" and the "have nots". This was evident in her description of an incident she had experienced years before in early recovery from clinical depression. I believe this to be illustrative of an intersection of her control issues and such an underlying belief system. In Francine's words:

Driving to work in the van, with dear Richard at the wheel, a car skidded across two lanes of traffic and struck our van on the rear side. It came out of nowhere, especially for me as a passenger. No warning. Just a hopeless crunching metal noise and our vehicle turned onto its side, skidded across three lanes, righted itself only to flip to my side, scraping along the sealed shoulder felt like minutes but was, in reality, only a few seconds. As the van spun and scraped, I knew that I was about to die. 'I'm going to die. I'm going to die. We're going to die. We're going to die.' These were my last thoughts as I closed my eyes to meet my maker.

The van stopped. I opened my eyes and quickly looked over at Richard. He was OK. Though in a daze and feeling as though I'd been transported to another realm, having experienced a rebirth of sorts, I managed to utter, 'We'd better get out before it blows up.' A sentiment formed perhaps from too many film and TV scenes where cars often explode after a crash, right?

To avoid death by explosion, we climbed out of the front, which had been a window but no longer had glass. I crawled a few metres from the wreckage and lay face-down on the grass. I stayed there without moving for about fifteen minutes. During that time, someone came and put a blanket over me. The ambulance, police, and even the local TV news crew (who arrived first, perhaps also expecting a fiery spectacle) were soon at the scene.

Strangely, Richard seemed like a helpful passer-by, picking up papers that had spilt from our briefcases upon impact. A police officer approached, asking if he'd witnessed the accident. I could only hear their exchange, for my eyes remained shut.

Lying there, fully conscious yet reluctant to face the world, I noted Richard's distinct reaction, as though he was marching to a different tune or reading from another script. Doubts crept in. Should I remain here with my eyes shut? Why is he up and about? What's the appropriate behaviour after a motor accident?

On that damp grass, feeling inadequate because I wasn't reacting like Richard,[8] I also reflected on what I'd believed were my final thoughts. 'Isn't one's life supposed to flash before one's eyes?' I pondered. That hadn't been my experience. 'Typical,' I chided myself, 'I can't even have the expected dying thoughts. Surely, I should've thought about my children, and the fact I wouldn't see them grow up.' My mother's words echoed, 'Triple F is the selfish one.'

Later, in the casualty ward, after gathering the courage to open my eyes and verify that I was still alive (which contradicted my knowledge that I was about to die), I asked a doctor what the

---

8   Richard's response to trauma – stoicism – was learned early in his life. It was the prevailing masculine behavioural norm for six-year-old British boys separated from Mummy.

normal response to trauma was: the eternal search for valida-tion. He affirmed that both reactions were common expressions of shock, with Richard's being the archetypal male response and mine, well, you guessed it, the female counterpart. Imagine that … gender-based responses to shock … who would have thought?

'From this example and many others shared by Francine over the years, it is evident that she internalised her parents' view that there was a right way and a wrong way to respond to one's experiences. It's apparent to me that this patient often struggled to ascertain if her actions or affect were "right."

'In conclusion, Francine developed endogenous depression as both her survival and sanity hinged on understanding her role and her lines, thereby maintaining an internal mirage of control. She tried to navigate a new environment with neither a "down under" rulebook nor a North American English/Australian English translation app – tools vital for her and other insecure people. To survive meant not only articulating the correct words but also using the right tones and emphases as directed. Patients with her family history unconsciously need to learn the rules before they're enacted: pre-emptive swot to avoid the swat.'

Who knew Dr Jaye had a sense of humour?

With this eloquent choice of words, she ends her discourse. The (head) space is silent, the listeners' preconceived psychological postulations preventing them from celebrating alternative or original perspectives.

Triple F Romantic Partners Association: her cognition

The longer-term and short-lived partners with whom Triple F has been romantically involved are seated around a sizeable (but not massive) boardroom table. Given the male inclination to intellectualise rather than discuss their emotional state, it's anticipated that statements from attendees will be delivered rationally.

Today, the sub-committee aims to reflect on Triple F's seemingly random neuronal firings – perhaps a reason the men in her life agree she was never a dull date or partner. The chair of the meeting is Sweet (and Sour) Richard.

'Good afternoon! It's 3 pm and I'd like to commence this November meeting of the Triple F Romantic Partners Association (TFRPA). Our main focus today is Triple F's cognition – specifically how her digressions affect those close to her. Please remember that general comments about your perception of her personality are welcome.'

A few short-term boyfriends chime in.

'She has an intriguing mind that frequently shifts from subject to subject. She'd occasionally diverge, describing the images her words conjured. Weird and hard to keep up with. For instance, one time when I said, "Frankie, grab an umbrella. It's going to rain cats and dogs," she cracked up, sharing that she envisioned poodles, spaniels, Siamese, Persians and others soaring through the air.'

'Yes, I observed that, too. Perhaps it was her way of keeping us entertained, increasing the chance we'd stick around.'

'In that case, it didn't work very well,' they all mutter, except for dear Richard, who is wholly engrossed or ensnared or something of the sort, as he remains with Francine.

'I also believe that she attempted to *exert* a great deal of control over me in our relationship, while concurrently displaying significant dependence.'

Agreement is expressed by the nodding of heads by the men from her teens and early twenties. Some disagreement comes from the men who came later as Frankie began embracing her feminism, which allowed her to establish some boundaries.

'I think that Frankie is just a typical neurotic Jewish American woman,' observes husband number one, the typical neurotic Jewish American man. The one other Jewish man in her past, the charming Jeff from her wilder days, agrees.

'Frankie is a typical alchy/addict,' comments husband number two, the typical alchy/addict. The other alcoholics around the table agree. And there are quite a few of them; perhaps it's a case of like attracting like?

'Excuse me, but you're all wrong,' Richard interjects, clearing his throat and readying himself to pontificate, as academics, clergy, and politicians often do. His words serve as a mirror, reflecting the woman in recovery.

'Francine is the sum of the influences and individuals who've touched her life – a fusion of everyone present. Moreover, given my belief in genetics interacting with cultural influences, I see the essence of Francine as being shaped by the myriad cells within her, carrying messages from the DNA – the trans-generational Jewish RNA – that encodes intergenerational trauma. Given this biological context and the background of most of you here, her evolution from Frankie to Francine is particularly noteworthy.'

With that, Richard closes the meeting, advising the members to read the rest of the book before their next meeting to better inform future discussions.

2
THE TODDLER PRINCESS: THE SHRINKS' VIEW

For many years, Triple F laid the blame – to everyone from shrinks to fellow bar patrons, from women in special groups to her peers in twelve-step programs – squarely on her parents, who she believed had failed her.

But was it really their fault? Maybe Triple F was born with a genetic predisposition towards neuroses, addiction, eating disorders, and clinical depression. Even if she'd had an ideal mother like Mrs Brady on *The Brady Bunch*, would Triple F's journey have been any different? For kids growing up in the 1970s, this idealised family was so perfectly harmonious that no real-life household could ever measure up. Maybe it was different for the next generation who had *The Simpsons* as a benchmark.

Listening in on therapy: the early years

She has recounted her story to so many counsellors that by the time she met Dr Jaye, Triple F's history had turned clinical. Like a poem recited too many times, it lost its impact with each telling. To be honest, her memories are either fuzzy or entirely hidden. *They* say that this is a sign of past sexual or physical abuse. The cause-and-effect relationship is debatable, as many people struggle to remember their early childhood. This might imply that experiencing some form of childhood trauma or dysfunction is not unusual.

Frankie's first stint in a mental health worker's office was at age sixteen, initiated by Henry. To the teenage Triple F, the psychiatrist bore a striking resemblance to the Kentucky Fried Chicken (KFC) Colonel Sanders. Perhaps his mind was on inventing more secret recipes rather than attending to the distressed girl before him.

'Doctor, I'm a screwed-up teenager because my father used to hit my older brother and he'd knock my sister's head against my brother's. I was constantly afraid I'd be next. So, from an early age, I became Daddy's little girl, his princess. It was how I survived, doctor.'

'Tell me, Frankie, when do you think that you first *consciously* made this decision,' he asks. For reasons best known to workers in these caregiving professions, there's often a need to tie specific traumatic events to certain ages. Perhaps they're looking for patterns or sequences of behaviour to pinpoint the cause.

'Gee, Doc, I've already told you that my childhood memories are few and far between. How do you expect me to remember when? Should I know? Is this a trick question to see if I'm numerically obsessive? All I can tell you is that I was very young. We're talking two or three. The sound of a head being bashed on the floor above is a strong stimulus for a sharp-witted toddler.

'And why are you asking about my making a *conscious* decision? Hmm. It would seem that working with children who have witnessed abuse is not your schtick. I wasn't deciding anything. I was surviving.'

'Well, Frankie, why do you think that Henry was violent towards your brother, Jacob, and your sister, Sandra? Were they very naughty? Did they upset him? And what about your mother. What did she do when your father was "punishing" the children?'

'Whoa, Doc.' (This is a different 'Doc' asking the same questions as they do … Triple F's answers vary depending on her age. This is her post-PhD response, which can be read with Helen Reddy's song, 'I Am Woman' in the background.)

'Why do you call it punishment? And what's this crap about being naughty? I mean, I don't know what Sandy and Jake did, or I do, but what difference does it make? He wasn't punishing naughty behaviour. He was abusing children.

'And, if you really want to know where it came from, I guess it depends on your theoretical orientation. If you subscribe to a feminist perspective, then, Doctor, he was just another male trying to assert his power in a patriarchal society. The usual stuff.

'Or perhaps you lean towards a holistic approach that emphasises the era Henry grew up in, being a child of the depression and the offspring of yet another man who couldn't love or, at least, couldn't show it. He was bright, my father, but the lack of money hindered his university aspirations, and then there was the Second World War. Maybe he was frustrated and found some targets.

'Wait, Doc, let's get serious here. Given your background and training, we'd need to delve into the deep-seated psychological reasons for Henry's violence. The insecurity masked by arrogance … the need for authority without any challenge to it. Yes, if we're exploring this avenue, we could potentially blame the victims, or at least my brother. Jake always talked back. How could he? Was he an idiot? Wasn't it obvious to him what would happen? But he constantly did it. Jake set off Henry.'

'Tell me, Frankie, what did your brother do?' The Kentucky Fried Shrink's question pulls her back. Frankie senses there's intense emotion and pain ahead.

'Well, um, Doctor, I don't really know. I was just a little kid. Was I supposed to have that insight? Was I supposed to know that he'd get in trouble every time that he was mean to me? Was I meant to regulate his behaviour towards me? I aimed to be the cute and nice little sister, but he knew that I was Daddy's princess. Henry wouldn't stand for any poor behaviour directed at me. Stop looking at me like that. I didn't bash their heads together. Didn't use the strap. I didn't take Jake and Sandy by the hair and bang their heads on the linoleum. I just sat there with my mother and listened while they *got* it. That's all I did. And I never smiled like she did. Anyway, surely Miriam's look must have been an anxious grimace – certainly, not a smile? I never felt good knowing they were punished. Never. Alright, stop staring. Perhaps, just perhaps, I felt a touch of relief. I was grateful it wasn't me. I was safe this time. Can you understand that? I wasn't glad that they were getting it, but I was fucking happy that it wasn't my head.'

She rocks slowly, tears trickling down her cheeks. The emphasis here is on 'slowly'. Triple F isn't one to cry easily. We're talking a mere seepage.[9] Frankie senses that a nerve has been struck – a truth, a memory – that, if anchored, might hold the answers.

'You sound very guilty, Frankie,' the ancient, bearded man observes. He must be somewhat moved by the tears; after all, it has been ten months, and they're making their first appearance. A slow therapy, indeed. 'You don't need to feel guilty. Anyone in your family's situation would've been relieved not to be the one beaten. It's OK.'

Bloody doctor. Invalidate my feelings, why don't you? Of course, you're a man, so what can I expect?

'Yes, I *know* intellectually, in my head, among those millions of brain cells, that I don't *need* to feel guilty. But dear old doctor, feelings are feelings. They are not rational. And I bloody well do

---

9   Sobs come much later in recovery when Francine learns to identify and label hurt and rejection and then, allows herself to feel them.

feel responsible. Often, Henry would punish them either because they upset Miriam or me because of something they did. I suppose that you guys would call this the "survivor guilt".

'And let me tell you, sometimes it's worse being the observer than the target. The continuous dread of what might happen can be more traumatising than the act itself. Later, I realised nothing is as terrifying as the fear itself.

'It's like acting, where you need to get your lines and actions right. But imagine the screenplay always changing, without informing the actress. That's a tough role.'

Effects of being the witness

Let's leave the Kentucky Fried Shrink (and others of his ilk) to secret culinary musings for a while. They are in possession of some germane life history data. Over time, they help guide Triple F through the quagmire. Francine starts to realise that, even as she emerges years later, triggers persist, and the habit of catastrophising enshrouds her for (theoretical) protection. Through Dr Jaye's compassionate gaze and the trust built over years, Francine revisits the time of Franny and slowly processes the emotions that Franny once hid.

Being cast as his princess in Henry's story no doubt contributed to Triple F's spinning herself into a silky safety cocoon. Hypervigilance equalled protection. She believed that by anticipating every outcome, she'd be safe.[10]

For those unfamiliar with the popular jargon of dysfunctional families, hypervigilance means attuning to one's surroundings so acutely that you can predict others' needs and moods. Many women who've survived domestic violence will recognise this. They've intuited this through consistent observation and adapting their behaviours to lessen the risk of violence. They learn to

---

10   However, in reality, the batterer's abuse almost always continues to occur.

detect the signs preceding fits of rage and act in ways to avoid being the target.

Growing up in an alcoholic and/or dysfunctional family leaves children feeling powerless. Trying to control people and situations gives them a sense of power and security – that they won't be victimised anymore. This feeling equates with a semblance of safety. For Triple F, a lesson ingrained from childhood was that relinquishing control meant paving the way for the worst possible outcome.

Stimulus/response: Toddler Franny sees a face contorted with fury and hears her siblings' screams. Instinctively, she embarks on a quest to understand the intricacies of the survivor/witness role. When she behaves brightly and precociously, Henry's face brightens with one of his infrequent smiles. Being intelligent, lively, and charming becomes her primary defence.

The role of companion

By age three, Franny's existential fieldwork had yielded an extensive (unwritten, as she's not *that* precocious) dossier on Henry. For example, she observed that he enjoyed speaking omnisciently. Franny mastered the art of asking the right questions (that prompted Henry's pontifications, grooming her for potential career choices, like social work, journalism, or teaching).

Looking back, it seemed to Triple F that every evening, Franny and Henry would take a walk. He would clasp her tiny hand within his, and together, they'd 'discuss' the day's political events and the scientific wonders around them. Here, 'discuss' means Henry's monologue interrupted by Franny's timely questions and admiring remarks.

Henry exclusively held Franny's hand; Jacob and Sandra received touches from him only in moments of aggression.

Miriam would receive a kiss upon his return from work at 17:30 hours. Such intimacy between Franny and Henry contrasted sharply with the family's generally stark emotional landscape.

Franny's appearance also seemed a prerequisite for this companionship. While Miriam and Sandra sported short brown hair, Franny's long blonde locks came with an unspoken rule: they mustn't be cut. However, at ten, Miriam decided the golden waves needed trimming. The Bible's Delilah might've inspired her. As Samson lost his strength with his shorn hair, so too did Franny lose something upon returning from the hairdresser. Henry, who rarely commented on looks, spoke with an uncharacteristic calm anger.

'What have you done to *her* hair, Miriam? How could you do *this* without talking to me first?' And thus began years of male objectification …

'But Henry, I never consult with you when taking Jacob or Sandra to the hairdresser. I didn't think you'd want to know.'

'All of her beautiful blonde curls … gone. How could you do this to me?'

To "me"? It appears that Henry was channelling his mother with this comment. 'Do this to *me*?' is a typical phrase reminiscent of a Jewish mother's passive-aggressive love, reinforcing the idea that 'Jewish mother boundaries' is an oxymoron.

A dangerous safety

By age six, Franny, perhaps expressing innate intuition or her hang-ups, began routines she'd maintain throughout her life: security rituals. These consisted of inspecting beneath her bed and inside her wardrobe. She'd then struggle to sleep for hours, only to seek comfort from Henry and Miriam watching the late news. Henry, following another ritual, would tuck her in, and sleep would eventually embrace her.

Special session of head shrinks

The head mental health sub-group traditionally dedicates its annual general meeting specifically to this behaviour and similar practices that Triple F engaged in over the years. There's been much debate about the origins of these fears but a shared understanding sees insomnia as a self-protective mechanism.

'She likely believed these rites improved her chances of survival. As if to spot a lurking killer waiting for her to drift off. It's more magical thinking than realistic risk prevention.'

'That could explain why Triple F started exhibiting insomnia early on. This sleeplessness resurfaced throughout her life, peaking during periods of clinical depression.'

Perhaps this type of psychological theorizing is another expressive outlet for frustrated crime writers or those who enjoy jigsaw puzzles?

The alternative health coach who Triple F saw during one of her periods of marijuana indulgence, and who is likely also continuously stoned, sums up the group's view:

'Hey, man, there's a definite connection here with the big "C"? The control stuff, can you dig it? If she fell asleep, she would be unable to fight back – as if she could. Far out, man – she would have none. Rituals are not only guaranteed to influence the rotation of the Earth, they have often provided her with a feeling of security. This is a no-brainer and having smoked weed for two decades I am eminently qualified to talk about the lack of cerebral functionality.'

Francine has discussed her adoption and discarding of various practices over the years with Dr Jaye. Although this therapist seldom speaks, either in therapy sessions or during head meetings, on this occasion, she articulates her agreement with the others. Reading from volume 8 of the 3,268 pages of Francine's case notes, she provides a summary of these behaviours and their longevity:

'When Franny was aged six to twelve, she felt a compulsion to return to the previous page of whatever she was reading to re-read the last line. During that time, she also counted footpath cracks.

'Francine spoke about Frankie's years of intense addiction and unhealthy eating patterns, noting the apparent absence of these obsessive habits. However, she recognised that her ingrained alcohol intake schedule and the mental tallying of every calorie she consumed were, in essence, other forms of obsessions.

'The resumption of ritualistic behaviours unrelated to alcoholism or eating disorders took place after she was finally treated for clinical depression. Yes, I do say "finally" since seven health practitioners, including a few present here, failed to diagnose this condition, which presented itself as anxiety.

'For several years post-diagnosis, Francine was particular about hanging laundry ensuring she alternated the coloured pegs in the sequence – red, yellow, blue, and white. She might have adopted this ritual earlier, but before moving to Australia, dryers were commonplace, rendering clotheslines unnecessary.

'She took up daily exercise – first becoming a "gym junkie" (her words) and later taking up solo early morning runs. These could be seen as other compulsive activities, especially as she would exercise despite sprained ankles or upper respiratory infections. Francine termed daily exercise as the caboose in her bulimarexia. And she referred to it as a relatively healthier addiction.

'Both OCD and bulimarexia stem from a desire for control. Today, I'll focus on the non-bulimarexic rituals, starting with Francine's recent ones, which arose during the Covid-19 pandemic, a notably challenging time for many. Unlike some Adult Children who have chosen to avoid the news, Francine adhered to a strict schedule for reading, listening and viewing the medical research, epidemiology, and daily virus statistics. The compulsiveness lay in the rigidity.[11]

'Another recent ritual involved running. While jogging, Francine felt the need to touch an even number of bicycle path bollards or U-bars. She realised during therapy that it was not a coincidence that this compulsion coincided with lots of life changes. Her standing as an advocate for women was waning; her children had left the nest, and her workplace status had shifted with the changes in the political environment. Laughing, she ultimately concluded, "Definitely an absence of the fantasy of power." She stopped needing to touch the bollards shortly after that session. In a later one, Francine explained why that, and others ended:

I have stopped doing whatever it was except for my current-news-reading and self-care routine[12], because each time, at a gut level, I came to see that it wasn't working (to control other people, places, or things). Plus, I got tired of the constraints each of the compulsions imposed: the costs exceeded the benefits. I'd reach a bottom and recognise that the magic was not working. Come to think of it, Dr Jaye, I've just had another therapy insight! The same thing happened with food and substance abuse stuff!

The soft-spoken psychiatrist pauses, watching the others nod their heads – the men in agreement and the women as an indication of empathy, encouraging her to continue.

---

11   This type of intellectualising was (and is) a common defence mechanism used by Triple F (in addition to denial, repression, and disassociation).

12   In addition to her daily hour run, Francine has set times each day for resistance work, abdominal exercise, yoga, and meditation. Lockdowns did not present any obstacles since all activities were solitary.

'Unlike many other ritualised behaviour patterns, the safety surveillance has persisted intermittently to the present.[13] Francine, upon entering an empty house alone, feels unsafe until she has checked all closets to make sure no "bad guys" are hiding.[14] The reason for the persistence of this ritual is obvious, no doubt, to everyone.'

Again, everyone present nods in affirmation. They have their own egos to consider and must appear to understand the obvious. 'No one has jumped out of the closet and attacked Francine. Therefore, the time that she expends is outweighed by the positive outcome of feeling safe – the benefit exceeds the cost.'

More ritualised behaviours (with Dr Ben Cohen)

Dr Cohen seems inclined to stick with Franny's parents. This is unsurprising given the Freudian orientation of his practice.

'I'd like to delve deeper into the relationship Franny had with her parents as a young child. Let's set aside discussions of what may or may not have been non-sexual incest, her sense that her mother didn't like her, and memories of heads hitting the linoleum that she might or might not have witnessed.

'In one session, I asked her what else she remembered concerning her interactions with Henry and Miriam when she was aged three to five?' Dr Cohen's next journal article was specifically focusing on the phallic stage of development. This was her reply:

Well, as I've told you before, I don't have many memories. The few that I do recall for some reason involve ritualised behaviours. Not

---

13   Wearing a mask, washing her hands, and spraying deliveries throughout the pandemic had been not only natural but comforting for Francine.

14   Triple F ought not to have watched 'scary' movies. After viewing Hitchcock's *Psycho*, she has never felt safe taking a shower when alone in the house. Films like *Psycho* can prompt such long-term reactions in those with PTSD.

like checking under the bed rituals or counting rites, but patterns of interaction that occurred at a set time in a prescribed way. Here's an example: each day, Monday through Sunday, I woke Miriam at exactly 8:15 to braid my hair. She would undo the plaits from the day before, brush my hair, and then re-braid it. Looking back, I probably could have done it without her for a few years. But this was our special time together, albeit about seven minutes. Then, when I was ten, as I mentioned before, she decided that this braiding activity was a nuisance, and off I went for the Delilah cut. Not sure if I continued to see Miriam in the mornings or if she had even more of a sleep-in.

Hey, Dr Cohen, another of these regular 'have to do' actions just popped into my mind. After my hair was braided and I got my bag ready for school, I always went to see Henry for a kiss on the cheek and to say goodbye. He'd be putting on his uniform, which made him even more remote than the civilian Henry. I did this every weekday, rain or shine, until one morning, I was upset with Henry. I don't remember why or what had happened, but I was determined not to kiss him goodbye. I left and was a block away when I experienced a tidal wave of guilt, or was it grief? Hell, I don't know which of the twenty-seven emotions this one was.[15]

I was compelled back down the road, into the house, and running up the stairs to Henry and his cheek. Breaching a habitual behaviour, which acts like a security blanket, requires a herculean effort. That is unless the 'ritual' is terminated by someone else, which happened with another Henry-Franny ritual. Given your focus on the genital stage of development, this might particularly interest you, Doctor. Notice how I now switch to the third person?

---

15 A 2017 University of California study identified twenty-seven affect categories, concluding that they are all interconnected.

When Franny was three, four, and five, she'd sit by the living room window every evening waiting for Henry's return. His bladder must have been trained to follow a strict schedule including a 17:30 urination time. With military precision, Henry would head to the toilet. It was understood that this was another special time for Franny and Henry. She would stand beside the toilet, chatting about her day, whilst Henry urinated. It was a sacrosanct moment until the evening Miriam moved towards the bathroom door as the two approached, and spoke:

'She's getting too old to be in there with you, Henry.'

'Oh, right, you have a point.'

Henry seemed to accept Miriam's viewpoint. But Doctor, what about Franny? Her keen intuition (aka hypervigilance) sensed an ulterior motive: an enactment of Miriam's jealousy. If that was Franny's readout, then it's not surprising that shortly after this incident, she began to believe that someone had been hired to end her life.

And, sorry[16] Doc, but in the updated version of this story, which post-dates our last consult, the memory of who she perceived as masterminding her intended demise is blank. We'll never truly know unless Francine finds a different shrink capable of unlocking deeply repressed memories.

'One other question might require a different specialist. Why did Franny see Miriam as jealous? Was it a Jewish predisposition for neuroses, or was there *something* real there that a sensitive child could sense? Both?'

---

16 Females – specifically the sub-species marked by a codependent sense of responsibility for everything including the weather – apologise with the regularity of the lunar cycle. Plus, in Triple F's case, there's a the double whammy of growing up with violence, which is also conducive to self-blame.

The big 'I'

Back to the saga of the snipping of the golden curls … do not despair for our hair-challenged heroine. She managed, through extra charm and precociousness, to keep Henry satisfied. Speaking of satisfaction … one does wonder in this scenario about the big 'I' – Incest. Did the roles of companion and Daddy's sweetheart involve sexual intimacy? Those who have theorised this explanation for her mental health issues have been unable to unearth any memories. Triple F's mental barriers are sealed tight, potentially muffling any sounds, if they exist, of a little girl screaming for help.

Over the years, her career paths and healing journey have led Francine to interact with people who have experienced therapeutic breakthroughs resulting in incest revelations. Is this a coincidence? Does it mean that a random sample of people includes many who have been sexually victimised by a family member? Or might it be the nature of her work and/or her recovery that has resulted in an exceptionally high frequency of such interactions?

Or is it a case of like being attracted to like? She knows that when she listens to survivors discuss their feelings during assaults, she feels a deep visceral resonance. At times, Francine has hoped that this explanation is the correct one. Incest would justify addiction, bulimarexia, phobias, OCD, complex PTSD, and other diagnostic labels she has been assigned.

However, it might resonate because Triple F is a survivor of what some popular self-help writers term 'covert incest'. According to its proponents, this denotes a category of psychological abuse which misleadingly empowers children.[17] They are

---

17 Consistent with the construct of non-physical incest, Frankie was treated more like an adult than as a child by Henry. She knew that her primary role in the relationship was to serve his (non-sexual) needs.

treated as equals, as partners in every sense except, in her conscious memory, *that* particular one.

As Henry's chosen confidante, she was special. However, Rapunzel survived, her needs and identity formation neglected because the relationship existed primarily to meet Henry's needs.

The master of the mind (with Dr O'Reilly)

'So, Frankie, what else can you recall about your childhood besides your father's abuse of your siblings?' Dr Liam O'Reilly, known within the Al-Anon community as a go-to expert, sounds increasingly desperate. It's their third consultation, and the young Al-Anon newcomer is currently grappling with panic attacks.

'Let's start with your family members. Describe your father. What did he do for a living?'

'Gee, Doc, can't you guess what Henry did? Here's a man who revered logic, dismissed emotions and instilled in his children the belief that intellect was paramount. A man who shed tears in their presence just once.[18] A man who asserted that there was no God. That they were their own deities – the masters of their destinies. You heard right – *masters*. Henry was, and remained until his death, a chauvinist with a gender-biased view of the world.

'Henry was unsurprisingly a military man. A leader of *men*. A war-hero fighter pilot who returned to Canada with an array

---

18 This took place on the only occasion that the family went to see a film – *Exodus* – together. Henry, likely triggered by the moving story of Jews who had survived the Holocaust who then experienced more persecution, was noticeably moved. His tears were visible to Franny. These became linked in her memory to violence when, in the car driving home, Jake angered his father who pulled the car over, leaned over the back seat, and struck his son's head.

of medals that paled in comparison to his internal scars. Forced to crash-land several times over two tours of duty, Henry was neither diagnosed with PTSD nor treated for it. It posed a challenge since PTSD only gained medical recognition about 30 years later in the *Diagnostic and Statistical Manual of Mental Disorders III*. Henry wasn't treated for what was then known as battle fatigue.

'He perceived himself as unbreakable – as superhuman and in control. His squadron even nicknamed him "God". This self-view left no space for the "God of Abraham, God of Isaac, God of Jacob", with whom Henry was raised.'

'So,' Dr O'Reilly clears his throat, a bit nervously. Could he see himself in Henry, causing some distance between himself and Henry's staunchly feminist daughter? 'And how did Henry treat Miriam? Was he violent towards her as well?'

'There was a time when I would've hastily and emphatically responded "no" to professionals like you. I used to perceive violence in a limited way, overlooking the myriad forms it can take. But age may be the best teacher.

'To my knowledge, Henry never struck Miriam. However, in other respects, we tread on a different narrative, Doctor. For instance, Miriam may have once been bright with the potential to be a person in her own right. Yet, Henry overpowered her, much like a tsunami engulfs everything in its path. He never allowed her a thought or idea uniquely hers.[19]

'I began to view her with contempt, influenced by Henry's unspoken but clear instruction to his three children. We

---

19 Take religion. Henry's atheism was a taboo conversational topic but was likely a reflection of ill-feelings towards his father (another taboo subject). Miriam's pre-Henry religious practices and beliefs were also never discussed. She would light the Chanukah menorah candles (without prayer or head covering).

instinctively knew not to approach Miriam with our troubles. This behaviour stemmed from two unstated beliefs: firstly, seeing her as fragile at best, and at worst, weak. Secondly, whenever Miriam tried to voice her opinions, Henry would suppress them with a demeaning tone that often belittled or mocked. She was portrayed as lacking the acumen or insight for problem-solving. There was this unspoken bond between Henry and me.'

'Ah, Frankie,' Dr O'Reilly's eyes gleam with anticipation. He seems to operate on the belief that parental mistakes are a prime source of issues. 'What secrets did you and Henry keep from Miriam?'

'Well, sorry to disappoint you, Doc. Again, with the implications. We understood that Miriam needed to be guarded from anything potentially upsetting, thus constructing an image of her as helpless and needing to be protected. Because you see, Henry tended to dichotomise the world's population with him on one side – alone – and everyone else – mere human beings – on the other side. Within this dichotomy, the female of the species, for whom affect outweighed intellect, were slotted in as the most inferior of mortals. That was where Henry put Miriam. "Don't tell your mother. It will upset her (and she is not strong enough to hear the truth)."'

This is why, in hindsight, I recognise the immense cruelty in this. It was a negation of Miriam's very identity. A chronic invalidation of who she was. The woman she could have become.

'Anyway, Dr O'Reilly, if I picture Henry as the militaristic hyper-rational guy that he was, well, I guess I'd have to describe Miriam as the stereotypical Jewish mother, like Sophie[20] in *Portnoy's Complaint*.'

---

20 Described in the *New Yorker* as 'long-suffering; expert worrier; unrelenting wielder of guilt as weapon ...'

Portnoy's Complaint

'Tell me more please, Frankie, about your mother and her resentments,' urges the psychologist who, holding a visiting post at a local university, seems to be gathering material for a budding academic paper. These questions evoke memories Triple F wishes would remain dormant. They hurt.

'Well, often my mother looked like she'd recently eaten a crab-apple. She compared her childhood, adolescence, and young adulthood to the experiences of her three children. I could sense that some of her bitterness was targeted at me. A sixth sense wasn't required since Miriam, the oldest of four children raised during the 1930s by her (no doubt traumatised) Eastern European Jewish migrant parents, was renowned for her sighs. Jake, Sandy, and I would hear about her summers working as a nanny from age twelve and how she became a bookkeeper by seventeen. Understandably, given this relative deprivation, Miriam bemoaned our lack of gratitude full stop.

'Along with low self-esteem about her mental acumen, not surprisingly Miriam had body issues. In fact, she was a strikingly good-looking, petite woman. Yet, she felt unattractive her entire life, perceiving herself as overweight and flat-chested. (Dr O'Reilly might've delved into Triple F's body image issues, but he was more fixated on familial roots.) She could have been a victim of childhood abuse or some other familial dysfunction. Who knows? That generation never talked about it. Not like mine.

'And Doc, when I developed breasts (late at seventeen), I sensed Miriam's resentment over their size. Years later, my university qualifications and promising career elicited mixed feelings from her: pride in my achievements and sorrow for her missed chances. I felt her resentment lingering, another unspoken presence among the many in Henry and Miriam's home.'

The psychologist perked up, showing renewed interest. 'Elephants in their home? I've heard that expression used by people in twelve-step programs?'

'Yes. I first saw that phrase in an Al-Anon reading, which described how bizarre behaviours are taking place in the home. Everyone carefully walks around it but for the most part denial prevails. It becomes a normal part of the interior design. My father's rage and violence epitomised one such elephant. We never discussed it. Verboten. Its existence was to be avoided. Mum's resentment was another.'

The Rules of Miriam (shared with Dr Jaye)

The first rule of Miriam

'Francine, can you elaborate on what you said to the psychologist years ago about your mother's resemblance to Sophie in *Portnoy's Complaint*?'

'Sure, Dr Jaye.

'Since seeing Liam O'Reilly in my early days in Al-Anon, I have learned more about how Jewish mother rules operate and, by attending ACA[21] here in Australia, how to thwart their assaults of guilt and shame into my psyche. Like, "Eat your dinner or it'll break your mother's heart." That type of thing: simply put, emotional blackmail. If you don't do blah, and if you don't do it perfectly, then not only will it break our hearts, but we'll still be there to make you feel ashamed. It's hard to explain, Doctor. Either you're a Jew or you're not. And if you're not, then it's likely you're unable to get it: the many ways that she lets you know that her love is conditional upon you being a selfless, perfect grown-up little girl.'

---

21 Adult Children of Alcoholism and other Dysfunctional Families.

'Let's look at the last bit, Francine. Something important is emerging. Tell me about this selfless grown up that you were supposed to be.'

'Overlooking a birthday, in her eyes, branded me as a child or adult who neglected her parents. An overarching edict also prevailed: self-care was synonymous with selfishness.'

Dr Jaye makes a rare interjection.

'Yes, I have heard your mother's voice in this room when you are struggling with certain feelings. "Sad", "hurt", "anxious", "envious", "resentful" – I have watched the internal conflict within you when you have started to feel them (and no doubt others). Miriam's voice, "What right do you have?" Now terror and fear on the other hand, those are acceptable.'

Francine absorbs Dr Jaye's comment. Although its truth resonates, she's compelled to defend her mother.

'I don't lay all the blame at her feet. She typified the Jewish mothers of her era. They were constitutionally or genetically unable to compliment or praise their children directly. Perhaps this frugality with compliments stems from millennia of persecution – a survival trait, the "ghetto gene" so to speak. Maybe it's rooted in Jewish customs — an effort to deflect the evil eye.

'In any case, I guess that I grew up thinking that I was average looking but that my intellect was above average (a belief shattered at sixteen when I failed to excel in Physics and Trigonometry). Within our sub-culture, intelligence didn't invoke jealousy, thanks to the Torah's emphasis on education. Bragging rights were reserved for proclamations like, "my son, the doctor", or "my daughter's husband, the lawyer".

'So Miriam's foremost rule, which haunted my psyche for years, shaping my life, was simple: Never think well of yourself or *they'll* get you.'

The second rule of Miriam

'Another rule, imprinted by my mother and lingering within, dictates: "Always expect the worst; then nothing will ever hurt or disappoint."

While this might seem unduly pessimistic to a goy — and I'm making an assumption based on your Asian appearance, Dr Jaye — such a mindset aligns with a culture that had every reason to foster a wary worldview. The Jews. Watch out or the goyim will get you. They have before and they will again. Expect the worst and be prepared. And for Henry and Miriam, no doubt being raised during the Depression contributed to such a gloomy ethos.

'Without a doubt, Henry's violence taught Jacob, Sandra, and me to always be on our toes. Don't let the defences down. Don't relax or he'll get you. If not physically, he'll zing you intellectually or psychologically. Keep the guard up at all times and always expect the worst.

'Until emails became commonplace, approaching the mailbox would set my heart racing as I envisioned the worst possible outcomes. With emails, this alertness persists, only now it's a potential continuous strain during my waking hours. However, there's a silver lining, Dr Jaye. Newer voices in my internal dialogue remind me that there's likely no bad news awaiting and that constant worry is futile. As our sessions continue, except during times when the voices of Miriam and Henry intensify due to stress, the other internal voices can now hush the pervasive gloom cast by my parents.

'The other thing about Henry and Miriam that I don't think was true for Howard and Marion Cunningham in *Happy Days* or Carol and Mike Brady was the way my parents put each of their children in their own little box, marking each with indelible ink for life. As I've told you before, I was the one labelled as a spendthrift and as more self-centred. Therefore, for the remainder of their lives, they saw me through those lenses. There was no room or allowance for change. No matter what I did and no matter how much I changed, Henry and Miriam had to ignore behaviours that didn't fit those labels, focusing instead on the behaviours that enabled them to say, "She's still the same." Like if I forgot to send a Mother's Day card in 2002, it became an enduring topic of conversation, but the cards from 2001 and 2003? Ignored.

'Do you see what I mean, Dr Jaye? Not a very positive childhood, was it? Or was it? And yes, you can hear Miriam saying, "That I should have had it so good." Likely, I've been talking to you about it by rote – as the story that I've created and told. Maybe my own lenses are biased with Henry and Miriam unfairly blamed for decades. Let me give you an example.

'During sessions with past therapists, I often recounted the tale of my first-grade report card. "Look, Mommy and Daddy! Look at my report card. Isn't it wonderful? I got all As." The subtext here was, "Aren't you proud? Don't you really love me now that I've shown you how perfect I can be?"

'Henry looked the card over carefully. No smile of joy. No hug. "Why did you get this A minus in mathematics, Franny? Surely at your grade, you can still manage to get an A."

'That's one of my classic stories of Henry and Miriam's conditional love that turned me into an addicted and disordered person. But, did it transpire exactly that way? My recollections are murky at best, and perhaps this narrative took shape in the office of a therapist, moulded to fit a convenient template.

'Here's an alternative view of the straight A report card scenario: Franny, for whatever reasons, felt the need to be perfect. Perhaps it was that gene for perfectionism. The A minus simply wasn't enough for me. When Henry and Miriam looked at the report card, they might have said, "That's terrific Franny. We're really very proud of you." But, because I wasn't proud of myself, I didn't hear it that way. Instead, I projected my internal voice onto them: "You're just not enough."

'I do have one memory from the time period, which supports this latter view of reality. I can remember with unusual clarity the school's award ceremony at the end of Grade 2. Having topped Grade 1 the previous year, I was anxiously awaiting a repeat win. This memory is vivid, unlike most from my childhood, possibly because such anxiety-inducing moments of high expectation have been a recurrent theme in my life. My heart raced in anticipation of hearing, "The best second-grade student is Franny."

'The principal announces the first award for the top reader. Unbelievably, it is my name. "But it can't be me," I scream inside. "You don't get two awards, which means I'm not the number one second grader. I'm not even the second best. Just the best reader … not good enough … not good enough …" Devastated. I walked up to the stage almost in tears.

'However, in the many years that followed, try as I might, I can't recall any words or implications from Henry or Miriam that could've triggered such disappointment. They seemed pleased. Perhaps this is an instance where my personal history needs revisiting. But, of course, it's up to you, Doc, to make that call – so to speak. Of course, I'm now picturing you picking up your phone.'

The typically reticent psychiatrist (an oxymoron?) remains silent for a moment.

'You grade yourself on most things – even in this room, don't you, Francine? Regardless of the memory version, being the top reader wasn't the High Distinction you aimed for.'

She chuckles, and Francine joins in. Once again, Dr Jaye's words have a way of normalising behaviours, thoughts, and feelings that some committee members in Francine's head labelled as shameful.

'So true, Dr Jaye! Guess I really don't need to do that any-more, do I?' With that statement, another subtle internal shift occurs, nudging Francine towards accepting herself as a flawed yet acceptable human being.

3
THE PRINCESS YEARS: UNEARTHING WITH DR JAYE

etting: the cosy yet clinical office of Dr Jaye. She has been attentively listening to Francine for well over a decade.[22]

Is Dr Jaye enigmatic, or is she the only therapist that Triple F consulted whose therapy construct includes an exclusive focus on the patient? Despite ten years of sessions, Francine knows no personal details about Dr Jaye. This sharply contrasts with many of the other mental health professionals Francine consulted throughout her life, who often blurred boundaries and over-shared about their personal struggles.

Over the years, at Francine's request, Dr Jaye established two clear guidelines for their therapy sessions: 1. The hour is Francine's time; she is free to discuss whatever she wishes; and 2. Francine's reality is *the* reality during their weekly sessions. Dr Jaye added this guideline in the seventh year, noting its importance because, 'You grew up under your father's influence where his perception was the only accepted reality.'[23] Recently,

---

22 The pandemic precipitated a different therapeutic setting – the laptop. As with the other Covid-19 changes in lifestyle, Francine adapted easily.

23 That could be one of the reasons (in addition to feeling safe) that Henry and Miriam (and other committee members) are generally silent during these sessions.

Francine has discerned a third unwritten principle: there's no need to perform in this space.

These principles resonate with Francine, whose story, in part, revolves around her complex relationship with rules.

More on Triple F and fear

'Back to my fear of being killed, I've recently wondered: do *normal* children have such emotions? Though, I'm not sure if "normal" even exists.'

Triple F doesn't expect a response. Dr Jaye has mastered the art of withholding responses. One of her most effective techniques is silence. The quiet often compels Francine to speak, filling the uncomfortable void.

'People usually hide their vulnerabilities. All I know is that I grew up suffocated by fear, especially during the night. My fear of the dark was palpable. We all can probably deduce why …

'I was frightened of anything bad that could happen. For instance, a news story about a plane crashing into a house on the other side of the country would become my most pressing worry. Or when Jacob volunteered at a hospital and told us about a little girl dying of leukaemia, I became convinced that I was next. Miriam might have been right about me being self-centred.'

The psychiatrist gently interjects, 'That inner voice is your critic, Francine. Growing up with Henry was traumatic. It's understandable for you to have these fears. I've met other survivors of childhood traumas who share similar sentiments.'

With just those few words, Francine feels at ease, recognising she's not alone in her feelings.

Dinner time misadventures

'What else can I share about those years, Dr Jaye? Dinner times were illuminatng. Ever witnessed a family of five hurriedly eat in mere minutes? That was our daily routine: dinner started sharply at 17:35 and ideally, for Jake, Sandy, and myself, ended by 17:45. Supper was the rare occasion when our family congregated. Such gatherings often led to potential confrontations, with Henry taking issue with someone's actions or Miriam bringing up something Jake or Sandy did that irked her. In such instances, Henry would react violently, by smashing the accused's head or offenders' heads together.

'Henry and heads – could this be the definition of a paradox? He revered their grey matter particularly when applied to maths and sciences, but he also banged them against the floor, walls, and other heads.

'Our dinners were anything but joyful. Most of us wished for it to end before it even began. Here's an unconventional way to gauge family dynamics: time their dinner. A shorter meal might hint at a more dysfunctional family. Though, one should control for intervening variables such as the number of courses or the nature of the meal. After all, some things are easier to eat than others.

'When things got a little tense around the table, I had a role to play. Franny was not only the family's mini-monarch but also played the clown. She was guaranteed to sense the tension before anyone else and would lighten the atmosphere by speaking in her precocious way.'

Dr Jaye speaks in her soft, soothing voice, 'You had to be in charge of what other people thought of you and felt responsible for easing the tension at the table. Naturally, these behaviours continue. In any case, your oratory is a skill that has served you well in teaching at universities, public speaking, and as an advocate! So too other ways you developed to stay safe.'

Once again, the therapist's words silence and shut out sentiments expressed in the past by previously noisy head committee members. In *that* moment, for *that* moment, Francine accepts and understands herself.

'Thanks Dr Jaye!'

Anger

'"Why were Jacob and Sandra the focus of Henry's rage?" you might ask me, Dr Jaye, if you were the sort who asked questions. Instead, you encourage me to ask them, which is not a bad process, especially for a Jewish person who answers questions with questions.[24]

'Could be that Jacob was not the son that Henry had wanted – not a miniature Henry? Everything about him seemed to rub Henry the wrong way. First and foremost, Jake wasn't intellectually centred and didn't excel in academic subjects. He was, however, excellent at sport, but Henry did not value sport.

'Moreover, Jacob had a few issues that Henry might have taken personally. He could have felt responsible unconsciously and therefore needed to dump his shame back onto Jacob? Jake was a bedwetter until a teenager. It bothered Henry. Also, Jake wasn't a fluent speaker. He seemed to think a lot before he spoke, and sometimes there was a stammer.

'Plus, he didn't have many friends. Sort of a loner. Just not the stuff that colonel's sons are supposed to be made of, I guess.

'And he lost out in the physical appearance round, too. It wasn't that he wasn't cute, but he was the spitting image of Miriam. There was no Henry to be seen. Maybe that's hard for a father? I don't know. Certainly, unlike me, there was no chance for Jacob to be the *narcissist's appendage.*'

---

24 Psychiatrist's note: The patient's last comment is indicative of transference. Francine is insecure about questioning my work, fearing (parental) anger, rejection, and abandonment.

Narcissist's appendage and other labels

At this point, let's break from the session briefly to see how that last term – narcissist's appendage – became a part of Triple F's vocabulary and usage. During each sixty-minute appointment, Dr Jaye would interject a few key words. These were generally not spoken in a separate sentence as an assertion or as an insight, but would be interspersed as a reflective comment leaving it for Triple F to hear and begin to process or not. During a year two appointment, for example, whilst reflecting on Francine's sharing about Henry, she said, 'And as the narcissist's appendage, you ...' Henry was never labelled as a narcissist. As these words were slipped into the session, the patient did not respond directly but began the slow process of digesting that perspective.

During the first or second appointment, Francine had asked Dr Jaye not to put her into any diagnostic boxes and therefore not to use psychiatric labels. As Dr Jaye's therapeutic model appeared to revolve around the client's autonomy and space, there was no debate, and a diagnostic-free (by the shrink) decade began. Or did it? There were other hints or words dropped by Dr Jaye over the years: generalised anxiety disorder, OCD, eating disorders, and more. By year eight, however, Dr Jaye delivered her formal diagnosis, which Francine was ready and able to hear – complex trauma.

Back to anger

Let's return to the session on siblings.

'Sandra ... I'm not sure where she went astray. But, there seemed to be room for only one narcissist's appendage in the house, and evidently, Henry saw more of himself in me than in Sandy. Sandy had an issue with her eyes – perhaps it's called a squint? And there was some problem with her discs that affected her posture. She wasn't flawless.

'From what I remember – though it's not much – Sandy often "copped it" mainly due to her conflicts with Jacob. And there was no fighting allowed in that house – no, sir! No anger permitted except from Sir Henry.

'It's clear that anger has been a defining emotion in my life – shaping my therapy, my experiences, my reality. I think it's time to discuss this anger.

'OK dear guru-like doctor. Anger. It was indeed the sole property of Henry where it festered to rage. There's no denying that every member of that household was teeming with displaced or stuffed anger. Even as a toddler, young Franny knew she wasn't allowed to express it. (There I go, Dr Jaye, speaking in the third person – being Franny can be too painful.) Yet, the truth was, we were often discouraged from feeling anything intensely. Each day, these feelings were suppressed, deepening and amplifying. Some of this emotional weight was permitted to be transformed into fear; being fearful was an acceptable state for the "princess". As a result, a significant portion of my rage was converted into apprehension, with the rest shielded by a seemingly insurmountable barrier. But instead of guarding a castle – if I may mix metaphors – it protected a dormant volcano, bound to erupt. And unlike mountains known to house dormant volcanoes, nobody, including myself, was aware of its existence within me.

'I'm certain that there was a lot of pain in there alongside the anger. As *they* say in twelve-step programs, hurt is just the other side of the anger coin. However, the pain was permissible. It's odd, thinking about it now, after all my discussions about Henry's uncontrollable anger, it hits me that he must've been bearing immense pain.'

Dr Jaye nods her head and says, 'Yes. Henry was carrying intergenerational trauma from centuries of pogroms and PTSD from war. Francine, your recognition is an illustration of your growth. You are allowing yourself to feel more now.'

The affirmation in these sentences visibly impacts Francine.

'Still, Dr Jaye, I need to delve into why Jake and Sandy faced such physical abuse. Talking about this is challenging, even considering my progress. But having seen you for this long, I feel this space is as safe as it can be for someone like me, riddled with trust issues.

'I can remember a few times when they "got it" and I was involved or in some way even (indirectly) implicated. Please promise, though, not to think too harshly about me. I didn't intend for them to get in trouble. Not exactly anyway. I mean I wanted Jacob to stop what he was doing because it hurt, or I was scared, but I never hoped for Henry's violent reprisals nor the haunting sounds of heads hitting the floor.

'Here's a memory from my early years: I was around three. Jake was playing with me. He always played rough; it was Jake's way. Perhaps a reflection of the violence he endured?'

No answer to that one; she might suspect it's rhetorical.

'He inadvertently twisted my arm, resulting in a trip to the military base hospital for X-rays. The few recollections I have are almost visceral, like the excruciating pain when the technician positioned my arm for the imaging. Upon our return, Jacob faced severe repercussions. If I were to believe Freud, who opined that accidents are seldom just that, did Jacob, at some subconscious level, intend harm, or was it truly an accident?'

Francine gazes at Dr Jaye, who returns the look with gentle silence.

'Years later, around the age of ten, while I was joyfully riding my bike down a slope in the street, engrossed in my fantasies, Jake approached from behind. Threatening to overtake me, he seemed intent on pushing me off the path.

'I pumped the pedals harder and harder, with my heart pounding loudly enough that I could hear it reverberating in my head. I made it. I got home before him, dropped the bike, and ran into the house screaming, "Daddy, Daddy, Jacob's been chasing me. Daddy, Jacob's been scaring me."

'Then I realised that there were visitors, and I calmed down quickly as the company mask went on automatically. After the guests left, Henry went upstairs to Jake's room. I could hear the sound of skull on wall or floor and my brother's cries. I don't remember what I felt then, but I can tell you what I feel now – an incredible wave of guilt. How could I have told Henry when I must have known that Jake would "get it"? How could I cause that terrible abuse?

'I don't know what you think, Dr Jaye, but there's a voice in my head committee that's fighting that view. Could be you. I feel it *might* be you, and this is what you're saying in a reassuring tone: "No, little Franny. You ran in and told Henry because you were frightened. It was an instinctive response to danger. You're not the one responsible. You didn't do it. Your father was an untreated traumatised man. You could not change his behaviour."

'Thanks for that reminder … feels like internalised therapy? I'm working on exorcising Jake in there who chanted in the past, "Your fault, Triple F. Your fault. You ran to a violent man and dobbed me in. You must have wanted me to get beaten. You must have known."

'Ironically, I do know from my academic research that children feel it's their fault when their parents split up. They blame themselves when someone molests them. So it's understandable then why, even if I weren't a 100% certified codependent, I would feel responsible for Henry's abuse of Jacob. But those children are not the ones responsible. They are not at fault. Victims? Innocent pawns? Whatever. But not to blame. So, to you voices who continue to castigate: be gone and don't return. At least not until the next major negative affect attack.'

Surrogate mother Sandy

'Jacob and I were never close as children or as adults. But I was intensely close to Sandra, except for the times when I plummeted from her pedestal.

'Sandy was possibly the most important person in Franny and Frankie's life. Such closeness that there were times in late adolescence, whilst under the influence of an hallucinogenic, when there was no Triple F. I sounded and felt like Sandra and believed that if I looked in the mirror, I wouldn't see myself, just Sandra. Pretty weird, huh, Doc?'

'Well,' she clears her throat, which might be a nervous mannerism. Dr Jaye doesn't like being asked questions. To be fair, she rarely asks them either. However, this time, Francine receives a rare response. 'You seem to have developed a lack of boundaries due to your early distressing childhood. It sounds as though your sister was an important figure in your life …'

'Yes, Dr Jaye. Three years older, Sandy seemed to adore me. I don't know if this was her survival role, the caretaker of the princess, the handmaiden if you will. But she did it well. As you know, I have few happy memories from childhood. Most involve Sandy.

'When I was sick in bed, I can remember her offering me a handmade menu with choices of juices, types of eggs, and toast. I would check off my preferences and she'd prepare them and bring them to me.

'This was a shift from the usual weekday breakfast-time. As you no doubt recall, from what is likely somewhere around page 2,667 of my therapy file, Miriam liked to sleep in. And from the age of six, it became my job − or rather, my honour

– to fry bacon and eggs for Henry. Sandra might have done this for a few years and then it was my turn. Sharing this with you, I feel a discomfort inside. There's an image of Daddy's little wifey making his brekkie … or perhaps that's me trying to see my normal experience as abnormal, one that many *Brady Bunch* homes around the world might have had. Dr Jamyang, are you thinking, "What's the big deal? She made her father breakfast. Her older brother and sister got beaten, but she didn't. Sounds like an idyllic childhood to me compared to many other patients."'

Gently shaking her head in the negative to indicate that she isn't thinking this at all, Dr Jaye responds, 'In another session, we might explore how and why you minimise your traumas.'

'Anyway, back to Sandra. My hero, my role model, my pseudo-Mum. She taught me how to read, how to tie my shoes, and invited me on her adventures. The black and white photos from long ago reveal a Sandra with crooked posture, eye squint, and thumb in her mouth, looking like she could have used a Sandra in her life. Over time, the posture improved, the eyes became clearer, and Sandy transitioned into adolescence. There was no space for her little sister in her teen world of partying with the "bad" boys.

'Sandra was the saviour of my childhood, Dr Jaye. Yet, our relationship has had its challenges over the years. As I mentioned earlier, either I was on a Sandy pedestal and we were the best of buddies, or she entirely rejected me, as she did in her teenage years.'

There is silence. Tears well in Triple F's eyes. Then, Doctor Jaye, invariably providing at least one validation or insight per consultation, speaks. In her inimitable manner, she articulates what might seem evident but is inevitably a perspective Francine desperately needs to hear.

'Sandy and Jake have never understood that witnessing is a severe form of violence, particularly when few protective factors buffer the negative effects. They resented what they saw as your idyllic childhood and have held onto that resentment from those early days until now.'

Francine has often contemplated this. It's probable she has discussed it in previous sessions. But hearing it from her therapist gives the concept weight and validity. She can now more deeply internalise this understanding – the therapeutic process in action.

Early school days

'So far, Dr Jaye, our discussions about the past have centred mostly around my family. Admittedly, there was life outside of the family. Yet, any pertinent memories seem sparse and distant. Why? Is this indicative of suppressed trauma? Or – and I'll answer the question as per our protocol – is it likely because past therapists didn't probe into school and friendships? Over time, memories recede further into the grey cells, with nothing bringing them to the fore.

'Initially, primary school felt like a haven. It was a place where I could excel, work hard, receive praise, and find acceptance among my peers. But that changed around the age of nine or ten. Quite simply, I was seen as a "tall poppy."[25] They'd say things like:

"Don't pick or elect Franny. She's always chosen!"

"She's the teacher's pet."

"Franny always knows the answers."

"She's the one the teacher always picks."

---

25 The tall poppy syndrome is an Australian term describing putting down a high achiever to create a level playing field.

'Teasing was probably quite widespread. But other subjects of ridicule didn't seem outwardly affected by the bullying. Looking back, their feelings were likely hurt. I suspect, however, that I displayed my hurt both inside and out. But perhaps others couldn't see my pain either.

'I failed to learn from these childhood experiences how not to be a tall poppy and subsequently faced similar challenges down under. A few years ago, Dr Jaye, my research gained media attention, leading to frequent interviews and high-profile public speaking engagements. While it did feed my ego, resentment from fellow academics and even within the feminist community had its painful repercussions. This probably played a part in leading me to this very room.

'Anyway, back to the past. I recall the relief I felt when Henry informed us he had been transferred. Our family was set to relocate once more, this time from Canada to the US. This move coincided with the beginning of my adolescence, which is often not an easy time.

'Speaking of moves, we relocated about every three years, and Henry and Miriam would have told you that I was "the child who loved to move." This was another label they assigned to me. They would also tell you how I was "the child who made friends immediately," bringing someone home at the end of the first day at a new school. Franny was proudly recognised as the extrovert and the social child.

'Was I truly that person? Maybe yes, maybe no. Consider my enthusiasm for moving. As you know, this optimistic attitude stemmed from the hope that in the next city, I would not only fit in but also feel like I belonged. However, it never happened, or at least it never felt that way, even when I was accepted into the "in" crowd.

'Did I have many friends? Was I an extrovert? Who can say? I understood that this was how Henry and Miriam wanted me to be. I earnestly attempted to live up to these labels that conveyed positive qualities, rather than the negative ones. Through others' eyes, they would have seen a bubbly and outgoing girl who auditioned for this and tried out for that, losing with grace and winning with pride. Inside, however, it was a struggle; I lost with devastation and won with apprehension that the victory would be short-lived, that it wouldn't endure.

'Needless to say, the same pattern emerged with academic accomplishments.'

The upside

'Well, Dr Jaye, my childhood might sound rather grim. Memory is funny – in the sense of being strange. I don't remember most of the day-to-day details. I mostly recall unrepressed traumas and exceptional events like the primary school awards. Does that make me sound like Miriam, whom I've accused of only remembering the bad? Certainly, that's not the case for me now when I think about my children. For them, I've done the opposite and forgotten the negative. This may be due to twelve-step programs that have taught me about gratitude, Dr Jaye. And, I've learned that pre-twelve-step experiences were characterised by stark contrasts. In recovery, nuances have entered my perception, although, as you've no doubt noticed, my old lenses can still be triggered at times. Certainly, life for Franny could have been a lot worse, right? And really, it wasn't that bad. I lived in my head. I've always done that. No matter what is happening on the outside, having a life inside your head means a place to hide, a refuge from everyone else. No one could take that away.

'When I walked into my first Adult Children meeting in Melbourne – a couple of years after that most horrid of times, which shall not be mentioned – my exploration of my family of origin began: awareness, anger, acceptance, and forgiveness. Not all my memories are bad. One example: Miriam enjoyed reading aloud to me. I remember the long version of *Winnie the Pooh* and sitting on the bed night after night whilst she performed. It truly was a performance; she read with such intensity and expression. If she'd been born to different parents in a different time, Miriam would have graced the stage. She just loved to read with flair.

'In their defence, I'd argue that Henry and Miriam did the best that they were capable of as parents, given their own unresolved issues at that point in their lives. Their unpacked baggage was heavy.

'Further, they had to deal with a child – me – who often harboured unrealistic expectations. In a sense, then, no matter what they did, it seemed insufficient. An example: each year, Miriam would outdo herself in organising my birthday party with games, food, lollies, a delicious homemade cake, and treats for the guests. Yet, I often felt detached. If you live mostly in your mind, as I did, the real event can never match the fantasy. I'd be consumed with worry, always on the lookout for potential problems. And if that doesn't tick off enough "Are you an ACA?" or "Are you a Codependent?" boxes, I'd also obsess over whether everyone was having a nice time or just pretending.

'I was distant, not truly there with my friends. How can you enjoy a party you're not present at? So, it isn't about laying blame. Miriam did her utmost, but I got in the way.'

Another silence ensues, which, unusually, Francine doesn't interrupt. Dr Jamyang speaks:

'Being hypervigilant was an essential part of your role. Needing to be ready to avert catastrophes. Needing to be up to the mark.'

Everyone in the committee absorbs this. Typically silent during therapy, the newer members, spearheaded by Dr Jaye, echo within Francine: 'These were the thoughts and actions of a survivor. Shame be gone!'

Escapes

Literary adventures

'I haven't told you about the main love of my childhood, besides Henry: adult literature. How many children can say they've read nearly their parents' entire library, including numerous book-of-the-month selections – Faulkner, Hemingway, Steinbeck, Uris – by age ten?

'In many ways, these weren't suitable for my age. I wasn't mature enough. *The Diary of Anne Frank* gripped me like a tube of extra strength super glue. And there were other holocaust books like *Exodus*, which also affected me profoundly. I don't know if this fits any of your psychiatric paradigms or theories, Dr Jaye, but this material fuelled my already overactive imagination. It might have caused my lifelong wariness of groups and awareness of human capabilities. By eleven, I had to wear glasses, which I detested and often avoided, opting for a more surrealistic view of the world.'

Queenie

'I also want to talk about another joy from those days – Queenie. "A dog," you might wonder. No. Miriam would not have animals in her house, which was kept antiseptically clean. An animal might leave a hair or touch the living room furniture, which was reserved for "guests". She would wax the wooden floors weekly, using an electric polisher. Its resulting scent still brings joy when I come across it, even though, perhaps as an unconscious act of rebellion, I'm quite the opposite in my own home.[26] Miriam's proudest statement throughout my childhood was, "My kitchen floor is clean enough that you could eat off it." But, Doc, who would want to? Nevertheless, it mattered to her, leaving an indelible impression of my mother, scrubbing the tiles with determination.

'Back to Queenie, whom you can see could not possibly have been a pet. She was in fact my second-hand, rather beaten up, but oh so very special, first bicycle. She had character and, yes, a name. We went on adventures together when I was forced to leave my reading sanctuary. The interesting thing about my relationship with Queenie was the ambivalence that I experienced, and which was the exemplar for most relationships (and everything) throughout my life. As much as I loved Queenie, I wanted a new bike; one that wasn't second-hand, without scratches and with gears.

'And what did this ambivalence produce? If you were Jewish, you'd know the answer. Guilt, disloyalty, and an unpleasant sense of being greedy. These are transmitted by Jewish mothers through the umbilical cord and in their milk. Dr Jamyang – you could be Jewish or Muslim or Hindu. You've told me nothing about your personal or professional background in over a decade. But I'd put money on not Jewish.'

Dr Jaye smiles in her enigmatic way, saying, 'This is your hour.'

Travels with the Colonel

'Now that I'm unearthing happy family memories since I know there must be some, I am reminded of our annual holidays. Not

---

26 That's not entirely true. One of the few domestic tasks that Francine finds pleasurable is cleaning the kitchen floor with a small brush and dustpan. As she dumps the swept-up debris, she feels comforted remembering her mother's words.

because these were the easiest of times. I mean, can you imagine travels with Henry and Miriam being fun? Non-stationary, cars are like jail cells. No way out. Cars have remained a lifelong unsafe place for me as I've told you before about the perils of road trips with Richard and me. Conflicts about navigation and then feeling trapped. Lots of stories in that space ...

'Anyway, these were *supposed to be* happy times. "Is that fun?" "Do you know how much money this is costing us?" "Do you know what we could do for ourselves with this money but no, we're spending it for you ... (to have fun so you damn well better have it!)."

'Travels with the colonel. Rise and shine at 0430. "0430?" This was Henry's choice. He preferred to beat the traffic, stopping for the day at 1530. We managed to get out of our beds and squeeze into the back seat. And there were no fights in that back seat or Henry would pull over and the wrongdoer (never me) would pay the price. We would have a lunch at the side of the road. Picnic would be a misnomer. No blanket or table. No BBQ. No basket replete with drinks, snacks, and serviettes. Miriam's economies meant sandwiches (and *only* sandwiches) by the roadside. When we arrived at the motel, Jake, Sandra, and I would hurry to put on our swimsuits. There you go, Dr Jaye! Definitely a good memory; lying in the pool on a floating device.'

'Is that sarcasm, Francine?' The psychiatrist knows that Francine has never gravitated to water sport.

'Not at all! You know I have few positive recollections from Franny's time. And that was one: the refreshing sensation of cold water following the heat and tension of the car.'

Olfactory reminiscences

'Could we go back to aromas and the memories evoked? That's a rhetorical question as it's my hour – my time! It's taken me years to sense a warm sort of "rush" linked to a smell, like the floor polish I talked about before. Another is the smell of freshly made bread first experienced in a relatively benign fortnightly excursion to the Jewish deli in Toronto. When we left the shop and were seated in the car, Miriam would pull off a piece of the rye, the pumpernickel, the challah bread (morsels of Jewish culture that hadn't been assimilated) for each of us. This practice differed markedly from the norm. It tasted special. Henry and Miriam were the sort of people, who, if they bought their bread unsliced, would use a ruler and a bread knife to cut each slice the same width. Everything in Henry's house was done with mathematical precision. Consequently, the idea of tearing off a chunk of bread was a deliciously forbidden act that gave a short-lived feeling of togetherness.

'But even the fortnightly visit to the bakery was an ambivalent experience after I saw the numbers on the older shop assistant's arm. Burnt into her. I'd try to look away. I didn't want to be one of those ghouls who gets off on the grief and pain of others. Inevitably though, my eyes were drawn to her arm like a magnet to iron filings, and I was transported to the death camp. I'd see the trains, the lines, the selection, the crematorium, the ovens. All of it.

'Thus, even the bread was tinged with a bittersweet taste.'

The itinerant hairdresser child molester

'Well, Dr Jamyang, I guess it's time in our therapy – OK, I'll own it – my therapy – for me to share certain early childhood memories. Difficult to talk about because the words I use will not convey what's in my head. If I were a painter and could draw an impressionistic painting of it, then you'd be able to see what it was like. The sexual abuse. I could procrastinate or leave it out but at what cost? These experiences were an integral element of my life.

'First off was Uncle Charlie, the husband of Henry's sister. He used to have me sit on his lap and would touch me inappropriately. I can't remember the details because after all, who can remember what happened when they were three? What I do recall is the anger that Henry expressed to my aunt. It is likely that something did occur as interactions between the households ceased.

'There's a high probability that most extended kin groups have a paedophile, I guess, and Uncle Charlie was ours. Unless you count Henry and the emotional version of the big "I".

'Then, when I was ten, the main sexual molestation incident in my childhood took place. I have described what happened to many shrink-types over the years. It has become a story told by rote and with clinical detachment. Apologies, Dr Jaye. It doesn't make what happened and how it affected me any less real, though. It had an enormous effect on how I saw myself and my attitude towards men and basements – people and places to avoid and be afraid of.

'Mr Johnson was a short man, probably about fifty. He was balding with a paunchy belly, and he had a wart or growth near his mouth. A traveling hairdresser, he was in our Toronto home doing my mother's hair. No one else was home. I was downstairs in the room that Henry had "finished" into a rec room. I was ten years old watching *I Love Lucy*. Having put Miriam under the hairdryer, he came downstairs and sat next to me on the combination guest bed/couch.

'This was ages ago, but my memories are crystal clear. I didn't feel threatened initially – just curious. He told me that he had set my mother's hair and that she was under the dryer.

'Everything took place in slow motion, without urgency or heavy breathing ... just a slow deliberateness about it.

'He moved closer and then put an arm around me.

'Why didn't I run away? Why didn't I scream? Just froze. Couldn't run or scream and sat there with *I Love Lucy* in front of me and this stranger beside me.

'"So, tell me, Franny, have you ever been kissed?" he asked in a soft voice.

"Of course. My Mommy and Daddy and Sandra kiss me."

"Where do they kiss you? Show me where they kiss you."

'And, moving like I'm in a trance, because really at this point, for yet another time in my life, I am giving away my dominion to a man, I point to my cheek since we were not a family that ever kissed on the lips.'

At this point, Dr Jaye interjects, which is uncommon for her. 'Disassociation. A natural response, Francine, in this context. And a psychological defence mechanism that you had been using for years as the witness.'

'Thanks, Doc. The penny just dropped … again. I can feel how I disconnected. Weird. It looked like I was there, but I wasn't.

'Back to the horrible hairdresser who then said, "Well, I'd like to show you what a mouth kiss feels like." As he speaks, Mr Johnson is moving his hands on my body – on my thigh – slowly. And he leans over and kisses my mouth, and I don't, I *can't* move. For what seems like hours but what was probably a quarter of an hour, just fifteen rotations around the clock, Mr Johnson kissed those ten-year-old lips and touched my body slowly, moving to the place where no one, to my knowledge, had ever been before and he caressed that part, too. Slowly, slowly. Unable to cry out, why couldn't I run? What was stopping me? Concern about causing anger? I don't know.

'And then we both heard the sound of the garage door opening and I said in a voice that didn't seem to be my voice, "That's my Daddy. My Daddy's home."

'He ran up the stairs as if the furies were behind him. And I sat stuck like a statue. Henry walked in and stared at me. I must have looked strange. Or did I start to cry? I don't know. He said, "What's the matter, little Franny? What's going on?"

'Somehow, I found a way to describe what had taken place, which wasn't easy since I didn't have the words. He turned rigid and if lips can turn white outside of tacky novels, Henry's did appear to tighten and pale as he said, "I'm going to kill him."

'Exit Henry. And what about Franny? She sat there unable to move. Still waiting to be rescued. But her rescuer had come and gone. His property had been violated.

'I don't know how the evening ended. It was never discussed. I learned later from Sandra that she and Jake were told what had happened and warned that they were not to speak to me about it. The police were called, and Mr Johnson was arrested. However, evidently someone advised Henry and Miriam that it would be worse for Triple F if she had to go to court. The alternative was to make sure that he left town.

'*Don't talk to her about it and she'll forget*. But it doesn't work that way – quite the contrary. Without someone to tell her otherwise, Triple F came to believe that there was something about her that had caused Mr Johnson to touch her. For whatever reason, she already took responsibility for everyone in her family; the belief that the stranger had been compelled by some magnetic force she emanated fit within that model. She began to see herself as excreting a scent that enticed men, saying that here's a girl/woman who really wants you to want her. Because, you see, with no one to talk to about it, how could she not? She had not run from the basement. She had not pushed Mr Johnson away.

'Now, was this a big deal, Doc? After all, I have known many women who have survived much worse sexual assault in their early childhoods. People whose fathers penetrated them. Mr Johnson didn't. He *only* touched and kissed me. Why, then, did his face enter my consciousness for years when a boy leaned in to kiss me, requiring alcohol-induced oblivion to be able to respond? Must be that neurotic gene again.'

In addition to her compassionate eye contact, Dr Jaye responds verbally, 'What happened to you was traumatic. Trauma is trauma. The part of you which says your angst was not or is not justified is the critic.'

Pondering the meaning of life

Before we leave little Franny, who is about to become Frankie for the next couple of decades, let's consider a snippet from one of her private chats with Henry.

'Daddy, have you ever thought that the world could be like an ant farm for the gods? They're watching us run around doing all the things that we do. We're the entertainment. And perhaps I am one of the ants being put into certain situations and assessed or critiqued on my performance? Have you ever thought about that Daddy?'

'Actually Franny, as you know I don't have any belief in the supernatural and believe that we "men" are the "masters" of our own destinies. No ant farms, no gods. Just the rational mind.'

4
PUBERTY DEEP COLOUR BLUE: INTELLECTUAL SUB-COMMITTEE

Intellectual sub-committee sitting

Until about a decade ago, one of Triple F's head sub-committees would hold an annual meeting in which a segment of her life was deconstructed, scrutinised and reconstructed. This remains an integral working group as intellectualising continues to be used by Francine as her careers suit these members well.

Reasoning and thinking served as a means of cutting off her feelings and disconnecting from stressful occurrences that took place. The Founder and Chair of the sub-committee is Henry, who role-modelled reverence for the rational. However, given today's program, which involves analytically deconstructing Triple F's early adolescence, Henry has chosen not to attend.

There is consensus amongst the intellectuals and religious representatives on the intelligentsia sub-group that this time period is particularly challenging for many pubescent individuals, and perhaps even more so for Triple F. Daddy's little girl was in trouble. Getting bigger and growing pubic hair. Triple F sat in the bathroom with some scissors and tried to destroy the signs of impending maturity. Can't be a little girl anymore. Then what will save her from Henry?

'They're in limbo. Child or adult? Part of Frankie felt like she wanted the former, but another part desperately sought adult status. Why are Western industrial societies unable to recognise how torturous they make this time period and learn from their "less developed" counterparts?' These words are spoken by the personification of all the anthropology professors Francine was mentored by and whose voices she has internalised.

The sociology mentors disagree: 'That wouldn't work because twelve- and thirteen-year-old children need to be kept out of the labour market.'

One eclectic social scientist offers a suggestion: 'As a community, we need a ritual, like a *bar mitzvah* or an aboriginal initiation rite, to mark the passage from childhood into adolescence. Part of the induction process would include clarity concerning the expectations and role of adolescents. The goal here is to reduce the current ambiguity and its resulting stress.'

Richard's case study of a tween

Richard, who is the principal speaker, has prepared an abbreviated version of a case study of Triple F's tween years. As he is constitutionally unable to complete a project on time (unless there are inflexible deadlines), the narrative (inevitably) contains both brilliant insights and omissions.

'I'd like to begin by acknowledging that what I am presenting today is drawn from the stories that Francine has shared with me over the years. Hmm, OK well, more often in the early part of our relationship when she was the object of my ADHD hyper-focus.

'Corresponding with this awkward time in a child's life, there was a family relocation from Canada to the midwest of the United States. Henry and Miriam found a house to rent in an elite suburb. This location proved problematic. The neighbourhood had an unwritten policy: no Blacks, Asians, Hispanics, or Jews. The family had slipped through since no one suspected the Commanding Officer of the near-by air force base of being "one of those". However, word did get out; likely when Henry, at Miriam's behest, attempted to join the country club. That organisation not only had the unprinted guidelines, but they included a question on their application form. Lying was not an option in Henry's ethical handbook. The family was blackballed. Over time, the neighbours must have heard that there were non-Christians in their goyim ghetto. The result was ostracism. I understand that Frankie's underlying (and unfelt) sense of not belonging and being different became exacerbated.

'This was further aggravated by educational differences between Canada and the US. Having taken years three and four in one year, Frankie was already the youngest in the eighth grade. However, as she had studied French since kindergarten and was several years ahead in the Midwest mathematics curriculum, she was unable to attend the local middle school, which only offered grades seven and eight. Consequently, she was sent to the large Junior High that was situated in the blue-collar part of the city since it had a Senior High School in the same building. This physical arrangement meant that Frankie could attend tenth grade mathematics and eleventh grade French.

'Being twelve years old and placed with students four and five years older would likely be challenging for anyone. Being undeveloped made it more herculean. Although she had been unsuccessful in her battle with pubic hair, Triple F had yet to proceed through the other stages of puberty (except for much increased perspiration). Therefore, what we have here is a physically immature person – riddled with insecurities – thrust into the hard-core teenagers' realm. A few may have regarded her as a mascot, but the majority treated her as an annoyance on the rare occasions that she spoke up in class.

'Unfortunately, Frankie was also having difficulties with the academic work. She felt as though she had peaked at the age of eleven and was heading down the slippery slope of failure.[27] Her French learning had been mostly conversational. In the eleventh-grade French class, the students had learned the grammar rules.

'From ease and a dearth of challenges, school had become another site for head committee members' messages of inadequacy and inferiority to reverberate. Henry articulated the view (both inside and outside her head) that mathematics was on an equal par with the meaning of life itself. To fail in that subject (which meant anything less than a B) was therefore quite incomprehensible to him – an act of insubordination. Frankie's scholarly descent was a further contributor to her unsuitability as a princess, along with her onset of puberty. It was during these two years that their relationship began to change. The walks upon Henry's return from work became less frequent as did the daily chats. Their companionship diminished, soon to disappear.'

Entertainer extraordinaire

'Among her fellow eighth graders, Frankie was seen as different. Homogeneity is a desired aim for tweens and teens. Most Southside students were from lower income areas; however, Frankie lived in *the* affluent area – strike one. She spoke with a Canadian accent, markedly distinct from the locality's nasal twang with its rounding out of consonants and dragging out of

---

27 The feeling of having peaked early is not exceptional, although Frankie's experience was befittingly earlier than the norm. She felt the onset of her academic descent aged twelve. The more common phenomenon is to feel a failure to live up to one's potential, which was reached or set in secondary school.

vowels – strike two. The third strike was attending the Senior High twice a day. This was not only atypical behaviour, but it violated other rules too. Seemingly, "tall poppies" were not acceptable in American middle schools.

'It is evident that Frankie was not winning popularity contests. Yet, this was only the backdrop to the principal event – the nadir of her life at Southside Junior High School.'

Richard slowly turns to a label in the folder marked 'Nadir – age 12'. He then opens a diagram on Keynote. Richard's academic presentations generally include elaborate figures with multiple dimensions, numerous boxes, words, hues, and complex feedback systems. All eyes turn to the screen scrutinising the columns, rows, arrows and colours.

'As you can see, the various pathways derived from Frankie's personality and her life circumstances contributed to this incident.'

Was the clarity that Richard saw and intended to convey in the illustration experienced by those in attendance? With erudite audiences, there is a negative correlation between incomprehension and frequency of questions. There is a positive correlation between incomprehension and head nodding or the appearance of comprehension.

'About the fourth week of eighth grade, all seventh through ninth grade students gathered for a special assembly with an entertainer on stage singing, dancing, and telling jokes. Near the end of the performance, he called for volunteers to join him: two boys and two girls. As the variables in the diagram show, their inevitable intersection culminated in Frankie raising her hand.

'In seconds, she was on stage with the other three volunteers. The four were advised quickly what their roles involved. Each was to sing a verse of the traditional spiritual, *"He's got the whole world in his hands."* Triple F was the last to perform. Those preceding her were ill at ease with trembling voices. She moved to centre stage and belted out her lines as if she were in an African American Baptist church. Swaying slightly to the rhythm of the music, Frankie sang with expression; after all, she was Miriam's, the expressive reader's, daughter, wasn't she? She experienced a rush of adrenalin flowing through her brain and body – euphoria that has generally accompanied performance for her.

'The man acknowledged Frankie's participation as "marvellous" and told her that she "ought to go to Hollywood."

'Walking back to her seat, she thought, "I've done well. Now they'll like me."

'As Frankie sat down, the girl who was sitting next to her spoke quite loudly; "You've embarrassed the entire eighth grade."

'Frankie's thoughts went into overdrive.

"What? Wait a minute. This is supposed to be my free pass to popularity. What's going on here? Once again, I thought I knew the rules and thought I knew what *they* would like. And I got it wrong. My hyper-vigilant radar let me down."

'Others muttered as the assembly ended and students returned to their classrooms.

"How embarrassing." "Why *don't* you go to Hollywood? You don't fit here." "Can I have your autograph?" This verbal barrage continued relentlessly over the next two years, as this age group is unforgiving. A haunting refrain: "Can I have your autograph?"

'Frankie was susceptible to being tormented as I have shown in the figure. I refer you to the various personality pathways coded red that contribute to this vulnerability. Some examples: a tendency to reveal hurt; over-reliance upon external referents; giving away one's power by caring what others think. She was unable to mask the pain; tormentors continued to heckle and ostracize as their efforts were effective. Sent to Coventry with a one-way ticket.'

Richard breaks his hyper-focus and looks at the audience. He can see that someone has raised her hand. 'Yes, do you have a question? Concerning the diagram?'

The female English teacher shakes her head and says, 'Not a question but a comment. I am feeling Frankie's pain. I found her in the girl's toilet one time crying her heart out. When I asked her what was wrong, she told me what they were saying and how awful it felt. I comforted her with the view that these other students were acting out of jealousy: her performance had been outstanding, and they couldn't cope with that. Someone being good at what they were unable to do.

'I guess my words may have helped. It seemed to me though that she was like a pressure cooker. Whatever had gone before was now added to the mixture cooking inside. Hopefully, I was able to open the valve and allow some steam to come out. It seems that life for the two years at Southside Junior High were the absolute pits for her. Add the usual struggles of puberty with these facts, and with her personality, and her defence mecha-nisms must have been fully functioning. We know that even in the best of circumstances these years can be extraordinarily difficult.'

'Indeed, it was so,' responds Richard, adding, 'Two years of almost total ostracism, further exacerbated by her isolation and lack of a confidante. However, she did tell me that her experience with you, Ms Hill, was her first lesson in the value of sharing and being heard. You were kind and you listened, but you couldn't make it go away. And it didn't.

'Frankie was unable to disclose to Miriam or Henry, con-strained by her beliefs that the importance of maintaining the illusion of being the popular daughter, the one who was an extrovert and made friends easily, outweighed approaching them for emotional support. These were her affirmative labels, and she could not afford to lose them because the negative ones were indelible.'

Stomach and sweat

Richard now changes the slide: a four-circle multi-coloured Venn diagram fills the screen.

'Aside from the assembly debacle, as you can see in this figure, there were a series of minor incidents. The diagram shows how these factors were contributing to her increasing inner hatred.

'Any daydream of control was waning. Stomach rumbling and sweaty armpits were signs of her inability to contain her bodily functions. Straining to understand the intricacies of geometry in a classroom with people five years older, into the silence came the sounds of … could it be a marching band? No, it was the rumblings of Frankie's 10:30 tummy. Her discomfort grew, which translated into increased perspiration.

'As you all are aware, Frankie chronically compared her insides to other people's outsides resulting in a view of herself as inadequate. However, in this situation she compared her outsides – wet and clammy clothing with underarm rings – with others' outsides – their seemingly dry blouses. Her underarm secretions increased in direct proportion with her awareness of the dampness appearing on the fabric of the blouses that Miriam purchased for her. Frankie was unable to discuss body parts and secretions with Miriam.

'This situation was further complicated by the need to wear white blouses (which showed perspiration) to allow a bra, which all of her female peers wore, to be seen. The bra that didn't need to be there in the first place. Because as you know, Frankie was a late developer. One of Mother Nature's jokes. She could have stayed Daddy's little girl longer. Didn't bleed until aged fourteen and no breasts until she was sixteen.

'The result was not pretty, as the intersectional area of the Venn diagram's four circles illustrates.'

The breasts that got away

'Her lack of bosom development contributed to Triple F's self-consciousness and almost led to serious ramifications. Requiring a physical examination, Henry took Frankie to the nearby army base where medical services were free for military family members. The male doctor was young (even through the eyes of a thirteen-year-old). He asked her to remove her shirt. Taking off that piece of clothing and revealing a flat chest was torturous as indicated by the persistent visceral response she experiences when recalling the experience. And there were somatic responses, as her blood pressure, recorded after the top was removed, was dangerously high.

'Henry and Miriam discussed it when they thought no one was in earshot. The doctor had advised that their daughter should not return to school until further tests were conducted. Frankie was ambivalent. Euphoric thoughts of escaping from Southside were offset by fears of her imminent demise. As Figure 2 indicates, this latter affect was the effect of Triple F's catastrophising, which also manifested in her dire predictions about her future as she was still convinced, at this point, that she would be dead before the age of eighteen.

'In order to check the reliability of the reading, Frankie was taken to a private practitioner who appeared to be an octogenarian. Her blood pressure plummeted to within the normal range. This dramatic drop is illustrative of at least two factors: the interplay of mind and body, and Frankie's ill ease with her own body. The latter remained an issue through adolescence and early adulthood.

'A lack of breasts could be concealed in regular daytime clothing. Swimming gear, however, proved problematic. Miriam had bought her youngest a two-piece bathing suit with no attached padded cups in the top. Atypically, Frankie talked to her mother about needing plastic push-up pads that would provide a deceptive image of a well-endowed female. Miriam purchased two such cups. There was no adhesive or means of attaching them to the bathers.[28]

'Frankie admired her reflection in the mirror – excited about showing off her *new* body at the lake where a group of kids from school were gathering. Unfortunately, it is not clear in this narrative how or why she had been included in a social activity by her peers. They might have had an inkling that she would provide a modicum of entertainment. In any case, she did.

'Initially, the atmosphere seemed positive. Frankie felt the semblance of confidence, which translated into friendly chatter and some freedom from her customary ill ease and awkwardness. Then, as she was jumping around in the water, one girl shouted, "Hey Frankie, you've lost something!"

'This was another of the incidents in Triple F's life that occurred in slow motion – at least in recollection. Looking around her, a bobbing white object came into view. It took her a while to realise that the item moving up and down in the water was one of her new breasts (so to speak). Looking down, she confirmed the sighting since her chest was now flat on one side and well-endowed on the other.

---

28 Both the swimsuit and padding were likely cheap. Miriam was raised to make her own window cleaner, re-use paper bags, and to spend the least amount of money possible for anything and everything.

'Everyone was staring and laughing. Boys and girls shouted, "Hey Frankie, your boob's floating away," and other jokes and comments along the same lines.

'She grabbed the cup and, kneeling below the lake's surface, tried to stuff it back in. She stood up and was greeted by more laughter since she had managed to dislodge both.

'I asked her during a reminiscing conversation why she reacted in this way. She replied, "I don't know why I kept trying to get them in. Why didn't I just cut my losses and run off in the first instance? I don't know."

'She never wore the swimmers again. Miriam asked her why, but Frankie was unable to share the mortification. If you're the popular child, the one whom everybody likes, how can you admit that people laughed and ridiculed you? She couldn't.'

(Not) dancing the night away

'To complete my critique of these two particularly problematic years, I will examine Frankie's experiences with the North American phenomenon at time: the junior high school dance. The terminology used to label the get-together was a *social*, which had a degree of irony as she continued to be treated as a foreigner or an intruder.'

At this point, Richard is interrupted by the social scientist cohort who contribute their shared perspective through a spokesperson, a well-published sociologist with whom Frankie had studied the sociology of youth.

'We have observed that these preliminary quasi-mating ceremonies may further reinforce insider/outsider status within the group. In addition, both their placement and participants' behaviours reflect the individuals' position within the informal institutional hierarchy and their membership, if any, in sub-groups. For example, cheerleader females and male athletes (the football players) form the innermost circle – literally and metaphorically. These people are homogeneous: Anglo, blonde, thoughts seemingly unconcerned with the environment, poverty, or the dangers of war. This circle is closed with their discourse and dancing limited to those in the "in-crowd." Some students like Frankie, who do not fit within any of the few existing categories, stood alone – (again) literally and metaphorically – on the outer perimeter. Consequently, these occasions can be painful ordeals for fringe-dwellers – particularly for those who are approval-seeking and externally referenced. In Senior High School, there are additional groups, which prove more suited for Frankie's membership or affiliation: "delinquents," "druggies," "drunks," "iconoclasts," "hippies/pacifists" and other "rebels."

Richard resumes speaking.

'Indeed, Frankie was such an individual. She hid her angst, though, behind a mask of stiffness and hauteur. The boys did not come near. I've examined photos of her taken before one of these dances and, although it certainly wasn't the best of times for her beauty-wise, she wasn't *that* bad. Not bad enough to merit the status of wallflower along with the geeks and nerds that inhabited the outside edge. Is it possible that, by virtue of her accelerated academic path or her Assembly performance, she was considered to be a nerd? One wonders if nerds know that they're nerds?'

Richard, as a public speaker, is renowned both for complex diagrams and a tendency to become distracted and meander from the topic. Today, he is determined not to do the latter, saying, 'I cannot respond to that question. However, the philosopher members of our sub-committee could undoubtedly ponder this important issue. It could serve as the basis for a publishable essay.

'Frankie would stand on the periphery trying to look "cool" in the clothing that Miriam had selected, which inevitably was not "cool." Waiting for some handsome lad to be her Sir Galahad and rescue her. And, in her case, there was the ghost of Mr Johnson, which contributed to a stiffness and awkwardness with boys – no doubt even more so than the unmolested child. This is purely hypothetical, as there is no scientific literature that I am aware of that has compared these two groups and their early tween and teen experiences with the opposite sex. Identifying a control group would be problematic given the silence and repression which may be the effect or sign of childhood sexual victimisation.'

One can observe Richard visibly stopping himself from further discussing other experimental design issues such as controlling for potential intervening variables. He returns to Frankie's search for her male rescuer:

'This action, by the way, was a precursor for how the teenage and young adult Triple F awaited an idealised man in shining (or slightly rusted metal by the end of the period) armour; although, latterly as a staunch feminist, denying that she had that expectation.

'Waiting for the phone to ring; for the doorbell to ring; for the man to look or speak to her. Waiting. Could be that the *teacher* was saying that it is patience Triple F needs. And still does, evidently, as the lessons continue.

'Again, she couldn't discuss her ignominious experiences with Miriam or Henry. How could the popular child fail to dance the night away? Instead, she'd report success as the belle of the ball. They nodded their heads in contentment since their labelling system was proving to be accurate.'

Transitioning to rebel

Richard is reaching the end of his brief overview of the life and times of the twelve- to fourteen-year-old Frankie.

'As we leave this part of her life, we should acknowledge that ill treatment by peers and the slow erosion of her position as Daddy's little girl has translated into her next metamorphosis: the princess egg turning into rebel larva. Henry stood for war; therefore, she advocated for peace. Miriam represented materialism and upward mobility. Frankie responded by articulating socialistic views, although she did not yet have the language or understanding. These mindsets further isolated her. If there were other novice Flower Children at Southside Junior High School, they were closeted.

'This time period terminated with another transfer for Henry. When told about yet another family movement to the southwest, about 1,000 miles from this antipathetic place, she was overjoyed. However, there was a sadness too as Sandra was not a part of the relocation as she was beginning her university studies the following month. Jake had already left home the year before, aged sixteen, to travel the first of numerous career pathways.

'Therefore, only Henry, Miriam, and Frankie moved to New Mexico. It was there in Albuquerque that the nascent rebel became more radicalised, no doubt contributing to Triple F's activism and advocacy.

'Speaking of New Mexico does remind me that Albuquerque was the city that Henry and Miriam chose as their home base when the colonel retired, aged fifty.

'Once every two months, first as the caretaker for Miriam when she was dying of cancer and then Henry who was in care after a series of mini strokes, Sandra, who never left the small Midwest town she moved to after graduation, would drive the same 1,600 kilometres that Henry, Miriam, and Frankie had travelled years before. Her choice, however, was to do the trip (each way) in one sixteen-hour go. I did wonder if, like Lisa Nowak, she wore a nappy to avoid toilet breaks.[29] Certainly, my impression of Sandy is that, in addition to her dedication to her father, she had a similar intensity and singularity of purpose.

'Yes, the preceding was a slight digression but the importance of conveying this image of Sandy outweighs the need for me to stay on track.'

---

29 In 2007, Lisa Nowak, then a NASA astronaut, when making a fourteen-hour road trip in order to confront her ex-partner's lover, allegedly wore a diaper in order to avoid taking time for toilet pit stops.

5
REBELLION: LISTENING TO THERAPISTS AND DRUNKALOGUE

From relative 'riches to rags'

This time, instead of being from a wealthier neighbourhood than the other students, the reverse was the case for Frankie. A significant proportion of the student body came from the most affluent area of Albuquerque, with mansions that looked more like hotels or apartments than one-family residences. Henry, Miriam, and Frankie had moved into a middle-class house a suburb away from these seriously rich folks. A bit more inferiority to throw into the Triple F pot. Nevertheless, tenth grade was a moderate improvement over grades eight and nine at Southside. When you're at a nadir (following the Southside debacles), where can you go except up? The learning material was getting harder with more effort required; however, this correlated with Frankie's decreased approval-seeking behaviour as the chapter title indicates.

Back in the basement

Their new home was a one-story dwelling with a basement. The ground floor had three bedrooms, but Henry and Miriam insisted that Frankie would be better off in the basement with her own living room, bathroom, and bedroom. There was a certain irony at play here: a fourteen-year-old girl, compelled by numerous forces to reside in the part of a house that evoked dread or even terror.

Henry and Miriam likely thought that they were doing their youngest child a favour, providing her with her own 'quarters' and the bit of independence that went along with that. Their denial of Mr Johnson was complete; that incident would not have factored into the decision-making.

Given her antipathy for basements, why didn't Frankie assert her needs and say, 'No, thank you. Nice thought, but I'd prefer one of the smaller bedrooms upstairs to the palatial quarters below deck.'

What was consciously or unconsciously motivating that choice?

Former and current Triple F therapists: response

'We can answer that question,' say the counsellors of Triple F past, present, and (possibly) future. Some appear to have double degrees in anthropology and psychology. First, several speak in one voice, as they do:

'Triple F needed to separate from Henry. Whether or not there was anything sexual going on, we know from our amalgamated files that her early childhood did show evidence of what we have come to refer to as covert incest. And, as the precocious Franny changed to a pubescent Frankie, she needed, no doubt unconsciously, to ensure that the relationship would not shift in *that* way.

'Spatially speaking, a different part of the house could be equated with the girls' hut in some tribes where it is mandatory for girls beginning menstruation to live apart from their family, usually under the tutelage of older women. Unfortunately, since Sandy was at university and Miriam was not by nature that sort of mentor, she lacked such guidance in this transitional time period.[30]

'We observe too that the physical separation was accompanied by a more psychic estrangement that started with the move into that house and continued throughout the three years that the subject lived there with her parents. It reached the point where they no longer communicated.'

Gabe speaks up.

'This is not surprising to me. There was little healthy space in Henry and Miriam's relationships with their children – either no boundaries and total enmeshment or brick walls that prohibited any contact or friendly gesture. It's a generational thing – passed on through time. This family could have benefited from attending Codependents Anonymous (CODA) or Adult Children of Alcoholism (ACA) meetings. In fact, and not coincidentally, two of the children's paths took them there as adults.'

You've come a long way, baby

At the ripe old age of fourteen, Frankie had discovered a commodity that made life seem a bit more liveable. It provided a pathway to seeming grown up, assured, and sophisticated. Winstons first, then Marlboros, followed by Kool Filter Kings, and finally, as a fledgling feminist, Virginia Slims Menthol. Cigarettes were Triple F's first addiction, or at least her earliest substance addiction. Never a social smoker, the first pack led to the next and so on and on and on. Smoking made her feel as though she

---

30 However, Frankie was well-prepared for her first period. By the time of its tardy premiere, she was knowledgeable about menstruation through reading, friends' disclosures, and health education.

had 'come a long way' – the advertising slogan used by Virginia Slims, from 1968 until they changed it in the early 1990s to 'It's a woman thing.'

It was a family habit. Miriam was a heavy smoker. In fact, she quite agreeably purchased Frankie cartons from the army base commissary, motivated by her repugnance for spending more money than necessary. She knew that if she didn't buy them, her daughter would purchase them at the supermarket, paying three times more. Henry had quit a few years before Frankie began and Sandy started smoking even younger. Jake was the only non-smoker; perhaps due to his dedication to sport and to his determination to respect a body that had been repeatedly violated.

As he smokes a cigarette, Gabe, who has worked with addicts for fifteen years, discusses what cigarettes gave to Frankie and what they took from her concurrently.

'The greatest gift of cigarettes for her was keeping the pain at bay. How many did she smoke to inter the anger and the rage that would rise to the top? Yes, they were her friend, and ultimately, they were, of course, as with all addictions, an enemy. Triple F needed to feel the hurt, sadness, and anger before she could heal.'

He speaks whilst taking deep drags, seemingly unaware of the irony.

Trekking along the substance abuse path

In the latter part of tenth grade, Frankie embarked on a twenty-four-hour train trip back to the Midwest to visit Sandra. This holiday proved to be a major turning point in her life: the beginning of a rather lengthy involvement with drugs (including alcohol).

Let's ask Henry and Miriam why they allowed their fifteen-year-old to travel over 1,000 miles alone? Since Henry won't publicly discuss family other than to mutter about 'the *kinder* and the *tsuris*' in Yiddish, we'll listen to Miriam who is one of the more garrulous members of the head committee. She explains why, by this point in her life, she felt sorely provoked and ready for an empty nest.

'*Oy vey ist mir* … children?! Where is the joy or the *nachas*? Jake is only twenty and on his second or third study major. First, he wanted to be a teacher, then a librarian, and now he's learning to be a nurse. Enough already. Sandra has brought embarrassment on our family by getting involved with a boy – a goy even – from the wrong side of the tracks. Having my sweet little princess of a daughter slowly change into a sullen and withdrawn teenager is the icing on the cake. What can I do? Give her enough freedom to self-destruct? At least, I have never pretended with the three of them that they have made me happy.'

The sexual smell

Something happened on the train trip. It would recur every time Frankie travelled by train, plane, or bus, or when she was outside of the school environment. Inevitably, an older guy or guys tried to pick her up. On this first solo adventure, a soldier approached her in the rail club car and started to talk. He guessed, or said that he guessed, that she was eighteen, which was flattering to a girl who had recently turned fifteen. Although Frankie probably did look a bit older than her age, the narrator assumes that this approach was a pickup line. Nothing happened between her and the guy … that time.[31]

The significance of this encounter then was not that it led to anything sexual, but that it contributed to what became one of

---

31 With the advent of alcohol, a couple of years (and chapters) later, Frankie did have amorous adventures on trains and boats and planes.

Triple F's intrinsic beliefs about herself – that she was a person who gave off a scent, a sexual odour. Whatever it was seemed to make men regard her erotically. And you can rest assured that many of the males who came into her life did the best they could to ensure that she maintained this belief, thereby taking the responsibility, the blame if you will, for their sexual aggression.

Pill popping

Frankie was overjoyed to see Sandy but felt concern by changes in her sister. She wouldn't have known the words to describe it back then, but now would say that Sandy had lost any control that she'd had over her drug problem. It was rampant. The second morning of her visit, Frankie woke up, watching her sister when Sandy thought that Frankie was still asleep. Sandy took over fifteen medicine containers and placed red, yellow, blue, green, black, and white capsules into a bowl. This was her breakfast.

Yes, this was her big sister, her most special friend, *and* unfortunately, her mentor. It boded ill for Triple F. Not to place any responsibility for Frankie's next decade of substance abuse on Sandy. As the twelve-step contingent opine:

'Frankie was an addict looking for an addiction to happen. The incessant need for approval; the high achiever trying to get parental love and affection; the person who took responsibility for the mood of everybody around her; the shame and the fear. And then there were the environmental factors which might or might not have been the principal contributor to all the rest: the physical abuse, the sexual abuse, the family with the three rules of don't talk, don't trust, and don't feel operating full throttle. Like we said, she was simply a drunk waiting for the drink.'

The second day of the visit, Sandra introduced her younger sister to marijuana; nothing happened. Later that evening, smoking weed for the second time, Frankie had a novel experience: an almost mystical release from the bonds of anxiety that had been building for fifteen years.

As with all drugs, this initial euphoria would turn into 'bummers'. But not for a couple of years.

Both stoned off their heads, they walked into the Student Union. A Jefferson Airplane song was playing: 'One pill makes you happy, and one pill makes you sad, and the one pill that mother gives you doesn't do anything at all.' Lyrics had never seemed quite that profound. The music entered Frankie's body, permeating her brain and giving birth to a fascination for combining chemicals and sound. In addition, food was delicious. The 'munchies' led to deluging her taste buds with rushes of flavour. It had never tasted as good.

Grass or pot was pleasurable and linked with Sandra. They giggled and laughed to the point that tears rolled down their cheeks. And, they had serious conversations about the meaning of life, which made sense of everything that had ever happened or would take place. Unfortunately, it didn't the next day. And so, it always went for drug-inspired insights and revelations.

When Frankie returned to Miriam and Henry, there was no more dope. It didn't reappear for about eighteen months (and the next chapter) when her first (almost) fatal attraction entered the story. Stephen came with a plentiful variety of drugs.

Marijuana was Triple F's gateway substance, unless one considers cigarettes as a drug. First, but definitely not the last. There are plenty of other substances to be ingested and numerous people to be hooked on in order to help her make the great escape. Looking for oblivion. Trying to feel as if she belongs when all her life, she has been the square peg that doesn't fit into the proverbial round hole.

The first drunk

Frankie's first drink of alcohol was also her premiere state of inebriation and related blackout. To hear about it, we time travel a number of years following that drunken début. It is now another début with Frankie invited to be the speaker at her home AA meeting on the first anniversary of her sobriety. The person sharing is expected to share their experiences (of alcoholism and sobriety), strength, and hope. One's first public 'story' gig, though, tends to be heavily weighted on the drinking part of the story – referred to in the program as a drunkalogue.

Frankie's drunkalogue

'Thanks for inviting me to share my story with you tonight. I can't believe that I had my last drink one year, three days and ninety-four minutes ago.[32]

'As a drunk, my behaviour and attitude were less than endearing. This was particularly true as a teenager when alcohol and drugs exacerbated the difficult time known as adolescence.

'I will not defend the person who I was by blaming my parents, my paedophile uncle, the man who molested me when I was ten, anyone else, genetic makeup, living in a patriarchal society, and other experiences of violence. I do trust, though, that you too have been there, or just a bit there and will not judge me too harshly.

'I was on one of *those* first dates; this one was with Matthew whose father owned a car dealership. Consequently, Matt drove nice cars, which made a date with him an attractive proposition. This night, it was a red Corvette Stingray convertible. We met

---

32 In AA, it is considered essential to know the exact date of one's last intake of alcohol. This allows for monthly and then annual sobriety birthday/anniversary celebrations.

some other kids from our school outside somebody's house. Someone brought out a quart bottle of whisky with the aim to get me drunk. I had never consumed alcohol before, which they all knew. The bottle was placed in my hands. I held it to my lips and felt the liquid burning down my throat. I shuddered and everyone laughed. I took another gulp and another and, quite honestly, began to like the taste. I drank that whisky like the baby suckles the breast. That amount could have led to alcohol poisoning, except that my tolerance was evidently high.

'What that alcohol did for me! I felt released – literally – from the weight of all the crap I was carrying. Laughing and joking with everyone, for the first time, it felt like I belonged. This rush was short-lived as I continued to drink, which, by the way, was my alcoholism in action. For me, a positive sort of *rush* meant needing to drink more to maintain it, or to feel even better. It seldom worked out that way, though. Instead, everything would become blurry.

'On this, the first such occasion, the last thing that I remember was making out passionately with Matthew in the back seat of someone's car. This was a first for me. Until this alcoholic state of oblivion, when my date leaned over to get what he undoubtedly believed was his due, my Pavlovian response was to turn my head away. As the boy's mouth loomed closer, I sensed or saw Mr Johnson who had molested me when I was ten. He was part of that heavy load of baggage I was carrying. Until the night I first drank alcohol and got obliterated.

'Mr Johnson had been exorcised with booze. And I, Frankie, raised with a quasi-Victorian morality by Henry and Miriam, was passionately making out in the back seat of a car. I say quasi, by the way, because sex was one of the 10,632 topics not talked about in the family. Their prudish response to anything sexual provided implicit messages.

'I remember waking up in my bed the next morning with a visceral sensation of absolute terror. What had happened? How did I get home? Was I still a virgin? The last question was the paramount one.

'Now, I've learned in this program that the lack of memory was the amnesia of my first blackout. This inaugural episode turned out to be one of the longest of those for me – likely a couple of hours. We've all heard people in these rooms talk about day-long and week-long blackouts; times during which they ended up in different cities without a clue where they were and how they'd gotten there. So, if this drinking business was a contest of how low we were taken by this disease as measured by the length of our blackouts, then I don't come in at the top or at a "low bottom" in AA-speak.

'The blackouts that I had were bad enough. I mean, when you're a control freak like me, it's bloody scary losing entire time periods of your life. It's a bit of a paradox, isn't it? Almost as if we're exhausted from trying to run the show and the whole world, that *we* – or *I* since it's my story – just say, "Screw it," get drunk and throw away that illusion of having control. Or maybe it isn't paradoxical at all because, in the beginning, alcohol made me feel surges of an unfamiliar sense – possibly power? That didn't last, or I wouldn't be standing here tonight. As the old timers say, "Alcohol gave me wings to fly but then it took away the sky."

'My memory deficit contributed to high readings on the remorseometre the next morning. If all that wasn't bad enough, there were the shocking sensations of a body withdrawing from copious ingestion of alcohol. The absolute hell of what I later learned is commonplace – the hangover. An unexceptional after effect for people who drank like I did.

'And, for the first – but not the last – time, I made a silent pledge of abstinence. Swore never to touch another drop even though a ninth grader, Melinda, who was soon to become my bestie and had been in the front seat, assured me that my state of *virgo intacta* had not been breached. More about Melinda in a moment …

'OK. I had guilt about making out with Matthew, doing God knows what and saying God knows what, and yet the next weekend I went out with him again. And yes, this was a first, getting asked out a second time. Matt obviously thought that he was onto a good thing; unaware that I had vowed, as you may recall, never again to drink.

'We went to a drive-in movie, renowned as the local make-out mecca. And it will come as no surprise to you that as soon as he had parked and placed the speaker into the car, Matthew leaned over for the first kiss of the evening. I reacted by turning my head away and asking, "What do you have to drink?"

'Unfortunately for Matthew, he only had a six-pack of beer, and I learned a second lesson about booze and me. There was a clear-cut correlation between the amount of alcohol imbibed and the banishment of Mr Johnson and the other thousands of inhibitions and voices that prevented me from comfortably engaging in physical contact with the opposite sex. I drank my share of the beer and felt a bit tipsy but just couldn't get to the point I tried to reach with any chemical-suspended sensibility.

'That was the last date with Matt but, of course, not the last assignation with alcohol.

'The following two years are hazy: shadowy memories within an intoxication-induced fog. Eleventh grade was the year of peers and parties. A pattern began to emerge. Melinda and I would attend a social gathering with both of us getting as drunk as the available stock permitted. These evenings would culminate in making out with boys and/or throwing up on someone's yard and/or in a blackout.

'One of the customs enacted by youth in that part of the country at this particular time was to buy a keg of beer and take it into the mountains for an illicit keg party. Looking back, I guess that there must have been a lot of spiritual forces watching over us as, to my knowledge, no one ended up dead or seriously injured despite driving to and from these clandestine gatherings along winding steep and narrow mountainous roads. My higher power – whom I call HP or PGA (personal guardian angel) by the way – was protecting me without a doubt. I had gotten my driver's license during the middle of eleventh grade and used to drive one of Henry and Miriam's cars to these keg parties with a bottle of wine or spirits stolen from my father's liquor closet between my legs. And indeed, I do mean liquor closet. As he was a senior officer in the military, Henry bought duty-free booze through the base commissary. He justified the pantry of alcohol as necessary for work-related entertaining. In hindsight, although it's not my role to call someone else an alcoholic, the size of his stash may have been a clue? He maintained a paper inventory of the stock – several pages – but I managed to outwit the colonel ... a story for another day.[33]

'Yes, I was likely the only person who brought my own stash to the "kegger". Reckon there's a few other folks in this room, though, who did the same! It made sense to me since my goal was stupor. Too much beer needed to achieve that state. With the knowledge that this program has given me, I can see that this type of thinking and drinking were signs that I was not, and never was, or would be a "social drinker".

---

33 Frankie used a piece of tape to mark the amount of liquid in a bottle. Having lowered that level, she replaced the pilfered alcohol with water. The last step was to carefully remove the tape. Cognac, which was Henry's beverage choice, was not touched. The dilution of the other liquor would not be challenged by its drinkers since they were Henry's subordinates.

'Unfortunately, at that point in time, though, there was little information available about alcoholism or addiction and adolescence. If my sixteen-year-old self had been asked to identify an alcoholic, I would have pointed to the derelict living rough on the streets. I would not have looked in the mirror and said, "Here's one". No, not for quite a while. Even though the alcohol had already turned on me. From the start there was an inflationary price to pay in guilt, self-hatred, and hangovers. But, until I reached my bottom and, with my PGA's help, made it into these rooms, it was an acceptable cost for the freedom that it provided. Further, an anaesthetic was required to numb the destructive forces that were now activated within me.

'My relationship with my parents had deteriorated markedly during this period. Alcohol evidently served as another means of separation, of cutting the umbilical cord. If so, it worked. We rarely saw each other except at dinner and our conversations were restricted to, "Pass the salt, please." I think that my mother and father were burnt out with parenting as I was the youngest of three. It might have hurt them too much to witness the metamorphosis of their sycophantic princess into an autonomy-seeking rebel. Who knows?

'If you had asked them about how I was at the tender age of sixteen, I think you would have heard words like "surly", "uncommunicative", "defiant" and "withdrawn" – the unremarkable descriptors for adolescents. What they didn't seem to see, or turned blind eyes to, was my continuous and increasing abuse of alcohol during this period. You'd think that setting a car on fire twice would have been a warning signal.'

A slight problem burning out cars

'Ah yes, let me recount my escapades with motor vehicles, alcohol, cigarettes, and my friend Melinda, whom I've already mentioned. She was my drinking buddy for two years. We were inseparable. Even crushes on the same boys didn't divide us. Like me, she was drawn to the booze. We became the dynamic duo, and through crises and drama, hung out together until I, or this disease, ruined the relationship.

'With long, straight, ebony black hair down to her butt, Melinda was part Native American, part Mexican, and part Austrian. Neither of us conformed to the blonde pep squad stereotypes. Our deviation from the norm – in my case, largely due to a chronic need to be different and to stand out from the crowd – united us. She essentially moved into the basement with me, but who would know, as my bedroom window was an escape hatch at all hours of the night, both in and out?

'Back to the car. You may have sensed that my parents were generous with money and material possessions. I think that it was easier for them to give *things* than to give *love*. And it may have been a means of alleviating their guilt. Who am I to judge, though? Their generosity meant that they allowed me to borrow their cars as soon as I turned sixteen and became a licensed driver, even after I burned out the interior of one.

'Melinda and I had been cruising the streets looking for some action, which meant boys, drinking anything with an alcohol content, and smoking cigarettes, windows open with our long hair flying in the wind. After taking her home, I parked the car in the garage and went to my room. Now what happened next, thirty minutes to an hour later, was archetypal "Colonel". A knock at the bedroom door. I opened it, and my father was standing there. He pointed to the garage and gestured for me to follow him. My heartbeat accelerated as we walked down the hallway. What was it? Had I left some incriminating evidence? And then I smelled it. He flung open the door and smoke billowed out. "I've called the fire department. Go to your room."

'And that's the end of that. One of my cigarettes, flicked out of the driver's window, had flown back into the rear part of the car and had become embedded in the seat. The entire back seat was destroyed.

'No punishment per se; just more contemptuous looks and total coldness … the withdrawal of anything that was still good in the relationship.

'Now, it couldn't have been more than two months later that Melinda and I were cruising around once again when I noticed an acrid smell in the car. What were the odds? Could this happen twice to one person? The back seat was smouldering, and the smoke was getting thick. Coughing and gagging, I drove the car about a block from the house, parked it, asked Melinda to inform the Colonel, and ran.

'By the time that Henry and I had our confrontation, he'd lost the first edge of rage and was smouldering like the seat, or that's how I pictured him in my head. As I recall, on this occasion, I was told that the car was off-limits for an unknown period, which turned out to be a couple of weeks.

'Henry and Miriam had trouble setting limits on me for some reason. I don't know why. For example, I remember asking them to give me a curfew. Yes, as incredible as it may sound, I wanted a night-time restriction like my friends had, so I could then break it.

'Henry asked, "Curfew? What sort do you think is appropriate?"

"How about midnight?" I suggested.

'"Seems pretty early for a sixteen-year-old, but if that's what you want." And it was what I wanted – a boundary. Somehow, in some twisted and absurd way, that signified that they loved me. And, as I said, additionally, it meant that, like my peers, I would be able to truly sneak out of and into the house illicitly.'

"If that's what you want." How often I heard that phrase as my parents bailed me out repeatedly. The program has taught me that they were inadvertently enabling my disease. It could be why it didn't feel good to receive things from them. Or it could be that I always felt like I was being bought off. Like, we can't give you what you truly desire – our unconditional love – so we'll give you something else. But that something else didn't fill the void inside. With the benefit of some years, a few children of my own, and twelve months of recovery, I wonder if that's not being a bit unfair to them. It might be that I was unable to feel their love, which was there all along. Or I may have had unrealistic expectations or needed a reason to justify my drinking. Certainly, over the last year, by listening to your shares, I have realised that I need to take responsibility for my addiction and stop blaming others.

'Uh oh, the hour is up, and I've only made it through the first eighteen months of my drinking. I guess I better keep coming to these meetings, and in time I will share the rest of my story. Thanks for listening and for helping me not to drink, a day at a time.'

6
TEEN RISK-TAKING: PGA'S PRELIMINARY HEARING

'The Head Committee has convened this special meeting to assess whether you failed to fulfill your contractual workplace duties as Frankie's Personal Guardian Angel (PGA)[34] when she was sixteen and seventeen years of age. The law has established that there is no statute of limitations for this civil matter, as derelictions of duty by a guardian angel may have life-long effects.

'The process for this investigatory hearing is informal. For each of the four alleged breaches, you may present information to describe your understanding of Frankie's behaviour and your role at that time. Expert evidence from other Head members may be used to explain how your fulfillment of duties might have been compromised. Our goal here is not to pass judgement but merely to ascertain whether there are grounds for further legal action.'

---

34 Initially, the storyteller pictured this character or entity as an androgynous (but embarrassingly more masculine than feminine) imp-like creature. However, over time, the writer came to see this higher power emissary not as an external being but like Francine's evolving higher power, as an internal loving presence and guide.

PGA's opening remarks

'Everyone present is aware of Triple F's childhood. Looking back at her aged sixteen, at this critical juncture in her life, what transpired seems inevitable. Miriam and Henry provided whatever she asked for and imposed a curfew. Yet, their generosity did not make Frankie feel loved.

'I contend that her adolescent escapades were thus inexorable. And, until she hit rock bottom with any of her addictions, including co-alcoholism or codependency, my vigilance and voice went unnoticed.'

Alleged breach #1: Failure to protect Triple F from addiction to the addict

'Full of insecurity and fear, I argue that, unconsciously, Triple F was searching for a saviour. Then Stephen, with the silver tooth, appeared.

'A silver tooth? Hardly the prince in shining armour of fairy tales. And it was not a back molar; rather, the top right central incisor was metallic. Frankie may have chosen Stephen as the subject of her obsession for that very reason. Rebellion meant doing the opposite of pleasing Henry. If Stephen's dentition wasn't enough to *alienate* him from Henry, there were other reasons. For example, Stephen was a high school dropout and several years older than Frankie. Even worse, he'd spent some time in jail. Moreover, unsurprisingly to the discerning members of this committee, Stephen had substance abuse problems, contributing to a lean, mean physique and a tough guy image that said, "I don't give a damn, and I'll probably be dead by thirty."

'Frankie and Stephen met through a mutual friend, Johnny Anderson. Johnny, a twenty-year-old with almost mythical status in teenage circles, was the wild kid who would do anything if dared or drunk enough, or both. Gradually drawn to each other at keg parties, Johnny and Frankie became friends. Their similar alcohol consumption patterns led to mutual admiration and a platonic friendship.

'The lack of a sexual attraction, unusual for Frankie with her seemingly carnal "scent", may have resulted from Johnny's infatuation with Melinda. Unfortunately for him, the feeling was not mutual. However, once Frankie became obsessed with Stephen, she persuaded her friend to spend time with Johnny and Stephen. The male duo's drug-taking and delinquent activities evolved into a foursome.

'Stephen was Triple F's first, but not her last, major fixation. She thought about him incessantly. When they were apart, she'd sit in her room, staring at what had become an instrument of torture and terror – the pink *princess* telephone. With grim determination, she willed it to ring, "God damn you, call me, Stephen!"

'Most of the time, the phone remained silent. A distraught Frankie felt unloved, unlovable, and naturally, abandoned and rejected. She would muster her courage and start to track him down, talking either to Stephen's drunk father, a drunken Johnny, or an off-his-face Stephen. As I mentioned before, but it is worth repeating, any intervention from me was problematic as it was another decade before she admitted her powerlessness over anything and sought a spiritual centre.

'When they did meet up, they consumed a considerable amount of marijuana and alcohol, accompanied by "dry humping" in the back seat of Johnny's car on a dirt road in the mountains, or infrequently, in Frankie's basement living room. Although the genital contact aroused her, regardless of how drunk she was, they did not go further. This was due to Stephen's inability, not her reluctance. His lack of eagerness to penetrate the Bastille may have been a consequence of amphetamine or speed consumption.

These drugs, which among other things suppressed his appetite, could also explain his slim build.

'Triple F's co-addiction to Stephen occurred despite my reminders that he was unavailable and would only increase her self-hatred and despair. She could not hear me. Several twelve-step members will now testify as expert witnesses to explain why I wasn't heard, thus helping me prove that I was not in breach but was, in fact, actively fulfilling my contractual and moral duties as a personal guardian angel.'

The twelve-step program women testify

Nancy, the AA spokesperson, speaks first, reflecting the unspoken hierarchy among self-help organisations. Nan is a no-nonsense hardliner with a clichéd soft heart.

'Frankie's need for Stephen probably scared the shit out of him. In this Fellowship, we say that alcoholics don't have relationships; instead, we take hostages. Stephen was Triple F's first hostage.'

The CODA spokesperson, Jennifer, a thirty-something-year-old, speaks next with some nervousness. Like many other Australian woman, she tends to frame most statements as questions. As a people-pleaser with poor boundaries, public speaking triggers her insecurity. However, she's not alone in having those characteristics on the head committee.

'I think that the more he tried to get away from her, the stronger her obsession and desire became? It seems that she had to convince him to want her? She needed to make him love her? This appeared to be the raison d'etre of her existence. *We* in the CODA fellowship call it relationship addiction, and *we* say that it's simply another way that people with all of that pain inside escape from their emotions.'

Sally is ready to speak now. She's a quietly spoken middle-aged woman whose codependency has manifested in relationships with abusive alcoholic men and with her adult children, who have battled with drug dependency. As a long-time member, Sally confidently views this time in Frankie's life through the Al-Anon lens.

'Typical of male alcoholics and addicts, Stephen was unreliable, as evidenced by his failure to call when he said he would. That unreliability extended into every facet of their relationship. If they planned to go out, he'd either be over an hour late or fail to show up. If he was coming over to watch TV in Frankie's basement lounge, again, Stephen would either be a "no show" or would knock on Frankie's bedroom window at some ungodly hour to explain what had happened. Dependability was certainly not one of his strong points. As expected with a co-alcoholic like Frankie, there was a positive correlation between being treated poorly and her enmeshment.'

Now it's the turn of the Adult Children of Alcoholism delegate, Irene, or Reenie to her friends. Like many ACAs, she attended four other twelve-step fellowships before walking through the doors of this one. She laughs about having to become *older* to admit to being an adult child.

'From our perspective, what happened to Frankie was inevitable and not the fault of her PGA. It's clear that Frankie was acting out of repressed feelings and other issues arising from her family of origin. This is never a starting point for spiritual connection.

'Her upbringing is the core issue. As an adolescent "adult child", Frankie was trying to manage her actions and emotions and those of others. We do this because we worry that if we loosen the reins, our lives will get worse.

'We can arrive in addiction land, too, for various reasons. Like Frankie, we're self-medicating the anxiety we experience. The reality, of course, is that we're unable to control situations or people – no matter how hard we try! And we medicate anger and sadness that we couldn't afford to feel as children. We end up with certain ways of being in the world; always seeking approval by, among other things, being overly sensitive to others' needs, and may lose ourselves in the process.

'Many of us are like Frankie and are attracted to people who are alcoholics or those with compulsive personalities who sadly are unable to be there for us. We like to rescue others, thereby ignoring our own issues.

'Further, I have to say, from the perspective of having witnessed each of her addictions, that this one – the addiction to the addict – was the worst. Ultimately, it took Frankie to a 'bottom': another futile attempt to escape from the familial pain and fear legacies. Unfortunately, that is the end point of all addictions in the long run.

'In any case, as I'm a people pleaser, I agree with what everyone else has said, too.'

Nancy has been shifting uncomfortably in her seat for the last two minutes. AA is her *only* twelve-step program, and she's struggling with some of the other women's comments – especially Reenie's last point. Her voice is authoritative and unamused.

'It is not for me to judge as we twelve-step members are not judgmental, nor do we label others as alcoholic or codependent or an over-eater or a gambler. "Recovery" in twelve-step programs involves learning to adopt behaviours and ways of thinking that are in opposition to the "sick" individual's default patterns. Becoming less judgmental of oneself and others is an example. However, as we are recovering and not *recovered*, there is some judgmentalism thriving in the AA ecosystem despite its members' intentions.

'Not to be judgmental of Irene, as a hardcore recovering alcoholic, it is obvious that Frankie's primary problem was unquestionably substance abuse. This is reflected by her choice of Stephen as a boyfriend. After all, what were this boy's strong points? He was neither witty nor an intellectual conversationalist. They never discussed topics front and centre in Frankie's mind like the meaning of life, politics, religion, or abortion. Instead, conversations – or rather Frankie's monologues – focused on their relationship. Or Stephen would talk about drugs as they were his primary and possibly singular area of expertise. The addict within her was drawn to him. He served as an addiction mentor or guru, introducing Frankie to several inexpensive and readily available chemical highs.

'As an expert in addiction, I conclude that Frankie's downward journey could not have been prevented by her PGA. The obsessive thinking that is a part of addiction shuts out the spiritual force within.'

Alleged breach #2: Risky behaviours involving drugs

Back to the PGA: 'This was a time rife with dangerous or delinquent behaviour. Again, Frankie was tuning me out. Drugs acted to *block* my voice from penetrating her consciousness. Did you get the pun? I do like puns – especially the spontaneous variety.

'Here's one example I'd like to share with you. The gang of four would go on weekly drive-in movie adventures. Several blocks from the theatre, Melinda and Frankie would climb into the trunk or the boot of the car. Johnny drove an ancient souped-up Cadillac with ample room.

'I see those of you only familiar with Francine shaking your heads, no doubt wondering how the sixteen-year-old dealt with being locked in a dark and confined space. Certainly, the adolescent's later claustrophobia didn't seem to feature, or, if it was present, it was masked with liquor or dope. [35]

'Once parked, Johnny freed the two girls and got out the invariable carton of twenty-four beers for his consumption. Stephen supplied higher proof alcohol for himself and the girls, seemingly having access to relatively exotic spirits like ouzo.

'After drinking each bottle of beer, Johnny would smash the glass against the metal speaker. Laughing, no one was concerned that there would be a confrontation with theatre management or staff. Johnny and Stephen exuded a *West Side Story* tough hoodlum image that ensured exemption from authority. No matter how many bottles hit the speaker and no matter how many other illegal activities they engaged in, the foursome was exempt from law enforcement or injury.

'Take paint thinner. It can be a dangerous substance to mess around with, although the kids didn't have a clue. This practice, known as *huffing* or *sniffing,* involves the individual inhaling paints or other toxic chemical products to feel euphoria and experience hallucinations. It's a short-lasting but intense high which can result in injury and/or death.

'They'd sit in Johnny's attic bedroom, passing the tin around, taking turns at sniffing, seeing bright spots and saying, "Wow man, can you believe these lights? Do you see all of those colours?" Neither Frankie nor Melinda enjoyed this drug, as two of the major side effects of sniffing thinner are

---

35 Likely, Triple F is congenitally claustrophobic. The 'cure' was alcohol, which acted to medicate her dread of confined spaces.

bloated abdomens and flatulence. The boys loved to rip out those farts, but the girls weren't as comfortable with their biological functions and suffered in silence or passed the can on without inhaling.

'As her PGA, I was kept very busy trying to be heard for the next decade, although I note this hearing is only looking at the first two years of her active addiction. Her avoidance of paint-sniffing was an exception. Generally, Frankie went along with whatever was on offer, such as Johnny liking to play car chicken. The goal was to terrify his passengers and those unfortunate people whose bad timing placed them in a vehicle approaching Johnny from the other direction, late at night on an otherwise deserted road. He would rev up the caddy and move over to the wrong side of the road, heading straight into the headlights of the approaching vehicle. And he never wavered. Kept going straight for that car until – thank God – the driver of that vehicle had the sense or the will to live and would swerve to the opposite lane. Melinda and Frankie would scream at Johnny to stop. They continued to travel with him: Frankie – because where there was Johnny, there was Stephen – and Melinda, because Frankie begged her.

'Other, somewhat less hazardous, activities involved taking the caddy out into the country and doing "donuts". I guess Johnny loved circular movement or he had a death wish. I don't know. He also enjoyed driving, very drunk, on the twisted and steep mountain roads going at excessive speeds. More about that in a bit.

'By hanging out with him, Frankie was acting out her own inner destructiveness. Those years were a tough gig for any PGA. But I was always there within her and kept her from annihilation. I just couldn't protect her from the predators.'

Alleged breach #3: Failure to protect Triple F from eating disorders

'My PGA duties went into overtime with amphetamines. Literally, since she didn't sleep. Through Stephen, Frankie was introduced to speed, which meant the introduction of eating disorders into her life.

'She had never been overweight. Muscular with a ballet dancer's legs, she longed for the impossible: either a petite body or a tall statuesque appearance. She was neither. Frankie believed though, beginning at age sixteen with Stephen, that if she were thinner, she would be loved.

'Abuse of speed translated into a dramatic weight loss. Plus, it led to chain smoking cigarettes, staying up for two or three nights, and heading downhill in the fast lane.

'I did manage to put the brakes on that round of pill popping. Weighing less than seven stone, Frankie began to cough up blood. She savoured the weight loss, but the bloody sputum did get her worried about dying. That sensation was unusual. She was living a lifestyle that mocked death – for instance, by playing chicken in Johnny's car – but simultaneously had youth's immortality, which allowed her to say, "I don't care if I die" because Frankie no longer believed that she could die.[36]

'I was whispering louder than the other committee members, including that voice of immortality. The blood made enough of an impression that Frankie consciously did not touch speed until a few years later.

'Although she stopped the amphetamines, her eating disorders, which as you each know have persisted over the years in various forms, were now activated. It was the start of looking in

---

36 The fear-filled Franny had morphed into the fearless adolescent teenage alcoholic, Frankie.

the mirror and no matter how skinny she was – and sometimes she was quite emaciated – seeing her body as overweight with a focus on anything that could be perceived as a bulge.

'Amphetamines marked the onset of an encyclopaedic knowledge of the calories of all foods and beverages. For years, Frankie automatically added the caloric count of every item that she ingested; her numerical obsession plus mental maths skills combined to make a cerebral kilojoule cash register. This was not the first time that I had witnessed this specific manifestation of obsessive behaviour. She used to count her steps to and from school each day. Counting was a somewhat effective means of filling her mind, to keep everything else at arm's length.

'Another expression of this numerical focus was weight. Triple F struggled off and on for years to get the number on the scale to go down, and when it did, then lower yet. She'd weigh herself at different times of the day, and after leaving Henry and Miriam's "home", would fast for a day or two if she were going to be weighed publicly, such as in a doctor's office.

'I would say that for a long time, Frankie gave calories a lot of power – maybe even more than the bottle. Certainly right up there with the alcoholics in her life. She spent a lot of energy trying to have some sway over both, that's for sure. Perhaps it's the basic paradox of Triple F, whose bulimic binge would be a few biscuits – not a packet.

'It took many years for her to realise that she could make a choice and give the scales away. I was doing the best that I could, but her *isms* were entrenched likely because of being reared by Henry and Miriam – no disrespect intended to you two. I'd like to think that I was ultimately able to help her to let go of that eating disorder pathway. But that's not until later in the story. At sixteen and seventeen, Frankie had just crossed the border into eating disorder land and my accomplishments as her PGA were frustratingly limited. Some of the therapeutic head community are here today to provide their views concerning bulimarexia and why there was no PGA breach.'

Many therapists concur on at least the following: that, to some extent, parents are the cause of their kids' mental ill health, right? Would those who have dealt with this issue please confer amongst yourselves and appoint a spokesperson?'

Expert evidence from the therapeutic community

After protracted discussion, those present nominated Dr Liam O'Reilly, who remains one of the most audible on the mental health sub-committee.

'I am delighted to offer my observations, or should I say our observations as I speak for the group or for the majority who continue to attribute the origin of any mental disorder or illness to the parent figures in a child's life.

'Undoubtedly, weight was a subject frequently referred to during her childhood. We could conclude, for example, that Miriam was focused on her body shape. For years, she ate only cottage cheese for lunch; a dollop of sour cream was a special treat. She'd express anguish if she felt that she had gained an ounce.

'We got the impression that Henry was behind Miriam's need to stay svelte. He didn't say anything directly critical to her. However, a particular look was apparent when he struggled to fasten the back of her evening gown. Miriam may have sensed (justifiably) that she was competing with other women for Henry's sexual partnership, hoping that the eradication of any flab would ensure his fidelity?

'We can recall another Henry-related incident that may have impacted Triple F. He made a disparaging comment to Sandra about her slight weight gain. Like Frankie, Sandra's size fluctuated between an American size four and a fourteen. Sandy deflated on the spot. Really, that's the best metaphor I can use. As the patriarch, Henry was commander-in-chief. For both daughters, he was the forerunner of subsequent male mirrors. Chronically critical, he inspected them like soldiers on parade. They felt that if Henry noted any gain – even a few grams – they fell in his estimation for lacking self-control, stamina, and the strength to thwart the enemy forces of gluttony.

'Henry's and Jake's metabolisms allowed them to eat anything without the scales recording a gain. Henry seemed then to have no concept of what weight was like for lesser mortals. The females of the family starved, binged, and purged to earn Henry's love and approval, which overrode their spiritual sense of self.

'In addition, as the Adult Child layperson, Irene, mentioned earlier in evidence, anorexia and bulimia were a means for Triple F to feel in control or to have that illusion.

'We mental health professionals agree with ACA on this. We know that these behaviours may be a response to experiencing multiple forms of abuse as a child, including psychological abuse and exposure to intra-familial violence. Eating disorders can be a communication tool, allowing Frankie in this case to release anger and to channel traumatic thoughts into the toilet. I know that for Frankie, these behaviours gave her a sense of security and independence.

'Therefore, Triple F needed to "work through" her family-of-origin issues before she was liberated from the bondage of bulimarexia. And so she did (for the most part)[37] in Australia with the help of her PGA and us!'

---

37 We must remember the exercise caboose.

Breach #4: Failure to protect Triple F from (other) self-harming

'Thank you for your insights, Dr O'Reilly.

'I will now turn to what the Tribunal has designated as a separate breach – self-harming. I disagree with the deconstruction as Frankie's addictions to substances and addicts and her eating disorders were types of self-harm. And I have explained already why my cautionary and protective voice was muted in those contexts.

'Her relationship with Stephen played out with dramas aplenty. These tended to correlate with Frankie's additional self-destructive behaviours. To fully comprehend the following incidents, you need to understand – if you don't already – that Triple F always did have a flair for the dramatic. She excelled at acting throughout primary and high school. As little Franny, she acted out theatrical productions for the family, earning parental praise, which, as you know, was a scarce commodity. Not to be offensive (again) to you, Henry and Miriam. Her theatrical talent complemented an active imagination and a way of seeing everything around her in intense colours, including the darkest black. She simply thrived in crises.

'Given these characteristics, plus extreme intoxication, it is not surprising that one wintry night, Frankie opened the back door of Johnny's caddy and jumped out of the moving vehicle into dark unfamiliar scrub. Of course, most of you know that angry exits from cars have been a recurrent feature of Triple F's romantic life. On this occasion, her action was preceded by a heated argument with Stephen that took place while Johnny was driving in his reckless manner along narrow and icy mountain roads.

'A drunk Frankie stumbled around in the bushes, sobbing piteously. Johnny reversed the caddy at great speed and the three of them searched for her, calling out her name in contrasting tones:

Johnny was impatient, Melinda's voice expressed concern, and Stephen, well, he sounded pretty pissed off. If the purpose of the action had been to re-endear Stephen, it appeared to have backfired. Guided by the yelling, Frankie found the car and huddled in the corner of the back seat sniffling. She wanted to be comforted, told that she was loved and to hear some conciliatory words. None of these transpired.

'Somehow she made it home in a not uncommon blackout, ensuring she passed out on her bed. We guardian angels do work overtime for drunks – not a scratch or bruise from this adventure.

'Frankie woke up with a familiar hangover, enveloped in a cloud of depression. The head musical director led the choir of internal voices: "I lost my love." "I am alone." "I am unlovable."

'As Miriam was out of town, Frankie decided to stay home. School was not an option in her current frame of mind. She began to drink the highest proof beverages from Henry's stock. By the afternoon, aided by booze and sad music, her affect had entered the acute stage of gloom.

'"Sad music?" you might ask. Unfortunately, the PGA role does not include being a DJ. Another part of Frankie chose to repeatedly listen to *their* love songs. Alcohol, candlelight, and nostalgic lyrics are the ingredients for a certain cognitive framework, which is difficult for me to counter: "Life is just not worth living." "No one loves me." "No one will ever love me." "I'm totally worthless." "It's all hopeless." "I screwed up." "I always screw up." "I'm hopeless."

'And could I remind the Tribunal that it was my voice that steered Frankie to self-help programs when she was still in her twenties?

'This was not the validating internal-talk that she subsequently learned in recovery. On the contrary, these ingredients were guaranteed to activate the more garrulous and oppositional members of the committee. As the alcohol intake and depression increased, their voices became louder. Not very surprising that Frankie found several razor blades in her hand.

'"That's really amazing," she thought as she carved the inside of her wrist and her arm. "I can't feel anything." An upsetting and frustrating outcome, no doubt, since at least a part of the goal was to feel pain: to punish herself, to punish Stephen and all of the other people whom she felt had let her down.

'Was this an actual suicide attempt on *my* watch? I don't know the answer. It certainly wasn't close to a successful try. *They* say that attempted suicides are cries for help. That could have been the case here. Or she could have been slashing up like some women in prison do. They have no other avenue or means to express their pain and anger that accumulate over time.

'The response to her action was like the reaction the female inmates often receive – more on that in a bit.

'She watched red lines and puddles form, noticing in a detached way that some of the cuts, in particular those on her left wrist, were deep and bleeding profusely.

'The phone rang. Although answering it seemed not to fit the scene, given a lack of screenplay, Frankie did pick it up and burst into tears when she heard Melinda's voice. Between sobs, she revealed that her arms were a mess – that she wanted to die because no one, including Stephen, loved her.

'Within half an hour, Melinda had arrived, bandaged Frankie's wrists and upper arms and gave her plenty of water to drink. She wasn't sympathetic. As I said before, if the intent was to garnish sympathy, it was doomed. After more than a year of close companionship, Melinda was becoming weary of her friend's theatrics. She left her safely tucked into bed, though. When Henry returned home from the base, Frankie simply called out from behind the locked bedroom door that she was going to bed early. Untroubled, Henry was likely relieved to be spared the presence of the sullen adolescent at the dinner table.

'Frankie slept, if a stupor induced by alcohol can indeed be termed sleep. When she awakened in the early morning hours, she noticed the blood that had seeped through the bundle of bandages. Her indifferent curiosity mirrored her affect during the act itself. This emotional detachment served to deaden both the physical *and* mental soreness, enabling her to dress for school in a long-sleeved top to conceal her wounds.

'Mid-morning during study hall, she passed out, falling from her chair onto the floor. I concede that, as her PGA, I aimed to garner some parental concern for her. Or it's possible that my role was irrelevant, and her fainting may have been due to blood loss or shock. Regardless of the cause, Frankie next found herself being carried to the principal's office by a male teacher.

'Word spread, and the faculty engaged in hushed conversations that lingered for the remainder of Year 12. Teachers consistently adopted a gentle tone with her, presumably fearing that standard treatment might prompt her to leap off the school rooftop or self-harm in the girl's restroom. Frankie leveraged this to her benefit.

'If Henry's sympathy was a goal here, it remained unfulfilled. Frankie lay on the couch in the principal's office, eavesdropping on his conversation with her father. Apparently, the colonel was engrossed in critical military duties and attempted to persuade the principal to arrange transport to the base hospital. The principal declined. Ultimately, it was decided that Henry would dispatch a driver and coordinate with the military doctor to discreetly suture her wounds.

'The driver was seemingly occupied with tasks of greater importance for Henry, as Frankie languished in the sickroom for over two hours. The situation felt surreal, a state she often found herself in during stressful moments.

'When she did finally see a doctor, Frankie was still numb. As he stitched her deeper cuts, he remarked, "You know, if you want to do this properly, you have to cut lengthwise, not sideways." This comment penetrated her dreamlike cocoon. Feeling invalidated and affronted, she retorted, "I didn't know that. Thanks for the advice, though. I'll be sure to do it properly next time."

'As I said before, Frankie's experience mirrored that of incarcerated women who self-harm, often resulting in their solitary confinement. In a way, that's what happened to her – emotional isolation.

'The driver took her home, where she anxiously anticipated Henry's arrival, mingled with a glimmer of hope. A recurring issue for Frankie, as you may have deduced from being privy to her thoughts, is her tendency to retreat into her mind. Recall the birthday parties and the subsequent disappointments? In this instance, she fantasized about Henry sweeping in. embracing her tightly, and lamenting, "Oh, my poor daughter. What have we done to cause you such distress? We love you so much, dearest Frankie."

'Like that was going to happen. And once again, reality fell short of expectations. What transpired was as follows: after Henry rapped on her bedroom door, Frankie opened it. He stood at formal attention and spoke briskly and succinctly: "I have made an appointment for you with a psychiatrist next Tuesday at 1500 hours. I wish to avoid distressing your mother. You are not to tell her what you've done." Then he turned away and walked up the stairs.

'Although Frankie kept yet another secret from her mother, the news of her suicide attempt inevitably permeated through the school community, reaching the ears of other parents. Thus, about two weeks after the incident, while Miriam was engaged in a friendly card game, she was asked, "How's your daughter? This must be very hard on you."

'That day, Frankie came home to find Miriam lying on the living room floor, Israeli folk music blaring loudly. Miriam was not the type to recline on the floor, nor had she ever, to her daughter's knowledge, blasted music. Being the intuitive person you all have come to recognise, Frankie deduced that something was amiss and made a hasty retreat. Miriam arose following her into the kitchen. There, with a bitterness in her eyes that reflected the accumulated resentments and disempowerment of some twenty-five years of marriage to Henry, she uttered one of the inimitable Jewish mother phrases:

"How could you do this to me?" Presumably "this" alluded to the suicide attempt or the non-disclosure, or perhaps both.

'For years, Frankie regaled others with this tale of Henry and Miriam's reactions to her cry for help. For decades, Francine reproached her mother for her self-absorbed reaction. She would lament to her audience, "Why didn't she hug me, care for me, shout her love for me?" A narrative guaranteed to elicit empathy from a counsellor, psychologist, psychiatrist, friend, acquaintance, or potential partner, it served to rationalise Frankie's harmful actions over the next decade. In a way, it was a "get out of jail" card for me as well. With parents like that, what could a Personal Guardian Angel do? Again, no disrespect intended to you, Miriam and Henry.

In time, Triple F began to see the world from your lenses instead of through her somewhat warped perspective. She came to see that your response, Henry, could have been a precursor to what is now termed "tough love." Alternatively, perhaps you were engulfed by such sadness, anger, and confusion that you were rendered speechless. You might have felt the frustration she later encountered while parenting teenagers: the desire to save them from their self-destructive paths coupled with the knowledge that she was powerless to do so. Francine found solace in twelve-step programs, which aided her in relinquishing control. Yes, Henry, maybe you were trying to do that without having the words.

'And Miriam, how dreadful it must have been for you to learn of Frankie's suicide attempt from an acquaintance, devoid of the support of therapy or spirituality. With motherhood, twelve-step programs, shrinks and me, Francine eventually comprehended and empathised with the pain you must have endured.

'Honestly, I don't know how people who never have children ever truly forgive their own parents and understand that, for the most part, they did do the best they could, given the circumstances. I hope those who are sitting in judgment today can accept that Frankie's conduct during those years was both inevitable and necessary, enabling me to guide her later along a spiritual pathway.'

7

SHARING FRANKIE'S
DIARY WITH DR JAYE

'Hey, Doc. In twelve-step programs, we say that a coincidence is God choosing to be anonymous. Well, a "coincidental" thing happened a few days ago. You know how, in therapy, we're up to my final year of high school? Going through the attic last week, I found a few diaries in my "memory box". Wonder why I brought it to Australia? We had such a limited amount of freight and baggage.

'And one diary is me writing about that time. So, I thought I could read you some extracts. A warning, though, there's a lot of F words and you don't seem like a person who uses profanity?'

Dr Jaye smiles, gently speaking her mantra, 'It's your hour, Francine.'

'OK, well here goes, but it's hard listening to my seventeen year old reflections. Poor Frankie was on the downward slope. At least in this room, I can feel some of the hurt, sadness, and anger that Frankie couldn't.'

December

Dear Diary. I've decided to finally be that cliché – a teenager with a diary. It was a birthday present from Sandy last year and is pretty cool with a real leather cover and lots of lined pages inside. Since there's no one to talk with about some things, will give this a go!

Far fucking out. You would not believe how everyone at school is acting around me. Bet the teachers and office staff are afraid that I might suicide at any moment.

I've started to rock up to class only when the spirit moves me. I've never 'ditched' before. But good little Franny has taken a hike. Bad ass Frankie has arrived!

When I get bored, I leave. Which is every day. Haven't had a teacher say anything when I walk out. When anyone does talk to me, it's like I'm a mental patient in a psych unit or they talk the same way that a grown up speaks to a three-year-old. 'Now, dear, do you really want to miss another week of school?'

Duh ... yes. If I can, I will. How cool is that?

...

Hi, Diary, my own dearest friend. The shit time with Dr KF Shrink has been worth it! Shared with him how important it would be to feel trusted by them. I suggested – rather cleverly if I say so myself – that they could show trust by letting me stay in the house alone for three weeks in February when they're away on their yearly escape.

Dr KF Shrink, who is way too old to be shrinking anyone, has convinced Miriam and Henry that they should agree. Today they told me that in February, I won't be farmed out to one of Henry's staff when they're in the West Indies.

They may live to regret that decision.

Francine stops reading and looks at Dr Jaye.

'When I was reading this before today's session, it occurred to me that it's possible Dr KFC was OK at his job but that I never gave him a chance. The other colonel – Henry – ordered me to go. This is not a case of the horse going to the trough willingly, as we say in AA. Being dragged there, I was pretty much refusing to drink.'

'Now, Doc, the next few entries are about sex – not a subject we've looked at outside of abuse. Maybe reading about it will be easier than talking?'

January

Dear Diary. I'm really excited!!!! Stephen rang earlier, saying that he wants to get back together when he returns from Arizona. This was the first contact with him since the tic tack toe on the arms incident. I guess he's forgiven me for that drama.

His reward will be my 'cherry' – big blush. The Mills and Boon books[38] I've been reading say that this is the most amazing gift I can give. I'm planning it fucking carefully. No spontaneous shitty deflowering for me. No, I want a well-planned and orchestrated beautiful event to file in my fucking memory bank forever.

Have arranged a cover story with Melinda and talked Johnny into giving up his attic bedroom for the night. During a phone call, I have promised Stephen, who's still out of town, a special birthday gift for my seventeenth birthday.

…

Dear Diary. Last night was the big night! My most shitty seventeenth birthday. We didn't drink enough. Unfortunately, nobody gave Stephen the script and I had seen this production so many

---

38 Frankie's choice in reading material had shifted from Franny's escape into the distant realities created by Hemingway, Faulkner, Uris, and Steinbeck. The shift was likely due to seeing other students secretly reading these enticingly covered paperbacks during study hall: seemingly an adolescent rite of passage for American females..

times in my head that there was no fucking way that reality could equal the fantasy of 'throbbing members' and my body 'quivering with delight'. When Stephen rolled off me, I almost said, 'Is it over? Has it happened?'

What am I doing wrong, dear Diary? Stephen has trouble staying hard. I must be a super crap lover. If it wasn't good, the problem must be me, right? And does no orgasm mean that I'm frigid? The dry humping we've done for the last year felt far fucking great compared to the actual ... fuck.

Francine looks up at Dr Jaye trying to gauge a reaction. As usual, though, she gives nothing away. Despite not sensing any judgment, Francine feels the need to explain further.

'I doubt anyone back then had much of a clue about female sexuality, particularly the importance of clitoral contact. A bogan like Stephen? He would've been utterly lost. Plus, it wasn't just alcohol for him – amphetamines were his go-to. I've read research linking those to erectile dysfunction.'

There's a moment of silence – providing Dr Jaye the space to speak.

'One thing hasn't changed though. Your *natural* response is to feel responsible for everybody and everything or for negative events or traits in your children and the universe in general. This is understandable, Francine. It's how you've survived. But nowadays, I see you catch yourself in the act. Sometimes you even laugh it off.'

Francine nods. 'Poor me back then, though. Stuck. Little wonder that grog beckoned.'

February

Hi, Diary dearest. Well, last night, we fucked again – or tried to. It was as bad as the first time. Henry and Miriam are overseas for three weeks and am home alone as instructed by the KF doc. God was he off! Poor Henry and Miriam.

Been drinking and popping dexies since the parents abandoned ship. But have stopped now. A fucking scary thing happened. Well, first, something amazing: I'm skinny enough that my bones are sticking out. So cool. This happens when you stop eating. But after three days and nights without sleep and non-stop smoking, I started coughing and blood came out. Bright red.

Man, oh man, I promise you that I will never do speed again. Never.

…

I have lost not only heaps of weight – enough to drop two sizes – but also the first love of my life. Before the parents returned, Stephen took off for Arizona without even saying goodbye. Yes, that's a lot of shit happening but it's OK DD, I'm doing OK. For one thing, I'm not obsessing about Stephen. Of course, without booze or speed my head is too fucking foggy to think about anyone or anything! I'm sure there's a lot of tears in there and probably anger but right now I feel zipped up.

Francine stops reading. She needs to explain to Dr Jaye that, when Frankie wrote about never taking amphetamines again, she believed that to be the truth.

'I was being honest, or reckon I can say "fair dinkum." I hear that expression a lot but haven't used it yet since, with this North American accent that won't disappear after decades, I sound like a try hard!'[39]

---

39 Migrants tend to adopt the colloquialisms and accents of their new homeland. Francine, as a proud and patriotic new Aussie, wanted to sound as Australian as she could. This became even more the case with the Trump era given that listeners conflated Canadian and US accents.

'Anyway, at the time I made the commitment to quit speed, I did believe that I wouldn't pick up again. That's just part of the cunning and powerful parts of this disease. Broken (or false) promises aren't just made to other people but also to ourselves.

'Reading about my seventeen-year-old's jutting hip bones, Dr Jaye, did you notice that my hand sort of explored one hip just now. Yep, still bony. Eating disorders are a lot like alcoholism; I'm recovering, not recovered from either. With alcohol, I can abstain. That's not a healthy option with food. Thankfully, I've moved beyond obsessing over kilojoules and can eat without guilt — as long as I exercise daily, of course.

'As I've shared with you before, I suppose that in some ways, jogging is an eating disorder finale for me. But as we say in the Program, it's only a problem if it causes me a problem. When I put a bandage on a twisted ankle and went out for a run, yes, Dr Jaye, I could see the lack of choice and potential long-term damage.

'Most of the time, running is when I feel closest to my PGA or HP. The committee in my head goes quiet because I'm in the present moment. And have I told you that, for the past couple of months, I've been listening to a running meditation with affirmations for part of my run?

'Bottom line is that I haven't been injured or ill in years. If I were, would I rest? Hmm. Reckon we both know the answer. I'm definitely a recover*ing* bulimarexic, much like I'm a recover*ing* alcoholic and codependent.'

Dr Jamyang makes eye contact with Francine. Her message is, as always, non-judgmental and validating but not directly relevant to the topic.

'That's good to hear. You seem more understanding and accepting of who you are. And it sounds like you're hearing less from Henry and Miriam too.'

March

OK. I've got to confess. Like wow man, guess I'm not super great at shutting down emotions after all? Yesterday I tried to kill myself for the second time. Or sort of tried. I swallowed a bottle of aspirin, about one hundred tablets. Melinda, who's been staying here, found me crying in the bathroom and she made me throw up.

I might have lost her friendship, too. She left last night, telling me in a disgusted tone that she's had it with my fucking melodramas.

...

The evil parents returned today to a disaster: broken windows and furniture, a car in the shop for major bodywork, and an anorexic daughter looking like 'hell warmed over' – Miriam's words.

The KF shrink may have advised them not to show anger or to question their suicidal teenager. Like there's no obvious price to pay here. Instead, it's my guess that the wreckage of the car and house now resides in what I call Miriam's 'MORGUE' (memory organ of rank, gruesome, ugly events). Clever, right?

What's more, dearest Diary, I am sensing Henry's swallowed rage. I better be extra careful.

Francine pauses and turns to Dr Jaye.

'Reading this diary isn't easy, but it's good for me. Like, the last bit triggered Franny. Other entries have stirred up anger and hurt. But I can identify and process those feelings here. It's a safe space.

'And, thinking back, I say, "Good on Melinda." Without Al-Anon, she managed to detach and get off the roller coaster.'

Dr Jaye glances at her notes – a signal Francine has learned means the psychiatrist is about to speak. Her comments, as always, resonate with Francine.

'Your mother's MORGUE was more than just a repository for bad memories. To me, it seems more like a hidden garden where resentments blossomed over time.

'And your note about your father at the end. You had already developed a finely tuned, hyper-vigilant survival mechanism, which is still accessible to you. Now, you can recognise when it's activated and understand that it's not abnormal for those who've experienced violence firsthand or as witnesses. You're continuing to learn how to let go of those safety measures.'

April

Haven't written in a while. Too fucking off my head with weed. Sandy came home for spring break with a stash of pills along with a substantial amount of pot. She left me about an ounce, which I thought would keep me in happy highland until she comes back in summer.

A few kids at school have discovered the joys of marijuana but are struggling to get their hands on any. Word's spread about my inventory with a few of these wannabe potheads asking me if they could make a purchase. Accordingly, Diary dearest, I decided to roll it into joints and then set up shop. Henry and Miriam are always hinting that it would be good for me to earn some money outside of my allowance. I aim to please.

Last night at 7:30, about a dozen of the wannabes arrived at our front door. My cover story for the parents involved an out-of-hours rehearsal for a drama class.

Anyway, DD, I'm feeling guilty. It's not about selling the dope. Someone's going to do that so it might as well be me, right? I mean, just take a chill pill.

No, it's Miriam and Henry's response. They were obviously pleased that kids were over and relieved that their popular daughter has returned. Far fucking out. Gonna smoke some weed and totally veg listening to Dylan. Catch you on the flip side.

...

Well, Diary, can't believe I'm writing this – cannot really comprehend that what I have dreaded all my life happened last night.

I lost my temper and broke at least two 'Henry' rules. He was talking to or at me in the doorway of the stairwell. I yelled at him, 'I hate you. I've always hated you!' You could see the rage ... fists clenched. My heart was pounding. Terrified, in that moment, I wanted to hit 'Rewind' and take back my words.

Henry pounded me on the head and kicked my tailbone (as if my butt were a football). The kick knocked me over and I fell down the sixteen steps to the basement landing in a heap.

'Is that all it is? Is that all it is?' Not sure if that was aloud or an inside scream.

Because at that moment I knew that nothing, absolutely nothing, is ever as bad as I had anticipated.

Tears begin to fall as Francine concludes her reading. For a brief moment, decades later, she re-experiences the sensation of being struck on the head and thrown down the stairs – this time not as a witness to Henry's violence, but as its target.

'Dr Jaye, fear moulded little Franny. And post puberty, when that role no longer fit, I was in hiding like Anne Frank – from Herr Henry, not the Nazis – in my downstairs hideaway.

'Repression might have erased these memories, except for the lingering injury. Even now, I can't sit for extended periods without discomfort, which serves as an uninvited reminder.

'I did eventually forgive Henry as I came to realise how anger and hurt are integrally connected. If only such epiphanies, like this understanding of fear, could be single-lesson events for me. Instead, I undergo cycles of dread, confront the reality, and time and again discover that the anticipation was far worse.'

Dr Jaye looks even more thoughtful than usual.

'In your writing and public speeches, you've identified as a survivor of sexual assault and as a witness to physical abuse. Those experiences seem easier for you to discuss than direct assault or abandonment, which have also left indelible scars.'

May

Dear Diary. It is interesting that in the six months that I have been seeing Dr KFC, he has never asked me about drinking and drugging. I sit in the black leather recliner telling an edited version of my life story. He nods wisely, giving minimal feedback. Sometimes I wonder if he's perfected the art of sleeping with his eyes open.

Francine hesitates, feeling guilty for criticising one psychiatrist in the presence of another. Dr Jaye might think she disparages her as well.

'Look, Dr Jaye, I'll defend him if you won't. My time with Dr KFC probably predates the broader awareness of teen alcoholism and addiction as social issues. The question might not have aligned with his therapeutic approach, assuming he even had one. Alternatively, he might've simply been an uninformed bludger. But let me share some more diary entries before our time is up.'

Hello, my friend. The marijuana business has been going well with my folks convinced that their Frankie is back on the popularity track. Oddly, they're kind of right. Here we are, nearing prom and graduation, and I've gone from the only hippie group (Melinda and me) to the 'in' crowd. These are the rich girls; the cheerleaders with straight blonde hair and the groovy clothes; the ones going steady with the jocks on the football or basketball teams – the people Miriam calls the goyim.

Far out. Far fucking out.

Francine looks up from her diary. 'Doc, you might be wondering how I became a member of that clique? Looking back, the key may have been that Marissa, one of the most popular girls, sort of adopted me as a project. Her parents were divorcing, making her more emotionally compromised than her peers – a victim of collateral divorce damage. Perhaps that's why she gravitated towards me, another soul acting out. It felt surreal, as if I'd successfully auditioned for a role in a teen movie.'

She glances at the clock. 'Anyway, back to the diary –'

Man, I haven't written in almost two weeks, DD. Been super-duper or doper busy partying for end of high school. Be there or be square! Alcohol and making out in the bushes. Each time, I think that this guy is the 'one'. Yeah right …

Two nights ago, I did meet someone super cool and fucking hot. Roger graduated last year. Casanova for sure. If he were a sailor, he'd have a woman in every port of call. And each girl would think that she was the only one. Playboy heartbreaker.

Today, the rush is worth it.

For an eighteen-year-old, Roger seems to know about fucking. What do I know, though? At least, compared to Stephen, he's a stud.

Yes, Diary, I had sex with Roger! And you'll never guess what happened. He took my virginity!!!! I know that's a lot of exclamation marks but how many people lose their virginity twice? Must check Guinness Book of Records.

Bit hard to pop the cherry if a guy's not hard.

...

Far fucking out, DD! You'll never guess where I was last night! Prom!!!! Man, I was like Cinderella wearing a floor-length mauve-coloured ball gown, which I picked out – not Miriam! My date was none other than ... wait for it ... the junior class president and captain of the football team! Can you believe it: the radical oddball and the super straight jock?

Francine is conscious of the time but wants to share a few more thoughts.

'Weird, doc, isn't it, how I can remember that night clearly. Not my usual memory MO.

'It was a fun evening and there weren't many of those back then. Maybe it went well because, for once, I had no expectations.

'As far as making it to the popular clique, my seventeen-year-old self had "made it" there on the outside. But inside, I felt like an imposter and out of place. Rush of gratitude right now to PGA for guiding me to people who share their "insides" enough for me to know I do belong and no longer feel "terminally unique." Also speaking of the Program – well, if back then I had understood that type, I wouldn't have had sex with Roger. However, as *they* say, hindsight is 20/20.'

June

Can you believe it, DD? Just two days ago, I graduated and moved out of the basement of their house.

I just want to feel safe.

Far fucking out, man. I'm FREE! Well, sort of free, with three months not to rely on Henry and Miriam until I go to university.

Has leaving been easy? No idea, to be honest, DD. Pretty much off my face non-stop. Being high continuously allowed me to escape from Henry — or from the parent's house, anyway. Henry and Miriam are still living in my head, though.

The therapist tilts her head slightly, indicating agreement.

'Hearing about your suicide attempt from a card-playing acquaintance must have been a tipping point for your mother. But as a mum, Francine, you realise that there was probably sadness for the earlier loss of Franny who, unlike Frankie, hadn't added to Miriam's catalogue of negative memories.'

8
SUMMER OF 17: AN OPEN MEETING

'Hi. I'm Linda, a very grateful member of AA and a prominent voice in Triple F's head committee. Our purpose today is to hear from those who can reflect on Frankie's life during the three months between leaving "home" and going to university. As today's meeting is deemed to be "open", could relevant cerebral passers-by share their observations briefly. But first, instead of starting off with a prayer, we'll have a reading more appropriate to this period of time – a poem partially derived from P Wiz.'

"No way José
That's simply not OK
She has never accepted her "warts and all"
To reach the bottom she still must fall.
"It's just a life struggle where the F is at
But don't you worry Dr F, it ain't gotta be like that
When you start winning give yo self a pat on the back
And all the bad things they be wishing
They're gonna take that right back."

The first step down

Annie

Annie, an innocent-looking girl, raises her hand. Linda signals that she can have the floor.

'I met Frankie right after she became my next-door neighbour. She arrived with a few posh possessions. Her message was clear: "I'm a rich girl just passing through slum town."

'I helped her to get a job at the New York City-style deli where I was a waitress. Turned out that Frankie lied and told management she was eighteen, which meant she could serve beer. Weirdly, in fact, I was a few months older but had to ask her to handle my beer service! She told me – and I believed her – that she felt uncomfortable lying about her age.

'She sure was smoking heaps of dope – trying to silence that guilt.

'Frankie was a seventeen-year-old on a mission. For a month she was either working or off her face, or both. Her goal was to earn enough money to lie on a California beach and see the Pacific Ocean.

'I learned bits and pieces about Frankie during those weeks. For instance, sometimes she'd get a dreamy look, and I knew she was thinking about Jeff. I met him once, and wow, he is a super dude with dark, almost black wavy hair and the deepest blue eyes that you'd want to stare into. Those of you who were around at high school with Frankie would remember him. Hey Jeff, would you like to share?'

Jeff (and Miriam)

Jeff, who is sitting nearby, blushes; 'Well, not sure how good look-ing I am. I think my claim to fame here is that I'm one of the very few Jewish guys that Frankie dated. What else can I tell you? We both thought the other was hot. Our political consciousnesses and ideologies were a match, likely the only two students in our high school year who had read Kahil Gibran and Omar Khayam.

'We didn't have sex, though. I might not have been messed up enough to appeal to her. I do remember our lying on the creaky single bed in that grotty old apartment and how we just held each other and hugged. Perhaps I was beginning to become aware of my sexuality? I know that Frankie has encountered quite a few gay men like me, who didn't yet know. Or at least that became Francine's "story": if a guy didn't want to do "it" with her, (or like Stephen and others yet [not] to come) likely they were gay? Yes, I see some of you think that's arrogant but at least in my case, it was accurate!'

'What is this – gay, schmay? Are these happy men?' That's Miriam needing to talk about a persistent niggling in her MORGUE.

'So, after four weeks of serving Reubens to goyim, my genius child saved enough tips for a student standby ticket to Los Angeles and a few hundred dollars more. First though, my *meshugenah* daughter sold all her worldly possessions, which weren't many at that first sale. Later, she sells all the good furniture, fine silver, china from Europe – everything Henry and I ever gave. And what does she get? *Bupkis*! If she needs a ritual cleansing better that she uses a *mikveh*. For any goyim here, if there are words you don't understand, you could begin to study Yiddish?'

Marissa

Speaking of goyim, another passer-by – the top of the in-group, Marissa – like Jeff, came to visit Frankie in the poor side of town.

'I did see some changes in her that I think could help us to understand what was going on. One incident stands out. Escaping from the heat and humidity inside, we were on the front steps of the tenement. An elderly woman collapsed on the sidewalk near us. Her head hit the pavement hard enough that blood was visible through her white hair. Frankie didn't move. I crouched down beside the lady, putting her head on my lap, talking softly. This wasn't hard, since blood has never bothered me, and she looked a bit like my gran. So, I stayed there with her until an ambulance arrived. Frankie stood at a distance looking away.

'It's what happened afterwards that is significant. After the ambulance took off, Frankie looked at me with tears in her eyes. This is what she then shared with me. I think it says a lot about her insides.'

Marissa, you are a hero to me. I couldn't do what you did, and that makes your act heroic and me a worthless piece of shit. That woman represents two of the things that I dread the most: age and ill health. I always avoid both. Like, I remember when I was about four, for some reason I was out with my older brother, Jake, which was unusual. He bumped into a friend with his grandmother or great-grandmother because she was seriously old.

'At this point, Frankie laughed and said that when you're four years old, a forty-year-old would seem ancient. She then continued to tell me her story.'

This woman's face, though, was covered with lines. And, when she moved closer to me, I froze and looked away from her. I could neither move nor respond. And even though I have a memory like a sieve, it's a picture that won't go away.

'Frankie sort of made a confessional. She wanted to be me: a Florence Nightingale, a saint, a healer, and a helper. She sensed that the image of me tenderly holding that old woman would stay with her forever. She suspected that she could never be that person, which filled her with self-loathing.

'Just want to say too, especially since there's lots of twelve-step program people here today, that I'm happy and relieved that Frankie hit her bottom so young and started to accept that she is who she is – her own strengths and skills that are different from mine!'

Heading West

At this point in the proceedings, Linda asks if there is anyone present whose life intersected with Frankie's life about this time who would be willing to contribute their observations. PGA, who had been kept especially busy during the time period beginning with the sojourn to California, is the first to speak.

'There she was, seventeen, all alone except for me and she wasn't listening. There were all sorts of dangers lurking but she didn't have a clue.

'Chaos, really. No forward planning at all, which many of you in this room will find surprising as you only know the recovering Francine who plans so far ahead that her children and partner(s) ridicule her. But here's an example of what she was like back in the day. She got off the plane without any idea of her destination. At that time, this was her traveling modus operandi. At the bus stop, she waited for a bus that had the word "beach" on its route sign. The first one with that word said "Santa Monica Beach", which was how she ended up in Santa Monica.

'Having booked into an ocean-side hotel that looked decent and was too expensive for a teenager with limited funds and fiscal sense, she wandered to the beach where she could hear the sounds of "Classical Gas" from someone's radio. Whenever she hears it, she is transported back there.'

Carl

'And that was the day she met me.'

A clean-cut quintessential American athletic-looking man, Carl, interrupts PGA, saying that he might be the best narrator for the next part of the story since he had been her one-week-long Santa Monica boyfriend.

'Lying on the beach within staring distance, for about an hour we stole looks at each other. I don't remember who spoke first but before I knew it, we were together and talking non-stop. I was on summer break from Penn State and was working on the boardwalk for three months.

'I know what you're thinking … I was thinking it, too. On the surface, I didn't seem to be Frankie's type. I did have some hidden characteristics, though, which drew her to me. She established in the first ten minutes that I wasn't averse to a bit of weed, and currently was in possession of a substantial stash. That helped my case. And, turned out that we both enjoyed playing sexy games while high. This suited her just fine.

'There we were – the evening of her arrival in California – in my room, stoned out of our minds and playing strip poker with a lot of nervous laughter and groping. It may surprise you, but we never had sex. Don't feel bad, though, since we did do just about everything else during the next week. I guess she discovered that my clean-cut exterior didn't match up with my insides. And yes, I understand that this was a lesson she would continue to experience repeatedly.

'Reflecting with the wisdom, or perhaps cynicism, of age, I find myself marvelling at her naivety in entering the bedroom of a man who was almost a stranger. I suppose at seventeen, one is either blissfully unaware of the twisted and violent individuals that lurk in the world, or one believes oneself to be invincible or somehow exempt from harm. Let me give you an example of how Frankie ended up in risky situations.

'One night, she decided that it would be fun to hitchhike into Hollywood. Neither of us had been there, and it seemed like *the* place to go when you're in Los Angeles. Why hitchhike, you ask? Well, Frankie told me that she'd taken to hitching rides back home. Could be this was an exception to her being a spendthrift and/or a by-product of the daring that came from drug-induced delusions of immortality?

'It was our third ride of the evening. Some hitches are like that. You get in and they only take you a short distance, which means you're out there looking for another lift. This third guy, and yes, they were always men, was friendly and after a few minutes, asked if we'd like to smoke a little grass. We agreed. And, to tell you the truth, I can't remember if it was me or Frankie who made that call.

'After going into the Beverly Hills mansion, a nervous Frankie and I were sitting side-by-side while Anthony, sitting across from us, passed us a silver cigarette case filled with these mind-blowing, huge, machine-rolled joints.

'At this point, I guess the only thing that we were worried about was the possibility that the guy was a "narc"; you know, an undercover narcotics police officer. Kinky sex just wasn't on our radar. But when I went to the toilet, Anthony asked Frankie some intimate questions although, in her dope-affected brain, she wasn't sure exactly what he was asking.

'Later on, she told me that he asked her: "So, have you ever thought about doing a group thing? I've done it and they're really good fun!"

'"Group thing?" She wondered if he was referring to group therapy since everyone knows that in Hollywood, shrinking is mandatory.

'Frankie didn't reply. The marijuana had slowed the grey matter appreciably, with the connection between the neurons putting her larynx on a delayed setting. Anthony ignored her silence and continued. "I mean, when there's more than just the two of you, there's a greater possibility that all parts will be in contact, which has to be what it's all about, right?"

'"Parts in contact?"

'Frankie thought this could be a reference to a psychiatrist and the patient's transference and how, in a group, everyone could transfer identities with everyone else? She did begin to feel some apprehension, though, which, when you're stoned means, "This is turning into a real bummer, man."

'When Frankie went to the bathroom, Anthony was more direct with me, suggesting that the three of us *do* it. Or maybe I'm a better listener?

'I wasn't impressed. My sexual game-playing was in a different league. So, when he left the room to get drinks, Frankie and I looked at each other and shared enough to know we had to get out of there. We escaped and, laughing like mad people, ran down the streets of Beverly Hills.

'Since then, I have wondered how close to danger we actually were that night. It didn't put us off hitching, though. In fact, still off our faces, we hitchhiked back to Santa Monica.'

'Are you going to San Francisco … flowers in your hair …'

Carl continues to talk, a bit sadly now as he is describing how Frankie left Santa Monica (and him), qualifying, though, that he wasn't ever the subject or object of her fatal attraction focus.

'It might have been that absence that prompted Frankie to move on to San Francisco. This was a place that she told me had been beckoning to her through the lyrics of songs like, "If you're going to San Francisco, be sure to wear some flowers in your hair." She sure was drawn to Haight-Ashbury – the supposed mecca of hippies at that time.

'She assured me that she'd write. She didn't.

'The last time I saw Frankie, it was just after dawn. She was standing on the side of the Pacific Coast Highway with her thumb out, wearing a mini dress and carrying two suitcases.'

After a now visibly moved Carl completes his 'share', Linda asks if there is anyone present who interacted with Frankie that day and/or during her week in San Francisco. Twenty men raise their hands.

'OK. Let's first narrow the next speaker to someone who gave her a ride that day.'

John

The four men who had picked her up appoint a spokesperson – John, a middle-aged, nondescript sort who was the last driver of the day.

'When I pulled over, it was already dusk. I guess she had been waiting a while for someone to stop who would be going the remaining hour to the city. She leaned into the passenger window saying, "Hi. I'm Frankie. Are you going to San Francisco?" I nodded my head, "Hop in. I'm going there."

'I asked her about her hitchhiking experiences that day and how she'd ended up in the middle of nowhere. She told me about the three truck drivers who had preceded me: "They were each lovely guys, stopping for food and offering to pay for my meal. No one put the moves on me or even flirted. The only problem today has been finding a driver going all the way to 'Frisco. The last trucker was going home and was turning off the Pacific Highway where you picked me up."

'I think she saw me as too old to be a threat.

'We drove along the coast road to 'Frisco for about fifteen minutes. Then I took an exit which did not have San Francisco signage. Frankie was obviously anxious now. When I drove along an unpaved road, the chatter stopped. Edging close to the door, she was likely thinking about jumping out. But what good would that do? There were no houses or people. Nowhere for her to run.

'Parking the car on the side of that dirt track, I turned the ignition off. Frankie reached for the door handle, but I leaned over and restrained her with my arm. Her body was trembling, and you could almost hear her thoughts: "This is it! I'm going to die or be raped or both now."

'"You know, Frankie, I have a daughter who's about your age," I spoke slowly. "As far as I know, she's never hitchhiked. But, if she ever does, I hope that someone will do for her what I am doing for you – that is, to provide this real-life warning. The person who picks you up could be a sicko who intends to sexually assault or murder you."'

He glances at the others present at today's meeting.

'Most of you know this was a pivotal episode for Frankie. I understand from PGA (who was working through me) that she never hitched again! I've also been told that Francine uses the story as one of her standby anecdotes to fill awkward silences in social situations. She describes the finale and its meaning like this: "I could feel my heart beating quite loudly in my ears. I sensed danger. What could I do? So, John did me a solid, although I didn't appreciate the technique at the time. But it worked."

'The last that I saw Frankie, she was entering a rundown building with a malfunctioning neon sign hanging lopsided, "Hotel, Rooms by the Week." Evidently, she rented a room there with only a single bed for the grand sum of $30 a week. You know the kind of place? Small with cracked walls, free standing sink, tiny window opening to downtown San Francisco and the sounds of sirens and screeching cars.'

Jackie and a few regulars reflect

A pint-sized fellow, resembling a former jockey who has hit rock bottom in the world of alcoholism, takes the floor. He looks like a gangster, which may have been an attraction for Frankie.

'Hi everyone. I'm – well – Jackie to my mates. Yep, you guessed it. A Cockney for sure from the East End of London. Left there when I was a lad to make a fortune riding the ponies in America. And I stayed, and still spend time at the track. Not riding, though … just trying to make me fortune.

'I met Frankie the first night she arrived at the place I called home. I was coming out of me room to use the toilet, saw her, and said, "Evenin." Such a sweet lass. We had many natters in the hallways and on the *apples and pears* (stairs, mate) that week as I tried to keep an eye on her. She liked my rhyming slang and started to say, "I'm still *coals and coke*." Thought it sounded cooler than broke.

'Bollocks! Don't look at me like I'm a *dodge and swerve*. Mate, I'm not a perve – just making sure that she was OK.

'I'd see Frankie a few times every day. She liked wearing dresses and shirts with layers – made her look like a proper wedding cake. But she thought she looked up the duff.

'Some people might have bought it, but not the hippies. She went on the *Uncle Gus* a few mornings and stood at the intersection of Haight and Ashbury, waiting for a flower child bloke to invite her into their commune or to offer her some of that marijuana stuff. No one did. Crashed in their pads until late recovering from the love-in the night before. No mate, the good guys in her story were blokes like me … well, the sort that go to the pub for a pint anyway.

'The cable car conductors let her ride up and down the hills without a ticket for hours. A few even *paid* her (instead) a quid or two for food, but she bought fags instead. That was Triple F. Chain smoking, she'd tell me how these tram rides were as entertaining as the variety of people on them – different races, social classes, occupations, ages, and degrees of bohemianism and conventionality. "Jackie," she'd say. "Don't you just love to people watch like I do? I make up stories about a person or a couple in intricate detail. For me, it's the same as reading an excellent book. The practice releases me from whatever is happening in my life, escaping into a literary or imaginary reality. Another great getaway with no hangover and cheap as chips, as you'd say Jackie!"

'Another favourite activity of this lass, which was special and endeared her to me and the lads throughout her life, is the way she talked to strangers, including shopkeepers, clerks, bus drivers, former jockeys – the lot.'

At this point, there are signs of life from a few standing committee members in the audience. Evidently, this last comment has evoked some divergent responses. Several are moved to speak.

'It's such an open thing to do, quintessentially Francine and what I love about her,' speaks sweet (and increasingly sour) Richard. A number of those who have preceded him nod in acquiescence.

'That's our little Franny,' Miriam and Henry say proudly. 'She would talk to everybody because she was born an extrovert. Franny was always popular at every school she attended. In fact, one evening when she was a teenager, about twenty of her friends dropped over! Can you imagine?'

'We believe that's a misunderstanding. These behaviours are simply ways of avoiding real intimacy. She just unloads all her *crap* onto strangers, then believes she's an open individual,' argue the codependency and other new age counsellors. They believe Triple F could add another twelve-step program to her membership list if People Watchers Anonymous was ever established to help those who use people-watching to avoid their own feelings or lives.

'We don't want to be accused of black-and-white thinking, though. We recognise there are many shades of grey between healthy and codependent. For instance, we know from sharing our case notes that this indiscriminate type of sharing has sometimes been helpful for Triple F. There was that time in her thirties, for example, when she was waiting for public transport and began to chat with another woman sitting on the bench. This was during one of Francine's many work debacles. Remember? It turned out that the other person worked for a union. She gave Francine pro bono advice on industrial action and employment law pathways that proved helpful!'

Matteo

An older man with grey hair and a beard, wearing loose trousers and a neatly tucked button-down shirt, indicates that he would like to contribute. He speaks with the accent of someone who emigrated to the USA as an adult from a Mediterranean country.

'*Buon giorno.* My name, it is Matteo. I feed Signorina F – no charge – every night around 9:30 when I closed the shop. It was the right thing to do. That first afternoon she came in, I could see that there was a problem. She stood a few feet from the counter for about a quarter of an hour. Other customers they came, and they went. I saw that she was looking at the cigarettes on the shelves behind me and at the sandwiches sitting behind the glassed refrigerated compartment in front of me.

'"*Ciao. Buon pomeriggio, Signorina.* You know, if you stand at my counters for much longer, someone's going to buy you. What's the matter? Can't decide what you want to eat? Can I recommend the chicken salad on rye? Just made it an hour ago."

'She looked at me with eyes that were both wise and innocent. *Lei era molto bella.* And then she started talking, and her openness … it was *piacevolmente diverso* – refreshing.

'"Well, to be honest, kind sir – and I do pride myself on honesty – I have a dilemma. My mouth is watering. I love chicken salad, especially like my mother makes! It feels like a long time since I've had a decent meal. In fact, it's only been a day or two since the cable car guys gave me some money, but let's face it, when you're a middle-class girl, even a single day with little to eat feels like starvation and poverty. The thing is, though, I only have enough money left to buy either cigarettes or food." She paused for a couple of minutes, then said, "And as the addict that I am, there is no choice, really. A pack of Kool Menthols, please."

'As I rang up her purchase, I could see the indecision and the hunger in her eyes. *Scusami*, there was a thing going on here that made me want to help.

'"Look. If you're hungry with no money, *piccola signorina*, you come back here after I close tonight – after nine o'clock when I'm cleaning. Knock on the door. I'll make you a sandwich, nice and fresh, and you can eat it here with a glass of milk."

'She looked unsure and told me about how that last ride into San Francisco had scared her. "Oh, *mio*," I thought. "Hitchhiking alone with that body and innocence. Her mama and papa – they are not thinking straight!"

'She did come back, though, that night and the following five evenings, telling me that her "bourgeois stomach had overruled the paranoia."'

Home again, home again ...?

Linda closes the meeting.

'Thank you to everyone who was able to share their experiences with our protagonist during this time period. Could we applaud these folks, please? A special thanks to Jack and Matteo. Triple F told me about how kind you both were to her. How you fed her, Matteo, for five or six days and never asked for anything in return. She fantasised about sending you a substantial cheque and/or expensive gifts to repay your kindness. However, her disease was raging for the next decade and she never even wrote to you, Matteo.

'And Jack: Frankie told me how you asked her to pick a number for you to place a two-dollar bet on a specific race. Off you went to the track, which I guess was your routine? That day, though, you won $50 on number four, which covered a student stand-by fare back to Henry and Miriam. And like with you, Matteo, she swore that she'd send the money back once she had some. But, as you know, she never did. Periodically, she felt waves of shame and guilt about both of you. You see, Triple F has her own MORGUE. She's never needed Miriam to remind her of her dastardly deeds. For years, Francine felt guilty – likely, she still does since she didn't make amends to you. We do have to *work* those steps although, as most of you know, there are no rules.

'And now, shall we end today's meeting in our recommended way?'

Linda is ready to close with the serenity prayer, however, someone is indicating that she would like to speak – that is, with both her voice and with hand and arm gestures passed on through the generations. Miriam's usage of Yiddish correlates with her angst.

Miriam

'Yes, I do like to *kibitz,* but this is not me kibitzing. This is a mother who needs to talk about the *chutzpah* of that *meshugener* daughter of mine! She graduated in that long white dress or robe and looked so beautiful it hurt. The next day she leaves. The *tsuris* with that one. Teenagers … you can have them. She gave us *bubkes*. She broke our hearts.

'Yes, I know the baby bird needs to fly away, but we heard nothing. Does she write a letter to her parents? No. Does she pick up a telephone? No. Who could sleep for the worry? Does she care about everything we sacrificed to give her a good life? She needed to have her head examined, or we needed to have ours examined since we gave and gave and gave and got nothing but *tsuris. Nu*?

'Then, out of nowhere, shortly before the start of university, she knocks at the door. Next, after staying in the guest room as a visitor for ten days, we drove Frankie to her new school. She didn't want either of us coming into her dormitory room – that we were paying for. As I said to Henry while driving back home, "*Oi mein Gott,* that I should have had it so good."

'Years later, when we were visiting her and our grandchildren in Australia – on the other side of the world – Francine talked about why she didn't let us come into her dorm. My daughter, the intellectual, said it would have been "too uncool and prolonged the pain of separation."

'I'm her mother. I will always love her. You can stop looking at me like I'm *Portnoy's Complaint*. That Roth was an ungrateful son. Makes us look like we're smothering our children. He may be Jewish, but he doesn't know from Jewish.'[40]

---

40 An expression used by Jews, like Miriam, who grew up in the northeast of the US, 'to (not) know from,' which means not knowing anything about something, is derived from Yiddish.

9
SHARING FRANKIE'S UNI JOURNAL IN THERAPY

'Hey, Dear Doc, as we're going through my life, I just found a journal from my first semester at university. Can I read some parts aloud instead of retelling the whole story?'

'Your hour, your time, Francine. That's the only rule in this space.'

'Thanks, Doc. I won't bore you with all 300 pages, but I'll try to pick extracts that might highlight any relevant history for therapy.'

Mid-September – mid-October

I've landed in a foreign land – a university with a conservative ethos. Most students seem like the in-crowd from high school: blonde cheerleaders and jocks. Almost everyone is part of a Greek sorority or fraternity, and all the newbies are pledging. Not me, though. I don't want to be blackballed like I was in the Midwest. Plus, my self-image is that of a more heavy-thinking person.

Dr Jaye nods compassionately at Francine.

'Perhaps there was a fear of rejection. That's a normal feeling for adult children who've been neglected.'

That word again, leading to more internal turmoil. Francine resumes reading.

Another non-pledge is my roommate, Shelly. She's shy, far from home, and homesick. It's hard to tell what's going on inside her. Under my guidance, she's tried marijuana, amphetamines, and hallucinogens like LSD over the past month. Although we use together, I don't feel close to her. She's a closed person.

Since arriving, I've made only one friend – beautiful Leila, whose room is a few doors down the hallway. She and her roommate are the only other 'non-Greeks' in the dorm. She doesn't drug with me, though.

I'm amazed at how she seems to have no vanity and is unaware of guys literally stopping and staring at her. Daughter of a famous professional athlete, Leila has everything a first-year student could want materially. But I sense sadness or maybe some madness too, or we wouldn't have gravitated towards each other.

'What do you think, Dr Jaye?'

Dr Jaye looks up from her notes.

'Not feeling good enough and consequently rejected or excluded are expected given your childhood, Francine.' She often doesn't answer direct questions. 'Both Leila and Shelly may have developed healthy boundaries.'

<u>Mid-October – mid-November</u>

So far, my undeclared major has been 'Getting High'. These months have passed in a chemically induced fog. Since I'm seventeen and can't buy alcohol, it's easier to access what sellers claim is THC, LSD, STP, PCP, etc. Wonder where they come up with all these letters?[41]

If there were more, I would take them. Whatever is on offer, I'm at the front of the queue. Whatever I take is never enough. Always, 'Can I have more?' 'Another hit, please.' 'I want a better buzz.' 'Higher and higher.'

Seems like each drug turns on me. Take LSD. The first time I dropped it was my only good trip. Then a lot of failed attempts to find that buzz. There's something about that first rush of euphoria. And you're looking for it again, but instead, I look at other people and feel afraid and disconnected. I try to see inwards and feel the same. A bad trip is fucking scary.

There's a pause as Francine senses that a Dr Jaye comment or two are about to take place.

'Francine, you were ingesting strong drugs. It's understandable for someone to take a second trip after a good first one, but it's interesting that you continued countless times despite experiencing the same negative outcome.'

Francine reads on.

Mid-November – mid-December

Silent Shelly, who needs to take a chill pill, stays in the dorm room most of the time despite my loud playing of Hendrix, Joplin, Led Zeppelin, Queen, The Beatles, Eric Clapton, Vanilla Fudge, Mothers of Invention, or The Doors. Yes, I have managed

---

41 THC (tetrahydrocannabinol) is the chemical in marijuana that is primarily responsible for psychotropic effects; LSD (lysergic acid diethylamide) is a synthetic psychedelic popularised by Timothy Leary; STP (or DOM – 2,5-Dimethoxy-4-methylamphetamine (standing for Serenity, Tranquillity, and Peace)) is a psychedelic amphetamine known for its long-lasting 'trips' and hallucinations; PCP (phencyclidine) or 'angel dust' causes psychoactive effects, physical euphoria, and also, of course, hallucinations.

to buy lots of records again after selling a huge collection for my California trip. She says nothing – just turns the pages of her notes and textbooks. So, I've been going to class most of the time, usually high. Gets me out of there.

Philosophy and sociology are especially interesting when I'm out of it, but Italian and history are boring.

Anyway, as always, I'm comfortable being the class dissident. The imposing environment here hasn't stopped me from expressing my stoned thoughts, which translates into high marks for participation. As for the lectures, I read the interesting parts of the texts and go to enough classes that I can pass the subjects where regurgitation is all that's needed. And I am almost acing the subjects that reward original thoughts.

'Looking back, Dr Jaye, I guess the first two subjects allowed for thinking outside of the box or encouraged it. In Italian and history, though, I felt more like a sponge, only present to absorb dates or conjugate verbs. Neither of these processes were compatible with the kind of existential questions that occurred with hallucinogen consumption. Confession then – I guess my drug intake did affect my university studies. And it affected my romantic life, as I had none that I can remember.

'I'll read the next entry, which describes a "trip."'

Last night, for some unknown reason, two boys – just friends – and I were walking along suburban streets in this college town at 2 am. Off our faces on STP. Owen is chubby, and the other, Larry, is skinny. Both are nerds. Larry likes to drop acid and STP because he's bored and says he feels better about himself on them. Owen told me he wants to see fractals.

I looked that up in my trusty Webster's Dictionary,[42] and it didn't make sense to me. As Henry says, 'Frankie, you're a loser who lacks the intelligence to understand higher level mathematics or physics.' OK. He doesn't say it that way, but it feels like he does.

As we walked along, I first noticed that the sidewalk had turned into a colourful tapestry, and then it changed into a slimy snake. Not sure if these are fractals? I looked at my two companions and discovered that they had become cartoon figures from Sergeant Pepper's Lonely Hearts Club Band.

My good trip was turning into a bad one. I started to giggle. Larry turned to me and spoke, which is rare. But when he does, it's with a nerd-like bluntness and a monotone. 'Are you unobservant? There is a police vehicle approaching forty-five degrees northeast. Do not look like you've taken illegal substances.'

As police weren't a part of my animated film, it ended abruptly, and instead, I was now playing the role of a college kid hanging out in the middle of the night. The cops drove by. Not sure why they didn't pull us over. Maybe we were camouflaged by the group of Greeks heading from a party at Omega Psi Phi Fraternity to the Alpha Psi Delta sorority house.

'This episode did ruin the trip, though. Bummer. Cartoon characters aren't supposed to monotonically make accusations and be unfriendly, are they?'

Dr Jaye continues taking notes. Surely a rhetorical question?

---

42 Curves or geometrical figures, each part of which has the same statistical character as the whole. They are useful in modelling structures (such as snowflakes) in which similar patterns recur at progressively smaller scales, and in describing partly random or chaotic phenomena such as crystal growth and galaxy formation.

Christmas break

Am going to write about what I got up to a couple of weeks ago. It was a crazy thing to do – even crazier than my regular crazy. Reckon it will be useful to record for meeting with a therapist sometime in the years to come.

Francine looks up at Dr Jaye.

'And here I am! Although I wasn't using the word "crazy" as a psychotherapist like you would use it to mean insanity or psychosis.'

Francine continues reading.

The dorm is closing for semester break, and I don't want to stay at Henry and Miriam's. Surprise, surprise – no money saved but travel bug present. Where to go broke? I've looked at notice boards around campus and found some people advertising lifts. Found someone wanting to share the driving of a rental truck to Chicago. Without thinking it through, I rang the number listed and arranged to share the driving (and the pay) with Lucas, the guy who had posted the ad. This seemed like a reasonable means of traveling. It's true that I'll have less than $50 to my name upon arrival in the big smoke. Second, I know no one there, and third, the drive is expected to take about twenty-four hours with us arriving on Christmas Eve. No accommodation booked or even scouted.

Dr Jamyang appears pensive.

'Hmm. Impulsivity was present at that time in your life, Francine. This is a significant change that we could look at in later sessions.'

Lucas was an odd fellow. He may have been a born-again Christian in silent prayer or a bit off mentally. No possible obsession fix for me with Lucas. Just the flat, ugly Midwest plains.

Can now say that I've been to a real farm! Day 2 began just past dawn with the truck starting to make weird sounds. We were luckily near a dirt road with a farm house nearby. Guess I learned that farmers wake up early! While he worked on the truck, his wife invited us in for (my first) home-cooked country breakfast. Not sure what was better? The food or hearing someone talk after spending twenty hours in silence with weird Lucas.

I see or feel that warm kitchen as yellow, which is very different from the gray meals with Henry and Miriam.

Truck repaired, we were on the road again and a few hours later, without further mechanical or homicidal incident, arrived in Chicago. Lucas (or Loopy as I had begun to refer to him in my thoughts) dropped me downtown – the lower end near the bus station. Bit reminiscent of my last hitch. Nowhere to go and with only about $40, things looked grim.

I found a YWCA and paid $10 for a room; a bed with walls might be a better descriptor. Bought a couple packs of cigarettes, figured out what a student-standby ticket would cost and used the remainder to buy a sandwich for dinner. And they say I can't budget!

The following morning, I caught the bus out to O'Hare. The first available flight back to Henry and Miriam had seats available. Guess there are few travellers on Christmas day.

I wonder if Miriam has been worried about where I am? She does worry a lot.

Francine stops reading and looks at Dr Jaye.

'I know that this last story may not seem to be relevant to therapy. No trauma, sex, suicidal ideation, or drug overdoses.

I thought it was important to share, though, for a couple of reasons. It was a common saga in the life and times of Frankie. This episode was relatively benign, although it could have had a much worse finale. As you said earlier, I acted impulsively back then. Hugely different from the present. My children wouldn't believe that their mother could both deviate from her routine and be such a risk-taker. Talk about extremes …'

January

Well, I guess I'm now eighteen but I have no fucking memory of that entire twenty-four hours. About forty-eight hours before the big day, I ingested some substances that must have been laced and then, laced again with amphetamines. Around 3 am of my birthday, I was out for the count, catching up on three nights without sleep. Anyway, I finally crashed, and whoever termed it 'crash' certainly knows what they're talking about. I must have slept almost around the clock and woke up to find that my day of birth had passed.

I wonder why I'm still here given all the illegal and unknown substances that I've taken over the past five months. Possibly it's so that I can tell the story someday?

I've been doing a lot of drugs here. Despite being off my face most of the time, I could stay on track grade-wise. I didn't get As first semester but I didn't fail – two Bs and two Cs. But I've decided that this isn't my scene and dropped out.

I've sold all my (much less) stuff again. Tomorrow, I fly to San Francisco to find the other flower children. 'Other' is the important word here. I do continue to feel that these are my people. Hopefully, I'll have better luck finding them than last summer.

There is silence as Francine closes the notebook.

Only two minutes left in her hour. As usual, Dr Jaye appears to be considering what she has heard, maintaining steady eye contact.

'Thank you for sharing this part of your life here with me. As you know from your own research work, leaving the perpetrator is difficult and in your situation as a seventeen-year-old going away to university, there was neither a refuge nor even an identity as a survivor. These months – the indiscriminate drug-taking and disconnection – are typical behaviours for adolescents who experience complex trauma as children and disassociate from themselves in order to survive.'

Francine leaves the room feeling, as she often does after therapy, a bit lighter.

10
RAPE: A HEAD
COMMITTEE MEETING

'Hi, everybody. I'm Gabe and I'll be chairing today's meeting. Most of you know me from my counselling work over the years in various rehabs, or you may have seen me at twelve-step meetings.

'I'm going to start by playing tapes (recorded with Frankie's permission) of three appointments in which she talked about the five-month San Francisco period, which, as we all know, was the climax of that time. Oh my God – that was a totally accidental and quite inappropriate double entendre.

'Frankie told me about what happened when she first went to find the hippies. Before I start, though, let me advise you, they are edited. Some of you know that unlike the relatively mute Dr Jaye, counselling with me includes a lot of mutual sharing and caring.[43] Frankie was one of the best clients, with lots of relationship advice for me. But I've deleted most of my voice, or we'd be here for a week.

'Here's the first tape.'

---

43 Gabe's self-disclosures during sessions with Frankie were a deliberate method of building rapport and trust. However, this therapeutic model may have triggered her codependent caretaking, which was never an issue with Dr Jaye.

Pre-rape tape

The idea was to find the hippies in Haight-Ashbury. Once again, though, there was a detour. Instead, I ended up in a place which, although close, was as different as chalk and cheese.

The truth is, I had no plan. I know that's odd compared to the me you know, Gabe. But I was different then.

Without thinking about it beforehand, I decided to ring Leila, my dorm friend, from the airport. She'd gone 'home' a few days before for semester break. After getting her parents' permission, she invited me to stay with them and even picked me up!

Leila's family lived in an alternate universe. 'Home' turned out to be an estate in America's most expensive postcode, at that time about fifty-four miles southeast of the hippies. Their lifestyle and family dynamics were totally different than anything I'd experienced.

Could be why it seemed somewhat dreamlike.

Leila's parents were incredibly kind and insisted that I stay in their home, at least until Leila went back to school. Her mother, la Français Nanette, was a tiny and très belle femme. I could see where Leila got her looks and elegance from.

Her famous father, 'Big Bill', used personal contacts to get me a job.

Both Bill and Nanette expressed (more than once) their concern that my parents had allowed their eighteen-year-old daughter to travel alone without providing any protection or care.

Of course, Gabe, this blame thing wasn't fair to Miriam and Henry, who played no role whatsoever in my leaving tertiary education or in travel decisions. In fact, they didn't even know I'd dropped out until the day before my departure when I rang to give them the heads up not to pay the second semester's tuition and fees.

After staying with them for three weeks, Bill found me a furnished bedsit and a job! Who didn't he know?

So, a month after arriving in San Francisco, I looked in the mirror — and not to be dramatic (who, me?) — saw a stranger with short hair wearing clothes for an office job.

Pretty bizarre or ironic, Gabe, if you remember why I was there. Supposed to be living in a commune, long hair plaited with flowers intertwined, floor-length, tie-dyed, and loose-fitting robe, taking drugs and talking about the meaning of life.

Instead, I was taking the weather off the teletype machine hourly, cutting out the relevant forecasts, photocopying them, and distributing these two-page reports into the pilots' cubbyholes. Mind-numbing labour, although moderately less boring than the first job Bill arranged, which was literally collating papers by walking around a boardroom table, eight hours a day for a week.

Anyway, Gabe, as I'm sure you know, this new outside 'me' didn't match my insides. Between feeling unreal and a lot of what I guess today was shame, I was drinking heaps or smoking dope whenever possible. Surprise! Surprise! Not. Self-medicating — nothing new on that front.

And, like you've shared with me, I was also drawn to another kind of addiction. Kept trying to fall in love. Do love that 'love' buzz that we both enjoy. But, for whatever reason, it wasn't happening despite some eligible candidates.

Like Pablo — the handsome Latino co-pilot at least twenty-five years older than me. We went out a few times — cocktails and caresses. But, no lights, bells, fireworks — nada. Maybe it was the wife back in South America, although, of course, he said they were separated. Yeah, right. Or was it the age difference? There was no way I was looking for another Henry!

And then there was Freddie. Hmm, he was this super straight luxury car salesman who played golf with Bill at their country club. Freddie – probably at Bill's request – wined and dined me at expensive restaurants, but again, despite wanting to feel really anything – either love or lust would do – there was just zero chemistry.

He was too all-American jock without any quirks needing to be ironed out. And like you, I do need to feel needed. From our experience of men, Gabe, don't you think the guys who do need someone are the least likely to show it, though?

Next came Leila's younger and very good-looking brother, Mark. Don't judge me, please, on this one! Yes, he was only sixteen, but I had just turned eighteen, don't forget! After Leila returned to university, he was the only person I knew in the Bay Area that I felt was on the same planet … especially when we were stoned.

Not one of my proudest moments – I turned him onto grass when living with their family. When I moved out, we continued to meet up and get high. In my defence, the corruption of Mark could've been worse, as he'd have gladly given me his virginity. But, fortunately, or unfortunately, depending on how you look at it, marijuana never gave me the same liberation from my puritan morality as alcohol. So, Mark was safe from sexual seduction anyway.

Gabe, further in my defence, not that I need to tell you as you helped me to find AA, all drugs including weed affected my behaviour – and not in a positive way. My personality, morality, values, and thoughts were dramatically altered by chemicals. I would unconsciously create a story that totally justified whatever bad stuff I was up to. For Mark it went something like this.

'Wow, man, the stuff is natural. I mean it like grows in the ground – obviously, it's meant to be consumed. Plus, this garbage about

it leading to heroin and other harder drugs? Just look at me. I've been smoking for a few years now and I don't shoot up. No way, José. Just the occasional LSD, PCP or any kind of speed, that's all. And you know why we smoke it and why I gave it to Mark, don't you? Some drugs are bad news but my friend Mary Jane, well, we're using it to help us find the answers to Earth's problems caused by previous generations. It's like a mystical journey and I need to share that with my sisters and brothers.'

Been there? Done that, Gabe? I see the slight nod and know there's no judgment here – at least not from you.

'OK. That's the end of the first recording. Let's take a short break before we listen to tape two, which can be triggering to survivors. So, heads up.'

The rape tape

Well, Gabriel, it's time to tell you about the rape. Would prefer to be like the ostrich burying her head in the sand, but it's hurting too much to keep inside.

My PGA had kept pretty good guard over me, but that night, I didn't listen to my inner guide. Maybe I was being punished for Mark. Bad karma?

There was no warning.

The evening had begun with Freddie and me drinking exotic cocktails that tasted like milkshakes up in the mountains at an exclusive restaurant. It was one of those times, though, where no matter how much I drank, there was no buzz at all. I was the kind of drunk, Gabe, who felt nothing until a short-lived buzzy high, which would transition without warning to a blackout with loss of control over pretty much everything.

After Freddie dropped this sober-but-drunk-me off, I was walking through the apartment foyer and saw Craig. I'd talked to him a few times in the basement laundry. He and a roommate, Martin, lived on the floor below my studio.

We hung out for a few minutes and then he invited me to smoke some weed with them. I didn't hesitate. Marijuana plus two good-looking guys and alcohol-affected thinking made it a no-brainer.

The three of us, in a dope-induced semi-coma, were stoned off our heads and having a conversation that felt heavy and meaningful. After midnight, tired and needing to get up at six for work, I thanked them and went upstairs to my bedsitter.

I had changed into my favourite nightgown – white with embroidered flowers on the bodice (amazing I remember that) – and was on the edge of sleep when there was a knock at the door.

'It's Martin. Can I come in and talk to you for a few minutes?'

OK. I get it now. What the hell would anyone want to talk about at 12:30 at night?

But my inner voice of caution was AWOL. A handsome fellow on the other side of the door wanted to interact with me. That's all that I thought when I let him in and opened the door to decades of self-blame and self-hatred.

That sounds like victim-blaming, doesn't it? Well, guess what? It's what we do until or unless there are enough voices that put the blame where it belongs. On the perpetrator.

Anyway, Gabe, some things are easy for me to talk to you about; others not so much. This is one of those.

Please don't take it personally, though. I know we both have that tendency. You're one of the most empathetic non-judgmental people I know.

Remember Mr Johnson from when I was a kid? He moved in slow motion. Martin was the opposite. Without a word, he pushed me down on the bed, tore off my white nightie, and tried to push his penis into my vagina. He couldn't get it in since I had my period. Saying, 'Oh, shit, blood is repulsive,' he then orally raped me with force. I remember gagging and thought I was going to throw up. The worst part was that I couldn't breathe and was afraid of being suffocated to death.

Why in hell didn't I bite it off?

I didn't fight. I didn't scream. OK, thanks, Gabe, I couldn't fight. I couldn't scream.

I did indicate 'no' saying, 'Jesus what are you doing? No, stop it.'

Yes, you're right, Gabe. I shut down and drifted away. My body went into shock – paralysed by the past.

As soon as he orgasmed, he stood up, pulled his pants up and left. I cried for the remainder of the night and washed my mouth until it was raw. I showered in boiling hot water to feel clean. It didn't work.

Did I call the police or tell anyone? No way. How can you talk about it when you can't even speak to yourself in a coherent sentence or even have the language to describe what had happened? No bruises, opening the door after midnight in my nightgown, stoned and drunk – my shame blamed me.

The post-rape tape

I did end up falling apart – sobbing during a phone call – with Big Bill. He decided that I was having some sort of nervous breakdown. Being Big Bill, he set out to track down Henry and Miriam who were on their annual holiday somewhere in Central America. Within twenty-four hours, Henry called me.

'Frankie, we've heard that you're very upset and we want to help you. What can we do?'

The warmth I sensed was undeniable, Gabe. I felt momentarily transported back to an earlier time.

'You can't do anything to help me, Dad. Nobody can.'

Mind you, his concern had already helped. I imagine that redemption or forgiveness feels like that.

We talked for a few minutes, deciding quickly that Henry and Miriam could best help by sending me to Europe.

'What?' You might ask. 'Overseas? How does traveling address the trauma of sexual assault?'

Fair enough questions … the Kentucky Fried Shrink did help me to understand that Henry and Miriam were more comfortable giving objects and money than 'being there' in other ways. When Henry asked what they could do, I said that I wanted to go to the Royal Academy of Dramatic Arts in London. He agreed.

Yes, Gabe, this was wacky even for me and my family of origin! I had absolutely no information about the Academy, and what is more amazing was that Henry did no background research. He simply said, 'Yes, dear. Anything that you want!' This from the man who would go to the library to thoroughly investigate everything from travel destinations to electrical appliance repair.

Big Bill and Henry decided that I needed to work another month for the airlines in order to provide adequate notice. Fair enough. They didn't know that I had been raped by a guy who lived in the same building as me and that I was a mass of quivering jelly each time that I unlocked my 'cell' and walked down the stairs and across the foyer to get outside.

Then things got worse. About two weeks before I was leaving the Bay Area, Bill and Nanette came over and confronted me, more with sadness than anger, expressing their disappointment in me. Mark had written to Leila about my introducing him to the 'herb' and after sacking me as her friend, she told her parents. Their belief in my 'nervous breakdown' saved me from being sent to Coventry but the warmth was gone.

And me? Well, between the rape and what I had done to Bill and Nanette, my insides weren't crash hot. No surprises for you on how I got through those weeks. I ingested, in one form or another, the chemicals necessary to produce a semi-aware state, a fog. That's how.

It was only about ten minutes in my life, but you can't measure the impact of life's events by the minutes, hours or days involved, can you? I guess that like Mr Johnson, Henry and others, I have given Martin a loud voice in my head.

I didn't see Martin or Mark again.

At the end of my notice period, I flew to Toronto where Henry had been posted. Walking into the terminal in a work dress and a bobbed haircut with a hat, Miriam looked past me, not recognising her hippie daughter. Henry approached with his colonel's stiff and formal gait. Not quite what I'd expected or hoped. In the scenario I imagined, the successful daughter, cherished and appreciated by her parents, disembarks. Gabe, stop giggling. It was total fiction, OK?

The reality was that in lieu of a hug, just these words: 'I've arranged military transport for you to Gatwick. It leaves the day after tomorrow at 0900 hours.' That felt reminiscent of how he had responded to the razor blade saga. I guess Henry didn't have the tools for dealing with a daughter who Big Bill had warned was a damaged fuck-up (or words to that effect). He had no choice but to shut down. He did that well.

Miriam burst into tears, and we clutched each other but it wasn't clear who was the neediest. It rarely was with my mother.

Reflections from regulars on the committee

Gabe switches off the cassette player and invites anyone to share their thoughts.

'Rape, shmape – she calls it that? Did he put it in the sexual part? No! Did she resist him? No. This is my promiscuous daughter trying to rationalise her actions after a night with a stranger. And, not just any stranger, but a goy at that. *Oy veh*, he probably wasn't even circumcised … To think what she's done to her mother.'

'I'll kill the son of a bitch. Touching my princess, my sweet and pure daughter.'

Nope, that's Franny's daddy's voice – no longer in the scene. By this point in Frankie's life, Henry's perspective and comments had drastically changed.

'Well, she might've played a role. She opened the door to a man after midnight. What did she think would happen?'

'Well, we'd like to kill him,' say the men in the chorus who she'd 'sleep' with post-Martin. 'There was something absent when being intimate with Frankie. We can't pinpoint it, but sometimes she seemed distant. Martin's assault might've played a part.'

'That's because she hasn't let go of men,' claim the lesbian group from the second wave radical feminists. 'We've been there. We understand the feeling – being held accountable by society's standards. We're her sisters in solidarity. Working through her pain and misplaced blame would be easier if she'd stop having penetrative intercourse.'

'That's a bit of a generalisation. I'm Anna from the Sexual Assault Crisis Centre. Francine has been a valuable board member here. While many on the Management Committee identify as lesbians, Francine isn't the only straight woman. Our aim is to aid those affected by sexual assault. We work within a trauma framework and prioritise safety, trustworthiness, choice, collaboration, and empowerment.'

'We represent AA, but it's important to note that we don't have *one* voice. Sexual assault isn't typically discussed in our meetings, unless someone, like Frankie, shares it in their recovery journey. During her first fifth step, Frankie confided in her sponsor, identifying it as one of her deepest fears. Linda listened without judging or offering therapeutic solutions, as is our recommendation, and shared similar stories of where her disease had taken her.'

'The same principle applies to us as Al-Anon and CODA members. We understand that this incident played a part in Frankie's dwindling self-esteem. We've guided her in realising its potential influence on her attracting troubled partners.'

'We're dentists from various eras. Francine has opened up about her experience, and we aim to make her visits as comfortable as possible. Some of us ponder why she hasn't moved on, but we respect and adapt to her needs, given her traumatic experience.'

Richard feels compelled to respond to that last comment.

'"Moved on?" From a psychotherapeutic perspective, that's nonsensical. A survivor like Francine may heal enough to avoid psychiatric institutional care, obtain employment, have a family, friends, and the other accoutrements of emotional health. However, we must remember that recovery from PTSD is lifelong. Trauma is stored in the body and rooted in the nervous system. It's too complicated to delve into today, but there is scientific, medical, and popular literature readily available online that explains how PTSD can be triggered both ad hoc and predictably. For instance, decades after the rape, Francine still cannot wear anything tight around her neck. If a hairdresser fastens the cape clasp too tightly, she starts to panic, fearing she can't swallow or breathe. Similarly, dental procedures are potential triggers, as the dental specialists present here have noted.'

Dr Jaye, smiling gently, adds to Richard's viewpoint.

'While the healing process is lifelong, it has accelerated for Francine with the absence of chemicals used to sedate the pain and anger. Both her involvement in twelve-step programs since her mid-twenties and weekly therapy with me for the past ten years have helped equip her with the spiritual resilience necessary to reconnect with her body and repressed memories.'

11
SIX-WEEK EUROPEAN BENDER: AN OPEN MEETING

'Hi, everybody. I'm Linda, and I'm an alcoholic.'

'Hi, Linda.'

'I've been asked to chair this meeting of the head committee and to be the primary speaker, although we do have a few special guests today – not resident members. We're here to look at Frankie's overseas adventures as an eighteen-year-old drunk. Let me be clear: it's acceptable for me to call her a "drunk" because she self-identified as such years ago. As some of you know, as an AA member, it's certainly not my place to label others with a drinking problem. Also, I'm not violating any twelve-step tradition by recounting parts of stories Francine (or "Frankie" back then) shared with me. I have her full permission.

'In one of her disclosures about drinking, Frankie told me about a period which started with her getting drunk en route to England aboard a military aircraft arranged by Henry. The passenger beside her, a civilian older than Henry, had brought liquor with him. To procure alcohol, which she believed would ease her flying phobia, she resorted to flirting. That flight was symbolic, if you will, of the next six weeks, which a few of the 12 step members of the committee refer to as "a six-week super-strength dual-focused binge and bottom (though not the ultimate one) in addiction terms: alcohol and romance." Personally, I just consider myself an alcoholic. But when Francine shared her quest for her knight in shining armour, her saviour, it sounded eerily like addiction in another form.'

In the front row, Miriam shakes her head, interjecting, '*Oy veh gevalt*. What did I do to deserve this? My youngest daughter was *shrek* – terrified of airplanes since she was two years old. Who knows why? I did everything I could. Bribed her to get on the plane by knitting an entire doll wardrobe. Even then she'd cry and tremble. What did I do to deserve this?'

'Thank you, Miriam,' Linda responds, keen to continue the meeting. 'This isn't your fault. Show me someone with a fear of flying, and I'll show you someone with control issues. Before her recovery, Frankie routinely soothed her phobia in airport lounges or bars, consuming alcohol consistently during flights. Smoking helped too– back when it was allowed on airplanes.'

England: Simon

'After spontaneously booking a week at a bed and breakfast, Frankie went to Hyde Park – a location she'd read about in the gothic romance novels she loved. Her fascination with all things British led her to a young man who bore a slight resemblance to Paul McCartney, albeit with a paler complexion and rosy cheeks.'

'That young fellow is with us today to share his experiences with Frankie. Please welcome Simon.'

'Hello, or shall I say, "Hiya"? I was Frankie's London love. But, regarding the term "lover", it depends on your definition. Our eyes met repeatedly. Then, a smile from her, returned by my timid one. Both heading to Speakers' Corner, we gradually closed the distance between us. After nearly twenty minutes of this classic British male courting, Frankie initiated the conversation.

'Within a quarter hour, we were no longer strangers. Like her, I was new to London, having arrived a fortnight earlier from Newcastle upon Tyne for a work training program. I did mention Laura, my girlfriend, and our plans to marry in a few years. At some point, I disclosed my virginity and my resolve to preserve "it" for my wedding night.

'Perhaps you're wondering why a shy lad from the north of England would be admitting such personal things to this lass after only making her acquaintance half an hour earlier? You permanent residents understand Triple F well enough though to know that within those thirty minutes she had shared most of her life with me in an open way that seems to invite disclosures from unlikely people like me.

'For the next eight days, we met each evening at a predesignated pub. I made finding the Black Tailed Mare in St John's Wood or the Cricketers Arms in Putney part of the excitement. This wasn't easy as I'd only been in London for a couple of weeks and there was no Google Maps or Google. But I managed to schedule each "date" at a different pub. We drank vodka and lime, threw darts, and sang when or if others were singing. When the place closed, we'd take tubes and buses – money was for having fun, not for taxis. And, outside her digs, we'd kiss and arrange the next night's adventure.

'By the eighth night, I had pain down below – too much arousal, no release. As Frankie enjoyed wordplay, I confided my *growing* need to give up my virginity to her, the overseas seductress.

'My declaration seemed to please her. It confirmed the views of those on her head committee (yes, she'd told me about you) who believed that she emitted an odour of sex. However, she did seem more distant as we made plans to "sleep" together the next night.

'Of course, the plan started with a pub visit. Frankie drank more than me, and quicker, yet she appeared sober. Her tolerance was always unpredictable. Since then, I've known a few mates who've been to rehab with similar tendencies.

'We got to my flat. Snogging, we took off our pants and shirts, but I was too shy to take off my underwear and too inexperienced to remove hers. It was bloody awkward and painful to remember. I wasn't surprised when she told me that she didn't want to have sex. To tell the truth, I was relieved. Instead of passionate love making, we tried to sleep in my single and still virginal bed.

'I slept and Frankie wept. She left at sunrise.'

France : Jacques, Robert, Jan

'Linda again, still a recovering alcoholic,' she giggles. This is one of the 3,896 AA rituals.

'Hi, Linda.'

Although the residents are a mix of twelve-steppers and non-Program people, they're all accustomed to this introduction and the expected group response. The practicing Catholics are habituated responders. In addition to 'Amen' and 'With your spirit' in mass, they have learned when to say: 'For we have sinned against you', 'And grant us your salvation', 'Lord have mercy', 'Christ have mercy', 'Thanks be to God', 'And with your spirit', 'Glory to you, O Lord', 'Praise to you, Lord Jesus Christ'.[44]

'Hi, everyone! On to Paris.

'After leaving Simon's flat, she headed for the train station. It may be obvious, but I'll say it anyway as I can tell Miriam's about to

---

44 https://www.catholicbishops.ie/wp-content/uploads/2011/02/Order-of-Mass.pdf for e-readers. *Excerpts of the English translation of The Roman Missal* © 2010, International Committee on English in the Liturgy, Inc.

explode. Frankie's time in London had not included any ventures into schools of drama. She excused this "oversight" by telling herself that traveling to France was an education in itself with the opportunity of further improving her conversational French.

'We alcoholics are experts at justifying and rationalising, aren't we?

'The language excuse didn't last long. When Frankie bought her first wine at the Calais rail station, which was dotted by vendors with carts of booze, the seller said, *"Parle Anglais s'il vous plait. Votre Français est terrible."* From then on, Frankie just pointed and said *"Merci."*

'France seemed ideal for a drunk: a landscape where lushes were relatively invisible. Drinking on the train was the norm as most passengers sipped a glass of wine with their meal. In contrast, Frankie sat alone with a cask in her lap, periodically holding it to her mouth, like suckling a baby, until the pain of yet another Sir Galahad failure receded into a boozy blurriness.

'Arriving in Paris, without any planning or booking, she ended up at a fairly nice bed and breakfast or *pension* run by Madame Lambert who is with us today to describe her observations of Frankie's time in Paris. Welcome, Madame.'

'*Bienvenue* Linda and *tout le monde ici*. This young girl – she was *trés belle* and how do you say it … a bit *cinglé* – what you call the English word is … loony? She liked the *vin blanc* very much – quite possibly too much but who am I to say this? If London meant a tour of the pubs *pour* Frankie, in my city, it was the sidewalk cafés and white wine.

'On the second day staying *avec moi* – *pardon*, the French just comes out of the mouth easier, that is, with me – she returned from one of these tours, *trés* excited. She had met a man, Jacques in Les Jardins des Tuileries. They began to talk … this is very strange to me, to speak with how you say a stranger – *un étranger.* She told me that a café was where they went next – sitting in the sunshine, sipping vin blanc for many hours. He did not speak *Anglais* and so they talked *en Français.* Her *Français* it was bad. But Frankie felt there was a – how do you say *le raccordement* or *le lien* or *la relation?'*

Madame Lambert is becoming visibly frustrated; one of the listeners comes to her aid: 'Connection – is that the word?'

'Oh *Merci, oui, c'est correct.* The young *mademoiselle* was sure that there was a connection with Jacques and at seven in the evening went to meet him at the café as they had made this arrangement. She sat there for many hours but Jacques, he did not return.

'"So?" you might ask. "Where is the *grosse affaire* – what you call the big deal? A stranger promises to see a girl again and he does not show up." It is what happened next that was *trés* loony …

'She spent five days searching for this Jacques. *Par exemple* – he'd mentioned that he played the football – what you call the soccer? Well, you can guess where she looked over the following days? I helped her because it is like Simon was saying – there was no Google Maps back then! *Tres difficile, n'est ce pas?* I found for her addresses for all the *terrain de sport.* There are many of these, but she went to all of them. *Elle ne pas avoir de chance* – what you say, "No luck."

'She said to me that he was a sky jumper or at least she thought that was what he was describing with gestures. *Qui sait?* – Who knows? This Jacques could have been saying he flew the planes or *peut être* he is a loony like her and thought that he was the Superman sometimes. But Frankie, she kept telling me how it was *"quel romantique!" Le coeur* – my heart – was moved and I looked for her in the *annuaire téléphonique* all the parachuting clubs near Paris. Frankie, she went to each and asked in her French for *un homme* named Jacques, average height and build, brown hair and eyes. You do not believe this story? I did not believe it *aussi*. I think she was having the thing that this man of some fame in *Amérique* told her – un *crise de nerfs* – a nervous breakdown.

'Her residence in my pension could be a comedy for the cinema. The men – they kept coming into the picture. *Effectivement*, even though she was experiencing a passion with this Jacques, there were a few more male roles we would need to cast. *Par exemple* on the third day, at a different café, Frankie started talking to another gentleman, Robert – or *peut-être* not a gentleman? He accompanied her to my home where she had the need to get a sweater. I saw her running through the dining room. She started to laugh with the … what is the word … hysteria? This Robert had started to chase her in the bedroom trying to get her onto the bed. After the third circuit around the room, she ran out into the hall, leaving this stranger alone in her accommodation. *Probablement*, this would be a funny scene for the audience, but it was not for the mademoiselle or for me. I could see her terror and she kept apologising to me saying: *"Je suis stupide; je suis stupide."*

'Robert left. *Peut être* this was through the back door? I was busy attending to *la petite cinglée*. Together, we drank the cognac I keep for such emergencies.

'The next one was Jan. He was a photographer – there are thousands of them I think, who walk around Paris and approach to see if you'd like your photograph with the Eiffel Tower or the Seine or another Parisienne landmark in the picture. He looked very much like an actor *en Amerique* – David McCallum. *Trés beau* in *un homme du monde* way – you understand? – man of the world. *Quelle surpris* – Jan was *trés gentil* – much nicer than we learn to expect from *un beau monsieur. Peut être* this was because he had *une vie difficile;* he was an escapee or an emigrant from East Germany or Hungary, I think. Frankie *et* Jan – such nice names for a couple, non? *Quel romantique mais* I think the mademoiselle was only interested in finding this Jacques. Jan and Frankie – they wandered around Paris together for a couple of days but her heart, it was not there. *Elle est bizarre, n'est ce pas?'*

Italy : Ercole

'Hi, again. Still Linda and still an alcoholic.'

'Hi, Linda!'

'Triple F explained to me why she chose her next destination and talked about Ercole. This is what she told me in her own words – as I remember them.'

Rome was a city that I had heard about and there was train service from Paris. The overnight journey began with me well-fortified with a supply of wine, crying about Jacques a bit as the train pulled out of the station. But the grief was apparently linked to that physical space. As soon as Paris was behind me, my spirits lifted (with the spirits imbibed no doubt) and I went to the dining car. It felt like another fresh start. And Linda, it was there that I met Ercole, my sweet little giant. Yes, Ercole is the Italian word for Hercules; the fact that this took three days for me to understand provides some understanding of the limits of a relationship in which one party knew no English and the other had studied Italian for one semester in school! Nevertheless, this was a longer relationship than the others in Europe as it lasted for almost two weeks.

Ercole indicated mostly through body language and a friend who spoke a bit of English, that he worked with his wealthy father in the mysterious family business (or at least, a mystery to someone with limited Italian). He found me an inexpensive room in a boarding house and each day after finishing work, he took me to see the sights of Rome and the surrounding area. There were plenty of wine bar stops of course.

Ercole adored me and would never try to do more than kiss. And, Linda, he was an excellent kisser.

After a couple of weeks, he begged me to stay in Italy and asked me to marry him, or I think that was why he kneeled down and offered me a ring.

There was a part of me that wanted to say, 'Yes, my sweet Hercules. Let's get married and live happily ever after.' But I couldn't say it, Linda, and it's very hard to tell you why as the reason makes me look shallow. I don't want to be that person.

My knight needed to be taller than me. That was it. Maybe it was a part of my disease though?

'I reassured Frankie that from my view, as her AA sponsor, she was simply a drunk behaving inappropriately or even insanely as we drunks often do.

'She was in an alcohol-induced haze and was incapable of doing little more than bringing the bottle or glass to her mouth and drink. However, I recognise that other twelve-step pro-gramme members, like those from Sex Lovers Anonymous (SLA) present today, might see it differently. They might argue that Frankie's romance addiction had been rekindled after just a few minutes' break.

'Alright, that was Rome. Before we discuss the trip back to Canada, I see a few individuals eager to share. Please, go ahead.' She gestures first to a sixteen-year-old in a cheerleader uniform.

'It's a bit hypocritical for someone who thought she was deep, looking down on us "superficial" pep squad and football-player types.'

Linda nods, acknowledging the girl's perspective, and then motions for the spokesperson of the conservative members of the mental health sub-committee to speak.

'We believe that Frankie was subconsciously using her fixation on height as an excuse or justification for her inability to maintain intimate relationships. This reflects her attachment issues, explaining her attraction to men like Simon, Jacques, and Ercole.'

Ship : Dutch crew

Linda surveys the audience, her expression more intense than before.

'Frankie relayed the subsequent events to me. For those unfamiliar with the intricacies of alcoholism, her behaviour might be shocking. I'd like to reference a quote many of us in AA mention, originally from F. Scott Fitzgerald: "First you take a drink, then the drink takes a drink, then the drink takes you." On her sea voyage, "the drink took" Frankie for almost a week. Here's what she remembered about it.'

I left Rome early one morning without telling Ercole – typical me at that time. Couldn't stand scenes of any sort but more importantly couldn't handle being found out for being a fraud.

At this point in time, after only a month in Europe, I'd spent, or drank, all the money Henry had provided. He'd arranged for some additional funds to be available, in case of emergency, from American Express. So, what did I do? Instead of getting free military transport back to North America, I spent several hundred dollars for a Dutch cruise liner voyaging from Marseilles to New York. Do I need to tell you that this act probably has the place of honour in Miriam's MORGUE, which, in a way, is reassuring, since it means that I haven't done anything perceived as that felonious since?

At this point, Miriam interrupts Linda's channelling of Frankie by making the classic Jewish mother sigh that originates deep in the chest and is guaranteed to produce guilt in her listening progeny.

'Enough already with the Morgue. Morgue schmorgue. Were we happy that our *meshuggah* daughter spent money like there was no tomorrow? We Jewish mothers have such a bad reputation when everything that we do, we do for our children. All that we want is what we know is the best for our children.'

'Thanks, Miriam,' Linda affirms Miriam by nodding her head and smiling. 'Anyway, to return to Frankie's hazy memories.'

It was a weeklong shipboard drunk. From 10 am when the various clubs, pubs, taverns, and bars opened until they closed at 4 am, I would drop by every day. Who wouldn't be drunk given that at that time, the duty-free booze was ridiculously cheap? Anyone would drink to excess, wouldn't they!

On the SLA side of things, there was an abundance of young blonde clones in white uniform. An unknown number of these crew members introduced me to places like the room where the deck chair mattresses were stored at night, where a couple could make out privately. And Linda, I believe that making out was the full extent of the sexual activities. Did you catch the critical word in that sentence? I can only speculate since my evenings or even late afternoons were a blur. Blacked out, somehow, I woke up each morning in my berth, but how I got there remains a mystery. Woke up? Does one in fact wake up if one has passed out? That's rhetorical, Linda. I know the answer.

Six mornings I staggered out of bed with a hangover, plus: cot-ton wool in the mouth; torn between extreme thirst and nausea; head aching with every sound reverberating through the body like an echo chamber. Then the ordeal of getting to the toilet.

And, on this voyage, each morning, the experience was pro-gressively worse. I know now that it was physical withdrawal. Each day, detoxifying was harder with my body's need for alcohol increasing. There was only one way for me to stop the sickness and my hands from shaking – the 12 o'clock Bloody Mary. OK, OK, I'll be honest, the 10 am – when the bar re-opened – Bloody Mary.

The 'wet' places were closed on the day we docked. Somehow, I managed to disembark with nowhere to go, about $5 and a body and psyche screaming for alcohol. I know you've been there, Linda. I've heard your lead at plenty of meetings. For me, though, this was new. Depressed, jumpy, hands trembling, exhausted, and with clouded thinking, I managed to ring Miriam reverse charges. She then contacted her high school friend, Florrie, who lived in Manhattan and arranged for me to go to her. Sometimes referred to as Auntie Flo, she had been a part of my life forever.[45]

Florrie was clearly shocked by how bad I looked. She quickly rang my parents, speaking softly. Her voice was like a lullaby as I literally crashed in her spare bedroom for the next sixteen hours. Think that this must have been the first real sleep I'd had in quite a while.

The next morning as I was leaving for the airport to fly 'home', Aunt Flo gave me a big hug and told me that I looked like hell

---

45 The childhood memories that Miriam shared with her children concerned her family of origin's economic (and seemingly) emotional poverty. Triple F visualised her mother's friendship with Flo, which continued until the latter's death, plus Miriam's connection with her two sisters, as light blotches of colour in this otherwise bleak picture of the past.

warmed over; that I needed to get my act together before I broke her friend's heart.

I wonder what they felt when they retrieved me from the airport. Probably, they'd had too many disappointments to feel anything. Flo may have forewarned them adequately.

I can't tell you about their embraces. There were none.

I can't repeat the dialogue. Not because it requires censoring or because it was too distressing but because there were no words spoken.

And you know, Linda, that I could 'drink out' on that episode. In fact, guess what? I did. Alcohol imbibing pity parties that included drunken references to the ice-cold parents.

Now, though, with sobriety and by having children, I can understand the pain that they were experiencing that day and, at least in Miriam's case, the worry that I might try suicide again. Eggshells were strewn through that vehicle and in their house for the two months that I stayed there, that's for sure.

Linda pauses and says: 'As most of you know, this wasn't Frankie's "bottom" although she didn't have another bender quite in that league and therefore never had physical withdrawal again except for hangover biochemical messages. No, it took close to a decade to bring her to her knees.

'That was Europe. Before we begin part two of this special head meeting, two announcements: First, let's have a break. The AA folks are hanging out for a smoke and we all could use a stretch, no doubt. Secondly, the feminist subcommittee has decided that Miriam should chair the next gathering. They'll explain why when we reconvene.'

12
FRANKIE'S 18TH SUMMER: OPEN MEETING, PART 2

Why Miriam needs to chair a meeting

The members of the feminist sub-committee are becoming uncomfortable with the development of Miriam's character.

'We are concerned that she has become a victim of stereotypes about Jewish mothers. Even if this were true, labelling her solely based on this stereotype would be unfair. We believe these images are perpetuated by the patriarchy and sit squarely within a framework where strong women must be undermined in some way. With the Jewish mother, the tools of diminishment are caricature and ridicule.'

'Some of our sociologist 'sister' colleagues have read Barbara Greenberg's (2016) *20 Ways to be a Jewish Mother*[46] and will look at Miriam through that lens.'

'Miriam did exhibit some of the classic traits – self-effacement, overt sacrifice – for example, opting for the chicken wings while reserving the meatier parts for her family; feeding her children and then, feeding them some more, all while expressing

---

46   See Barbara Greenberg (2016) '20 Ways to be a Jewish Mother', *Psychology Today* blog

concurrent concerns about weight gain; valuing education; teaching them about charity and exemplifying it through her generosity towards the three of them.'

'However, various factors limited her ability to embody all the behavioural expectations of that role. She wasn't the quintessential overbearing Jewish mother, nor could she always shield her children.'

'The traditional Jewish mother is rarely cold and withholding. Family is paramount, with her children's needs at the forefront. Further, she encourages them to talk about their problems and offers unsolicited advice, encouraging them to see highly recommended therapists. Indeed, the Jewish mother would detest being accused of neglect. Thus, she remains highly attentive, often being acutely aware of her child's life intricacies.'

'For this archetype to be fully realised, a complementary traditional Jewish partner is often needed: a man who willingly relinquishes certain domestic territories to her. Henry was not that man. Over time, Miriam's identity was chipped away, her enactment of the role becoming not just limited but at odds with the "Miriam" that Henry was shaping, or perhaps imposing.'

'Still, we recognise her underlying strength and distinct attributes that have been suppressed. We aim now to offer her a spotlight, ensuring she's the lead rather than a mere supporting act. By enabling her to articulate her "reality", this might be a transformative moment for her.'

Henry leaves the room as Miriam takes the stage.

Miriam speaks

'Me, the chair*woman* today? Sent to work to take care of goyim children when I was only a child. And now a chairwoman ... Who would have thought?

'I can tell you what I saw when Frankie lived with Henry and me for two months after her trip to Europe.[47] I also gleaned insights about that period when visiting Francine during one of our trips to Australia. Yes. And not to tempt the jinx, but Sandra and Francine both confided in me when they stopped being *meshugenah* teenagers.

'Francine said that back then, she could hear me in every glare, sigh, and shrug. And she was right, although what she wasn't *hearing* was the worry. It was only after years with those therapists and twelve-step people and by becoming a parent, that she understood what it was like for Henry and me. And, to give her credit where credit is due, Francine then treated us like royalty. *They* call it making amends?

'Speaking of psychiatrists, I was with my two sisters, arguing over which one's daughter loves her the most. My sister Helena said, "You know, my daughter Evie sends me flowers every *Shabbos*." "You call that love?" said my sister Edie. "My daughter Karen calls me every day!" "That's nothing," I then said. "My daughter Francine is in therapy five days a week. And the whole time, she talks about me!"

'You see there's more to me than the sighing and *kvetching*.

'Speaking of *kvetching*, I am going to *kvetch*. What could Henry and I do? Frankie spent all the money we had given to her, which was supposed to last for a year abroad. Gratitude? Ha! What did we get? *Bupkes*. God knows how hard I tried. But would she speak to us? Only if she wanted money, then she talked.

'"Instead of her parents, who did she talk to, and go out with, drinking and doing God knows what?" you ask. Laura, a

____

47 Don't get me started on that European vacation. *Mein Gott*. My daughter thought money grew on trees.

thirty-eight-year-old *shiksa,* the separated second wife of Henry's Jewish lawyer and friend. Her seventeen-year-old son James was even more withdrawn and sullen to her than Frankie was with us. It could be why she decided to have our daughter as her pal for the summer.

'I'm sorry. I don't want to *kvetch* about any of my children. God knows. This daughter, I would *kvell* to my sisters about her beauty, intelligence, and her delightful personality when she was younger. Henry and I, we *shepped naches* then from her achievements, which were many. But I could see something inside – a preciousness – which got worse as a teenager. All we had done for her, and did she hug and kiss me, her mother, her flesh and blood? No, she hugged that Laura who had more alcohol and younger men than sense. That middle-aged woman who dressed like she was Frankie's age and her hair – that a woman almost forty years old should wear her hair long with a headband, it's an *umgunud* – a disgrace.

'What did I do to deserve this? Where did we go wrong?' Miriam's eyes are teary now and she needs some privacy to process. She has learned from the two of her children active in "recovery" that space and boundaries are both important to self-acceptance.

'I know that Laura and James are here today and want to talk to you *briefly* about how they knew my daughter. I will go to the bathroom for *five minutes.*'

Laura and James

As Miriam walks away, Laura and James step behind the rostrum. Laura, who has not aged well, looks haggard and hungover. She speaks first.

'Well, Miriam got part of it right. I did love to drink and still do! Had an eye for men. That *has* changed since men my age are looking at girls young enough to be their daughters. I watch Netflix instead.

'What a summer Frankie and I had, though. Wish I could tell you details but it's a bit blurry. One memory: I can recall a day in late July when we decided to go on a train ride to Ottawa. We drank before, during and after. One of Frankie's cousins was involved in this story, and I have remembered tears. But that's all that either of us has in our memory banks. We were aiming for oblivion, which is a fancy way of saying that we spent much of those months blacked out.

'Yes, I can see the judgment in some of your eyes. First there's the twenty-year age difference but that doesn't stop men, does it? Why the double standard? Second, there's the drinking that you've just heard about. Considering what I now know about alcoholism, and I do know quite a bit – in and out of rehab and AA – I'd have to say that she and I shared a lot in common in that area.

'At that point in time, I was heading for one of my bottoms. Still am, since recovery (from what AA people call the disease) has eluded me as it has my son, James. But since all three of us have a disease, give me a break!'

She turns to her son.

'James, will you tell the people about what you were up to with that older woman?' she giggles. 'Not too much older – just one year!'

James isn't laughing. His 'struggles' at seventeen have persisted over time. This might be due, at least in part, to an inability to 'come out' to Laura, friends or (crucially) to himself.

'Frankie and I became friends on the DL. We only talked when my mother wasn't around. Did I say "talked"? OK, I admit that we did more than talk, and yes, it was a lot more, not a bit more.

'We tried to have sex a few times, but I wasn't able to stay hard for some unknown reason! I remember Frankie saying to me: "To my knowledge (barring blackout balling) two of the three boys I've tried to have sex with consensually have had trouble with their erections." I guess it wasn't hard (excuse the double entendre) for a codependent girl like her, who felt responsible for everyone, to start to wonder what *she* was doing wrong.

'One night, my mother, Frankie and I went camping. Truth is, Frankie stayed in the car drinking. She wasn't a camping person; telling me that it was #10,567 of the things she felt bad about. After Laura passed out in the tent, a few metres away, Frankie and I made out in the backseat. Frankie was turned on but for me, it was probably guilt that caused my erectile dysfunction?'

More from Miriam

At this point Miriam returns from what she calls the restroom and the dysfunctional duo exit stage right.

'And then there was Jonathon. He was Henry's other friend back then. Henry didn't have male friends, so this was an unusual time period in that he had not only one but two. He did have a lot of women friends later – after he left the military at age fifty-one and took up skiing, cycling, and mountain climbing. I always referred to these women jokingly as Henry's "girlfriends." I remember Francine's response on the phone when I told her how her father was camping over night with one of them and that I had packed a homemade lunch and dinner for the two of them. She seemed shocked and hinted that she was suspicious about what her father and the current "girlfriend" were doing (in addition to climbing or skiing). She didn't have the Yiddish words, but she was implying that her father was a *momzer* – hmm what you would call a ... hard for me to use this word but a ... bastard. I needed to ignore her and not respond.

I haven't stayed married to Henry without learning how not to see or hear things that could hurt deeply.'

A few women in the audience gasp. Others nod, signalling either agreement or empathy based on their own experiences. Miriam pauses abruptly, sighs, then continues.

'OK. Better that I return to today's topic. Jonathon was a frequent visitor at our place that summer. His marriage was in trouble – not that it's for me to say – but he said that his wife had left him. On my last visit to Melbourne, Francine opened up about what was going on back then between her and Jonathon. How she sensed an interest from him. I've never had men do this to me – God forbid – or if they were flirting, I didn't know about it.

'She was in the kitchen getting a glass of water (that's what she said to us at the time; she was actually getting her half hourly liquor from Henry's stockpile and filling the bottle with water). Jonathon – such a *schmuck* – followed her and wrapped her in an embrace. Francine's thoughts at that moment? "Not again! What is it about me? Do I emit some sort of sexual smell?" Who knows? As I said, I can't relate- this has never happened to me.

'Still, she kissed him back with, as she described it, "some passion". Francine thought her eighteen-year-old self was attracted to the idea of kissing a good-looking TV celebrity friend of her father. The twenty-year age gap only heightened the thrill. This dance of temptation continued for weeks.

'All right already. I see your raised hands. You want to talk, then talk already!'

Discussion as the meeting ends

A gentleman, bearing a remarkable resemblance to Einstein, stands up.

'Thank you, Miriam. As you know, I'm Dr Cohen, representing the Neo-Freudian faction on the head committee. Let me be perfectly clear. I speak specifically for the Jungian psychoanalytic theorists. I assume you are familiar with the Electra complex? Frankie harboured feelings for Henry. Freud might suggest that, because Henry stayed with Miriam, Frankie felt rejected and abandoned. At eighteen, she was trapped in this phase of her psychosexual development. Engaging with one of Henry's friends was therefore an unconscious means of hurting her father and potentially a way for her to have sex with him through projection.'

'No, no, no!' There is a chorus of negation from the non-Freudian and non-Neo-Freudian adherents. Liam O'Reilly speaks for that group.

'Bullshit. Let's call a spade a spade. Henry hurt her. Simply put, Frankie only wanted her father's love, and he couldn't give it to her. Accordingly, she wanted to hurt him. Hurt and anger are, after all, two sides of the same coin. How better to hurt him than by betraying him with his friend? And we have the proof! She told me what happened in one of our last sessions.'

I didn't have sex. Chickened out. He'd invited me over and I arranged to visit one afternoon. I got there, sober, and felt incredibly awkward and out of place. Like one of those pictures where you must pick what's wrong with it, what doesn't fit. It was me, as usual. I wasn't meant to be there. When he led me to the couch and started making 'moves', I ran out of the apartment.

If it was all a game, I didn't know the rules. I remember Jonathon's face as I left. There was a sadness and a knowing look there. I think he knew that he'd just been a pawn in my madness. I never saw him again. Apparently, the friendship with Henry ended, too.

'As Frankie did not have sex with Jonathon, there was no sexual transference. Therefore, our conclusion is logical and consistent with the facts.'

'Thank you, Dr O'Reilly and Dr Cohen. Your mothers must be proud.' Miriam took over the proceedings as the meeting was drawing to a close.

'This special meeting of the head committee has reached the end of its allotted time. I would like to thank you for having me act as the chairwoman today. It has been a privilege and an opportunity for me to exercise some dormant skills. After all, I was born in my time.'

She lets out an enormous Miriamesque sigh. This time, though, she is not alone. Something about Miriam has resonated with many women in the audience. A collective exhale fills the room. Miriam feels an unfamiliar strength. In this moment, she undergoes a transformative experience, and the butterfly begins to emerge. No doubt, many now perceive her differently from the *Portnoy's Complaint* mother figure they had previously envisioned.

'To conclude, I'll read an excerpt from a letter Francine sent to me. She was elaborating on what she had told me when we were visiting the grandchildren. Maybe this was a part of her *work* on a step from one of those meetings she attends? I felt a mix of sadness and gratitude.'

And then, in her distinct manner, she read the words with great emphasis and feeling.

And that was the summer I turned eighteen, spent living with you. I am deeply ashamed. I partied with Laura, flirted with James and Jonathon, and committed other acts I regret. I believe I embarrassed you in front of Aunt Helena, but my memories are hazy. I stole from Dad's liquor cabinet. Whenever you were both out, I would listen to the only rock music you owned, a tape of Simon & Garfunkel's greatest hits. Drunk, I'd weep and harm my arms with razor blades; never deep enough to require medical attention, just a lot of slashes to feel the pain and to express the anger and the shame that were welling up in my psyche. Because Simon & Garfunkel sang about 'darkness my old friend', and darkness was indeed my old friend. They sang of the spring-time of life, my current phase, and I mourned its fleeting nature and the futility of my existence.

Years later, when I hear these songs, I'm transported back to your house that summer. And every time that I listen now, there's a healing. When I cry, it's for the eighteen-year-old who felt lost and unlovable.

It was not about you, dear Mum. Please forgive me.

13
DISSENSION IN THE HEAD: A CORNER TURNED

arol is a university psych services counsellor available to troubled youth (and there were many) free of charge. She was Frankie's second mental health practitioner (or the first, if you consider that the KF Shrink had been mandated) in a series of therapists. Through their guidance, Triple F managed to unburden some internalised torment, moving forwards in her metamorphosis from egg to butterfly.

However, not every head committee member shares this sentiment.

Carol's retrospective report

'Frankie visited me several times a week for a few months. Mostly, I listened. From my notes, here's Frankie's voice at that time.'

Well, Carol, I ended up at this college since my father, Henry, arranged it all. Without realising, he chose a much better place than my first university: no fraternities or sororities here; instead, New York Jewish radicals, political activists, and lots of dope!

I spent the first few days walking around just saying, 'Far fucking out'. I'd dropped out of school eight months earlier to search for my people on the west coast, but my path had not intersected with the Haight-Ashbury hippies. Now, I was seeing them, or people who looked like them, at the institution which Henry had chosen.

Also a blessing, as a second semester freshman[48] as you know Carol, I don't have to live in a dorm. Instead, I'm living in an apartment with two cool girls – 'Heroin Heidi' and 'NYC Frieda' – and a couple of super straight girls. They resent our drugs, politics, and ideas of communal living. For example, Heidi, Frieda, and I are happy for the group to share everything in the kitchen. Could be because we don't pay for anything?

Carol, it's the classic struggle between the bourgeois capitalists and the fun-loving bolshie socialists. And given our proclivity for marijuana with its inevitable 'munchies', the refrigerator has become a battleground; containers armed with name tags are raided by cannabis-affected invaders. Really, that's Frieda and Heidi when she's not nodding off. Not me. I'm neutral like Switzerland.

Truth is, food isn't high on my priorities. Diet pills. I'm skinny and smoking like a chimney and my brain is in fourth gear! What was a total drag before with the 'Greeks' and too much LSD is now the opposite … So, my grades are excellent.

I'm here to see you because, despite all this good stuff, I'm down. I honestly don't feel as though I deserve to live because I am such a flawed person.

'At that point, you see, Frankie had no reference point or role model for accepting herself as a human being.

'Not to minimise her suicidal ideation, perhaps it is that way for many adolescents. Such a difficult time as we have discussed at

---

48 Frankie emphasised *man* as she became conscious at a young age of the power of language to create a male reality.

previous meetings. Who knows? Most people don't walk around disclosing inner despair, do they? Certainly, such thoughts are not uncommon among the students with whom I interact, although admittedly they're not a random sample of eighteen- to twenty-two-year-olds.

'Frankie confessed that, following her pattern since puberty, she was perpetually seeking a romantic partner or at least someone to obsess over. Her radar had detected Brad, another student living in her building. However, he reminded her of Simon, whom she'd met in London. (Yes, she shared her overseas adventure with me, although she didn't say that it was essentially a six-week bender.) Both young men seemed emotionally stable and weren't predatory.

'Frankie was more enamoured with Brad's car, a racing green MG sportscar, than with Brad himself. They'd go for long drives in the countryside. Conversation was difficult due to the loud engine, which Frankie probably appreciated as it saved her from engaging. Admittedly, that's my own assumption, which I didn't delve into during counselling. She only visited me for a few months, after all, and I'm a university counsellor with a bachelor's degree in counselling.

'Like many her age, Frankie pursued relationships with virtual strangers. We first observed this behaviour in Europe.'

Carol points to Triple F's personal guardian angel, now back in the committee's good graces.

'Lucky for Frankie, her PGA was still working tirelessly. Everyone, let's give PGA a round of applause.'

Almost everyone claps with varying degrees of enthusiasm.

'The lack of targets for obsessive thoughts may have contributed to the depression she presented with. I have learned about codependency since those days and understand now that transferring one's feelings and thoughts onto someone else is problematic without an individual to serve as the sponge.

'Reflecting on it with hindsight, Frankie's mindset might have been worsened by PMDD, undiagnosed clinical depression, PTSD, and/or substance abuse. Unfortunately, my training back then included neither the diagnostic criteria nor treatment plans for any of these conditions.

'Regardless of such challenges, our conversations seemed to brighten her spirits. While some might deem it cliché, especially given its origins in twelve-step programs, I genuinely believe that a problem shared is a problem halved, or at the least, diminished.'

Committee reflections upon the arguable value of therapy

Sweet Richard, who is human and therefore not always that sweet, does sometimes reveal a less affable side, especially towards Francine and their children. As he's now speaking to the members living rent free within *her* head, they're hearing that family voice.

'As most of you know, I was sent off to boarding school at the age of six. To survive, one learned to live by "coping". We simply did not dwell upon our difficulties. Instead, we became experts in being reserved and practical – doing what needed to be done. In diametrical opposition to this "soldiering on" ethos, North Americans' tendency for introspection might seem like rubbish to us. Plus, Francine did grow up with Woody Allen-type mentors doing what we poms sometimes label as self-indulgent *therapeutic* introspection.

'Nevertheless, I would note that there was one period shortly after we moved to Australia when Francine clearly grappled with serious mental distress. I witnessed the transition from her "normal" state to a semi-psychotic condition. She tried to describe what it felt like, explaining through tears that she felt as though she was trapped inside a glass jar unable to feel connected to me or the children.

'Leaving the house was a nightmare but staying inside was a prison. She tried to shop but would end up spending an hour in the frozen vegetables section of the supermarket, overwhelmed by choice and indecision. Every routine task or interaction was extraordinarily stressful.

'Unable to sleep for months, in the middle of the night, like Lady Macbeth, Francine paced the hallways.

'I spent hours futilely researching medical journals at the university library. This is how I show love. And, like Francine, it is how I deal with emotions and my inability to help her. Indeed, intellectualising is one of the traits that we have in common.

'Carol, it's unfortunate that your diagnosis of clinical depression was only made retrospectively. If it had been a part of Francine's medical history, one of the many "professionals" we consulted might have noted its return. Three general practitioners, two psychologists, one psychiatrist, a masseuse, a hypnotherapist, and an acupuncturist did not see the "black dog" lurking behind her masked presentation of anxiety and full-blown insomnia. The acupuncturist did come the closest. Based on her symptoms, he was surprised by the lethargy of her pulses. Almost makes one believe in these … hmm … unconventional health fields … *almost.*

'I started out with minimal regard for the mental health profession. These experiences reinforced my views.

'Furthermore, I believe that if the North American therapists whom Francine saw in the years before I entered her life, and before our move to Australia, had posed the right questions or truly listened, then her issues with drug and alcohol abuse, eating disorders, addiction to men, and even this major depressive episode might have been avoided.'

Richard's last comment evokes a quick response from Nancy, representing the AA members.

'Triple F's journey is *her* journey. Therapists couldn't have changed it. Everything that took place happened for a reason. Like each of us who has had the opportunity to find a twelve-step program, she needed to "bottom out". It's the only way we take the first step. And she has had to feel that powerlessness over each substance, person or "ism" to take the second step and then work her way through the twelve-step pathway.

'However, I will concede that the psychiatrists, psychologists, and counsellors, including you Carol, whom Frankie consulted, never broached the subjects of drugs or booze. No. It was AA that tackled that malady. And while we aren't dogmatists, we firmly believe that one needs to address addiction before confronting other issues.'

Carol, speaking on behalf of the pre-recovery professionals Frankie consulted, responds with a hint of defensiveness – which is to be expected after Richard's and Nancy's remarks.

'We couldn't live life for her or perform a lobotomy to remove the traits that make Triple F who she is, could we?

'Our role is not to heal or to mend but to guide the patient or the client through that process. And I did assist her. In fact, near the end of her counselling with me, she expressed gratitude that for the first time since adolescence, she had stopped searching for her soulmate.

'And we know what happens when the person stops waiting for the water to boil?'

14

MICHAEL (TAPES 1 and 2): HEAD COMMITTEE MEETING

'Hey, everyone! It's me, Gabe, chairing again. Please take a seat. We've got a lot to cover today, looking at the first half of Frankie's time with Michael. Next week we'll look at the latter three years.'

'The tapes we'll be listening to were made with Frankie's consent, of course. And, just like with her sessions about the rape, I've deleted my voice.'

Tape 1: playing house

I met Michael – Mikey, or Mike – at a demonstration. Yes, I called him all three names, and, as you'll hear, even more as we go on.

When the loudspeaker blared out instructions to form a two-person line, holding hands with someone, my partner in the queue was a tall boy who, from the corner of my eye, seemed decent: average build from what I could see underneath his poncho, long reddish-blonde hair, green eyes, cheeks flushed from the crisp autumn air, and a nose that clearly shouted, 'Jewish on both sides'.

I wasn't really judging or on the lookout for any romantic spark, was I?

190

We began to talk and it turned out that the shnoz was a clue that he was in fact Jewish. Not just a Jew in ancestry like me but the middle son of members of a New York conservative temple. They had three sets of dishes, and on the right side of the front door of their home hung a mezuzah, which every family member touched upon entering.

Like me, he was eighteen, but unlike me, it was his first year at college. Amid the protest chanting, we found some common ground. He smoked dope – which I found reassuring – and we had a shared love for music: Chicago, Vanilla Fudge, Cream, the Doors, the Beatles, Led Zeppelin, Pink Floyd, Queen, and the Rolling Stones. Mike seemed, at his core, a hippie just like me.

I started to feel that this could be someone special. Despite (or because of) not actively looking, it seemed that a potential boyfriend had appeared.

Gabe, you know neither you nor me is inclined to take things slow in relationships, although I always vow to tread lightly each time. But it just doesn't pan out that way. So, it wasn't really a shock when, early on, I found myself in love with Michael. Very quickly, our relationship became ... well, the answer would depend upon who was labelling it. If it were a word association test, like tree is to wood or marijuana is to stoned, it would be Frankie and Mike are to sweet, or Frankie and Mike are to utterly devoted.

And we truly were. When we met, Michael was a first semester undergraduate living in a dormitory. Like me and most others back then, as he had no idea what he wanted to do or be when he graduated, he was taking general arts and sciences classes. But, starting with the second semester, he enrolled into whatever I did. And, by the middle of winter, Mike was living with me, Frieda and Heidi in a house we'd escaped to that was ready to be demolished.

In those days, the four of us lived in a tenement, with mattresses spread on the floor, beaded room dividers, Indian tapestries, and erratic iron space heaters. They would either blast intense heat or offer no warmth at all against the bone-chilling cold. We'd often wake up either drenched in sweat or noticing our bedside water had frozen over.

At the beginning of Mike's second year, we rented our own place. It felt like setting up a cubbyhouse. Fittingly, it was Henry and Miriam who supplied the furniture, linens, and kitchenware. The colonel chose to take early retirement at the age of fifty. Opting to buy a trailer and embark on 'walkabouts' or 'caravanabouts', he and Miriam sold their home, and in doing so, provided me with much of their furnishings.

'At the end of this session with Frankie, I offered some feedback that I've deleted from the recording, but I'll summarise for you now.'

'First, I pointed out that since she had fallen in love with that French fellow she knew for a few hours, her feelings for Mike seemed suspect. I managed to get her to concede that the intensity of their bond ticked the boxes for dependency or codependency.

'Now, before I play the next tape, are there any comments?'

Miriam and Beverly, Michael's mother, speak in unison: 'This was a huge mistake.

'(S)he was too good for her/him. They were too young, just kids. But what can you tell them? Nothing! What does a mother know? Nothing! We tried but who would listen? Them? No! They thought they had all the answers. So, what could we do? Help pick up the pieces when it was over.'

It's just Miriam now. She adheres to the belief that behind every woman is a man preventing her from falling apart.

'And my Frankie, she needed a stronger man to take care of her, to make her whole. Poor Michael wasn't up to the task. He was still umbilically tied to his mother. He was like Humpty Dumpty, needing someone to piece him together!'

Beverly shifts uncomfortably, taking umbrage at the depiction of her son as a fractured egg with mother issues. She views the situation somewhat differently.

'That family … Jews in disguise. The problem here was Frankie's latent anti-Semitism.'

Henry, however, dismisses Beverly, a habit he frequently exhibits when women voice their opinions.

'Our children only marry losers – except for Richard – so, Michael was the third in line. First was Jake, who brought home Sonya, a woman he'd barely known a week before marrying. A full twenty years her senior, an Iranian Muslim who had finished sixth grade, she had the temerity to call us, "Mother" and "Father."[49]

'Then, with Sandra, there was Wayne, the son of a small-town Methodist preacher. Apart from being possessive, he drank too much beer, and his views on social issues were too right-wing, even for my liking.'

Tape 2: changing Frankie

During the six years I was with Michael, I changed.

I began to excel academically. After a three-year hiatus, I was once again achieving top marks on tests and having

---

49 Sandy and Frankie, also visiting during the Easter break, found this hilarious. Poor Jake. To his credit, Henry could no longer physically abuse him. However, at that juncture, Jake faced criticism from his new bride on one side and a stunned – actually, more than stunned, let's call it incredulous – silence from his parents. In any case, Jake had the last laugh. A few months later, he divorced Sonya and shortly thereafter came out of 'the closet'.

my essays read aloud as exemplary. I can't pinpoint exactly why, but I attended all my lectures, prepared for exams, completed the necessary readings, and even submitted every assignment.

And Gabe, this may be hard to believe, but I barely drank. Mike preferred dope and other hallucinogens. He loved to 'trip.' I tried to tag along but inevitably found that LSD turned my mind inside out, which was not a pleasant experience.

Hey, another epiphany! Or maybe we've had this one already? Possibly, people with control issues don't choose these types of drugs because they lose that illusion of being in control.

We only had alcohol if we were given a bottle as a gift or when we visited family or went to friends for a social gathering. Like once a year we'd drive to Sandy's in the Midwest and the four of us would party at their club. Gabe, no surprises here. Alcohol meant my morality changed and I flirted with anyone – even my brother-in-law! My sister had told me that Wayne had a 'foot-long dick'. When we slow danced, he thrust said dick into my stomach. She hadn't exaggerated. And if that wasn't bad enough, he was whispering that my breasts far exceeded Sandy's in size and touch.

And yes, my boobs were big! Munchies-sized. My marijuana measurements grew first to 36, 24, 36; then expanded to 38, 26, 38. But, for the first time, though, I felt comfortable with my body. Mike seemed to revere my curves – in particular, my breasts, which, until childbirth and breastfeeding, were excellent, Gabe, although I know not a part of the anatomy you have any interest in.

Gabe nods as he switches off the tape recorder, having observed several twelve-step program members raising their hands, eager to share.

AA Nan, Frankie's temporary sponsor during rehab, speaks with Triple F's consent. She discusses her perspective on how Frankie's time with Michael fits into the narrative of her alcoholism. Frankie had revealed the comfort she found in Wayne's admiration.

'I helped her recognise that her alcoholism influenced these feelings. It's the shame-driven thinking that perpetuates our drinking. Embracing the steps can start the emptying of this reservoir of shame.

'Frankie was a binge drinker. During her time with Mikey these benders took place less frequently. Relative to the time in Europe and then the summer with Henry and Miriam, Frankie was on the wagon.

'She is one of our members who used a lot of "controls" on her drinking – a tendency more prevalent among women. As you can see, her drinking history was punctuated by periods of abstinence, perhaps by crossing addictions? With Mikey, she veered towards marijuana, romance, sex, and notably, codependency, which always seems to lurk in the background.

'Her sister Sandra, who joined AA a few years before Frankie, didn't limit her alcohol intake. She quickly hit rock bottom, transitioning from pills to alcohol. Unlike Frankie, Sandy hid her drinking. For example, when visiting Henry and Miriam, she'd bring a stash of whisky. Emptying half a can of diet coke, she refilled it with booze. Henry and Miriam didn't have a clue.

'In contrast, during her visits, Frankie was mindful of her consumption. It was ironic and exasperating that Henry and Miriam scrutinised Frankie's drinking but overlooked Sandra's.

'However, this disease is not about how often we drink or how much. It's what it does to us – how it alters our behaviour. Speaking of which, when Frankie drank and was out and about, she was a flirt. Alcohol ignited a desperate need to be admired and desired by all males in attendance. In Frankie's defence, though, she would (almost) never have slept with them. In fact, the apex or nadir of her flirtations (depending on your values) during the Michael years was kissing another man.'

The Sex Love Anonymous (SLA) delegate, Sam, who identifies as non-binary, nods in agreement.

'Ah yes, crossing to romance addiction happens a lot in our female members' histories. The chemical high from endorphins, especially during the early stages of passion, is palpable.

'Sex wasn't quite as buzzy for Frankie, though. It was scheduled for every other day before sleep. There was no spontaneity and little excitement although they *worked* their way through a guidebook to over 100 sexual positions, which Mike had bought.

'Plus, it wasn't until their fifth year together that Michael found a reference to the clitoris in another book he was reading about female sexuality. A diagram mapped its location, guiding Mikey to successfully achieve the quest. And Frankie got hooked on another high as the effects of an orgasm are like the rush that results from injecting heroin.[50] We do *get* that in SLA!'

Return to Tape 2

Anyway, back to Mikey, Gabe. He was super affectionate. Love notes were standard. The anniversary of the day that we met was routinely celebrated; and, in time, our wedding date. Flowers sent on many occasions and when rare circumstances forced us to be apart, phone calls several times a day.

Shared words were ritualised, too. I called Michael, 'My mighty man, Mikey' or, when in a hurry, 'Mikey'. My special name was 'Pretty Princess Frankie'. Pretty ironic, eh, Gabe?

---

50 Adam Safron describes orgasm as a 'correlate of elevated opioid concentrations.'

The names didn't stop there, with our body parts including genitalia labelled. And, yes, every night, before turning out the bedside lamps, we ritualistically said goodnight to each other.

The committee can hear Frankie laughing while telling Gabe that this process took a minimum of five minutes. The room is silent for a moment – a stunned sort of silence. Then there's a clamour of voices. Gabe turns off the recorder and points to Liam O'Reilly.

'It is my view that this last routine was another manifestation of both their lack of self-identity and a further loss of their individual selves'

As expected, the Neo-Freudian Dr Cohen disagrees.

'Naming Mikey's balls was an attempt to fornicate with Henry. Indeed, one scrotum was named Henry but Hank for short and you have to know by now that the real Henry would never be called Hank.'

'Well, speaking as the men who came before Michael, we have to say that Frankie seems to have learned a lot since she was with us. Back then, she didn't know what we had, let alone any ability to talk about testicles and give them a name.'

'Hey, you've got to be kidding,' assert the men who followed Michael. These guys were PC – the post-clitoral age.

'Our Triple F had the male anatomy down to a fine science, but she'd never waste time making cutesy talk. She was too busy worrying about when or whether she was going to get her orgasm. Thank God that she learned how to get there herself, less pressure on us to perform.'

At this point, Miriam interrupts.

'Such talk. Orgasm schmorgasm. Names for his ... you know and his other ... who knows? What is this? Who names these things? And, every night, to take the minutes to talk to all of them?

It's what I've always said about her laziness. All that time when she could be washing the kitchen floor or cleaning the bathroom tiles with a toothbrush, but what is she doing? Our daughter? Talking to his … his … you know what I mean. Who needs the aggravation?'

Miriam's bitter tone matched the Michael years' extensive contribution to her MORGUE. It now included the memory of how the 'good' silver, 'fine' china, the crystal, and furniture had been sold. Even without knowing the heavily discounted prices, Miriam maintained a well of resentment.

Silence descends. Garrulous Gabe has been mute. Now, he needs to talk or be heard.

'Well, we're *almost* in agreement that Michael was the wrong partner for Frankie. Only one problem, though: she locks us in the boardroom during an addiction. In fact, you might say that this muting is one of obsession's payoffs, at least at the beginning, before it turns sour. When it does go "off" and the committee is liberated and listened to, they make up for lost time, bellowing to be heard and vying to be the first to tear away the denial and show her what she's been doing wrong.'

He turns the tape back on.

Over time, we stopped functioning as two people and did almost everything together. We took almost all the same classes. Since Mike couldn't decide what to major in, he followed me. I switched from anthropology to sociology and finally to psychology. Michael made the same shifts.

Same thing when looking at graduate schools. With no vocation or desire for employment, further education was the obvious choice. But, to study what? I applied not just to different universities but a variety of disciplines including social work, psychology, and sociology. Ditto with Mikey.

Decision-making would be simplified by accepting whatever course was offering the best deal financially.

Penn State offered me a teaching assistantship in their PhD psychology program, which paid more than the other offers. Decision made. Mike was accepted into the same program. Showing an unusual degree of autonomy, he opted for the clinical component whilst I chose the experimental program. Neither of us felt any real affinity for the discipline.

This may have looked like I was the boss, Gabe, but I wasn't, really. It was more a reflection of Mike's being stoned most of the time and without any vocation. And my outsides gave the message that I knew where I was going but as you know, inside I was just as lost as him. Dilettante drifters or middle-class spoiled brats, we'd opted for what looked like the easier and softer way.

The recording ends.

Dr Jaye has decided to share some of her insights about this relationship and how it contributed to what she calls Francine's 'butterfly moments' or mini metamorphoses.

'Francine disclosed that her time with Michael felt surreal. Reflecting on it in therapy, she has sensed the disconnect.

'"It feels like someone else was playing house with Mikey, not the person you see now, Dr Jaye."

'I was able to reassure her: "The child Franny, who is present now, also lived inside the young Frankie. The same core fears persisted. The same yearning for a semblance of power. But today, Francine, you can identify those emotions and discover healthy ways to manage them. The enlightenment and awareness we've cultivated together wouldn't have emerged without your experiences with Michael."

'In my opinion – and yes, I do rarely express one – this cloying and dependent relationship was doomed from the start. If one partner felt suffocated or, even began to evolve, how could the pair survive? Answer: they couldn't. But it took a few years and a baby to find that out.

'Gabe could you please play the next recording?'

15
MICHAEL (TAPES 3 and 4): HEAD COMMITTEE MEETING

Tape 3: Following the charted path

*G*abe you would have loved this wedding. I know you adore the eclectic! We stood under the traditional Jewish floral chuppah in a conservative Jewish temple as two friends played guitar and sang a Beatles medley. I wore a white cotton dress with embroidered flowers and an empire waistline to hide my larger-sized body. A floppy white hat and a wicker basket of daisies completed the 'look'. Michael had a vested blue suit, care of Ben, who sold men's formal clothing. Speaking of which, the engagement ring, honeymoon, and wedding reception included a discounted component offered by different members of the New York network of second and third cousins.

Surrounded by a grandparent, four parents, four siblings, and a dozen friends, we exchanged our vows. As is the custom, Michael stamped on a wine glass, which, in hindsight, was quite fitting for someone marrying an alcoholic. His grandmother called out, 'Mazel tov.'

It was done. Unreal, but done.

Later that night, in the New York city hotel, we did – or tried our best to do what we'd seen in the movies: champagne and passionate sex. But Gabe, through it all, I wasn't present. As per my MO, I was removed from the scene like a spectator at the wedding, the reception, and Bermuda resort. Surprise, surprise ... not. Once again, nothing was taking place as it had inside my head.

Oh, well ...

A couple of weeks after the honeymoon, we headed to Philadelphia. This was the start of three years of graduate school. A time that we breathed, lived, and even partied psychology.[51] You know, Gabe, looking back through the twelve-step lens, I'd say that this time could be designated as my foundation workaholic period.

Through that lens, our poverty – my small stipend plus a bit extra from Mike's limited marijuana trade – was another limit on my drinking. We only drank at the occasional gatherings of our friends who were either studying or teaching in Psych.

And there was our pledge, made after Year 1 of the PhD, to quit smoking cigarettes. This was part of the 'prepare Frankie's body for pregnancy' plan. Since I've seen you, before and after meetings, Gabe, smoking like a chimney outside with more than half of the members, I guess that you don't know about nicotine withdrawal? It's the worst. Without a doubt.

We kicked the habit, though! Used more than twenty paint-by-numbers kits to keep our hands and minds occupied.

And cigarettes weren't the only thing I gave up. Since ciggies went with drinking, smoking dope, or doing speed, I quit them, too. Stayed clean over the fourteen months (and eleven pregnancy tests) that it took for me to get pregnant and while Samuel was in utero, of course.

---

51 The social group was limited to psychology postgraduate students (and the occasional departmental staff member). Party conversations tended to be erudite – an intellectual preening.

This heralded other changes. The pregnancy meant that plans had to be made for the year of observational PhD fieldwork to fit with having a baby.

Michael, as the emancipated pro-feminist that he was, volunteered to be househusband for that year and to defer his research.

'Excuse me. Turn this thing off for a minute.'

Once a colonel, always a colonel.

'Pro-feminist. What a load of garbage. No motivation, no balls. Not only didn't this kid have a clue what he wanted to study, he let Frankie lead him around the country like a dog on a leash. He may have been chronologically twenty-one, but in many ways, Michael was about fifteen.'

Gabe, pushes 'Play', saying first: 'Certainly, Henry, what Frankie told me about next could be seen as indicative of your former son-in-law's immaturity.' Henry does evoke more formal speech, even from laid-back counsellors.

Michael seemed to need to tell lies: the Playboy *and* Hustler *saga is an example. He hid them in the bathroom and read them secretly in there. Or that's what he claimed he'd been doing after I found them on top of the medicine cabinet.*

However, Mikey was always remorseful when caught lying. If I occasionally saw a sly look, any concern was offset by the tenderness there too. He seemed to love and want me.

There is no opportunity for Gabe to open the floor for comments as a visibly upset Beverly ignores protocol.

'My son! That my son would be doing these things in the bathroom ... no, it was *her*. She didn't let him do what a man needs to do. My Michael wouldn't read those types of magazines unless he was driven to it.'

Henry also has a view to add.

'The material I can understand, but to get caught at it? Just look at what he was doing in the bathroom? A real man doesn't masturbate. A real man (cover your ears, Miriam) satisfies these sexual urges with chronic infidelity.'

Francine's CODA friend, Jennifer, has another explanation for the alleged bathroom porn.

'Unbeknownst to Frankie, Mike never stopped smoking. Isn't it amazing how we convince ourselves that black is white because it's too painful to deal with reality? Late afternoons in sub-arctic temperatures, he'd pick her up, with the car windows rolled down. The open bathroom window, *Playboy* magazines, and lengthy stays in the toilet ... she could sense that something was going on in the loo. Her knight in shining armour was getting rusty.'

Tape 4: Sammy

I loved being pregnant – almost every second.[52] *Just by existing, I was the centre of attention with no performances required. And Mikey was at my beck and call. He was thrilled at the prospect of fatherhood and loved to lay beside me, hand on my abdomen, feeling the movement of our child in there. Whenever I had a food craving, whatever it was, Mikey was on call. Speaking of which, between no cigarettes and pregnancy, my weight was entering the stratosphere.*

---

52 Being with child can answer the prayers of codependents with PMS. Atypically, their oestrogen and progesterone levels are harmoniously balanced. Another bonus: since adult children and codependents have a need to be needed, being a foetal caretaker may induce a state of bliss.

I always wanted to be one of those women whose bump becomes large with no changes to the remainder of their bodies except for bigger boobs. Michael didn't seem to mind, though, and I felt healthy and fantastic. That might be why a comment he made a few months after we broke up, when I was anorexically thin, was particularly hurtful.[53]

A perfect pregnancy with no morning, afternoon, or evening sickness was followed by a near-perfect natural birth.

Gabe, I don't need to tell you how weird that last statement might seem. After all, we're talking about an addict, albeit one on all sorts of wagons. Feel fat? Take speed. Low? Have a drink, and another, and another. Ironic, then, that when it came to childbirth, I was a fanatic about experiencing the agony. Pretty weird kind of hippie cognitive framework, eh?

So, Sammy emerged naturally and quickly.

I've brought some photos to share. You know what they say about a picture …?

See how tiny he was at birth despite my giving up the cigs. And here's Sammy sound asleep in the carriage with Mike sitting on the couch staring at him. And look at two-week-old Sammy lying face-down on Michael's stomach. He liked that. They both did.

Here are Beverly and Ben holding Samuel aged three weeks. There's a cloth on their shoulders because Sammy started to throw up in an arc after each feed. He's now below his birth weight which, remember, was low to start with.

'It could be your milk, dear.'

No, Beverly, not my milk, just my genes. See, Gabe, not only do I have a genetic predisposition for addiction and (no doubt) other

---

53 Mike had said, 'Why couldn't you have looked like *this* when we were a couple?'

mental disorders but turns out I'm the carrier of pyloric steno-sis,[54] which Samuel was born with (and later, his sister, Rosa).

You can see in these next photos Sammy is even tinier and surrounded by diapers. I look stressed, don't I? Concern and responsibility – maybe it's my milk – the putrid emissions of a bad mother?

I brought you a few snapshots from the Children's Hospital where four-week-old Sammy had surgery. Close-up of my face, which shows the stress from having listened to the crying and distress for the hour it took the medical staff to insert an IV into his miniscule vein.

Such a sad place, Gabe. You know I saw a dead child being wheeled off the floor; parents sitting in waiting areas or pacing the hallways through the night. Although Michael held my hand, I felt alone and afraid.

Here are some photos after we brought Samuel home from the hospital. See those huge mournful brown eyes, framed with long thick eyelashes women pay for? He's asking, 'Why?' But I had no answers. Might be why, in the album marked 'Samuel – ages one to four months', there are no pictures where I look relaxed and comfortable. I wasn't.

As I'd lived and breathed psychology, I focused my energy entirely on him. In contrast, Michael, in the photographs, appears tension-free – joint or pipe nearby.

Gabe hits pause.

'Hey folks, as you know, I've deleted my voice from these recordings, but I'd like to share just a few of my notes from that session.

---

54 This is a serious condition in which the muscular valve (pylorus), which is located between the stomach and small intestine, thickens from birth. Preventing food from reaching the small intestine, it causes the infant to projectile vomit.

'There is a disconnect between Frankie's internal picture of herself as an "earth mother", feeding Sammy on demand and blaring music for him to learn to sleep through noise, versus the tense Frankie we see in the photos. In those images, she tip-toes around the house to avoid waking Samuel and is intent on establishing a strict feeding schedule.

'As a codependent ACA, Frankie wanted to be the perfect mother. But, given that perfection is out of anyone's reach, she appeared overly anxious and super-responsible in the photographs she showed me.

'OK. Let's listen to the last part of the fourth and final tape I'm playing today.'

When Sammy was four months old, we moved 760 miles south so I could begin my observational PhD fieldwork in a metropolitan hospital. The focus was on understanding medical practitioners' and police officers' attitudes and behaviours toward battered women. Domestic violence intrigued me, even though it was barely addressed in our coursework.

The plan was that Tuesday through Saturday for a year, from 4 pm until midnight, I'd leave Michael and Sam. Mikey seemed happy deferring his PhD and instead being a stay-at-home daddy.

Gabe, I know you never judge, but surprise, surprise, I'm judging myself. A 'good mother' wouldn't leave her baby and if she had to, she certainly wouldn't enjoy the experience. I loved the emergency room though and felt very drawn to its vibe and rhythm. And, okay, stop giving me that look, Gabe. Yes, I admit, I was attracted to the doctors and the cops. Their assertive presence was a stark contrast to the laid-back Daddy Mikey.

This was the beginning of the end. When police officers and interns are flirting with you, well, what can I say?

The committee has much to say regarding Frankie's wandering psyche. First to speak is Miriam, followed by Henry.

'This was my feminist daughter? She disregarded poor Michael, who was only sublimating his own career to help her. That was typical of Frankie – always thinking of herself and being unreasonable! If she wanted a doctor, why didn't she marry one? She chose Michael; made her bed and should have stayed in it."

'Who could blame her for looking at the physicians, and yes, even those in law enforcement? These are men who earn their living, not boys who stay at home minding the baby. While I, being a moralist, don't condone her actions, I do grasp her motivations.'

'Hey this really had nothing to do with Michael being a house-husband.' Jennifer and Irene, speaking in one voice, identify the codependency and adult child core issues.

'Frankie could intuit that Mike was drifting away from her. He had begun to go out with a network of friends – "the boys" – once or twice a week. Understandable considering he was home all day with Sammy. To Frankie, the super sleuth who could sense withdrawal of affection at 100 metres, Michael was changing. Most change is terrifying to ACA codependents as we are terrified about the unknown even when the "known" is dreadful.'

'We can see that when Frankie responded to flirtatious Gary – a married doctor whose wife was eight months pregnant with their third child – she was afraid of being rejected by Mike. This is an underlying motive that we understand and accept. It was a legacy of childhood emotional neglect. Apologies, Miriam, but it is what it is. We do understand that you have always done the best that you could.'

'Wrong! The answer is alcohol, plain and simple,' Sally and Nan are in Al-Anon and AA agreement. 'Frankie needed to self-sabotage in order to continue down her path of alcoholic self-destruction which she'd begun in adolescence. Michael, as an external control, was collateral damage.'

Dr Jaye, unusually, wraps up today's discussion.

'These are interesting theories, some of which Francine has integrated into her "story." In our eighth year of therapy, she provided further insight into this phase of her life, which I'll now discuss.'

16
THE RETURN OF THE BINGE: LISTENING IN ON THERAPY

Francine's now in her eighth year of therapy with Dr Jaye. To date, they've looked at Franny's childhood, Frankie's adolescence, the early to middle 'Michael' period, and Francine's current trials and tribulations with family and work.

Today's therapy session begins with the final stage of Mikey.

'Dr Jaye, after conducting participant observation and interviewing in the hospital for four months, I slowly morphed into another version of Frankie. Yes, surviving as a child meant adopting the values and behaviours of Henry. Over time, these chameleon-like adaptations happened without my awareness. This hospital persona became more conservative and cynical. You'd understand this since you went to medical school and must have had a rotation in Casualty?'

Dr Jaye nods, allowing Francine to continue uninterrupted — a contrast to Richard, who cuts her off if her words exceed what he deems as "headlines."[55]

'When I saw people come into Emergency drunk, women with unexplained bruises, or toddlers with injuries purportedly from

---

55 This habit is evidently yet another characteristic of ADHD. Interestingly, Richard, like others of his ilk, does not reciprocate with brevity of discourse. Instead, he frequently lectures or pontificates at length.

accidental falls, I began to look at people differently. Were they being honest or hiding violence and addiction?

'Then, I'd go home to a hippie who didn't have a clue about this different world. It felt like we were living on different planets, except for our co-resident – Sammy.'

She pauses, giving Dr Jaye the *look* that invites a response.

'This was not atypical behaviour for a "codependent adult child" – your term and label, not mine. This chameleon-like ability suggests a potential lack of boundaries, a shifting identity, and a drive for approval. Or we could look at this as a skill that had served you well – and continues to do so – at least in academia. Additionally, there's a third, blended perspective, Francine. Always consider the nuances.'

'Indeed, Dr Jaye. Recognising those nuances, rather than viewing things in black and white, is part of my recovery journey. Along with identifying, accepting and changing the other 15,893 legacies of growing up with Henry and Miriam, and the intergenerational trauma.'

Dr Jamyang offers a warm, understanding smile. Francine continues, valuing this time as one of the few moments she feels genuinely heard.

'As I became integrated into the Casualty environment, the police officers frequenting emergency would strike up conversations with me. They seemed to flirt with every female staffer. You'd know about that from your experiences as a medical student and resident?'

No response from the good doctor. The focus of therapy is on Francine, not on Dr Jaye. After eight years, *nothing* personal has been shared about the psychiatrist to the patient. This was not the case years earlier with Gabe.

'Gary, a robbery detective in his forties, entered the scene. Gary adored me but had only a minor role in this story – not my type. He was the catalyst though for the suggestion I made to Michael late one evening. It went like this. "I think that we should have a vacation from our marriage. All parents have visited in the last few months, and no one is expected here so no one needs to know. We take six months to do our own thing and then get back together. It's the perfect time since Sammy is too little to know what's going on. We were eighteen when we met − children really."

'This was out of the blue, Dr Jaye, and not rehearsed. Or it may be possible that extemporaneity has become part of my narrative? Likely, I was being as honest with Mike as with myself. Problem is the bar was low. It could still be − that's a warning to you.'

Francine looks at her therapist to gauge any non-verbal reaction to that last comment. Dr Jamyang meets Francine's gaze steadily as always. Her look says, 'No warning required. I trust your ability to be truthful with yourself.'

'Michael was receptive, which was unexpected. Although he seemed to be a bit hurt, there was no outrage. On the contrary, he seemed eager.

'A month-long discussion about logistics followed. We had to wing it in isolation, which, you know Dr Jaye, is not easy for a person like me. I ended up drinking alone − a bottle of sherry gifted by Miriam and Henry. This of course led me to light up after more than two years' abstinence. That first cigarette quickly escalated to two packs a day, which meant my weight plummeted.

'Which brings me − in my typically roundabout way of speaking, a manner Richard once enjoyed but no longer tolerates, yet you seem patient with and manage to follow, Dr Jaye − back to Gary, the married detective.'

'If you're visualising, picture a slim and trim Frankie making out passionately on Gary's living room floor as his wife was literally giving birth to their third child at the hospital. In my defence, we didn't exactly have sex. The infidelity was limited to that one episode of dry humping fully clothed. It was bad enough, though, to remain in the top ten of my personal MORGUE.

'In fact, many, if not all, of the contenders for MORGUE championship gold occurred over the following few years, at the peak of my alcoholism.

'Thank God for AA, Dr Jaye! When I made it through their doors, the Fellowship offered me a precious gift regarding Gary. My behaviour with him was interpreted as a symptom of the *disease*, or so *they* said. Like *all* the twelve-step tools and pressies, self-forgiveness has proven transitory though requiring vigilance. Those less accepting and unforgiving factions in my head committee want to be heard!

'Actually, back then, only the alcohol-driven negative voices were present, leading to escalated drinking and drug use. This, in turn, resulted in more regrettable actions, perpetuating the downward spiral.'

Michael heads backstage

'In mid-January, when Samuel was eight months old, Michael moved into a bedsit. We had agreed he'd continue to look after Sammy at my flat during the five shifts I worked at the hospital doing fieldwork. This arrangement meant he could answer the landline when Beverly and Ben called, ensuring no one in the family would know about the "vacation".'

Tears trickle down Francine's face as she continues: 'I convinced myself it was just a six-month hiatus. But, Michael went off script our first night apart. He rang the day after to provide a detailed account of the evening's adventures, which included chatting up nineteen-year-old student, Susie, at a venue featuring one of his favourite bands. He and Susie had christened the sleeper sofa.

'And you think I'm a codependent, Doc! This guy couldn't last an hour without a relationship. Okay, I'm not able to judge. At that time, I wouldn't have known a boundary from a bar of soap.'

Francine chuckles, 'Now at least I can recognise them when I'm about to trespass or have just breached one! Two weeks later, arriving home early from the hospital, I found Susie and Michael making out on what had been *our* sofa. It must have hurt but as you know, Doc, at least for me, sometimes anger and hurt get mixed up. In this situation, anger was easier to handle. It's always more empowering, isn't it, than pain? Pain is what victims feel.'

Dr Jaye prepares to interject, a rarity in their sessions. 'Francine', she speaks kindly, keeping her patient's gaze locked into the warmth of hers. 'The environment you grew up in was terrifying. And yes, I'm aware you weren't a child soldier in Sudan or a Holocaust survivor. I also know you minimise your childhood traumas suppressing feelings of vulnerability and fear. But you're entering a new stage in your therapy, and I sense those repressed feelings beginning to surface.'

At that moment, Francine feels young Franny's terror. But she's also apprehensive. A new phase? 'New' is daunting, and 'stage' suggests she's been graded and promoted to the next level, which adds more emotions to the mix. These will wait for another session as today's focus remains firmly in the past.

Greg enters downstage

'Several long-term voices in my head began pointing fingers at me: "Susie is karma for your fling with Gary." That particular chorus amplified the familiar tune of unworthiness. Frankie, ever ready to reject and revolt at the slightest hint of impending abandonment, chimed in, "Well, to hell with him. If he can stray, so can I."

'Enter Greg, a good-looking police officer who frequently dropped by Casualty. He was a chain smoker and drank beer non-stop when off duty. That's what we had in common except that, instead of beer, I drank whiskey. I bumped into him after work a few times at the local bar, which catered to shift workers. As Michael was going to have Sammy for the next weekend sleepover, *we* began to plan a weekend away in the mountains. *We*? More likely *me* fantasising yet another Hollywood romance film. This was back in the day, Dr Jamyang, when I hadn't yet learned that life doesn't generally proceed according to plan. You are allowed to laugh here, Doc, as that's a joke since it obviously remains a lesson unlearnt.

'Greg was just one in a line of bad boys. Perhaps I was inadvertently emitting a siren's song? Whatever the rationale, the next few men in my life were messed up alcoholics. Back then, though, I didn't have those words.

'Hmm, as always, it's hard for me to talk about sex in this room. I know – or kind of know – that you won't judge me, but I sense that you could be easily shocked, although you wouldn't show it.'

The therapist remains silent as Francine realises that these cognitive inhibitions are likely her own – transference.

'OK. It could be my own morality, prudishness or whatever.

'In any case, the bottom line was Greg's impotence. Specifically, he wasn't interested in sexual intercourse. He preferred to climax in other ways, which would be OK if there was any reciprocity. There was none, though. Greg was a user. After two days of pandering to his desires and receiving nothing in kind, I emerged inwardly dirty, like a prostitute without the *income*. Yes, Dr Jaye, there I go with my puns again. Maybe it's Franny easing the tension or helping to hide it.

'Those two days were like a black-and-white R-rated film. The woman reaches for the whisky bottle at the side of the bed as the man sleeps beside her. She drinks to tune out the committee. An unusual gathering as they are in consensus in their condemnation. Or likely those are the ones that she can hear. No individual voices, just a group chant: "Slut! Whore! Worthless tramp!" The liquor works its magic, and they are silenced briefly.

'I returned home a hungover post-marital virgin, so to speak. Two weeks later, when Michael again had Samuel for the weekend, on impulse, I decided to stay overnight in a motel with the aim of finding oblivion. Yes, dear Doctor, you heard correctly – "on impulse." Frankie – the adolescent or alcoholic me – scored high on impulsivity compared to the person you know.

'"Why a motel?" you might ask. To fit the inner sordidness, I suppose.

'You might be tempted to ask if I knew beforehand that I would ring Greg and invite him over? I do remember believing that this time it would be different. There was still a lingering hope that he'd be the answer to the pain.

'Fat chance.

'That night, the more I drank, the more morose I became. For me, the effects of alcohol were always a lottery. Not only was I unable to predict when my state of relative sobriety would shift to blackout oblivion, but I wasn't able to foresee when I'd become maudlin, or alternatively when I'd need to be centre stage dancing on tabletops. A lottery with a guaranteed loser every time – me.'

Francine addresses the space just to the right of her therapist. Making direct eye contact is currently out of the question, given that this particular memory still awakens a deep sense of shame. It is her standout MORGUE memory.

'Dr Jaye, as far as I know, you're not in AA. I hope you won't judge me but can see what happened as part of the disease?

'Greg agreed to come over, although I had to talk him into it. I'd convinced myself that not only did he love me but that the sex was going to be passionate and reciprocal.

'Well, surprise, surprise, that's not quite what happened. Within ten minutes of arriving, he'd taken off my clothes, ejaculated in my mouth, zipped up his pants, and left.'

Francine lacks the fair complexion prone to blushing. If she could, her skin would be ablaze. She averts her gaze even further to the right of Dr Jaye.

'In my distress, I curled into a foetal position – looking for nurturing from the mythical mother? After a while, I stopped and knew that I had to leave the room, or I'd begin to play games with razor blades. The whiskey bottle was empty.'

Enter Tom centre stage

'Around one in the morning, I found myself at a twenty-four-hour "family-style" restaurant. Collapsing into a booth, I ordered a coffee and began to look around. I could see a tall, lean guy moving around the kitchen. There was something about him that attracted me immediately: those Paul McCartney eyes.

'Remembering Greg, I began to cry again.'

'"What's the matter? Is the coffee that bad?" I looked up to see the guy with those eyes.'

'WAIT! STOP THE CAMERAS!

'If only.

'This was one of those critical moments where the "if onlys" will echo for a lifetime. If only I had turned away. If only I'd told him to go back to the kitchen. If only I'd told him to get fucked. If only I'd said, "What's your problem? Can't you let a young drunk woman cry alone?"

'But I didn't, and as a result, Danni and Rosa eventually came into my life. I stared at those eyes and that charming grin and thought I'd died and gone to heaven.

'Hell would be more accurate.

'As he empathised with my story, I felt an invigorating high, akin to what a gambler might experience when hearing the jingle of a winning slot machine. I walked into that diner as a self-loathing wreck, but exited with a renewed sense of worth. If this isn't indicative of an addictive personality, then what is?

'And so Tom entered my life. Perhaps it's the reason he stayed for quite awhile, Dr Jaye. Tom, the alcoholic, the ex-heroin addict, and the fugitive wanted in two states. Tom, the poorly educated hillbilly. Tom, incapable of either fidelity or friendship. And Tom, the unabashed lover whose sexual stamina many men would envy.'

17
TOM (TAPES 1 and 2): HEAD COMMITTEE MEETING

Tape 1

'OK, everybody. Most of you know me: Gabe, a recovering alcoholic counsellor. I'm pretty in touch with the emotional head space and just want to address some bad "vibes" I'm picking up. Maybe these are coming from some of you in the therapeutic community who are asking, "Why is *he* chairing another two meetings?"

'The answer is simple guys. I'm the only one of us who recorded counselling. The rest of you took notes and/or stared into space.'

'Here's what Frankie had to say in this first tape I'm playing today.'

The second time I saw Tom, I did kitchen prep work without pay just to be near him. After the shift ended, we spent a few hours at a local watering hole drinking Canadian whisky on the rocks (me) and scotch on the rocks (him).

From there we headed to my place where we had sex, which was like what I'd read about and seen in the movies. Keep in mind, Gabe, that back then, sensitivity to the female anatomy wasn't featured. Instead, machismo and endurance were high-lighted in film.

Frankie's description of Tom as a lover is evoking a response from some present. Accordingly, Gabe stops the tape.

The radical second wave sisterhood faction speaks as one.
'Frankie was breaking at least four rules here. A feminist does not want a lover who is dominating, a bit rough and controlling.'
Miriam has a few words to add on this topic: 'So, this is my daughter, the feminist. Ha, feminist, sheminist. Inside she's just the same as me.'
Normally muted by marijuana, Michael is fuming.
'For six years, I was as good and considerate a lover as any teenager could be and look what it got me! *Bupkis*! She dumps the SNAG[56] and ends up with Mr Neanderthal. *And* she loses weight. True, I told Frankie that I loved her body as it was, which wasn't a lie. I just didn't know how much better she could look.'
The 532 women with whom Tom fornicated prior to Frankie and the forty-seven he had sex with while he was in a relationship with her confirm her sexual experience.
'The guy was quite simply a stud. Not big on honesty, kindness, and fidelity, but how much can you expect from one person?'
Gabe wraps up the discussion as it's time to return to the recording.
'I would like to note that Tom's prowess in the sack was likely due, at least in part, to abuse of booze and a variety of other drugs. Length of time pre-climax correlated with chemical consumption, which means that we'd expect that Tom's entry into rehab about halfway through their time together would have translated into speedier intercourse. Frankie told me that it did.

---

56   SNAG is the acronym for Sensitive New Age Guy.

'Back to the tape …'

Tom was having sex with his roommate, Karen. We agreed to share him with me awarded Friday, Sunday, Tuesday and Thursday nights. Four out of seven felt like I was the more desired.

But the idea that I wasn't enough did hurt and led to a couple of months of fighting, which escalated to breakup #1. You see, Gabe, there were no muted colours here. Paint Tom and me with bright reds and oranges within a black background (which occasionally became the foreground).

It's hard to talk about that first separation. Lots of regret still. I was a different person when I drank and drugged. But you know all about that, right?

Take casual sex. That was diametrically incompatible with my sober morality, which, post-rape, bordered on prudishness. Yet I was like a wind-up toy that's been wound too tightly. Imagine a flower bed but instead of roses, petunias or tulips, there are men waiting for me to pick them. And so, I did. One at a time.

First, there was the Adonis-like Patrick whose genitalia rivalled my sister Sandra's foot-long Wayne. Then came Walter, allegedly separated, but not according to his sister, who found out about the affair and no longer wanted to be friends. It got worse, though, hanging out with Tom's friend, Mark, whose pregnant wife and three-year-old were out of town. Hanging out was our code for drinking and drugging. Again, though, like with Gary, there was a moral line that no amount of alcohol could erase. That is, if you use a Bill Clinton definition of moral lines. Like Ms Lewinski, I provided a helping hand.

There were other men and potentially violent situations but I was kept safe by HP or my PGA — maybe they're one and the same?

And my 'outsides' looked good. The PhD research fieldwork continued five days a week, 3 pm to 11 pm. One-year-old Samuel filled my mornings and days off. There was an ease within me when it came to Sammy. A joy. He was my anchor; a point of gravity and what I now recognise as a control.

*At night, though, and on the days that Samuel spent with Michael, I would pick up the drink or the man or the substance **and** the man to ward off my ever-present companions: an underlying trepidation and self-hatred. And the (not so) funny thing about that process is that, rather than helping, each drink, drug, or sexual activity only increased those companions' presence and voices. But when you're in the middle of the insanity, as everyone in 12 step programs know, you can't see it.*

Suicidal ideation, last encountered in adolescence, returned. Some on the committee were demanding retribution for Patrick, Walter, Mark, and the others.

Late one night, a bottle inside and another beside me, I retrieved the gun provided by a few friend cops from its hallway closet hiding place. Then, sitting on the bedroom floor, I held the revolver armed with one bullet to my head.

Is this a hyperbolic memory or was I seriously playing games with the gun? Probably a bit of both.

Did I squeeze the trigger? 'Irrelevant,' according to the cerebral naysayers the next morning.

'You have broken another of the myriad of rules: a good mother does not sit on the floor in a drunken state holding a gun to her head.'

Hungover and remorseful, I made my way to a neighbourhood counselling centre. Now, Gabe, we both know that a treatment program would have been a better choice but at that time I had zero knowledge of the disease and thought that alcoholics were men living under a bridge.

The psychiatrist I saw there, no doubt responding to the Russian roulette episode, prescribed anti-depressants and referred me to a counsellor for weekly chats. I didn't go and I stopped the medication after a week. It wasn't working. Swallowing the tablets with vodka or bourbon might have played a part in the pills' inefficacy?

Once again, a mental health practitioner did not ask about the (mis)use of alcohol and other drugs. The therapist, if asked to define alcoholic, might have agreed with how I defined it before I came into twelve-step programs. Without addiction or trauma in his radar, he focused on treating my symptoms with medication. He was in good company.

That one-session nameless shrink feels the need to defend the diagnosis or lack thereof and asks Gabe to hit 'pause.'

'This young woman, although presenting with sporadic suicidal ideation, did not manifest any other visible symptoms. On the contrary, she appeared to be a mature and well-balanced doctoral student and new mother, albeit with low affect. We spent most of the time discussing her PhD fieldwork at length as it was relevant to my own work.'

Nancy, Frankie's rehab counsellor, wants to ensure that everyone present understands Frankie's behaviour in the context of the *disease.*

'As we say in AA, "It takes what it takes." Meaning we each have to reach our "bottom" to make it into recovery.'

'Without the program, she lacked faith, the antidote to fear. No "day at a time" to make life seem manageable or even doable. No first step yet and no acceptance of powerlessness over alcohol and alcoholics.'

Resume tape 1

If I had possessed a crystal ball and looked into it, I'd have seen that what had appeared to be the 'final' drunken cursing and abuse scene with Tom was small potatoes compared to what lay ahead. I did not.

Instead, in desperation after a couple of months apart, like a heroin addict needing a fix, I rang him, and we arranged to meet the following day for a coffee.

Tom was sweet, affectionate, and communicative. These weren't words usually associated with him. But that morning, we talked for hours about what had been going on in our lives. Karen was out of the picture; she had moved out. He told me that he had no sexual interest in the overweight sixteen-year-old replacement flatmate/waitress. And I did believe him because, Gabe, as you know from your time with Jimmy, there's a part of us that must. The alternative hurts too much.

Without Karen in the equation, it felt like we were forming a family. Tom would come over in the morning without sex on the agenda. Instead, he'd kneel to make his six-foot-two-inches closer to Sammy's size. They'd play for hours. Sammy quickly grew attached. This element of domesticity was evident when, after a couple of weeks, Tom asked me if I'd add his clothes to my daily load of laundry. Each sock, pair of briefs, shirt, and piece of clothing was placed with love first in the washing machine and then the dryer, folded and put into the basket.

My laundry service included delivery. Arriving at Tom's apartment, I knocked quietly since he had worked the previous night's graveyard shift. No answer. As the door was unlocked, I walked through the living room to Tom's bedroom where he was asleep on the floor mattress. Only one problem with this picture, Gabe. Have you guessed?

Lying next to Tom with her arms wrapped around him was the naked teeny-bopper roommate.

Oddly enough, I felt calm … or numb. Who knows? I wasn't doing much on the feeling front in those days. After all, this was me – the Tom-addicted Frankie. I did methodically throw the clothing around the living room as I left quietly.

Tom rang me later. Guess he couldn't see a way of denying it. He went with remorse, claiming that it was a one-off marijuana-related accident. Yes, he said 'accident.' 'I'm kicking her out and it will never happen again, Frankie.' Obviously, that was a message that I literally inhaled.

After Gabe turns off the tape player, Sally explains Frankie's 'inhalation' from the Al-Anon perspective.

'Just as severe hangovers and guilt don't stop the alcoholic from drinking, as this tape has shown, knowledge of deceit and infidelity does not end addiction to the alcoholic. She was on the downward course necessary for redemption. *It takes what it takes.* Frankie was now well and truly hooked, which meant that Tom moved in with her and Sammy soon after this incident, as we'll hear next. Please, Gabe.'

Tape 2

For the next two years, Tom and I partied hard. And for me, considered to be an AA high bottom drunk but a CODA low one, remembering is even more important.

We swallowed or snorted whatever he had handy; that is, everything except heroin. Tom had told me shortly after we met about how he had used smack but had stopped a few months earlier. 'I came off it in my apartment using three or four casks of wine to get me through the first few days,' he'd explained. I was impressed that this guy had managed to kick a heroin habit. Didn't see the forest for the trees, did I?

Initially, we did alcohol in the same way; that is, excessively without ever leaving a drop. Going out for dinner usually meant drinking cocktails until the kitchen closed for the night. But Gabe, don't worry about caloric intake. There were the olives in the vodka martinis, cherries in the Manhattans, and complimentary bowls of nuts!

Some nights I'd drink him under the table. Other times, my erratic tolerance would decrease quickly, and I'd land in blackout land to be joined later by Tom. Just two alcoholics having a riotously good time that neither would remember.

Almost out of time but I'd like to share more about Tom in the remaining ten minutes. It's taken me years to see that he wasn't a villain. Instead, I'd say he was the victim of a damaged childhood.

In a drunken conversation in the early days, Tom, close to tears, told me how his mother, Louise, had never visited him in prison. Then, when I met her and Tom's stepfather, Tony, on our first holiday trip just after Sammy's first birthday, I learned that both were major league partiers. At first this was appealing, since Lou and Tony bore no resemblance to Bev and Ben or Miriam and Henry. Tony would joke about Lou's behaviour during blackouts – how sometimes, she thought the bedroom closet was the toilet. Lou would come right back at him with a litany of droll anecdotes about Tony's drunken debauchery.

The second night of this first visit, we went out for dinner. Like our Tom and Frankie dinners, the four of us drank continuously from five in the afternoon until about two in the morning when we gorged on barbequed ribs. The last thing that I remember, prior to blacking out, was sitting on Tony's lap in the car. I was told later by Tom that he'd cleaned up my BBQ rib vomit trail from the front door of Lou and Tony's house, down the hallway to the bathroom.

Novel way to meet your future in-laws, huh?

As Michael was happy to take care of Samuel for a few more days, we decided to head to the Appalachians to visit Lou's (and Tom's) hillbilly extended family. It was there, Gabe, in a cloud of marijuana smoke, that Tom, an alcoholic drug addict wanted by the law in two states, asked me to marry him.

My affirmative response was a one-way ticket to a relationship rollercoaster. Over the next eight years, I often felt scared and desperate, but it was never monotonous, predictable, or unromantic.

As the second tape has now ended, Gabe opens the floor for comments. First, Henry and then Miriam:

'He was a loser. She wasted years of her life with a drug addict hillbilly who couldn't add six and six.'[57]

'*Oi vey.* My daughter the idiot. Who does she pick as husband #2? A goy, yes but not just any goy. This one had no education. He drank too much, and he messed around on her plenty even before the ceremony. Did she care? No. I remember when she telephoned Henry and me to announce her engagement. My brilliant daughter, almost with a doctorate then, she says, "It may be the disaster of the century but it's also the romance of the century!" Romance, schomance.

'Henry and I, though, we always stood by her. You'll see. All the phone calls where she cried to us about what he was up to. And

---

57 Wrong, Henry! In fact, Tom's IQ was well above average. He did have an undiagnosed learning disability. An ability to mask it could be seen as a sign of high intelligence. ADHD wasn't being screened for back then, either, but we now know that chemical dependency is about twice as common in people who have it.

I listened without trying to fix it. Who could fix it? She made her bed. Now she had to lie in it.'

Miriam doesn't get the last word. She rarely does and must be satisfied with having the last sigh.

'As a representative sample of "Tom's women", we must say that Frankie wasn't capturing his true essence. Words may be an inadequate way of conveying Tom's power over us. Within the man's silent and seemingly strong exterior, the child, Tommy, needed a mother or someone to nurture him. Each of us desperately wanted to be that person. The charm, the magnetism and the raw animal appeal coupled with the little boy we could sense within triggered our need to rescue.'

'It's true that he was a bastard and quite the master of emotional and sexual abuse, but through it all, we remained loyal, true (emotionally black and) blue Tom women.

'Like Frankie, we know now what mental games were being played, although of course we didn't at the time. When he left, and yes, he always did leave, we had too much accumulated shame to know whether he was the wrong-doer or just an innocent pawn in our own downward trajectories.'

18
TOM (TAPES 3 and 4): HEAD COMMITTEE MEETING

'For our next session, as she did when talking about Sammy's operation, Frankie brought in a couple of photos. This may have helped her to talk about painful experiences.'

Tape 3

Gabe, here's a photo of Samuel, age seventeen months, taken about a month before the travels with Tom began. Sammy is standing at the curb waiting for Michael to pick him up for the weekend. He's wearing a blue leisure suit. You can see long tendrils of hair covering his neck and an intense facial expression. Sammy was a serious little boy. He's watching each car intently as it passes by looking eagerly for Daddy Mike.

The routine changed a month later with Tom's loss of employment. We decided to move down south near Tony and Louise since my hospital research stage was now over. We loaded up our worldly possessions (mine, as Tom had none) and headed south. Over the next eighteen months, we moved four more times, I followed Tom around Florida, grasping Samuel tightly with one hand and my typewriter case gripped with the other. A thesis needed to be written. A child to be loved and adored.

The amalgamated shame subcommittee isn't happy.

'Good mothers, trying to break the generational cycle of abuse, do not take the nineteen-month-old away from his biological cannabis-smoking-but-very-affectionate father and substitute with an addict unable to show affection.'

Sally is quick to defend her sponsee.

'Like any addiction, choice wasn't a factor. Frankie was hooked on Tom. It was inevitable. Her disease was hitting rock bottom.'

And there's another voice here today defending Frankie's parenting at that time. Samuel wants to share a letter his mother tucked into a 'special Sammy's memory box' when he was twenty months old.

I'm writing this, Sammy, for when you're older. You can read it then and remember. Daddy Mikey is picking you up tomorrow morning, and you'll be away for a week. He loves you too, baby, and wants to spend time with you so much.

I love you very, very much. I'll miss you, from early morning when I normally come into your bedroom to 'liberate' you, and you greet me with a big smile and a hug – right up to bedtime when I tuck you in, read your bedtime stories, and then you roll onto your side and drift off to sleep like a good little boy.

Today, we sat on the couch, each eating an apple. It was your first, and you were serious about munching it just like me. We then played with your green truck, and you laughed as I pretended it crashed off the coffee table. And we did 'huggy' a few times – you'd dash into my arms from across the room, grinning broadly, then pivot, run back, and then go again with me saying, 'Huggy, huggy, huggy bear!'. We did our other usual stuff, like playing with light switches and bouncing on the bed.

Being such a good fellow, you even helped unload the dishwasher. You carefully carried each fork, spoon, and butter knife to me.

We also went for a walk. It was so windy! Each time a car drove by, you'd stop and stare as it passed. And boy oh boy, did you ever walk! Finally, I had to pick you up and turn you around for us to head back home.

You picked up blades of grass and leaves, presenting them to me as gifts.

Tonight, when you had your bath, as I laid you back in my arm to rinse your hair, you stared at me and smiled serenely and trustingly.

It was a precious day for me to keep forever.

Tape 3 (cont.)

OK, guess I need to tell you about wedding #2, Gabe. Here are a few photos to help.

There we are poolside at Louise and Tony's. You see the woman next to me? That's Frieda. She's the only person (besides me) who witnessed both the Michael and Tom knots being tied. No Henry and Miriam in the picture. They used their annual overseas holiday as an excuse. Sandra's life and her drinking were already too unmanageable to plan and execute a trip, and Jake, well, he was in the midst of a non-contact period with family as he prepared to 'come out'.

Here's a photograph of the cake arriving unescorted in a taxi's back seat. Tom and Tony had gone to fetch it but decided to have a drunken afternoon instead.

Speaking of which, Gabe, everyone in that first photo, except for nineteen-month-old Sammy, including the judge who slurred the vows, was wasted. Note, though, that despite or because of inebriation, Tom, sexual Olympian, scored a ten for wedding night endurance and frequency. Maybe he'd been faithful that day.

So that was the wedding – no doubt an event that no one remembered.

A few days afterwards, we relocated to the central part of Florida. The restaurant chain, which Tom had been working for, was opening another 'store'.

Surrounded by all of our belongings, Sammy and I were left at the 'dirt' house[58] by Tom on his way to another part of the state with our only vehicle.

Some people live with unpacked boxes for months. Not me. I always had an urgent need to have everything in its place – bookshelves, knick-knacks, the lot. This was especially true for Sammy's room and his toy shelves where all trucks had to be lined up in the correct way. The rocking horse placed in the same corner in each place we lived, etc, etc. A manifestation of a deep underlying insecurity or yet another sign of anal retention, or both coming together in OCD?

Anyway, back to the unpacking – I asked John, the shy, good-looking seventeen-year-old son of the landlord if he could help me put up some shelving. He offered to return that evening with his dad's electric drill. By the time he knocked at the door, little Samuel was fast asleep, and I was in the middle stages of inebriation; the point where everything felt good but not drunk enough to engage in adultery. After John completed the carpentry tasks, I did invite him to dance, though.

---

58 Frankie coined that nickname for Samuel given the absence of grass or landscaping. The label was a portent of what was to come.

One dance and one kiss – the extent of my infidelity whilst cohabiting with Tom, which, as you'll see, was nowhere in his league. And yet, being the shame-ridden or moralistic person that a non-intoxicated Triple F was and is, I carried baggage about this for years.

The seven months of isolation on the outskirts of a small coastal village with no friends, car, or work outside of home went something like this:

Two-year-old Sammy and I had a regular routine. During the day, we played at home and/or went for walks to nearby playgrounds, shops, and to the sea. All audio was by me for the first months as Samuel did not speak a word until he was twenty-six months. No 'baby talk'. When he spoke, it was in complete sentences; almost as if he had been soaking in all my words, pondering, and now was ready to verbalise them.

While Samuel napped mid-afternoon, I worked on my thesis.

Then, at four o'clock each day, I'd open a bottle of whisky or vodka, which I'd slowly sip through the evening while writing my dissertation from 7:30 – Samuel's bedtime – until midnight when Tom returned. The first draft of the PhD thesis, some 300 pages, was written during that period in the 'dirt' house.

There were few visitors. John didn't return. Sandra did manage to organise a trip with her three-year-old daughter Brooke and nine-month-old Sean. She and Wayne had reproduced after their divorce. Now, they were in the process of severing all ties for good.

Sandra was a mess. She got off the plane drunk and remained in that state the week with us.

'Man, does she have a problem,' I thought, when early one morning, I spotted her giving Sean a bottle of milk and herself a bottle of beer. As soon as the two hands on the clock joined at

the top, I joined her, though, Gabe. Except that I skipped the beer and went directly to real liquor.

A year later, when Sandra landed in a rehab program for chemical addiction, it was the long-term model. Tom's stint in a similar facility was about fifteen months later and mine came a year or so after his.

And that's it for today, Gabe. Sorry I've gone over time. How about next week we'll have a short session? Not that I'm trying to take charge of counselling. Who, me?

'Hi, everyone. I'm Nan, a grateful member of AA. I'd like to share a bit about how we in the program see these moves. They're what we call *geographicals*. Frankie thought that if they were physically removed from Tom's parents' alcoholism, then they – him in particular – wouldn't get as drunk as often. Unfortunately, she found that, as we say about geographicals, she had to take herself and Tom, too.

'Nothing changes.

'Also, could I please make a few observations about this stage of Frankie's addiction?

'For the first eighteen months of the relationship, at night-time after Samuel was asleep or earlier if he was with Michael, she matched Tom drink for drink and drug for drug.

'Incrementally, however, this changed. As her focus moved more towards Tom's drinking, Frankie began to consciously and unconsciously control her own intake and behaviour.'

Tape 4

OK, Gabe – back to Florida we go.

Our next stop in that state was a return to Tony and Louise's neighbourhood for two months.

Henry and Miriam were in the city (Miami) at that time as Miriam's sisters who lived there had organised a thirtieth wedding anniversary 'do' for my parents. The day after the party, they visited me and Sammy, which I figured was related to my phone request for a loan to help me travel north for the doctoral dissertation defence. Their wanting to discuss it face to face wasn't a big deal as they'd always come through materially, if not in other ways.

Henry cleared his throat.

'Frankie. I've given your application for financial assistance a great deal of thought and have decided to comply.[59] *However, I will defer the payment until a week before you are due at the university. We are concerned that the money will be spent in other pursuits.'*

Gabe, for the second time in my life, I lost my temper with Henry. Remember what happened the first time? I was kicked down a flight of stairs. Well, this time, I did the kicking (out), screaming:

'Leave my house right now. Out! Out! I don't want your money. You can take it and shove it! Just get out.'

As I'm saying this, even though I've already shared it twice in fifth steps, there's still a lot of crap inside. Poor Henry and Miriam. To be spoken to by their daughter like that.

Not to defend my behaviour but intertwined with the anger, there was hurt. In my screenplay, the proud parents provided the airfare with joy and pride. Once again, I was searching for acceptance from outside, not getting it and hating myself more. Another in the interconnecting downward spirals.

---

59   It's worth noting again that this was Henry's manner when speaking to Jake, Sandra, and Triple F throughout his life. Formality and remoteness further delineated the hierarchical nature of the relationships.

'How dare he not trust me with money?' I muttered, when a more accurate question could have been, 'How could he possibly trust me when it came to financial affairs?'

There was my track record. Not a good one when measured against their standards. They'd never bought anything on time or with credit, whereas I hadn't purchased any object of value without a payment plan. This was anathema to Henry and Miriam.

My history of selling everything that they gave me could have further reduced their confidence. There was the trip to Europe, too – a squandering of that gift. And my choice in partners was seen as appalling. Further, despite my best drinking impression management, they were concerned about my alcohol and drug intake.

Given that context, it's surprising that they gave me the money. However, unsurprisingly, after a few days, my self-will and temper deflated, I had pleaded successfully.

Such supplication was becoming normative. Conflicts between me and Tom were taking place regularly. Invariably drunk, he'd return home late from a 12 - to 14 -hour shift at the restaurant. I'd question where he'd really been and complain about his absences. He'd react with anger telling me to 'Fuck off,' or 'If you weren't such a bitch, I'd be home more'.

My rage smouldered, and, if Samuel, at this time my primary alcohol inhibitor, was away with Michael, and I was alone, I'd seek solace in the bottle.

Sammy's time with Daddy Mike led to frequent drunken dramatics, which you'll see tended to involve cars and my begging for Tom's forgiveness.

Here's an example. Tom and I decided to have dinner at a seaside restaurant. As was our practice, we'd sit in the al fresco dining area but forget to order food before the kitchen closed.

Our alcohol consumption correlated with a shift in conversation from light banter to heavy acrimony.

One evening after our non-existent 'dinner', I was driving home on a six-lane highway when Tom became verbally abusive. I pulled over onto the shoulder and told him to get out.

'Fine, and fuck you, bitch', was his parting shot as I took off with a screech of tires.

Predictably, I returned a few minutes later, driving slowly now as I searched for him. And, again true to form, I pulled over and pleaded.

'Tommy, please get in the car! My bad for telling you to get out. I'm a horrible person to have done it. I love you, Tommy. Please come back. Please!'

Another evening, a different restaurant, same plot, and a similar dialogue. This time, Tom decided to leave in the middle of the meal, taking the car. Without any transport, it took me over an hour to walk (or stagger) home. By 2 am, he hadn't returned. I knew that he was with another woman. Not a new suspicion, Gabe, but I've sort of neglected to mention it. Desolate and suicidal, I reached out by telephoning the local Helpline. The counsellor's initial recommendation was that I stop drinking (that night). As the only bottle of booze in the house was now empty, that was easy. Her next suggestion was harder: follow up with a counsellor alone or with Tom.

'No way. I might be advised to leave him. Or I could be asked about the role that alcohol was playing in my life.'

Tom returned close to 4 am. Having barred him from the bedroom by locking the door, within half an hour I was in the living room where he had passed out on the couch, pleading with him to come to bed. Desperate to be held. Needing to know that I was still loved. Still?

So, you see, Gabe, begging had become a routine practice. And I'm glad today's a half hour. Thanks for the hug.

With the end of the fourth tape, the Al-Anon and CODA members of the committee are nodding their heads. As Frankie's first sponsor, Sally speaks as their representative.

'Amazing isn't it how low a person addicted to an addict can go in that addiction. Tom was to Frankie as heroin is to a junkie. And, as with drug addiction, Frankie felt increasingly worse about herself with each incident: shame-producing supplication and subservience. Same downward journey that takes place with any substance abuse. Cunning, baffling, and powerful.

'To beg the abuser to return and hurt us again fulfils the insanity criterion implied in our second step: "Came to believe that a power greater than ourselves could *restore us to sanity.*" It needs to get worse for us to take the first step and accept our powerlessness. Can't get the second step without the first.

'We do believe that everything happens for a reason. There could never have been a transition to Francine, who could reach out and help other women and children, without the life and times – however painful and fearful – of Franny and Frankie.'

19
SHARING THE TOM ERA REFLECTIVE JOURNAL IN THERAPY

'**G**'day, Dr Jaye. Funny thing happened a few days ago. I found *this* journal which covers a lot of the really hard time period with Tom that we're about to cover. It was hidden away but I guess it's time to read at least some of it. "No pain, no gain" as we say in the Fellowships.'

February

I have decided to start a reflective journal (RJ) to mark the rite of passage to being an (almost) doctor! There's no one in Jacksonville for me to talk to. Maybe journaling will be like chatting with a (quiet) friend?

A few weeks ago, Sammy and I followed Tom here. The distance from Lou and Tony hasn't meant matrimonial bliss. Actually, the relationship with Tom has gone further downhill. We're not partying much together anymore.

Instead of buying myself a quart of whisky, I now buy several 'vodka martinis for two'.

'I'll have my first drink at four o'clock; the second one at 5 pm'. 'No more alcohol after 6:30.' Or 'I will stop drinking when the second or the third is empty.'

There are times, dear journal, when the absence of stupor feels pretty crap. And the controlling can be exhausting mentally.

'Dr Jaye, that last bit must seem peculiar or even oxymoronic? Over the years, we have established that one of my middle names is "Control." So, you'd think this type of drinking would be like water off a duck's back?'

Predictably, Dr Jaye looks intently at Francine before she speaks.

'What you have described involves on-going thought, or what some *might* call obsession. There was certainly a payoff, which would be the same as the payoff for any obsessive thought. By focusing on your own and Tom's alcohol intake, you facilitated the repression of emotions you could not afford to feel at that time. As we've seen in therapy, that outcome is the primary purpose of this type of cognition.'

March

Sometimes, I do let go of limiting what I drink and kill two birds with one stone by swigging Tom's scotch and then diluting what remains in the bottle. More liquor for me and less for Tom. Ideal result!

'Well, that last entry I just read out reminds me of what Sally, my first Al-Anon sponsor, said to me after hearing my first open AA meeting 'lead' about how I diluted Tom's booze. Evidently, if she'd known about this earlier when I came into Al-Anon, she *might* have gently pointed out that the typical co-alcoholic pours the booze down the sink. It's the "double winners" who drink it.

'Thinking about those days reminds me of something that AA Nan, my hospital counsellor, said at rehab that really resonated. She wrote on the whiteboard: "Social drinkers do not think about how much they drink." That statement broke down a lot of my denial. I'd been comparing my drinking to Tom and Sandy.

'Mind you, that was before drink driving safety campaigns. Now, many non-alcoholic drinkers do limit their alcohol consumption if they're going to be behind the wheel. I know I've been to work "dos" where people have said that.'

April

Writing on the plane heading back from my doctoral defence. God, I hate flying.

Tom has been home alone for a few days since Michael has Sammy. Alone? Highly debatable since last night close to midnight, I rang him. No answer. I started imagining scenarios from a fatal car accident to a sexually satiated Tom in somebody else's bed.

Dear RJ, the preferred fantasy between those two is Tom's imminent demise.

Just before 2 am, he answered the 232nd call. Slurring, he assured me that he'd been bar hopping with one of the cooks from the restaurant.

I guess that what they say – we believe what we want to believe – is true or, it might be that for me, it's more about believing only what I'm able to believe.

...

Been back a couple of weeks. My PhD oral exam was a success. The examiners were impressed that the entire thesis, written in absentia, needs little revision. Why doesn't it feel like I thought it would? Has it ever?

Francine stops reading. Another of her inner discoveries is emerging.

'Those head committee members I've told you about, Dr Jaye? Let me say again first that they're not voices in the psychotic sense! Just thoughts associated with specific people who take up space in my mind.

'Well, quite a few of the residents didn't agree with the examination outcome.

'"You fluked it." That's the inner critics, who, at that time in my life, were in the majority. "If they knew your real stupidity and incompetence, man would they take away the PhD. They probably just wanted to get you out of the system."

'And then there's what my critical parents were saying out loud (and internally).

'"So, now what? Do you have a job? No! If you'd become a secretary, you'd have been earning and saving money for the last ten years. Wait, not the saving part – not Frankie. Instead, what do you have? No job. My daughter the doctor, *ench*!?"[60]

'To other people, though, Miriam offered a different message.

'"Yes, my daughter Frankie just received her PhD in psychology. She wrote a brilliant thesis about emergency departments and those poor miserable women who let their husbands beat them up."

'Yes, that was my mother, Dr Jaye. And no surprise I'm sure for you but Henry, who worshipped at the shrine of science and mathematics, had little to say except a few indifferent comments comparing the social sciences to the *hard* sciences unfavourably, implying that a PhD in the former was of minimal worth.

'"Her disciplinary strengths are synthetic, soft and female."'[61]

---

60   The *ench* sound, which is not pronounced phonetically, is a guttural noise communicated by Jewish mothers world-wide to express scorn. It is often accompanied by a shrugging of the shoulders.
61   This is arguably not just a masculine belief but reflects a similar gendered hierarchy in academia and other professional arenas.

May

My doctoral stipend has now lapsed. We're living on Tom's wages.

Samuel is my sole companion, joy, and raison d'être. Colour our times together in mostly bright and warm hues.

Wherever we've lived since Sammy was a toddler, he and I walk to the nearest public library several times a week. As we both love books, libraries are a free treat. Same for parks and playgrounds except they're even better. Outside is always better. The air inside Henry's house was hard to breathe.

There is a moment of silence.

'Francine, as a child, the inside of any house you lived in was trauma-filled. You were frightened and disassociating in order to survive. Remember escaping on Queenie, your old bicycle? School was not pleasant either and you felt rejected. Plus, the sexual assaults took place indoors.

'But out in the open air? Safety. The chance to breathe. Is it any surprise how much your daily run means to you? And, of course even more with Covid, lockdowns and staying a Novid.'

Atypically, Dr Jaye continues to speak.

'And Francine, you had to be guarded in your childhood. You were never allowed to be the unfettered Franny. But, that child within could play and be present with Sammy. And with your other children and grandchildren. There is an advantage to having your inner child nearby.'

With a different sort of sigh than her mother (one of relief), Francine continues reading.

I haven't had a drink for five days. Want Tom to see that it's possible. His drinking has gotten worse and when he's drunk, which is all the time, he's not nice. Good thing he comes home after Sammy is asleep.

There's no one to talk to about what it's like living with him. I know that he's screwing around. Have sensed it for ages but yesterday it was sort of confirmed. When I rang the restaurant, the waitress (who it turns out had been fired a few hours earlier) told me that he'd left, as usual, with another waitress, Mindy.

'They go out all of the time,' she said. 'Like when you were out of town, I saw him pick her up at 11 one night, after her shift.'

RJ, I feel stunned even though I've known all along ... sort of. But thoughts are one thing; their validation another.

So, I came up with a plan to catch him in the act.

I went next door and asked the mother of a four-year-old who Samuel plays with occasionally, if she'd watch him and if I could borrow her car. Then, playing private investigator, I drove to Mindy's house. No sign of our Dodge. From there, I went past the motels in the area. Again though, no sighting.

'OK Dr Jaye, I admit that the PI bit sounds slightly crazy. Well not "crazy" in psychiatric terms of course – just sort of nuts, as in a tad whacky?

'Turned out that if I had driven further along the strip running adjacent to the beach, I would have found the Dodge parked in front of a Holiday Inn. Only the best ocean views for Tommy.'

She is silent long enough for her therapist to speak.

'That must have been a difficult time period for you Francine. Isolated from friends, no alcohol or PhD work to self-medicate.'

Dr Jaye's words help Francine to feel the pain and understand her actions.

'It got worse, Doc, as you'll hear with the next entry.'

I decided not to tell Tom about my suspicions (and the corroborating evidence). Yeah, right. Dear journal friend, when he came home last night, I couldn't help it. Predictably, he denied the allegations arguing that the waitress had been retaliating for losing her job.

When I accused him of lying, he was furious: 'You're a paranoid bitch, Frankie. Always creating dramas when they don't exist. You need to be centre stage.'

The shifting of blame began. As per our usual dialogue, I was the one apologising and begging for forgiveness. But this time, it included something really, really difficult to write about. But I think it's important that I get the exact words onto paper.

'No, Tom, please don't. It hurts.' I am crying.

'Come on, baby. If you want me to stay with you …'

Afterwards, I went into the bathroom to wash the stinging hurt and tried to scrub off the filth. I felt raped.

Silence.

'I felt raped, Dr Jaye, because I *was* sodomised without consent.

'I realised that years later when interviewing survivors. Some told *my* story — of giving in and lying there, passively coerced by a partner who threatened to leave, withhold affection, or find someone else if not acquiesced to. Such threats prey on those who already feel worthless inside. When the abuser commands, "Roll over", you comply. With each instance, the self-loathing intensifies.

'Their naming what had happened as rape allowed me to do the same.'

Dr Jaye's eyes convey compassion.

'And Francine, you have paid it forward with your writing and public identification as a survivor, which I know has not been easy.'

June

What to do now that I have the doctorate? Henry and Miriam have asked me this for ten years. I don't have a clue!"

...

You won't believe what's happened, RJ?!?! I've got a job! I've fluked into a university position up north: a research and teaching centre dedicated to violence against women!

'Guess I don't need to tell you about the self-doubt and the creeping feelings of hypocrisy?'

Once again, Dr Jamyang's next words help Francine to understand and accept.

'Yes, that makes sense. As your research highlighted, many survivors of family violence struggle to recognise the abuse until the relationship concludes.

'You had to work through the denial. But, without that period of your life, how could you have helped others?'

Tom seems to be excited about the prospect of moving north even though this time, he is following me. I do wonder sometimes if it ever bothers him that I have twelve years more education and will be making more money than he earns?

'Well, over the years I've thought about what seemed to be Tom's feminist enlightenment. It's possible that, within this hard-drinking and drugging mute philanderer and philistine exterior, lay a pretty enlightened fellow for those times, Dr Jaye. After all, atypically, he was pretty domestic: cooking was an effortless talent.

'There are a few alternative theories – as you know, I'm not short on those. Maybe Tom drank his feelings? Or, also likely that the hold he had over me, coupled with other women, were sufficient ego supplements to outweigh my degrees, salary, and career.'

August

Once again, we have packed up our stuff and headed off in a rental truck. Fifth time in twenty months.

This time though it means moving away from Mindy, further distant from Tony and Louise, and towards my financial independence. Things are going to be better now. I hope.

September

A couple of weeks after we arrived, Tom got a restaurant assistant manager job about an hour's drive from the small university town where we now live. This means that he's gone for even longer hours than in Florida and the workplace is too far away for me to check up on him.

Mind you, I haven't really had time or head space to worry.

I've been adjusting to major changes – some good and some not so good. First the latter. Now that I'm working, Samuel must go to childcare, and I feel sad and guilty – same as when I left him to do my fieldwork.[62]

On the positive side of the ledger, for the first time in my life, RJ, I am employed in a paid full-time position, which I absolutely love!

'I felt like Superwoman, Monday through Friday, entering a metaphorical call box, a confident, articulate and ardent feminist professor would emerge. I'd walk from the crèche to my office – a

---

62 The guilt of being a 'working mother' was her companion throughout the child-rearing years. It did not seem to be experienced by the fathers, whose Y chromosomes may include a gene for guilt-free parenting.

beautiful room with the sun from two large windows offsetting the dark mahogany bookcases and wooden panels.

'And Dr Jaye, I did feel ecstatic about that job from the start until its calamitous end seven years later. Ah, yes, my career history … possibly our second decade of therapy?'

October

Academia is my habitat. It feels more like home than home ever has.

Guess I'm a natural teacher. That's the feedback from Bill, my department head. Teaching is sort of like acting; being centre stage in the classroom. Students come up after class to compliment my energy, enthusiasm and passion. Feels good.

…

Six weeks after starting this job, I've been feeling nauseous and my breasts are swollen. You guessed it, RJ! I'm pregnant – due in spring when Samuel turns four.

On one level, this isn't a surprise – yet, on another, it is.

I hadn't written in here about contemplating having Tom's baby after the revelation about Mindy. I had my IUD removed months ago.

'Given that the pregnancy was planned, are you wondering why I was taken aback? Guess back then, planning didn't necessarily mean I considered the consequences fully. Impulsiveness?

'It was a deliberate choice. After the sexual assault, the thought of having a baby surfaced. Dr Jaye, this might sound irrational- particularly when living with infidelity and other psychological abuse; weight gain and body changes aren't typically sources of security. But I guess I thought that if we had a child, Tom wouldn't abandon or reject me. Maybe it would keep him faithful or make him love me more … Right. We know how that tends to pan out. But I wasn't alone. Many women in my research and in twelve-step meetings have shared similar sentiments.'

Dr Jaye doesn't respoind directly, but her words are comforting.

'Parenting has proven to be one pathway for you to achieve self-actualisation. Determined to break the generational cycle of dysfunction, you stay connected in these relationships, being "present" except during your months of clinical depression.

'Indeed, there have been some claims from your youngest of "smother mothering". Every parent is flawed. You're only human. Your children haven't endured the abuse, neglect, and traumas that you faced. However, like everyone, their upbringing wasn't without its imperfections. You're not the Buddha.'

The last remark is signature Dr Jaye.

20
FRANKIE'S CO-ALCOHOLISM BOTTOM: OPEN MEETING

'Hi, I'm Sally, a grateful member of Al-Anon. In today's open meeting, we're looking at what brought Frankie into Al-Anon. I'll begin by sharing some of her story, but please do remember this meeting is open to anyone with experiences or insights from this time.

'Living with Tom, erratic behaviour had become the norm. His crawling into the house at two in the morning was no longer unusual. Demanding dinner at that hour was expected, as were Frankie's pleas for him to stay.

One evening though, something outside of the (bizarre) norm occurred. Tom returned shortly after dinner. He went into the downstairs bathroom, and soon after, three-year-old Samuel entered the living room in tears: "I was trying to make a big poo. Why did Daddy Tom pull me off the toilet, Mommy?" Sammy, or specifically, his right to space, had been violated. This made Frankie's skin crawl.[63]

---

63 This took place prior to absorbing the Al-Anon lesson that Tom was not a bad person but a sick man.

'The incident with Sammy provided the shock Frankie needed to finally leave the marriage and the home, which had, for the past four months, been the backdrop for numerous co-alcoholic dramas. Frankie, six months pregnant, quickly packed some bags and took Sammy to university guest housing. About a week later, they moved into a three-bedroom apartment near the campus. In the Fellowship, we might call this a *domicile geographical*.

'Fast forward two weeks: early evening and Samuel was asleep. Toys, books, and assorted items were neatly organised. The wooden rocking chair sat in one corner while the large Tonka trucks were parked tidily next to the shelving. The bed-cover and curtains were a collage of *Sesame Street* characters with pictures of Cookie Monster and Bert and Ernie decorating the walls. Mindful of ensuring at least a semblance of security with continuity of interior design, this room was an almost exact replica of its five predecessors over the prior two years.

'As Sammy slept, Frankie sat alone in the living-room, surrounded by unpacked boxes. She was consumed by obsessive thoughts: "I *have* to see him. I *must* have him. I *need* him."

'*We* say that's what lies at the core of codependency: the irrational need for one to have their perception of reality validated by another. In this case, Frankie desperately wanted Tom to see that his worldview and opinion of her were skewed.

'This flawed thinking led Frankie to do what any self-respecting co-alcoholic does after being "dry" for a few weeks – she sought out Tom. Earlier that day, she'd met her downstairs neighbour, who had two teenage daughters. The older daughter, Tracey, agreed to babysit Samuel, enabling Frankie to visit Tom at his workplace.

'Upon her arrival, Tom took her to the back room for "privacy". Tearfully, she pleaded with him to move into the new apartment. He smugly agreed to drop by after his shift, around 10 pm, to "talk", while making it clear he had no intentions of moving back.

'And why wouldn't he be smug? As she found out later, he was occupied having sex with most of the waitresses employed in that establishment. At the time she moved out, he was seriously involved with one of them.

'When he *stopped by*, she performed as dictated. Emotional coercion can bind a person with ties more durable than rope. And, when she woke up the next morning, she felt putrid inside, both physically and mentally. But in her eyes, she'd "won". Tom returned.'

Views from others

Sammy wants to add the memories he recalls from then. He speaks as the three-year old with lived experience.

'Mommy and I were having sleepovers! She had a cold and snored at night-time.

'Mom explained to me that her tummy looked bigger because I was going to have a sister or a brother to play with soon. I was a little worried about her being somebody else's mum, but she told me that I would always be her baby even when I'm grown up. We pretended sometimes that my head was a baby, and she'd hold my head and talk to it. It was really funny when she'd say that she was tickling my tummy, but she tickled my nose.

'We went on lots of adventures to her office and the place where she usually had lunch. Big boys and girls came over to us when we were eating our suppers and breakfasts too. I listened to them talking to Mommy, but I couldn't always understand everything they said. "Oh Professor, what a beautiful little boy! He has the longest eyelashes ever. And you are truly amazing.

Such an inspiration to us. A great teacher and a mother, yet you do so much work for women who are treated violently by their husbands or boyfriends."'

Interesting. Sammy remembers all of this positively.

However, once inside Frankie's head, the North American students who put her on a pedestal change their tune.

'You stood in front of us and discussed gender inequities while you were in an alcoholic and abusive relationship. We admired you and the aura of womanly power that you conveyed: mother, pregnant, wife, and psychologist. We wanted to emulate you. We grew our hair long like you and stopped wearing makeup. We quoted you and encouraged our friends to hear you speak. You should have told us the truth.'

'Wait! Wait! Stop this litany of abuse, please,' chime the chorus of women in Australia who have read Francine's books or heard her speak about family violence and sexual assault. 'We felt the connection. We knew that she was not just another airy-fairy ivory tower dweller. When she explained why we couldn't leave him and how we felt inside, her truth resonated. For some of us, this meant that the dismantling of denial began, and we started to talk and heal.'

Descent – part 2

'Thanks for sharing.' Sally is keen to proceed and get to the Al-Anon part of the story.

'Tom lost the restaurant job for undisclosed reasons and got work at a nearby petrol station. His drinking became more deliberate. No more pretence of socialising with friends. He'd return around eight in the evening, already intoxicated, and sit in a stupor, finishing off a bottle of scotch.

'Around this time, irrefutable evidence of Tom's infidelity surfaced in their final (previous) home landline bill. There were several calls to an unfamiliar number in the nearby city where Tom had worked. With a sense of dread, but a greater need to know, Frankie rang it. A woman answered, "Hi, Belinda speaking." Frankie recognised the voice and the name as a waitress with whom Tom had worked before he was sacked.

'"Could you please explain why Tom was telephoning you when he and I were separated?" she asked, hoping that there would be an innocent explanation.

'Belinda was bitter. In that bitterness, she was honest: "Because we were having an affair. I thought he'd left you for me, but the son of a bitch was just using me the same way he used all the other girls at the restaurant."

'Now, everyone in this room knows that codependents are chameleons. We are champion survivors, living at least double lives, and sometimes more! What Frankie did next illustrates that.

'Arising from the foetal position, she first led a workshop for counsellors and then retrieved Samuel from crèche, returned home, played with him, cooked dinner, and put him to bed having read the requisite three books.

'Having survived that revelation, she rang Tom's former assistant manager in Florida, Jim, to find out what the truth was concerning Mindy, the prior alleged girlfriend waitress. With a "loan" repayment long overdue, Jim was primed to spill the beans. Frankie learned about the routine afternoon trysts between Tom and Mindy at the Holiday Inn, the depth of the affair, Mindy's love for Tom, *and* the lengthy list of women who had preceded Mindy.

'Frankie told me that she had believed that infidelity was something she wouldn't put up with – each time.

'I've helped her understand the power of addiction for the addict and why she stayed even after Tom admitted to these affairs. The addict knows when it's time to bluff and when to "fold". Mindy, Belinda, and the nameless others were filed for years in her emotional storage compartment labelled, "Do not open". This is how we survive, isn't it?

'Life went on, much as it had before. Her pregnancy was nearing its end. Perhaps the regularity of Tom's peculiar alcoholic behaviour made it seem normal. Tom returned home drunk early in the evening, instead of two or three in the morning, and would drink scotch until he passed out.

'Knowing **where** he was offered her some comfort. For this, Frankie had her obstetrician to thank. The doctor, upon learning that Tom was arriving home drunk in the middle of the night, every night, offered to speak to Tom about his drinking at her next prenatal appointment.

'"Frankie tells me that you've been stopping off at the bar for a drink on your way home … (as any ordinary fellow would …). It would be better if you would drink at home until the baby is born. Pregnant women are, well, you know, a bit more needy at *this* time."

'Tom listened, though he was angered that he'd been dobbed in as an inconsiderate husband. However, it probably wasn't a coincidence that this change in his routine coincided with his career shift and the end of his affair with Belinda.

'It became clear to Frankie that the solution to Tom's alcohol abuse wasn't just drinking at home instead of at the bar. He needed to stop drinking altogether. This reality became even more evident after the birth of Daniella.'

The bottom

'As you've just heard about Daniella's time in utero, you'll know it was far from stress-free. Her first moments were also fraught.

Frankie was in the delivery room by 8:10 am.[64] Tom arrived from work at 8:15 am, the doctor used the forceps at 8:18 am due to a concerning drop in the baby's heartbeat, and Daniella was born at 8:20 am.

'Would this baby be the answer to Tom's drinking?

'Not quite.

'He left the hospital mid-morning to celebrate and wasn't seen for the next thirty-two hours. Samuel, who a neighbour had taken to childcare, hadn't been picked up, leaving a hospitalised Frankie to make arrangements. She felt both responsible and ashamed.

'Tom showed up late the next afternoon, moderately drunk (as opposed to paralytic) with two similarly inebriated mates, seemingly without a care in the world. In his absence, Frankie had decided on the name Daniella Louisa. At some level of her subconscious, she hoped the name "Louisa" might awaken Tom's paternal instincts.

'It didn't.'

Views from within

'Hi, everyone. I'm Triple F's sister, Sandra.

'Around the time Sally's been discussing, I had completed a long stint in rehab. I was attending twenty AA meetings a week and that's no exaggeration! I'd speak at length on *every* phone

---

64 The ten hours leading to Danni's appearance should eradicate any doubts anyone might have about Triple F and control. Late evening, Frankie began to experience contractions. Given that she and Tom were arguing, and her head cold made natural childbirth breathing problematic, she decided that this was not the time to have a baby. Therefore, instead of timing contractions, Frankie slept intermittently. When her water broke just after Tom left for the half-hour drive to work, labour rapidly accelerated. A mature-age student kindly took Frankie to hospital and dropped Sammy at childcare.

call about the *disease*, my higher power, and the twelve steps. We all know that as an AAer, we're not supposed to label others as alcoholic, and I didn't. However, I refused to visit if *Tom* was drinking. Maybe these calls helped Frankie to understand that Tom was sick and that she needed Al-Anon?

'As we say in AA, "It takes what it takes." And although this wasn't Tom's bottom, Danni's arrival was my sister's bottom for co-alcoholism. On the day she returned home with Daniella, she rang the number for Al-Anon in the phone book and was told where she could find a meeting that night.

'She was ready. Sceptical, yet willing to try anything to stop the pain. We talked the day after her first meeting, and she said that she no longer felt alone. Al-Anon was a lifeline, especially during Danni's first five months before Tom's trip to rehab.

'Frankie liked the absence of rules or bosses and no need to believe in a God. No one seemed to judge her for refusing to recite the Lord's Prayer at meetings' end or for not saying "God" at the beginning of the Serenity Prayer. I'm a bit the same myself, to be honest.

'For instance, instead of saying "It works if we *work* it", I say: "It works if we *let* it." I shared that with Francine when I visited them in Australia, and she started to say "let" and not "work" too. She felt she had spent too much of her life "working the program". Far better to *let* it work.'

Sally smiles at Sandra.

'Sandy, you were essential in guiding Frankie to Al-Anon.'

'I remember her early days in the program. Of course, like many of us, she first walked into these rooms blaming herself for everything, from the weather to strangers' moods. She felt guilty for Tom's two-day bender, its impact on Samuel's self-worth, and even Daniella's birth trauma.'

'It's not clear to us why Frankie was experiencing shame instead of anger.' This perspective comes from members of the mental health sub-committee who see the DSM, the *Diagnostic and Statistical Manual of Mental Disorders*, as their bible. Effects of growing up with violence were not included in that volume.

'How could my daughter, who was raised to be a thinker, turn to a religious and a fanatical organisation? First Sandra and then Francine. Despite my influence, they exonerate morally deficient human beings like Tom by labeling them as sick without a sound empirical foundation.'

Next, Miriam echoes Henry's disapproval and contempt, but in her uniquely Miriamesque manner.

'Of course, she felt ashamed! I raised her to feel shame. It is a part of the thread of Judaism passed through the mother. But this disease? Shmease! If she took care of him properly, I don't care what anyone says, he wouldn't have to get drunk every night. If I've told her once, I've told her a thousand times: forget your schooling and all those degrees and take care of Tom. Give him a substantial supper every night and he'll be OK. It's the shortcuts that you take, Frankie – the frozen food, the packaged foods, the meals from restaurants. Never, in over thirty years of marriage, have I served Henry a frozen dinner. Always it's been from scratch. And look at us. He treats me like a queen. Protects me and even thinks for me. What more could a woman want?'

Indeed.

'Hi, I'm Irene a grateful member of ACA. Francine and I met at an Al-Anon Adult Children meeting in the Fitzroy suburb of Melbourne. The idea of shame, which some of you are having trouble understanding, is normal for people who grow up with alcoholism and other dysfunction. Sorry, Miriam, but Franny grew up with the belief that she was responsible for everything, including your well-being and Henry's violent tendencies.

'And it's those feelings that make a chronic alcoholic and addict partner either a dream or a nightmare come true for an "adult child".'

Sally agrees.

'I was there when Frankie took the first three steps in Al-Anon. She walked into our rooms bound by the chains of accountability for Tom's drinking and behaviour. By listening to us share our stories, experiences, and our hopes, she came to see her powerlessness. With that gut-level acceptance came the second step: a belief in a power greater than herself, which could restore her to sanity. And Frankie had no difficulty recognising her erratic behaviours! With this revelation came the third step – the act of surrendering and allowing a Higher Power to lead the way.

'Good place to close the meeting. Remember, though, that these steps don't make us recover*ed* but recover*ing*, which means many more descents to that madness.'

21
SHARING FRANKIE'S CONSCIOUSNESS-RAISING JOURNAL WITH DR JAYE

'Another journal from the past! Do you mind, Dr Jaye? The attic is proving to be a treasure trove. And these diaries truly evoke memories. At least now I can process the pain without necessarily numbing it, unless of course, we count exercise or work.'

September

I've connected with someone quite different from most Al-Anoners! We've grown close, initially drawn to each other by our mutual refusal to use the word "God".

It feels like ages since I've had a true friend.

Sylvia is a bundle of nerves. She joined the Program solely to help her husband, Kevin, find sobriety. Since he's still drinking, I don't think she'll stick around very long but I reckon that our friendship will endure.

Kevin, an academic like myself, has countered Sylvia's interventions in a manner fitting an intellectual – by doing research. He's curated a list of artists, novelists, and playwrights whose histories suggest a link between creativity and addiction. He claims that sobriety would mean that his creative juices will dry up, too.

'In a way, Dr Jaye, Kevin's rationale for drinking did make sense. People with vivid imaginations often perceive things many overlook. I believe this trait promotes both originality and deep-seated fears or pain. And, of course, some use alcohol to dull the latter.

'Here's one example of how I can imagine just about anything! This was years ago here in Melbourne when my children were young. I arrived home on a summer weekend afternoon to find the other family car gone. Samuel was overseas visiting Daddy Michael, but the remaining members of the household were absent. The front and back doors were unlocked, two TVs turned on, Daniella's shoes lay scattered in the kitchen (usually a sign she was at home), and an ice block was melting away on the bench. A hint of worry nudged me, which I quickly dismissed, thinking, "Don't worry. There has to be a reasonable explanation."

'The minutes ticked by. The first scenario that entered my mind: someone was ill and had to be rushed to the hospital. Not the worst possibility. Had the injury been critical, they would have called an ambulance, and the car would still be in the garage. I walked out to the driveway looking for traces of blood. Finding none, my panic subsided momentarily. But soon, another thought surfaced: perhaps Richard had suffered a heart attack, and Daniella, ever eager to drive despite her age, seized the chance to get him to Casualty.

'Soon after, Richard returned from the shops with Danni, Rosa, and Peter.

'My accusations of inconsiderateness met with a standard "Sweet and Sour" soft- spoken response: placating, yet subtly implying that I'm a needless worrier.'

The story concluded, and Dr Jaye weighs in.

'Francine, children exposed to violence often develop a keen sense of foresight, always anticipating potential dangers as a means of self-preservation. In adulthood, this predisposition to catastrophise can persist as their default cognitive setting, with their imagination continuing to create mental dramas in order to counter the unexpected.

'Do you remember telling me about your anxiety checking the post, and later, emails? Such reactions are not uncommon given your history. You mentioned it's been improving?'

'That deep-seated need for predictability is, of course, exacerbated during unpredictable events like a pandemic, which is why Covid was (and may continue to be) such a trigger for trauma survivors.'

Francine feels soothed now at several levels. In just a few minutes, Dr Jaye has done what she does best – normalise Francine's 'insides'.

October

In Al-Anon, I have learned plenty of handy slogans like 'a day at a time' and 'keep it simple'. There's another one that you don't see on the flyers or the posters: 'Compare and despair'– comparing our insides to other people's outsides.

I've been doing that a lot in the consciousness raising group Sylvia set up – especially with Lucy. She looks and sounds like a feminist academic who's read the original Friedan and Greer, whereas I feel like a fraud. Surely, she belongs in a stage four or five CR raising group?

Dr Jaye speaks: 'What you're describing sounds like impostor syndrome.[65] It's not uncommon for seemingly successful women to have those internal doubts.'

---

65 Impostor syndrome is marked by 'feelings of self-doubt and personal incompetence that persist despite your education, experience, and accomplishments': Healthline < https://www.healthline.com/health/mental-health/imposter-syndrome>

'Right, that does resonate. In academia, I've occasionally felt like a fraud, but never within Fellowships or as a mum or even in my advocacy work.

'Thanks for helping me see that.'

Mid-November

I've learned in Al-Anon that Tom has a disease. And, more importantly, I now know at least intellectually that I didn't cause it. When I can relinquish that misplaced responsibility, a newfound sense of freedom emerges, just as they promised.

He's finding it harder to blame me now because I've stopped reacting. Incredibly, Tom's drinking is getting worse. With eyes that clearly conveyed, 'I'm in a total alcohol blackout here,' he staggered past six-month-old Danni, who was sitting on my lap as we watched Sammy play with his Tonka trucks.

Then, in an almost unprecedented act, he mirrored his mother's behaviour. Tottering into the kitchen, he peed into the sink. If people in blackouts think, he may have been thinking it was the toilet. Clearly, he wasn't aware of peeing on the dishes. But Sammy and I knew.

This morning, we had a brief conversation. Unusually, no hysteria, accusations, or anger – only sadness.

'Tom, you are an alcoholic and you need help. Please either get treatment or leave.'

He looked at me with those sad (and moderately bloodshot) bedroom eyes. Perhaps at some level, he could sense that this time is different.

'Frankie, I can't quit now. I'll have to move out.'

How many times before had I watched him packing a suitcase, and how many times had I pleaded? 'Please, Tommy. Don't go. I love you, and I need you. Please don't leave me. Please.'

Not this time.

I did cry after he left. But there's a difference. Al-Anon has helped me to surrender Tommy. It's the first three steps. Mind you, I have only admitted that I am powerless over Tom's drinking. Not over anything else. They say surrendering takes years plus needs to be done all the time. Easy to slip back into default ways of thinking.

Francine looks up, smiling.

'Hey, Dr Jaye, from what I've shared about Miriam, can you imagine what she'd have said if I'd told her about Tom urinating in the kitchen? No? Well, here's my guess.

'"Nine in the evening and she had dirty dishes in the sink? Is this the way that I raised her? No. Never did she see a dirty glass, bowl, or plate in the sink longer than seven minutes after dinner. Never. But this is what all that education did for her. And she wonders why he drank too much? Well, it's not my way to judge but if a woman can't keep her man happy, well, he does those things."'

Laughing while her therapist smiles, Francine returns to the next entry.

Two days after he left, Tom rang. I didn't know then that he'd just been fired (again).

'Frankie. Who do I call to get into treatment?'

The magic words had been spoken. Euphoria surged. As is my way, within seconds, a narrative formed in my head: sober Tom, me, Sammy, and Danni living happily ever after.

Sally had told me to give Tom her husband Jim's number if Tom ever wanted help. So instead of me picking him up, that's what I did.

Apparently, when Jim returned from depositing Tom at the chemical dependency place, he told Sally that Tom is 'one very sick guy'. Validation of my 'reality' that I could arguably do without.

Late November

Well, we went to see Tom today since the rehab allows visitors after a week. I intended to be a good Al-Anoner and not expect anything. As if.

In my script:

'Oh, sweet Frankie, my love and saviour. I now realise how cruel I've been to you. It was the alcohol. I do love you and regret the pain that I've inflicted. Thank God you learned how to detach in Al-Anon and helped me to get sober.'

There were no such apologies. But I heard him admit that he was an alcoholic, which went some way in breaking down the vestiges of my recurrent denial.

Early December

Between the women's group, which I continue to attend while Tom's in rehab, and Al-Anon, I'm learning a lot more about feminism and also how to listen — well a bit better.

Tonight, at the CR meeting, Gail, a year sober in AA and fighting to regain custody of her two kids, dug deep and told us why she lost them.

'I'd get drunk and beat them. I couldn't cope with the noise and their demands. I don't know. There'd be like a roaring in my head and then I'd totally lose it and start screaming and hitting them. It's a miracle that I never broke any bones. My poor babies.'

We sat there momentarily silenced and stunned. Or at least I was. Visceral memories of Henry and Jake.

The Group is committed to non-judgment. Plus, Al-Anon has taught me about the disease. Gail is not to be judged for the things she did whilst actively affected by the disease.

A spontaneous (?) group hug took place. We're here to support our sisters. Yes, we do confront when necessary but primarily we validate each other's journeys.

Mid-December

Survived Family Week at Tom's rehab! Five days of group counselling, educational films, and a bit of couple's therapy.

I've listened but spoken enough that everyone knows that I'm a professor who goes to Al-Anon. Hmm. Will talk to Sally about my motives. Ego is the likely suspect.

Anyway, despite my credentials, on the last day, one of the counsellors, Julie, gave me a special gift – a book about identifying and working on low self-esteem.

Why me? Why not timid Mary married for thirty years to that chronic alcoholic? Now there's a woman who could really use it!

The good doctor has something to say.

'Francine, since Julie was trained to understand alcoholism and its effects, it's probable that she was able to see the child Franny and the alcoholic Frankie hiding behind your "I have it all together, after all, I have 'Dr' in front of my name and I'm in recovery and a loving mother" persona.

'I can see, though, how this present would have likely contributed to why you saw yourself as inadequate.'

'No doubt, Dr Jaye – although not likely I could have named those emotions back then. I had a limited repertoire.'

Late December

Tom is not missed. Our family unit is Samuel and me and in the last six months, Daniella. Tom hasn't really been present even when physically here. In an alcoholic stupor, hungover or dry, he has seldom participated in family excursions, crèche events, or day-to-day childcare and playtime.

So, this period alone with the little ones is easy. There's no added burden – the opposite, really. I sing loudly, entertaining the children with my dance moves as I do when happy.

'Dr Jaye, in the same carton of memorabilia where I found this journal, there was a note from a university student, Amy, who was our babysitter at that time. If it's OK, I'll read it to you since what she wrote was more upsetting than the memories the diary has awakened.'

'Your hour, Francine.'

Hey, Dr F. Over the last month, I've noticed a much nicer vibe in the apartment. Some things are the same. Before leaving for university, you still do everything: fix Samuel's lunch, get him dressed for childcare, breastfeed Danni, wash the breakfast dishes, do marking and brush your hair. You always seem to do them effortlessly. But you're laughing now as you buzz around.

And I feel safer. After Tom moved out, but before going into rehab, he stopped by saying he had to pick up something and stayed for a while, watching me feed Danni. I felt very uncomfortable. Not for the first time.

He has this way of looking at me as if I'm naked. It feels good but bad at the same time. Dr F, you're my lecturer, my employer, and my mentor. I want to be like you except for being married to a 'Tom'. Sure hope getting sober changes him. xx Amy.

Francine is visibly upset – a mix of hurt and anger. Her therapist can comfort her simply by acknowledging that they are the expected emotions to rediscovering that her ex-husband had flirted with at least one of her students.

She continues reading the next entry:

At tonight's group, Lucy had a major league 'ah ha' moment.

'Sisters. Big news from me today. I've decided to go to AA meetings. Thanks, Gail. Your stories have given me lots of

identification with the how, the why, and the effects. Alcohol is a problem for me, too.'

Tearful and trembling – possibly she'd binged the night before – Lucy looked relieved, as if a heavy load that she'd been carrying had been released.

We applauded. The Group celebrates such moments of insight.

Gail seemed to be particularly pleased. Success! She's told us that AA doesn't recruit but works by members sharing and listeners identifying. Lucy is now her 'pigeon': a term for a new person in the program.

I wonder how Lucy fares in AA and how AA will fare with Lucy.

January

Tom came home today. They kept him longer than anyone else to date – six weeks! Seems that by the age of twenty-six, a substantial chunk of Tom's liver has been destroyed.

It was weird and scary having sex. Weird because Tom seems to have lost that amazing sexual stamina. Scary as I'm not drinking either, now. I quit six weeks ago on his first day of rehab. So, sex with both of us sober is strange.

Not drinking hasn't been hard for me. Pregnancy and focusing on Tom's disease mean that I haven't consumed any alcohol for the past fifteen months and twelve days but who's counting?!

'You're not in AA, Dr Jaye – or I don't think you are – but still you might find it interesting that when Tom had a one-night relapse after six months of sobriety, I picked up, too. Then, when he returned to the fold the next day, I too reaffirmed my abstinence.'

<u>Mid-January</u>

'I've decided to leave Kevin.'

This week, it's Sylvia making a life-changing pronouncement. There's something about Sylvia. I can imagine her dressed as an old-fashioned schoolmarm, cane in hand with Kevin bent over, mouth open, begging for more.

'I could live with the boozing and the occasional fling with the graduate students because I understood that he's an insecure boy looking for Mommy in a liquid or solid state. But this is unacceptable.'

We wondered what had happened. Sylvia had stuck with Kevin through years of drunken debauchery.

'He brought his research assistant, Luciana, into our house to help out as a part-time nanny. I should have known ... and she made such beautiful paella. I'll miss the paella and the kids love her, but I guess that they'll still love her since they'll see her when they see their dad.'

She burst into tears. Her bitterness had morphed into misery. Sylvia wasn't leaving Kevin. As per the norm in academia, he had left her for a graduate student twenty-five years his junior.

We silently watched her cry. It's another Group policy not to immediately hug or comfort since that could be cutting off the crier's pain, which needed to be felt. That was our operational theory, anyway.

Her announcement shocked us. Sylvia has been The Group's exemplary woman of steel and she's been beaten by one of them. Pretty frightening for the rest of us.

Lucy cleared her throat.

'There's another change to report. I've split up with Gordon (her husband of ten years) and I'm having a relationship with a special woman. Yes, you know her.'

Marina is blushing. She was The Group's *token lesbian. Not so much, though, now with Lucy and Marina holding hands and looking at each other tenderly.*

A fortnight earlier, Lucy had dropped her other bombshell. She's gaining many insights through The Group.

'Reading this to you today, Dr Jaye, it feels as if Frankie was merely an observer in *The Group,* watching others make major changes in their lives. My ability to be candid with them, and more importantly, with myself, was limited then by the secrets I held. However, things said by some during meetings eventually led to profound self-realisation.

'You know, years later, when my mother was dying, Sylvia and I re-connected via email. We've since rekindled our roles as supportive "sisters of choice", communicating across continents. That's a story for another session. In addition, another person in *The Group,* Lucy, lingers in my head offering occasional criticism of my feminism in practice. It's apt, as I always felt she judged me, perceiving me as a pseudo-feminist.

'In hindsight, though – and this might sound either paranoid, or arrogant, or both – that negative "vibe" I was picking up might have had little to do with her perception of me as a failing member of the accredited sisterhood? You see, Dr Jaye, Lucy had a short-term appointment at the university while I was on a tenure track. And she was notably shorter and heavier than I was. Is it possible that she was comparing herself with me and feeling inadequate?'

The psychiatrist looks thoughtfully at Francine and then closes the hour with a reassuring statement, bolstering her patient's self-worth.

'We've talked before about how your intuition has served you well. And continues to do so. I have no doubt that if you sensed "bad vibes" from Lucy, they were indeed emanating from her.

'Your ability now to understand that her projected negativity might stem from her own insecurities signifies your personal growth and healing.'

22
IN BETWEEN REHABS: 12-STEP REPS SUBCOMMITTEE MEETING

'Welcome everyone. I'm Linda, a grateful recovering alcoholic.'

'Today, we're re-visiting the fifteen-month period between Tom completing treatment and Frankie entering rehab.'

'Could I ask Gabe, who is a member of several twelve-step fellowships, was Tom's rehab counsellor and later became Frankie's therapist, to be the first speaker please?'

Gabe's recollections

'Sure, thanks Linda. You know me. Always happy to talk!

'Well, we know that Triple F is a visual thinker. Literally sees words as pictures. For instance, I remember telling her that recovery can be rocky sometimes. Frankie told me how she translated my words into piles of rocks sitting in meeting room chairs.

'She certainly has an interesting, vibrant, and sometimes cluttered mind, doesn't she?

'For instance, she perceives past and present experiences in colours or auras. Not sure about future ones. Accordingly,

Frankie described this time as pale grey, contrasting with the previous reds, oranges, and blacks associated with her times with Tom. There were no dramas with him, hence little communication.

'Both of them were sober or dry, and family life was the closest to "normal" they would ever experience.[66] Once a week, they'd go to an open AA meeting together. Frankie would listen to the readings and the shares, relating everything to Tom.'

The codependency treatment centre rehab staff nod in agreement. They're not surprised that Frankie stopped drinking when Tom did and that her focus was on *his* disease.

'Tom saw me for one-on-one aftercare directly following rehab but then stopped abruptly. And I met them together three times to begin marriage counselling. Let me say that three sessions to fix that relationship were not enough. Not sure, though, that 300 or 3,000 would have done the job.

'I did try, folks. I gave them some tools for facilitating healthy communication. Nothing worked. Here's an example. I showed them how to call "time out" when a conversation was escalating to anger. Frankie told me later how, if she was starting to lose her temper and Tom used the signal, she'd respond with anger: "Don't stop me from talking and expressing my feelings!" If she made the "stop" sign, he walked out of the room.

'Well, as a counsellor, you can only lead the horses to the water, but can't make them drink.

---

66 Sammy describes that time period: 'Daddy Tom is babysitting sometimes. He doesn't smell funny anymore. And his eyes are seeing me now. He puts a dummy in Danni's mouth and he and I watch football or basketball or ice hockey on the TV. Daddy Tom is different from Mommy. He hardly talks and he likes to rest a lot on the couch. Mommy is always talking to me or singing. Mommy never lies down in the living room. She does sit on my bed every night to read me the books that we pick out at the library.'

'It was disappointing when Tom stopped seeing me. Tried not to take it personally, but as an ACA, I felt the pinch. It's possible that me being open about my sexuality might have put him off. Those with a machismo or womaniser disposition seem wary of gay men – not to stereotype, of course.'

A brief silence fills the room. Laughing nervously, Gabe continues.

'When he stopped seeing me, I took over from Liam and became Frankie's therapist, meeting up every two weeks for over a year. I'd like to think that our sessions together complemented Al-Anon meetings and *The Group*.

'Not sure, though, who was helping whom? Here, to give you an idea of what I mean, let me play a bit of another counselling recording. This time, I haven't deleted my voice.'

Gabe hits 'play', and two voices can be heard.

I just can't get him to talk to me, Gabe. I've tried everything that you suggested but he keeps it all inside.

Then, we hear Gabe's voice followed by Frankie.

Don't I know what that's like. Jimmy[67] is exactly the same way. Sometimes I feel as though I'll explode if he doesn't speak! I think that something serious is going on for him. It could be his work. I told you last time about those colleagues who are harassing him? Well, he just won't share with me. Should I be doing something different?

Come on, Gabe. Stop being self-deprecating. Where are those boundaries? What does Dr P[68] tell you? If Jimmy won't talk, that's Jimmy's problem. Either accept the limitations of the relationship or get the courage, as the Serenity Prayer says, to change the things that you can – how you respond!

---

67 Gabe's lover and partner.
68 Gabe's therapist.

Gabe turns off the tape recorder. Trying not to be defensive, he does want to explain how or why such a therapeutic model worked with Frankie.

'First to the mental health colleagues present, this sort of co-counselling is common in twelve-step programs. In fact, as the twelve-steppers here can attest, that's *how* it works. Frankie had to listen to herself when she was advising me. Change the things she can … herself. Unfortunately, though, she then took what *we*, in fellowship land, call "the easier and softer way".

'Frankie was good at listening to my angst, maybe because, like many of us in certain programs, she came alive in crises – her own or others. And there weren't many catastrophes in her own life at this time.

'But Jennifer, as the CODA rep, is the best person to talk about dramas and codependency.'

Jennifer

'Thanks, Gabe, although Irene might be better than me at explaining how and why we codependent adult children thrive in crises. Public speaking isn't my thing, but my sponsor has suggested I try to take on more challenges. So, here goes.

'Aside from Danni and the blood vessel saga, which I'll discuss next and clearly had "codependency" written all over it, the only other drama during those fifteen months was Tom's and Frankie's one-night relapse. That is until Frankie's flirtation with John began, but Sandy can tell you *that* story. By the way, you might have noticed that I'm referring to Francine as Frankie. Seems right since that was her name back then. But the woman I know is called Francine.

'OK, a bit of background first. When Danni was six months old, a raised skin bump, which the doctor said was not a concern, became visible on her left cheek.

'Then in April, the baby – now ten months – woke around 2 am crying. This was unusual. She'd been sleeping through the night since she was two months old.'[69]

Miriam raises her hand to speak. Jennifer smiles, encouraging her to talk.

'The earlier that children sleep through the night, the worse they are as teenagers. I know this to be true from what I saw with my daughter's no-goodnik adolescents. Also, there is an ancient Jewish belief, passed from mother to daughter, which goes like this: "Since you had it easy once, now you have to get through the hard times."'

Jennifer nods her head and thanks Miriam for her 'share' before continuing the ruptured blood vessel story.

'Frankie got out of bed, half asleep, went to Danni's room, picked her up and brought her to their bed to breastfeed. She kept the lights off to encourage the baby to sleep. When Danni was asleep, Frankie placed her back in the cot.

'Imagine her horror when she got out of bed in the morning and saw a red stain on the carpet! She could see that the front of her nightgown was covered in dry blood. It took her about a second to put two and two together.

'As she put it to me, "heart beating loudly", she ran into Danni's room where the baby was lying on her stomach in the middle of the cot. The sheet was drenched in blood. No sign of breathing. Then – and this is the interesting part of the story from a codependency perspective – she started screaming: "Oh God, please let me die right now. I can't go on without Danni. It's all my fault. She's bled to death because I'm a bad mother. I didn't turn on the lights."

---

69 So, too, Samuel, Rosa and Peter. Perhaps all four intuitively recognised that their mother and sleep deprivation were not a great combination.

'While her mother was losing her grip, Danni, covered in blood from the top of her head to her pyjama-clad feet, stood up holding onto the cot railing, chortling without a care in the world.

'We CODA members understand why Frankie immediately felt culpable for what she thought was her child's death. As I told Francine, I would have had the same thoughts if it had been my son, James. Healthy boundaries with our children are challenging.

'Gabe, I know that little was known about codependents when Frankie told you this story. You wouldn't have recognised it as symptomatic of what I see as her core issue. This is just my perspective, of course, and no disrespect is meant for our upcoming speaker. Nancy?'

Nancy

Nancy, Frankie's counsellor in rehab, has the reputation of being a 'hard-ass AAer' (yet with a heart of gold). She wants to talk about what *she* sees as the real *disease*.

'Starting with Tom. Admitting he was alcoholic seemed to be as far as he could go in recovery. He'd go to a few meetings a week and did get Raging Reggie, known as Double R, as his sponsor. It looked promising. But there was no embracing of the fellowship; it was more a test of endurance. As we say in AA, it's not enough to admit defeat. We need to surrender. Tom was a ticking time bomb waiting for the next drink, snort, or fix.

'Now, on the other hand, Frankie had long been aware that her own drinking was problematic and by the time she and I shook hands, she was well on her way to surrendering. For those fifteen months, though, by merging her identity with Tom, she stopped drinking except for the "relapse". And, during that time, she went to Al-Anon meetings and spoke daily to her sponsor – our next speaker – Sally.'

Sally

'Yep. She rang me every day. Frankie *did* Al-Anon and therapy the same way she *did* study, parenting, partnering – trying to do each perfectly, which makes her a classic Al-Anoner. She was desperate to learn how to live with a recovering alcoholic without walking on eggshells or worrying about Tom's "program". And Frankie, like all of us in Al-Anon, wanted to do the first three steps on Tom and let him go! At least now, there was some awareness and a slight navigational shift in putting her focus onto herself.

'Part of the change in focus might have been due to the children. Frankie's face did certainly light up when she talked about them, which she did frequently. I learned that Danni was always on the move while Sammy was a more stationary and solemn child; the latter evidenced by his walking relatively late. In contrast, Daniella was four months younger than Sammy was when she first walked. It was the day after the blood vessel burst. While waiting to see the plastic surgeon, an upright Danni moved from chair to chair in the waiting room until, quite naturally, she moved across the room.'

Miriam asks to speak again.

'I'd like to add something more about my granddaughter, Daniella. She walked the same way that she crawled – constant motion. But when she did stop moving, she enjoyed lying on the floor totally engrossed for hours watching the weather channel. She was in a world of her own. I would be knitting Barbie doll clothes and tried to talk to her, but nothing went in. Such a loveable girl. Just not quite ever there. If I were a hugger, her I would hug. Who knows what *she* did by marrying that no-goodnik goy?'

'Thanks, Miriam, for your insights.[70]

70　Miriam could be describing the behaviour of a child with ADHD. However, Daniella was not tested (or diagnosed) as a child or as an adult.

'To return to our meeting's topic: sorry to report that the medical emergency with Daniella did not bring Frankie and Tom closer together. He *dealt* with it in his habitual manner, which my dear friend Irene will now explain from the ACA lens.'

Irene

'Thanks, Sally. Not sure I can add much, though. Yes, that sort of response is common for an alcoholic who's an ACA. Tom would shut down if he was experiencing an emotion other than the two or three that he was comfortable with. Alternatively, he exorcised them with alcohol or painkillers.

'When his mother abandoned him, seven-year-old Tommy learned to not feel afraid or deserted. Interesting that in contrast, both were safe feelings for Franny. Likely a result of the patriarchy.

'Yes, the "P" word's a clue. After thirty years of recovery in Al-Anon and ACA, I've put on feminist lenses. Through them, it looks like many of the ACA effects are gendered.

'Anyway, back to Tom. In our Program, we say that maturing may stop earlier than addiction as the child plays a family of origin survival role. Plus, we believe that real change is limited until we get honest with ourselves and stop blaming other people, fate, or karma. Don't reckon from what I've heard that Tom got far with that part of recovery.

'Now, Francine's path was different. She found CODA and ACA early on here in Australia. Her discovery came after that delayed clinical depression diagnosis. Horrible time. Unimaginable, really. Big hugs, Francine.

'Breaking the rules of dysfunctional families became one of her passions. But, like the rest of us, or the women anyway, she's learned slowly that we're recover*ing* imperfect human beings. Pretty hard to break those rules perfectly, that's for sure!

In any case, as Sally was saying – about Francine and her kids – she's always doted on them. Possibly to the point of enmeshment although it's not for me to judge my sister in recovery – especially as I'm the same! For her, the ticking time bomb was knowing that each child would grow up and leave. Abandonment popping up again. Not surprising at all – a relic of our trauma.

'Another ACA trait, which Gabe mentioned, is how we may create crises. These can act to divert the things that we're unable to feel. Reckon this was where the John drama fit in. And it was lovely, too, for her to have a man around who talked.

'Now about John. In case you're concerned that she wasn't experiencing guilt back then, don't be. There was the puritan morality stream of consciousness saying: "Although you didn't actually have sex at this point, if Jimmy Carter felt lusting was equal to adultery, then you were unfaithful."

'Roaring Reggie echoed in her head, too: "Hypocrite. For years you focused all your attention on Tom and getting him sober. Poor guy finally stops drinking and what do you do? What goes around comes around."'

Sandy

'Get out of my sister's head, Double R, and accept that your "poor guy" pigeon was egotistical – an unreconstructed addict – unable to love or to parent – or to stay clean.'

This last comment is made by Sandy as she moves to the rostrum. Well-known for being both an AA hard-liner like Nancy and the confidante of her younger sister back in those days, she's ready to talk about Frankie's misadventures with John.

'First, a bit of AA info for those of you here today who are not in twelve-step programs. The sponsor/sponsee tie is like a parent-child relationship. And, like parenting, there are a range of styles. Some of us – like Double R – are controlling. Others are more nurturing, guided by one of our sayings: "We'll love you until you can love yourself."[71]

'We do *suggest* that you don't sponsor anyone until you're at least a year sober. Another suggestion concerns having boundaries with the sponsee. Now, Tom didn't follow our advice. When he was close to six months sober and had been around AA for about a year – remember the one-night relapse – he began sponsoring John, a master's student at the university where my sister worked. John would hang out at their apartment. While Tom watched sport on the television, he and Frankie chatted about social and political issues. A friendship grew.

'And folks, they were just friends. That is until my (at *that* time *dear*) sister decided to quit smoking when Danni was eighteen months. I told her it's the toughest addiction to stop but she wasn't listening. I waited another thirty years to quit and look at me. No cancer.

'What does this have to do with John? Well, after three days of serious withdrawal, it looked like my once dear sister had won the war using will power (instead of higher power). We know how well that works. She was a crazy person without being able to smoke her anger and pain. I could see that minus the dramas of active alcohol abuse, her obsession with Tom wasn't working either. Frankie needed an alternative way (or person) to plug her feelings – John.

---

71   More about how AA works from Sandy: 'There are no rules as our members tend to be people who score high on anti-authoritarian indices. Instead, there are "suggestions". The idea is, if the member doesn't do what is suggested, as in get a sponsor for instance, then she or he will drink again. At one level then, we're using fear to help our pigeons stop drinking. At the same time, though, we're encouraging those who walk through the doors to find a higher power, which, if believed in, will remove one's fears; that is, the unhealthy ones that have consumed each of us. Faith will replace these except for the healthy worries about relapsing.'

'They started to meet for coffee and stroll around campus. And, for months, that's all they did until one afternoon when they were walking from university to her home, somehow … hmm somehow … their hands touched and fingers intertwined.

'Frankie told me later that it felt like a force greater than themselves. Yeah right. I did point out to her that this was her *disease* talking. Emotional maturity stops when you first pick up alcohol or another addictive substance. She was an unmanageable teenager. Linda? Could you please finish this story providing the local AA perspective?'

Linda

'Happy to share what Frankie told me months later, Sandy, as well as what I gleaned about *the flirtation* through our AA scuttlebutt.

'Around that time, Tom, thanks to Sylvia's ex, Kevin, had become friends with Robert, a wealthy contractor and entrepreneur. They'd hit it off, which wasn't surprising since Tom was not just a lady's man but a man's man. And Rob appreciated Tom's involvement in AA since his wife Meredith had recently started going to meetings. Think he saw Tom as keeping an eye on her? Interesting idea, wasn't it?

'Being Robert's henchman and aide-de-camp meant that Tom was now away from home more than ever, accompanying Rob on sailing and fishing trips. In addition, Rob made Tom the manager of two apartment complexes that were part of Rob's real estate empire.

'Not great at showing what was really going on inside, Tom did seem to be happy with this job. The pay was decent, and he likely received some internal accolades, which must have helped to suppress that core sense of inadequacy that, as we mention in the program, he hid so proficiently.

'Home life? Well, Frankie confided that it was about as good as possible, given that the marriage should never have occurred. He'd come home from work (unless out of town with Robert), seemingly abstaining from alcohol and other mood-altering substances.

'Yet, something remained amiss – either within the relationship, within Frankie, or both. Her mental fixation on John was escalating. This was about to translate into trouble. The flirtation was graduating from meaningful looks to hand-holding. The latter was spotted by an AA member the afternoon that Sandy mentioned. For the record, not by me. The *sighting* spread through our small-town fellowship grapevine.

'Tom confronted Frankie the next morning: "What the hell is going on between you and John?"

'Frankie's immediate response was neither remorse nor guilt. On the contrary, how dare *he* confront *her*? His infidelity was legendary. In stark contrast, it had taken six months for John and Frankie to hold hands. At that rate, it would've been two or three years before they had sex.

'Frankie spoke without an internalised red light, as was her way until well into her time as Francine. Out poured the litany of harms inflicted by Tom. This verbal regurgitation was spectacular, yielding its short-lived sense of empowerment. Inevitably, separation was suggested, and Tom quickly packed and was out the door.

'OK. That brings us to the end of today's special meeting, marking the close of those fifteen months. Thanks to all who helped set up and to everyone who participated, including those who listened but didn't speak. As we say in our fellowships, "Take what you like and leave the rest behind!"

'Oh, and just a reminder that the next time the full head committee meets, we are honouring Frankie's PGA/HP for guiding her to sobriety.'

23
GETTING TRIPLE F SOBER: PGA AWARD CEREMONY

'Hi, everyone. Gabe here. I've been asked to chair this special head meeting.

'We're here to honour Triple F's PGA, otherwise known as her higher power or HP. Some of us blamed PGA in the past when Frankie was on a drinking binge. Tonight, we take what is no doubt the harder path and give credit where credit is due.

'When Tom walked out, Frankie was left with anger and the other usual suspects from which she tried to escape: hurt, pain, and the feeling of being unlovable, to name just a few. Every self-respecting alcoholic in this room knows what came next. A trip to the liquor store was required. And a twelve-hour bender began.'

'PGA, thanks to you, ten memories of (what we hope was) Frankie's last drunk have firmly stayed with her. Without these recollections, she might downplay the gravity of her binge. The *disease* wants her to forget, to surrender, to continue the cycle.'

'We celebrate *how* you directed and *developed* that indelible mental montage. Over the previous fifteen months she had been attending AA with Tom, she was consciously filtering what she heard through a "Tom-centric" lens. Nonetheless, you attuned her subconscious to countless women's stories, enabling her to see her own alcoholic behaviour.

'Let's play the video first and then we'll look at the other bases for the award.'

Video: Frankie's last drunk

Scene 1

Here we see Frankie staring at bottles in the liquor store. First, she reaches for a martini for two. Then she spends more than ten minutes looking at the whiskey section, comparing prices by size and quality. We can almost hear her stinking thinking.

'If I buy a quart, I'm going to drink it all. If I do, I will be obliterated. If I'm obliterated, I won't know or care what I'm drinking. So why spend the money?'

She buys the large bottle of rotgut whiskey.

Scene 2

The camera is now focused on Frankie starting her car. She has taken what she thinks of as her friend, the bottle, in its brown paper bag and propped it between her legs.

Driving along a main road heading home to her children, Samuel and Daniella, she lifts the bottle to her mouth, savouring a few swigs.

Scene 3

A couple of hours later we see Frankie driving again, but this time with the children in the backseat. She sips undiluted whiskey from a coffee mug, held with one hand while shifting gears with the other hand.

Scene 4

It's dusk now. The camera zooms in on a long-haired woman who looks like an undergraduate, sitting on the grass surrounded by colleagues and acquaintances, crying.

Scene 5

The sky is now night black. We see a drunk Frankie running around the playing fields searching for Danni, not yet two years old, who has wandered away. When she finally finds her, she hugs Daniella with tears of self-pity falling onto the toddler's wisps of hair. Little Danni wriggles, attempting to free herself from this unfamiliar-smelling, oddly-behaving mother.[72]

The camera lingers.

Scene 6

Transitioning to her apartment, it's almost 10 pm. Frankie discreetly conceals the nearly empty bottle under the bed. She's apprehensive about Sylvia, who's due to fetch her, discovering the extent of her consumption — that would certainly cancel their night out.

Scene 7

The next couple of hours blur into Frankie's first memory lapse of the evening. In the midst of this blackout, she and Sylvia end up at a bar. The footage becomes hazy.

We can see Frankie just outside the loo, using the pay phone trying to persuade Tom to come home. All right, possibly the word 'persuade' isn't entirely accurate. Beg? Beseech? Implore? Grovel? Cry? He says he'll think about it.

---

72 Since her arrival at Al-Anon, Frankie's rarely touched grog; first to show Tom that life without alcohol was doable and then to join him in sobriety.

Immediately after that call ends, Frankie's making another call but, in this shot, she's sweet-talking John. The intoxicated Frankie suffers from drunk dialling.[73]

Scene 8

Sylvia and Frankie are in another bar. The camera is slightly out of focus, with the glazed-eyed woman now drinking martinis. It's blackout time again.

Doesn't last long. Coming back from that oblivion where saturated souls dance alone, Sylvia is looking at her with contempt, saying, 'For Christ's sake, Frankie. Wipe your nose. The snot is falling into your mouth. You're worse than Kevin. At least he only screws all his graduate assistants. He doesn't cry in public. You're a more disgusting drunk … disgusting drunk … The words reverberate and remain.[74]

Scene 9

Razor blades again and a suicide note is left for Tom. The children fast asleep in the adjacent room. We can see, though, that as you may have guessed, Frankie's not dead. Just a bit cut up, she's lying down on the bed, which has begun its merry-go-round routine. Twelve hours' worth of martinis and whisky are midway from stomach to mouth as alcohol's centrifugal force smashes her body into unconsciousness.

Scene 10

And then there's the torturous emergence from that alcoholic comatose state.

---

73 Like so many other drunks, she's the centre of the universe.
74 This is as painful as Scrooge with the ghosts of Christmases Past and Future.

'Lost Tom. Lost John. All alone. Terrible mother. Lousy wife. Horrible friend. Might as well die. Drink up and do the deed. Die bitch die.'

'I don't want to die. I'm scared of dying. I'm scared of drinking because I'll die. I'm scared of living because it all hurts too much. Too scared to die and too scared to live.'

The courage to act was in the bottle. Unable to hide from the anguish and humiliation, she reaches under the bed. Hand on bottle, a centimetre from her lips, PGA, you then played Frankie this video in its entirety. Frankie was now able to connect these visual scenes with fragments of the stories she'd heard subconsciously in AA.

'Normal social drinkers (NSDs) don't take fifteen minutes making a choice about what liquor to buy.'

'NSDs don't drive and drink out of a bottle in a brown paper bag.'

'NSDs don't drink and drive with children in the car.'

'NSDs don't drink whisky covertly out of a mug.'

'NSDs don't cry drunkenly on their workplace grounds.'

'NSDs don't get so drunk that they are oblivious to the whereabouts of their one-year-old child.'

'NSDs don't hide their alcohol to preclude someone knowing how much they've had to drink.'

'NSDs don't phone their estranged husband and their boyfriend telling both how much they're loved and needed.'

'NSDs can remember everything that has taken place. They do not have blackouts.'

'NSDs don't cry until mucous drips from their noses without their noticing.'

NSDs' friends don't look at them with repulsion and tell them how they resemble their alcoholic husbands.'

'NSDs don't think about dying and self-harming with razor blades.'

'NSDs don't whirl around the room on a bed turned to carousel and pass out.'

'NSDs don't wake up with hands that tremble as their body is withdrawing.'

And, amidst her fear of living and dying, she remembered a woman who had spoken about fear being at the crossroads of hitting bottom. How it gets the alcoholic to ask for help and how it keeps some from picking up.

End of film.

Leading Triple F to Gail, Nancy, and Linda (and others in Australia)

'PGA, you're also being honoured tonight for ensuring that Triple F's path intersected with certain women guides who have supported her recovery, speaking with a clarity that resonated.

'The morning after her final binge, feeling utterly defenceless and frightened, Frankie chose to put down the bottle and pick up the phone.

'"Uh, Gail, I've really screwed up and need help. I don't know exactly how to say it, but I think that I have a drinking problem. If I drink now, I'll explode at some point. Alcohol is like a powder-keg for me. Sometimes it's dormant, but occasionally the crap inside drives me to oblivion."

'"Could I be an alcoholic? I know Tom is, he's done things like urinating in sinks and crawling into the house. Sandra is definitely one too; she had beer for breakfast. And then there's you, Gail ... you know what I mean?"

'Frankie waited for Gail to tell her that she's wrong; that she doesn't believe there are signs here of alcoholism. After all, Gail knows that Frankie hadn't had a drink since Tom went into rehab except for their one night "relapse" and that there have been many times when she controlled how much she drank.

'Gail, however, didn't have any doubts.

'"Oh Frankie. I'm delighted that you've reached this point. I've waited for over a year now. I knew that you were one of us but it's a program of attraction, not promotion."[75]

'Gail then persuaded Frankie to attend five meetings in quick succession, which she did. Nothing magical occurred, though. Her urge to drink away the pain remained a background hum.

'That humming noise got louder when, a few nights after Tom left, John escorted her from an AA meeting and *somehow* they ended up in bed.'

At this point in the ceremony, two individuals are clamouring to be heard. Neither Miriam nor Raging Reggie can let the word 'somehow' go unaddressed.

'*Somehow* they ended up in bed! Like a strong gale came into the living room and lifted them down the hall and onto the bed? We have words in Yiddish for women like this, but I won't use them here. I'm already repressing this incident from my MORGUE.'[76]

'Really nice. Poor Tom, faithful for at least a day or two, trying hard to stay sober. OK, turns out he was secretly smoking dope, but we AAers didn't know that. She cuckolds him with John, whom we had told, "No relationships for the first year!" We didn't order it, but we did *strongly* suggest it.'[77]

---

75 AA view: It's not up to us to label you as alcoholic. We'll help you self-identify by pointing out features of our personalities and our drinking that most of us seem to share. If you experience a sense of connection, then you're in the right place.

76 Given Henry's chronic infidelity, Miriam had mastered this mechanism.

77 Reg: for the record, Tom and Frankie were separated. John was, in fact, *almost* one year sober. Also, the awkward act didn't last long – less than a minute from go to woe. Sobriety or John coming to terms with his sexuality or both? It was the relationship's finale.

'OK thanks, Miriam and Reg. Let's get back to the purpose of this meeting.

'PGA, Gail was the first of these pivotal people whose paths you arranged to intersect with Frankie. Gail believed that Frankie was battling alcoholism. Not surprising as the view held by most in AA is that if you get here, you belong here.[78]

'After the night with John, Frankie's inner knowledge that drinking would lead to self-destruction, delivered her to a twenty-eight-day residential treatment program.[79] And there we find the next person you brought into her life – Nan, the rehab counsellor who helped Frankie take the first three steps in AA.

'Frankie's acceptance of being powerless over alcohol did magically give her a break from the pain. And then, through one-on-one counselling and sharing of the inner garbage, she became lighter yet, offloading a segment of the shame that Tom's treatment program nurse had seen in her a year and a half earlier.

'Under Nancy's tutelage, the second step seamlessly followed the first one. She had no choice but to believe in you, HP - that there was something – out there or within – greater than Henry. It was the second step or drink again. The second step or feel like a victim.

'Nan was the right person for Frankie to listen to. She helped Frankie understand that the end game wasn't to become Saint Frankie. On the contrary, her old or default ways of being in the world would continue to be present in a variety of contexts. Part of this stemmed from what Nancy called "spending way too much time in your head". She advised her

---

78　The underlying hypothesis: What sane person would identify as alcoholic (if not one)?

79　Tom was left with no choice but to return 'home' as carer for the children.

to add a "Don't" before each "Think" in the slogan, "Think, think, think".[80]

'And it was while not thinking and standing in nature next to a creek that Frankie experienced the third-step euphoria of surrender. No more grim determination vis-a-vis *that* addiction. The opposite works as the steps *only* happen when she stops trying to force them and feels trust in you, PGA.'

'The first three steps in relation to alcohol[81] were followed by doing an AA fourth step with Linda's support. This first inventory of character defects and assets was heavily weighted with the negative – the shortcomings. Page after page of fears. Sheet after sheet of resentments – likely just the tip of the anger stuffed inside.'

'There was minimal catharsis in the writing of that first fourth step, but cleansing and absolution did occur with step five. Kind Linda, her first AA sponsor, listened attentively to each word without a hint of judgment.

'"You drove drunk with a one-year-old and a five-year-old because you are an alcoholic. You are not a bad person. You have an illness. You are not bad."

'Thanks, PGA, for the forceful voices of Gail, Nan, and Linda that have remained within Francine. They helped to mute other, more negative voices, like those of her parents, that denied her alcoholism.'

'"Our daughter, Francine, is not and never has been an alcoholic. Now Sandra, I can believe. But our Francine, always popular, bright and beautiful! She joined that AA nonsense because

---

80 She could see the potential for 'analysis paralysis'. There were a few clues – the self-portrait with an over-sized head and a tiny stick figure body, which Frankie had drawn in 'group,' and her career choice as an academic.

81 Frankie let go of alcohol, but Tom remained an obsession or object of her addiction.

she's weak and wanted to do whatever Tom was doing. He went to AA, she goes too. This is the great feminist. Once again, I must say it – feminist schmeninist."'

'"I both agree and disagree with Miriam. I believe that Francine does have a problem with alcohol. She lacks the will power and the strength of a rational mind to consistently curb her intake and her behaviour. I do not believe, however, that she needs to attend meetings and follow the creed of Alcoholics Anonymous. Self-control – that's the answer."'

'No surprises here, Miriam and Henry. As a Jewish son with Jewish parents, I ask you to please lighten up on your daughter.'

Good on you, Gabe.

'Other alcoholism deniers on the committee are mental health folks. We therapists sure have our own schtick. For instance, Dr Ben Cohen – always with Freud this and Freud that – has the following theory about Triple F's alcoholism. According to him, the answer lies in Frankie's unresolved Electra Complex.

'"She unconsciously selected a surrogate Henry, an organisation founded and dominated by males. By joining it, figuratively speaking, she unites with you, Henry, which is the dream of every daughter. However, I'd add that her joining AA was a rejection of you Henry and your norms, which is illustrative of the Electra Complex. Her actions are the embodiment of what our founding father believed."

'And, then there's Liam O'Reilly, an Al-Anon advocate, who disagrees with the previous theory but has another family-of-origin-related codependency hypothesis to explain why Frankie identified as alcoholic. Here's how he put it at one of our sub-committee sessions.

'"Hang on, you old-fashioned fellow, and I do mean *fellow*. The critical relationship here was not that between Frankie and Henry, but her tie with Sandra! We're looking at a classic codependent relationship. Sandra was her hero. Franny and Frankie were Sandra's shadows. Remember when Frankie got stoned and thought that she *was* Sandra? Once Sandra entered the *fellow*ship and identified as an alcoholic, it was only a matter of time before Frankie followed."

'Lots of naysayers inside her head. Thanks, HP, for quieting them.'

Helping Frankie stay sober: first three years

'In Frankie's first three years of sobriety, her world turned upside down – crisis after crisis – but she didn't pick up a drink. For this, you need to be commended, PGA.

'But first, some context – merely four months into sobriety, she became pregnant, despite having an IUD. Tom's enthusiasm might've been in question, but Frankie's elation more than compensated. She saw the pregnancy – Rosa – as a gift from you, PGA. Tucked into a wicker basket with her strawberry quilt and her pink onesie and matching bonnet, newborn Rosa came with Frankie to her eight AA meetings each week.

'Rosa was an easy baby, sleeping soundly after only ten days – sparing Frankie the ordeal of sleep deprivation. In sobriety, she felt in harmony with your will. Rosa – the marvel – walked at eight months. Sammy and Danni were both happy and thriving. Her students loved her. All seemed to be well ... on the surface.

'However, a lot was going on below *that* surface. The subterranean stuff meant that just after Rosa's second birthday, Tom left the family home (for good) without preamble or conflict. His rationale and explanation? Frankie's "constant" nagging about the pain pills that he was being prescribed by several medical practitioners.[82]

---

82 Frankie had crossed back into Tom co-addiction: counting pills prescribed by dentists and doctors for back pain and searching for codeine caches.

'He was packing up his pickup truck in the driveway as she sobbed and pleaded for him to stay. As the truck pulled out, desolation and abandonment engulfed her. Not one of Frankie's finest moments. But she didn't drink, clinging to the slogans plus a couple of extra gems. "Everything happens for a reason." "God won't give you more than you can handle."

'Then, a few weeks later, another blow: irrefutable proof that Lily, her beautiful best friend, recovering heroin addict and first AA "pigeon" was having an affair with Tom before and after he left.[83]

'Lily's betrayal added more rage and self-hatred into the mix. But again, Frankie didn't pick up a drink or drug.[84]

'At the same time, loss and anxiety were coming from workplace crises. Shortly before Tom's departure, the newly appointed dean turned down her tenure application. This was a real shocker as she'd received consistent outstanding annual evaluations from her department head, which the former dean signed off on each of the six years of Frankie's employment.[85]

'These were confusing times. Her identity as Tom's wife, best friend, and sponsor disintegrated. Her identity as a much-loved professor seemingly well adapted to the university ecosystem was becoming blurry.

'PGA, without you, Frankie would have picked up a bottle of whiskey or vodka to medicate the pain and allow the anger to spew. Instead, she upped her meetings to seventeen each week and chose to live one day, sometimes just one hour, at a time.'

---

83 AA *strongly suggest*s the need to set boundaries with a sponsee such as not inviting them into your home life.

84 Maybe she simply shut down. Repression and emotional disconnection had been life-long survival tools. She felt that you were over-estimating her handling capacity, PGA.

85 A story for another day: Triple F's (mis)adventures in academia.

Francine thanks her HP/PGA

'Dear HP, this award is about far more than my sobriety. Recovering has meant becoming able to see the other offshoots of my "ism" and these side effects of trauma[86]: people-pleasing, perfectionism and control "issues", which result in eating disorders[87] and addictions, including not just alcohol and cigarettes but also baking and work, to name just a few.

'I've had to become willing to work with you on each. But that's OK because, except for the months of undiagnosed clinical depression[88], I know that I'm not alone.

'Thank you, most powerful female force, within.'

---

86   Chicken or egg? The answer depends on which mental health sub-committee member is speaking or which twelve-step fellowship representative's viewpoint is solicited.

87   That stick figure in the rehab self-portrait was prophetic. Anorexia and bulimia soon reappeared.

88   The major depressive episode was marked by an absence of hope. One woman in AA inferred that Francine was responsible for the "spiritual bankruptcy" she saw within her.

24
EPILOGUE (MORE ABOUT FRANCINE): SHARING WITH THE COMMITTEE

Down the track: Francine, about being sober 'down under'

'Hi, everyone! Well, you can tell from my voice, even though I've lived here more than half my life, that I'm a migrant to Australia. Darn it. I try hard to sound like a *real* Australian. This is the country that I love, and I consider it my home. Guess you're stuck with your eleven-year-old's accent, though.

'How I got here … a real adventure!

'Richard, Samuel, Daniella, Rosa, and six-month-old foetus (soon to be Peter) embarked on a journey across the globe. Our entire life was packed into six duffel bags and a few suitcases.

'The children were excited about global travel, although it must have been harder for Samuel as he spent school holidays with Michael. Danni and Rosa, on the other hand, had only seen Tom once in the year before moving to Australia.[89]

---

89 Tom and Lily took them for Christmas with Louise and Tony. However, when Frankie rang Lou after a few days to talk to Danni and Rosa, she was told that they were no longer there. Abduction? No. But that concern may have contributed to the global move.

'Most of the time. I do trust that everything happens for a reason – Richard, his job offer at Melbourne University, my various career calamities. I even came to see that Lily was a gift from PGA, freeing me from the toxic relationship with Tom.'

Committee chatter

First up, Sandy, harbouring decades of mixed feelings[90] about her younger sister leaving North America, possibly deriving from *her* abandonment issues, shares her piece.

'I'm very glad that moving to Australia worked out for you, Francine. It's too bad it meant that you weren't around when Mum had cancer. You did visit, though and, as my sponsor back then pointed out, you showed me how best to help her by modelling how to do it. Then, of course, there was Dad's stroke twelve years later and the resulting dementia.'

Henry, all faculties present, interjects his positive view of the relocation.

'Two years after your mother died, our "friend"[91] Sue passed away. My annual visits to Australia – a country I like a lot – went from two weeks to eight weeks.'[92]

90　When Sandra talks to or about Francine, her manner is, at the least, guarded, and at the most, unforgiving. Francine's descent from the pedestal escalated when Henry's health declined, and the sisters disagreed about prognosis and treatment.

91　Remember how Miriam would talk about Henry's adventures with 'girl *friends*'? Shortly after her best friend Miriam died, Sue emerged as Henry's de facto partner. It was obvious to at least one person (Francine) that this intimacy predated her mother's death.

92　Unwittingly, 'Franny' was present 24x7 during Henry's visits. His favourite alcohol was purchased, drinking companions arranged, and side-trips organised. Access to a computer (of his own) allowed him to check his bank accounts hourly – a source of delight. Henry's enjoyment during a visit visibly waned as the days passed. Francine and Richard did heave sighs of relief when he departed. Her exhalation included shame for feeling it, though.

Linda and Nancy express the AA view.

'We were worried you were doing a "geographical" when you moved around the world. We weren't concerned, though, that after Tom left, you were smoking sixty cigarettes a day. That was average for anyone in AA back then. And we weren't overly fussed that you were drinking twenty cups of black coffee and only eating a raisin bran muffin late at night. That coffee consumption is the norm for a recovering alcoholic attending eighteen meetings a week. And yes, eating disorders seem to be what many of us women in AA cross over to as a means of purging undigested feelings.[93]

'The bottom line today is simple. You haven't picked up a drink and, although bulimarexia has continued in various forms, if you count your current hour-long run every morning, you're doing just fine, Francine. You're a work in progress, to be sure.'

Samuel, as the oldest, is the spokesperson for Francine's adult children.

'There's only one Mama who could have taken her three and a half children on such an amazing journey across the world. It's you, and you're definitely special to us and many others around the planet. You taught us we can each make a difference in the world through our actions, and that honesty leads to a more joyful existence. Congratulations on decades of sobriety, Mum. Danni, Rosa, Peter, and I are very proud of you, not to mention grateful, as our lives have turned out unfathomably better because of your efforts. We love you, Ma. And don't let the ghosts of grandma and grandpa get to you!'

---

93 Regulation of each kilojoule that enters the body can be self-medicating. Anger and rage are momentarily muted by the illusion of being in control.

Down the track: Francine pondering partnership with Richard

'Well, I'm not sure if the relationship with Richard was and/or is another codependent one because I'm in it. Likely it is so, given my codependency.

'Certainly, there was an incredible spark right from the start. Our first date went for twelve hours. In that time, we talked more than Tom and I had over eight years. As you know, talking wasn't Tom's and my forte. I was on cloud nine at least for the two years that I was the centre of Richard's attention. Of course, I didn't know, until he received a long overdue diagnosis of ADHD years later, that I had been the object of hyper-focus, which shifted to his scientific research - puzzle pieces connecting for me.

'In some ways, the reality is that Richard is as unavailable as Tom and can be even more bristly at times. When he's engrossed in something, I practically become invisible.

'To his credit, though, Richard hasn't just been a stepfather to the three older children; he's truly stepped up as their father.'[94]

Committee comments

'That wonderful Richard. What a *mensch*. How many men would take up with a woman who already has three children? And with those feet? I always said you'd never get a husband with those feet … but somehow you had three by thirty. And he brought you to this beautiful country. Loved to come for a visit each year but leaving broke my heart.'

---

94   Neither Tom nor his parents made any attempt to see Danni and Rosa after they moved to Australia. Richard was and is their only father. However, they have not been cheated of a 'real' dad. Richard sees and treats each of the four children in the exact same (ADHD-erratic) way.

'Hi. I'm Jennifer, a grateful member of CODA and another voice here to help you, Francine, recognise your worth. We're aiming for progress, not perfection. Your quest for a partner after Tom was much more measured than your times in Europe or after parting with Michael. Remember, a watched pot never boils. And then Richard came into your life.'

Richard has decided to speak but has agreed not to exceed one minute. Can he?[95]

'When I was diagnosed fifteen years ago, my library expanded with some forty-three books about ADHD, including a few that explore what it's like to live with an adult ADHD partner. From my reading these, I understand that you may feel lonely, ignored, unheard, and unappreciated by me. And, although I freely admit that I'm unreliable and have no concept of time, I do become irritable when you remind me of anything and accuse you of trying to manage me. Again, those are expected responses for somebody with ADHD.

'Francine, much of the friction in our relationship derives from your taking my ADHD behaviours personally. But it's not about you. My struggles with focus and task management, as well as my unreliability and skewed time perception, are all part and parcel of ADHD.'

Down the track: Francine, about being an academic and advocate

'Years ago, at my first ACA meeting in Melbourne, the characteristics of an adult child of alcoholism or dysfunction were read out at the beginning. I identified deeply with each one: seeking approval coupled with an overdeveloped sense of duty; feeling intimidated by those displaying anger; either being an alcoholic

---

95 Listening may be problematic for the person with ADHD.

or married to one, or perhaps to another compulsive personality like a workaholic; harbouring childhood traumas, which obstruct the ability to both feel and articulate various emotions; possessing severe self-critique underscored by an immense core of shame; and having a dependent nature riddled with abandonment fears. And that's just scratching the surface!

'I heard others in 12-step rooms describe the possibility of change. Work the steps, go to meetings, read the literature and talk to members. They shared feeling *less* isolated, *less* afraid of authority figures, *less* reliant on others to define them, *less* recreating of abandonment, and more able to respond as actors, not reactors.

'In addition, as I came to understand more about the effects of growing up with Henry and Miriam, I've experienced acceptance of my childhood, which was followed by the need for action. "Action" for me to has translated into helping victim survivors to identify their traumas, understand that they are not to blame and for me to serve as evidence that the three rules can be broken.'

Comments from passers-by and a few residents

A spokesperson for those who have attended her lectures or read her books speaks:

'Hey, Francine, you were one of the first to break the "Don't talk" rule by saying in your books, classrooms, and public addresses, "I'm a victim and survivor". We're hugely grateful. Your story resonated and we were no longer alone.'

A few undergrads of the thousands who Francine taught are present today.

'Our mental light bulbs concerning gender and law have been ignited. Words cannot convey adequately the importance of your kindness, generosity of spirit, support, guidance, and encouragement ... with your inspirational teaching and ability to encourage students with a belief in our capacity and ability. We are beginning to understand parts of the huge icebergs of biases, invisible until now.'

Her adult children also celebrate their mother's work. Danni's here to read the *Insta* she recently posted for International Women's Day.

'"Happy International Women's Day … Here's a few of my mum's books on domestic violence, partner rape, and law reform. She's tirelessly advocated to elevate women's stature in the community and promote awareness and justice for women's rights and equality. Love ya, Mum 🩶"'

Down the track: Francine on being a mother

"Action" translated into my *trying* to change the generational cycle of dysfunction by conveying messages such as: "You are unconditionally loved." "You are the children of alcoholics and addicts." "You are at high risk for addiction."[96]

'However, it's a family disease and not something I can cure – as hard as I have tried. Perhaps, though, i was able to give them sufficient information to shorten their own journeys into addiction-land or not travel there at all. Who knows?

'First Sammy. In Year 11, his usual position as top student was on the descent.[97] Cannabis, with its accoutrements of malaise except for the energy needed to scream in a death metal band, was used to make downward mobility more bearable. But with weed, cognitive endeavours became more problematic.

---

96   Each learned enough about the *disease* and its effects to be able to label their mother's behaviour as codependent when she's in 'control' mode.

97   Francine did sometimes wonder if her enthusiasm on Award nights contributed to Sam's need to be the best.

'The result was plummeting self-esteem, which inevitably disrupted the family dynamic. Sammy's relationship with Richard reached its nadir – marked by a loud, unsettling episode with Sammy wielding a baseball bat. But was the connection between him and me more protected or more codependent? I'll share a note he wrote to me aged eighteen, which shows one or both.'

I apologise for yelling at you all the time. I love you very much and I'll work on not doing it anymore. It's just teenage angst! You've always been kind to me, and I just want to say thank you for all the things you've done for me. I know I've been far from the perfect child and must've put you through so much stress over the years ... but I hope you now realise how much I appreciate all you have done for me all of my life ... You like good music, are very helpful with my schoolwork and are an inspiration in the areas of fitness, intelligence, and loving kindness and compassion for both your family and for people who are marginalised in our community ... I just want you to know how lucky I feel deep down inside that you are my mother.

'In his mid-twenties, Sam did put down the dope and slowly re-discovered a love of learning and writing. Today, he has a wife, children, and a successful career. He's consciously abstinent from alcohol and marks the day he quit smoking with pride.[98]

'Let's look at Danni next. From toddlerhood, she gravitated towards hanging out with friends, preferably outdoors playing netball and tennis. Once home, she invariably had a friend by her side. Then, in her early teens, there was a shift to different extra domestic (and unknown) activities with a different friendship circle.

---

98 Sam's path of recovery has included healthy and unhealthy mechanisms for coping with his on-going anxiety.

'On the rare occasions that Danni was alone, she'd immerse herself in still life drawing and writing poetry. Here's a sample of a poem that she made into a birthday song for me when she was fifteen.[99]

Mum, have you had a good year? How old are you now?
Do you fear? I can't remember your age, it's unclear
It would have to be the late 20s or near
A person of power, presence, and praise
Always thinking of me on my birthday, giving me toys
Your life to me has been a tough but
Magnificent adventure
Too bad now Mum it's time for dementia
Aerobics queen and a body to show it
It's not hard to tell that I am a dodgy poet
Couldn't afford a prezsent, wrote it,
It's not just how it looks but what shows
In it

'Danni used alcohol and drugs when at the tops and bottoms of her rollercoaster ride. [100]

'The ups and downs continue today, but without self-medication as Danni has chosen not to drink – at least for today.'[101]

'Turning to Rosa – her two teen years lost in addiction-land were full-on and terrifying. Let me share an English essay that

---

99 Her aptitude as a poet was evident to Francine, anyway.

100 Rosie nicknamed her older sister rollercoaster or 'RC'. In her twenties, Danni's lows became a time of suicidal ideation.

101 Francine has desperately tried to help Daniella when she's down. Each time, she futilely encourages her mood-swinging daughter to get an accurate diagnosis. The depression periods are painful ordeals, which force her to trust that Danni's PGA won't let her die.

Peter wrote in Year 9, which describes her behaviour and its effects better ....than I could.'

Twenty minutes and counting. It's not as if anybody there had misconceptions about what was going to happen, they just prayed with all their hearts that it wouldn't ...

My sister Rosa. Over the past year good had gone to bad, bad had gone to worse and then worse still. She had slipped and slid down the terrible snowballing crash course of drugs. I remember the yelling distinctly. On an almost daily basis she would naively fight an uphill battle against my parents, not knowing what strain she was causing on not only them but on the family. She was still their daughter. They recognised it was a disease and tried all they could to help. All attempts seemed to end in my mother's tears.

When she finally walked in the door that breezy summer night, you could see it in her eyes. I remember thinking to myself, 'You couldn't even go this one night without? Not even for my birthday?' Completely immersed in her own self, she began to talk. I don't know what she was on, Ecstasy, speed, something, but for the next hour she talked non-stop and fast. She talked as if she had only one hour to tell all the secrets of the universe. My parents along with the rest of the family listened on with mute faces, distraught on the inside. She hadn't even recognised the occasion, not a simple, 'Happy Birthday Peter!' I didn't feel any rage or anger, just disappointment. As abruptly as she arrived, she departed. Off to another party or rave, whatever she could get her hands on.

The silence broken by my father's offhand question to try to smooth things over, his voice sounded strange. 'So, how about the dessert menu?'

'Doesn't Peter write well?[102] When I found this assignment, I mentally travelled back there to the restaurant and to those scary years. Al-Anon did help me to detach with love.[103] Not easy but necessary. I don't know how people without a Fellowship get through these times.'

'Like his siblings, Peter declined Alateen.[104] But I hope awareness of their addiction adventures may have been enough warning for him.'

Committee comments

'Hey, ma!

'It's Rosa, calling in to the meeting on FaceTime from a spiritual retreat somewhere[105] with a message from me and the other three.

'Thank you for giving us this beautiful gift of life. Your endless support, friendship, love, and acceptance. We just wanted to say a little something to let you know how much we love you.

'And Ma, you didn't cause my problem with Ecstasy. To be honest, maybe it was peer pressure? Not sure about Sam and Danni, though …only kidding.

'When speaking to my teacher here, he has helped me to see that you do an on-going "moral inventory" and admit when you're wrong. Not something that Grandma or Grandpa ever did

---

102 Predictive of his future career choices?

103 Francine has tried to give her children heart-felt praise and celebration of their personhoods. She has 'been there' for each of them; possibly too much 'there'.

104 From the Al-Anon website: 'Alateen, a part of the Al-Anon Family Groups, is a fellowship of young people (mostly teenagers) whose lives have been affected by someone else's drinking whether they are in your life drinking or not.'

105 She left the advertising world for non-drug-induced mystical life experiences.

– at least not according to your stories or what we saw during our childhoods when they came here to visit.

'We do feel truly blessed to have a mother who believes in us and we're grateful for all that you have done and continue to do for us. Love you, Ma!'

Dr Jaye takes the floor next, keen to offer her insights on trauma, parenting, addiction, and love.

'It's crucial to acknowledge that, like most individuals, each of your children experienced trauma in some form, Francine. Many of us instinctively try to mask its effects, for a while at least.

'First, there was Sammy's trauma as an infant in the hospital, followed swiftly by his father's departure when he was a baby. That's a raw experience of abandonment.'

'Danni, though externally unperturbed when Tom left, revealed her inner turmoil through her subsequent actions – like when she took apart the swing-set that you've discussed with me. Disconnection was her way of dealing with trauma. When you were leaving for hospital after seven months of undiagnosed major depression, nine-year-old Daniella, instead of crying like her big brother, asked you to play scrabble – disassociating from her pain of being abandoned.

'Rosa lost her Daddy when she was a toddler and a few months later, from what you've told me, her babysitter and other primary carer, left her without even saying goodbye. Like Danni, she didn't seem upset on the outside, but she had just turned two. Her personality traits of stubbornness and independence became even more marked. I recall you sharing anecdotes about her steadfast refusal, even at two, to let anyone pick out her clothes. Her chosen outfits – invariably an eclectic mix of mismatched skirt and top paired with socks of contrasting hues

– were a testament to her unyielding spirit. If any child could will themselves against abandonment, it would be Rosa.

'I know that part of you, Francine, admires Rosa's fierce independence. At the same time, however, you feel blame that she and Danni were abandoned by Tom. "If only I had chosen better …" I can discern the younger version of you, little Franny, yearning to make everything right in order to feel safe.

'And, when you were clinically depressed and not able to be present for them – first emotionally when undiagnosed, and then, physically while in hospital – Peter was two years old. Richard stepped in, caring for the children and bridging the emotional gap as best he could. Yet, the stark truth remains: for a considerable span, your children lost their primary anchor – their mother – to a psychiatric disorder. The bedrock of their world crumbled.

'This illness was not in any way your fault. We both know that if you could have done anything to prevent it, you would have. Even now, years on, those dark days are potent triggers for your PTSD, and I have observed the distress that its memories evoke.

'Francine, you're neither Buddha nor God.

'Despite your fervent efforts, you couldn't shield them from life's adversities. No one could. Like other humans they have issues, but each has a unique personality, challenges, and talents.

'Take Peter – the historian, screenwriter, and by choice, psychoanalyst's patient – a precocious child with the ability to fully tap into both sides of his brain.[106] This was illustrated at the early

---

106 Peter's older siblings are similarly equipped with equally dominant left and right hemispheres. As is her wont, Francine worries that Peter might be overly gifted. Sometimes she can 'see' a greyish-black aura around him as he bemoans the work that pays the bills and is uneasy about maintaining success in the other right-brained career, which feeds his soul.

age of seven by those two notes you shared with me that he left for the tooth fairy.

#1 Dear tooth fairy,
My tooth is known to have been sucked up by a vacuum cleaner.

Signed, Peter Sutherland

#2 Tooth fairy, please give me back all my teeth.

'Definitely signs of an interesting mind and the gifted adult he'd be as are Sam with his prose, musical instruments and linguistic and cultural studies, Danni the poet, artist, and secondary school PE and music teacher, and Rosa with her successful and diverse pursuit of physical and inner fitness, which she effectively teaches to others.

'Your children, like other human beings, have their "issues". Still, you've offered them love, support, and invaluable tools. I believe they recognise that you've always done your best and view you as the warm and loving person you truly are. Just remember the Mother's Day song Peter and Rosa, aged eight and twelve, composed and sang to you as you enjoyed breakfast in bed.'

First verse:
My Mum is the best
She cleans up all the mess
She writes lots of books
And she gets lots of looks
Chorus: She's my Mama, lives at …
Repeat line.

'I've shared enough today. As a therapist, my goal is to help you look within and understand yourself. Therefore, in my opinion, the most suitable person to end this meeting is you, Francine.'

Down the track: Francine, on becoming Francine

'Thanks, Dr Jaye.

'First, a heartfelt thank you to all of those on the head committee who have contributed to this and previous sessions. In Australia, the pathways, programs, and individuals like Dr Jaye, Irene, and Sally emerged, subduing and ousting some of the more negative North American influences.

'Today, although I've evolved beyond being a caterpillar in Dr Jaye's butterfly analogy, there are days when my wings frenziedly flutter against the headwinds of self-will, creating a stifling inertia. It just means that I'm hanging on to something or someone.[107] But, then come the tailwinds that herald sweet surrender.

'My character defects, or the ways that I learned how to survive witnessing violence, do remain as my default responses. Perfectionism, taking responsibility for everything, and having to feel in control are examples. These effects of trauma don't disappear by sheer force of my will. I tried making them go away decades in recovery. However, I am now able to ask for these legacies to be lifted – a day at a time. All that's required are willingness, self-love, and recognition that recovery and healing are processes – not one-offs. An acceptance that my inner demons will never be exorcised. That now, instead of battling them, I dance alongside them.

---

107 The struggle to surrender Sam, Danni, Rosa, and Peter, when each was, or is, in a dark place has been the hardest 'letting go' for Francine. Perhaps a mother never loses the fear that she caused, contributed to, or could somehow cure her children's 'issues'?